ROOTED AND REMEMBERED

A NOVEL

Share your stories –
they will become
someone's
history!

C.J. FREDERICK

C.J. Fred

Contact information: www.cjfrederick.com
Connect with C.J. Frederick: www.facebook.com/cjtellstales

Front Cover Design by: Ars Rönnei Media
Interior Design by: Indie Publishing Group
Editors : Susan Fish, Catherine Muss
Publisher: Carapace Books
Illustrations: Various (for commercial use)

ISBN (paperback): 978-1-7382856-0-0
ISBN (ebook): 978-1-7382856-1-7

First edition.

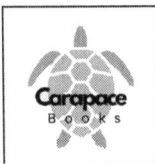

Carapace
B o o k s

To Betsy Jane, who lived her life doing God's good work.

To James C., who carefully listened to his grandmother's stories and decided to share them.

To Butch and Yvette, who first encouraged me to write stories.

To NFF, who cannot help but be helpful.

To all the giving trees under whose welcome shade we sit.

To the land that harbours our stories.

CONTENTS

PRIMARY CHARACTERS

The Carolinian Forest, Ontario, Canada

- A doe
- A buttonwood seed

Calcutta, India

- Eliza Dacosta (b. 1871), mother of Ellwyne, wife of Edward Dacosta
- Bessie Smyth (b. 1845), mother of Eliza, grandmother of Ellwyne
- Ellwyne Dacosta (later Ballantyne) (b. 1895), son of Eliza and Edward
- Duff Ballantyne (b. 1875), second husband to Eliza, stepfather to Ellwyne, father to Valetta
- Valetta Ballantyne (b. 1902), half-sister of Ellwyne

Scotland

- Donalda Elliott (b. 1877), second wife of Duff Ballantyne, stepmother to Valetta

Ontario, Canada

- Betsy Jane McAlpine (b. 1882), wife of James A. Carruthers, mother to Archie A., Elizabeth Mae, and William "Bill"
- Christopher "Kersty" Carruthers (b. 1834), patriarch of the Carruthers clan, father to William (b. 1867), Robert (b. 1869), James A. (b. 1871), and Neil Carruthers (b. 1886)
- James A. Carruthers, son of Kersty, husband of Betsy Jane
- Archie A. Carruthers (b. 1909), firstborn son to Betsy Jane and James A.
- JC Carruthers (b. 1946), son of Archie A. Carruthers, grandson of Betsy Jane and James A. Carruthers

England

- Rose Anderson (b. 1896), girlfriend to Ellwyne

PROLOGUE

The fertile farmland of Southwestern Ontario, with its swaths of fields, wasn't always sculpted to look like pieces of patchwork. A few generations ago, it was a vast forest dominated by towering deciduous trees and a labyrinth of interconnected roots burrowed beneath the soil. Starting in the 1830s, waves of European settlers, having been promised free land—land they could never acquire in their homeland—transformed the landscape from a hardwood forest into the agricultural farmland quilt we see today.

Although it has now largely been cleared for farming, Ekfrid Township still retains some elements of its natural wilderness prior to settlement by Europeans. Most farm fields in the area have corners still populated by massive deciduous trees reaching towards the sky. The heart of this story takes place on a homestead there, around the turn of the twentieth century.

Centered around a Scottish settler family and their relationship to the land, both in its transformed and pre-settlement states, this story explores how the land harbours the roots of countless stories—those we can hear if only we listen.

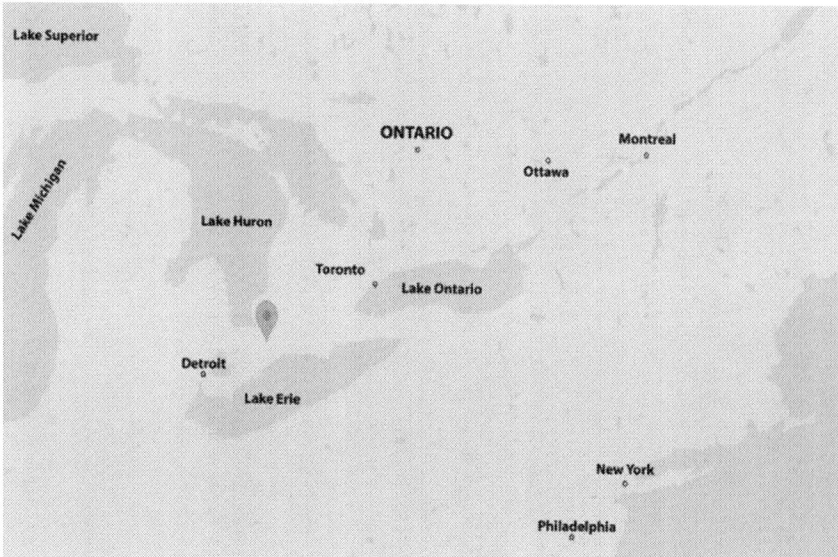

Before settlement by European colonists, the land in Ekfrid Township was the traditional territory of the Anishinaabeg, Haudenosaunee, Attawandaron (Neutral), and Wendat nations. The author acknowledges their rights and relationship to this land and the unknown stories it surely holds, the ones that have gone unheard.

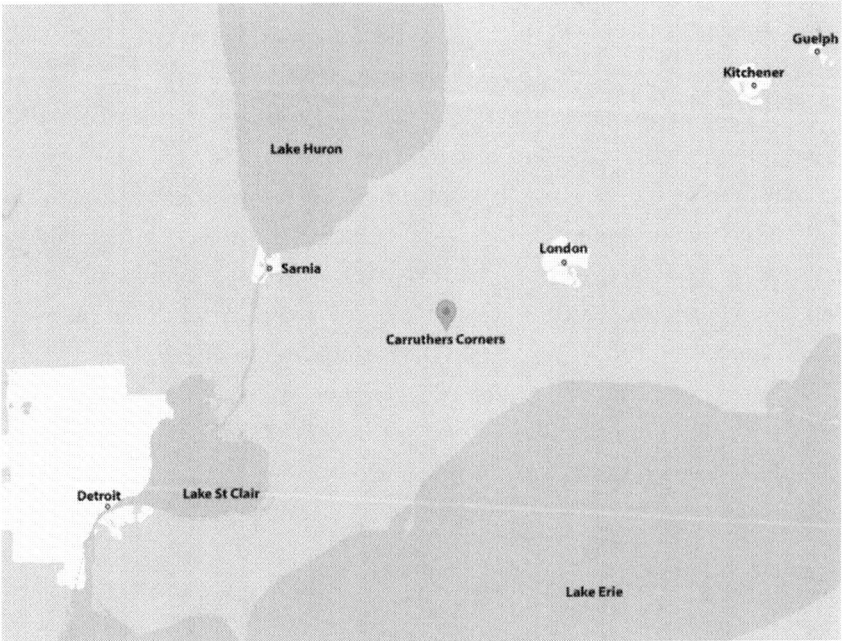

SOMEWHERE IN EKFRID TOWNSHIP, ONTARIO, CANADA, JULY 1902

PUTTING DOWN ROOTS

HER SURVIVAL THAT day, as it turned out, depended on the most trivial of decisions: a swift, instinctive reaction to the slightest of sounds. On a sweltering summer morning, the kind where the stale air has little movement, the deer had decided to pay heed to a noise so insignificant that she could easily dismiss it as nothing of consequence. While grazing in an open field close to the bush, she heard it. Frozen, she perked her ears backwards and listened. There it was again, closer. The snapping of a twig, the sound of a foot being pressed gently onto the ground to avoid detection. Feeling the eyes of a predator burning into her hide and sensing not a moment to spare, she leapt forward, sailing through the air like a kite aloft on a stiff wind. As her hooves touched the ground, she propelled herself further and continued to pound her way through the trees, dodging left and right to find a clear path ahead.

From behind, she heard the thrashing and snapping of branches and leaves as the wolf dashed towards her, its jaws snapping for its next kill. Speed was her only advantage. Her heart drummed in her chest. Racing, she hurled her legs across the hardened ground, her hooves digging into the forest floor only where it had softened from the recent rain. From her peripheral vision, she could see the blur of a furry grey coat receding as she continued to press ahead.

After many minutes of sprinting while darting

through the heavily wooded bush, she sensed she had lost the predator. The thrashing sound of steps from behind had quieted. She slowed her pace; the only sound she heard was the gasping of her own breath. The only movement she felt was the rapid beating of her heart as it tried to stay contained within her chest.

Thump-thump, thump-thump.

The doe stopped near a thicket. It would provide her with a place to hide until she knew it was safe again. Turning her head to make sure she was alone, she ducked into the thicket for cover. She rested, grateful for the slightest of sounds that had alerted her to danger and given her the chance to continue breathing.

Thump-thump, thump-thump. Alone with the sound of her heart.

She waited, blinking as her eyes adjusted to the shade. Time passed. Shifting and moving onto her rump, she was willing to wait. The sun rose higher in the sky as the hours passed. She stayed in place, waiting.

And then it came.

Silence.

It's what she was waiting for. The lack of sound told her it was safe to make her next move. Other than the buzzing of cicadas and the babbling of the river, she was enveloped in silence. She emerged from the thicket and edged towards the riverbank. Her flight through the bush had led her in an uncertain direction. She bent cautiously to dip her nose to the cool, rippling water of the river that snaked through the forests and farm fields as it made its way to the large lake. Although white oaks and some sugar maples lined the banks of the narrow river, it was the buttonwood trees, with their broad leaves and mottled bark, that were the most plentiful. Ever mindful for predators, she had waited for hours until she felt safe to emerge from her cover. The blazing heat, mixed with her recent exertion, had built up a strong thirst. She knew she had limited chances for water throughout the day and that she should seize every safe opportunity to drink.

As she sucked up the water, the breeze shifted, and the tree branches swayed overhead. At that moment, a single buttonwood tree seed floated from above, twirling as it fell, and landed on her downy coat.

She didn't notice.

After one final furtive glance, the doe satisfied her thirst, darted back into the bush, and disappeared.

The doe wandered through the bush, unfamiliar with where she was or where she was going but looking and listening for any signs of impending danger. The chase had heightened her already keen awareness. Her ears pricked at the slightest sounds. She found a raspberry bush and plucked berries and leaves from it. The angle of the sun was changing. Sensing impending darkness, she decided to find another safe resting place before the sun lowered to the horizon. She leapt into the air and flew through the trees, dashing from side to side to avoid the trunks and branches of the large trees that impeded her path. Having rested, quenched her thirst, and satisfied her hunger, she felt a surge of energy and took flight.

Running for miles, she dodged from one open field to the next, taking cover in the fragments of bush that abutted the farm fields. As darkness fell, a sprinkle of rain began to fall from the sky. The doe darted into the next bush that she found to wait out the shower until the sun rose again in the morning. A new day would present its next series of challenges. She entered a corner woodlot thick with maple, hickory, and elm trees. She shook her coat to disperse the droplets of rain that had gathered on her back. Her body twisted from side to side. The single buttonwood seed flew from her coat, twirling as it fell onto the softened ground at her hooves. As she walked towards a dry place to sleep at the base of a towering maple tree, she stepped on the buttonwood seed. The ground, wet from the recent rain, opened as her hoof pressed the seed into the soil.

Beneath the soil's surface, a complex, knotted network of roots, large and small, from the trees all around vibrated and hummed with the welcome rain. The roots drank the water and stored it, soon to send nourishment upwards to the towering branches.

The buttonwood seed, now immersed in the loamy soil, alone and hidden from sunlight, waited.

And then it came.

Silence.

THE CORNER WOODLOT, EKFRID TOWNSHIP, ONTARIO, CANADA, NOVEMBER, 2012

ACTS OF REMEMBRANCE

THE BUTTONWOOD TREE had awakened, stirred from a lengthy slumber. The corner woodlot buzzed with excitement and noise beyond the usual chirps of birds, creaking of branches, and rustling of leaves. Picking up the metal plaque, the tallest man in the group paused to marvel at the magnificent tree before him. It stretched over seventy feet into the air and had a glorious crown of broad leaves, crooked upward-pointing branches, and a shimmering trunk draped in the greyish-white cloak of a queen's robe. Its mystical white and silver, almost ghost-like outline, easily visible from several hundred yards distant, glowed as if lit by an inner energy. "How high do you want this, Dad?" he asked the grey-haired man standing behind him.

"As high as you can reach, Christopher," he said. JC Carruthers was in his sixties and had the roughened hands of a farmer. He was accustomed to giving instructions.

Christopher placed the plaque against the tree's bark and straightened it as someone handed him a hammer and nails. He pounded four nails into the tree, which fastened the modest sign about six feet from its base. Stepping back, he said, "How does that look?"

"It's perfect," replied JC, his eyes dancing with delight. "Betsy Jane and James A. would be so

proud." He looked all the way to the top of the tree, squinting as his eyes adjusted to the angle of the sunlight.

"Is everyone ready then?" asked the photographer, who had been busying herself with her equipment.

The small group had been chattering about the day's events but quickly formed a line of twelve at the base of the tree behind them. They quieted as she raised her camera and aimed it toward them. "We're ready!" proclaimed JC, who had his arm around the shoulders of his lanky son, standing beside him. "We've never been more ready." A few people chuckled.

"Say cheese." Everyone smiled. The photographer's camera clicked and recorded the moment in time. Although the people were the focus of the photo, the tree and its newly acquired plaque were the intended backdrop. After snapping the shutter a handful of times, she let go of her camera, which hung around her neck. "Okay, Mr. Carruthers. I'll email you copies of these photos when I get home."

After the photographer left, the group formed a circle at the base of the magnificent tree and stood wordless, heads bowed, and hands clasped. They paused for quiet reflection, each person focused on the solemn act of remembrance, the reason they had gathered at the corner woodlot.

Silence.

And through that, it emerged: *thump-thump thump-thump*.

Beating hearts the tree had waited more than a century to hear.

The silence was interrupted by a child's questioning voice. "How did this become Ellwyne's tree anyway?"

PART 1
SEEDLINGS 1902–1910

"From tiny seeds grow mighty trees."
—Aeschylus

1

CALCUTTA, INDIA, 1902

HE CAREFULLY INCHED the black cast-iron toy horse across the piece of wood. A puddle had formed during the previous night's rain, and, for the horse, it was a broad and treacherous river. Reaching a dry spot on the other side was a minor triumph.

"Now you have crossed the river," he exclaimed as the horse landed safely. Monsoon season had just begun in Calcutta[1]. The heavy rains usually lasted three months, from June to September, giving the city its entire annual rainfall in that short period. "Line up! Everyone can cross the river on this bridge," he said in a deeper voice.

Next, he moved the cast-iron soldier across. "There you go, Captain. You're on the other side." He lined up the soldier next to the horse, so engrossed in the bridge crossing that he didn't hear his mother's footsteps behind him.

"Ellwyne, we need to get ready for church soon." She smiled as she watched her boy, certain he hadn't heard her. Her six-year-old son was normally a serious boy, and she was relieved to see him captivated by his pretend world.

"Don't worry, mister," he continued, as he coaxed a reluctant black and orange caterpillar across the stick from one side of the puddle to the other.

"What are you doing?" she asked him.

"I built a bridge and everyone's afraid to use it, so I'm helping them cross," he said.

1 The British called it Calcutta, but the village on that site was known as Kolkata, and the city has reverted to that Bengali name.

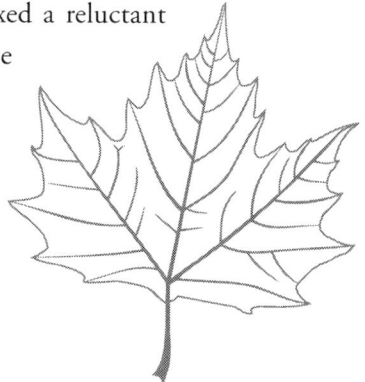

Eliza sighed. Her son had listened closely to her stories and committed them to memory. She was proud and heartbroken at the same time. He had never known his father. Eliza had married Edward when she was twenty-two. Edward was from a wealthy family with roots stretching back to Portugal, while her own parents had emigrated from Scotland to British India. Though their families had arranged their union, they fell in love shortly after they were married. Edward called Eliza "my darling" and almost never referred to her by her name, while she had called him "my love." He had been educated as a civil engineer, specializing in bridge construction. With his family's money backing him, he hadn't needed to work but chose to do so. He had a mechanical mind and enjoyed the many challenges facing the infrastructure of British India. In 1897, after five years of marriage, Edward had fallen sick with cholera. Despite efforts to save him, after a few weeks of illness, he was gone.

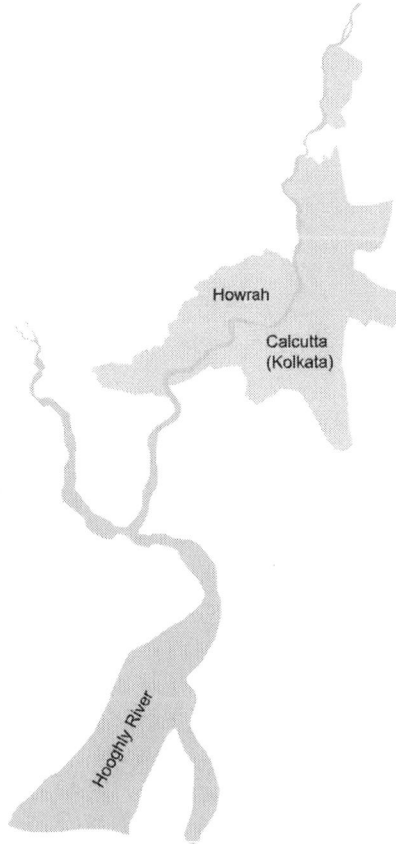

Howrah

Calcutta
(Kolkata)

Hooghly River

Her beloved husband left behind two important legacies: their remarkable son, who shared their jet-black hair and his father's dark eyes, and the elegant bridge that spanned the Hooghly River connecting Calcutta to Howrah. It was the first bridge built that could withstand heavy monsoon flooding. Ellwyne's memories of his father came from a treasured photograph and his mother's stories together with the most frequently told story about the Hooghly River Bridge.

"We can take a carriage ride over Papa's bridge later on, if you're quiet in church."

Ellwyne looked up at his mother. She appreciated that his dark brown eyes were so much like his father's. "Is it safe?" His nose wrinkled.

"Of course. Your papa made it so." He grinned, picked up his cast-iron toys, and followed her into the house. She knew he would have more questions later.

🍁

"What was my papa's name?" Ellwyne asked while they walked through the market. He was starting to recognize letters and tried to pronounce the words aloud by sounding them out.

Eliza stopped and pulled Ellwyne to a quiet area of the walkway. She felt pride when speaking of her late husband and was pleased when her son asked about him.

She gazed at the sky. "Edward Arthur Dacosta," she paused, looking down at Ellwyne. "Your father's name was Edward Arthur Dacosta. Edward, like the king. Arthur, which is also your middle name. And "dacosta" means "by the river" in Portuguese, which is why your father was drawn to Calcutta in the first place. He wanted to help with the problems of the river."

His eyes brightened with curiosity. "What was he like?" His eyebrows were permanently arched, as if he were about to ask an important question.

"Like a king, both clever and handsome," Eliza replied. She gazed at her ring finger and the gold band studded with diamonds and rubies still worn to feel close to her true love. "As I told you, no one could figure out how to keep the bridge from washing away down the river during monsoon season, but your papa solved it." She brimmed with pride. "Most of all, he loved you, Ellwyne, and wanted to take care of us."

He stretched out his arms and placed his hands on his hips. Eliza could see the gears turning inside his head. She knew that her son, like his father, spent time absorbed by thought. She prepared herself for the more difficult question that was coming.

"Why did he leave us, Momma?"

"He didn't want to leave us, Ellwyne." She knelt beside him, grasped his hands, and looked into his eyes. "Sometimes people get sick, and sometimes they don't get better," she said with a sigh. "Your papa tried to stay with us, but he was called home."

He peered at his mother with a look of alarm. "Will I be called home?"

"Yes, Ellwyne. Everyone is eventually called home." Long ago, Eliza had decided never to lie to her son about his father. "But you have lots of living to do first, so let's not think about that now," she said, giving his hand a squeeze. "Now, do you want to take that ride across the bridge I promised you?"

His eyes lit up. "Yes, Momma, I want to travel across Papa's bridge."

"Let's go catch a carriage. I'll show you how cleverly designed the bridge is. And maybe one day, you'll become an engineer like your father."

"Do you think so?"

"Yes, I believe you can accomplish anything you want, if you make up your mind to do it."

Eliza Dacosta was soft-spoken and had an elegant manner that made her appear fragile, like a glass figurine that would shatter to pieces if dropped. After becoming a widow, she spent more time in the company of her mother, Bessie Smyth. Thanks to Bessie's youthful appearance, they looked more like sisters than mother and daughter, which Bessie held as a source of pride. They shared the same raven-black hair and dark eyes, which contrasted with the porcelain skin they protected from the sun beneath parasols or wide-brimmed hats. Like most grandmothers, Bessie had a fondness for the black-haired boy, her only grandchild, and fussed over him at every opportunity.

"Let's go out into the garden, Grandmother," Ellwyne said. He usually visited her house on Tuesdays and Thursdays after his lessons. He liked to spend the afternoon in the garden with her. It was enclosed by a white brick wall that made it feel like a world separate from the bustle of the city around them. The fragrant, colourful flowers that bloomed burst with splotches of red, orange, and yellow. The brilliant red roses were Bessie's favourite, and she paused to breathe in their aroma before venturing further. Ellwyne often asked if he could pick a rose bloom.

"Before you ask, yes, you can bring a rose home to your mother," she told the boy.

The centrepiece of Bessie's garden was the magnificent, carved rosewood bench. Each leg was shaped like an elephant's head with a sturdy trunk. The seat had a temple design with swirling pillars extending in four directions, but the back-rest was the focal point. A carved peacock's plumage stretched across its width, and intertwined flowers mingled with the tail feathers, making it impossible to identify flower or fowl. As grand as any piece of sculpture displayed in a museum, the bench provided a tranquil spot to sit next to the birdbath. As though at a busy train station, the birds lined up to take turns splashing in the water held within the marble bath. It attracted colourful songbirds and butterflies stopping to take a sip.

Ellwyne ran ahead, exploring the paths that wound through the manicured plants and bushes.

"Be cautious of the peacocks, dear!" Bessie warned. Her garden was host to several peafowl, birds that stopped in to drink out of the birdbath and, sometimes, lay eggs near the dahlia bush. The iridescent blue-and-green plumage of the male bird was eye-catching, but they tended to be aggressive if approached too closely, and she didn't want Ellwyne lulled into thinking they were friendly.

"I'll be careful," he said. A series of paths led to the outer edges near the brick wall where the fruit trees grew. He wandered through, stopping to inhale the scent of citrus at the lemon and lime trees. Mangoes, hanging off the trees like Christmas ornaments, were greenish orange and at the peak of ripeness.

"May I pick a mango?"

"Only if you share it with me." A moment later, he brought two mangoes to his grandmother and set them gently in her lap.

"Here."

"I said we could *share* a mango," a slight admonishment filling her voice.

"We will," he replied. "But I also picked one for Momma." He looked up at his grandmother from beneath dark lashes.

Bessie's heart melted, and she regretted her first answer. "Ahh, sweet Ell. You're so much like your father." She pulled him in for a hug.

Ellwyne beamed. He wanted to be just like his father.

2

CALCUTTA, INDIA

THEY DELIVERED UNWELCOME messages for a living, and in a city the size of Calcutta, the channels of communication rarely stopped. Three thugs stood scowling outside the Bank of Calcutta with their eyes glued to the entrance. The tallest man had a ruddy complexion not well-suited to the searing Indian climate; he kept a hat pulled over his ears to protect them from the sun. His biceps bulged through his cotton shirt, flexing as he made a fist while he shuffled from one foot to the other. The other two men had more compact builds and framed their leader like tattered bookends in need of a good scrub. They all wore the dust from the streets of the city after having tailed their prey for several miles and watched him skulk into the bank twenty minutes earlier. Now, they were waiting in the afternoon's blazing sun for him to reappear so that they could pounce on him and deliver their boss's stern and final warning.

Inside the bank, the moustached man waited in the queue for the next available teller. He was impeccably dressed in a tidy three-piece suit, with polished black shoes that click-clacked as he crossed the bank's marble floor.

He stuck out his chin and cleared his throat as he prepared to speak. "I'd like to withdraw twenty-five pounds from my account," he snapped, tapping his toe as if in a rush.

The teller, a middle-aged man, whose grey side-burns contrasted with his dark-rimmed spectacles, left the window to sit at a desk where he pored over ledgers, turning pages, and making calculations on another paper. With each figure he recorded, he

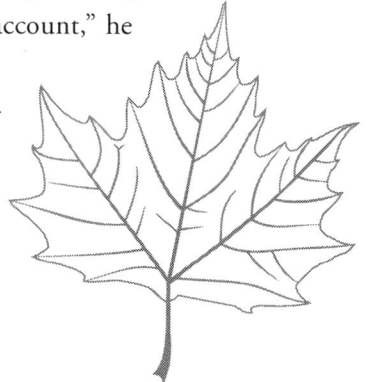

bobbed his head and tapped his fountain pen on the sheet of paper. He grunted disapproval as he summed the totals.

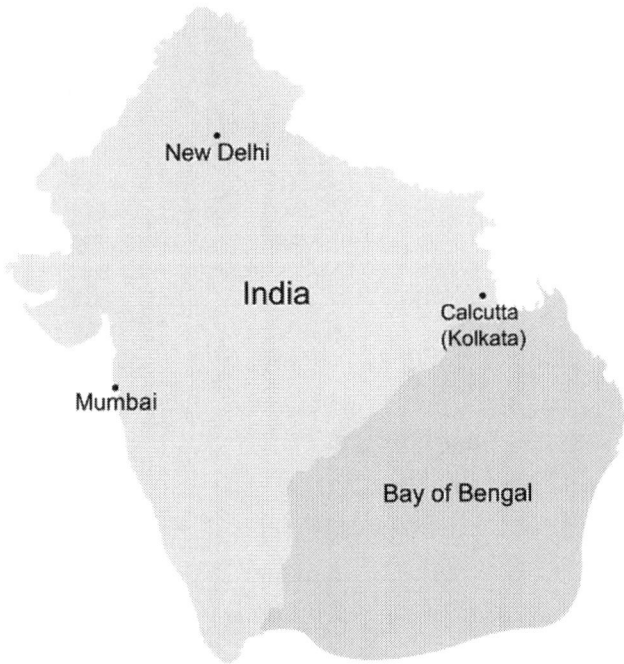

New Delhi

India

Calcutta (Kolkata)

Mumbai

Bay of Bengal

The moustached man, growing more impatient, willed him to pick up the pace by glaring at him, but the teller carried on with his methodical calculations. Row by row, line by line. After many minutes, the teller returned to the window. "I'm sorry, sir. You have only twelve pounds left in your account ..."

"Give me all of it, then." He lowered his voice as if trying to avoid drawing unwanted attention to himself.

"If we give you the remaining twelve pounds, that will close your account." The teller spoke as if this predicament occurred daily. "Is that what you'd like to do?" He did not look up from the ledger.

"Fine. Close the account," the man snarled. "I can always take my business elsewhere."

"Certainly, sir," said the teller without emotion. "Please give me a few moments to draw up the forms." He sauntered back to the desk and his ledger.

At the next window, a tall, slender, dark-haired woman with porcelain skin stood waiting for service. A dark-haired child clung to her skirt, humming to himself, oblivious to his surroundings. "If you're quiet and well-behaved, we can get some sweets on our way home," the woman said to the child, which the man presumed was her son.

The teller drew open the curtain. "How can I help you, madam?"

"I'd like to withdraw twenty-five pounds," she stated matter-of-factly as she handed him her passbook. It was difficult to hear her soft voice over the din of the bank, but the man leaned in to hear the entire conversation.

"Certainly, Mrs. Dacosta." The teller then disappeared into the vault. When he returned, he counted out the money and placed it on the counter in front of her. The woman picked it up in her gloved hands, placed it in her billfold, and tucked it into her clutch. "Is there anything else I can do for you, ma'am?"

She shifted forward. "How much do I still have in that account, if I may ask?" she whispered. The man at the next window leaned in closer.

"You have nine thousand two-hundred and eighty pounds in that account, ma'am." The man looked up to assess her reaction.

The woman smiled, a look of relief washing across her pale face. "I'm so happy to hear."

"A word of advice? Don't go broadcasting it around."

Her face flushed. "Yes, of course. One must be cautious in this life."

He nodded. "Now, is there anything else I can help you with?"

"No, thank you. That's all," she said with a slightly broader smile, reached down to take the boy's hand in hers, and walked towards the exit.

The teller returned to the man's window with a form for him to sign. After he signed, the teller placed twelve pounds on the counter in front of him. The man snatched the money and hastily put it in his billfold, which he placed in his breast pocket, and hurried out of the bank.

As soon as the man stepped onto the street, the three thugs descended upon him like starving hyenas ready to devour their next meal. On the crowded street, a disagreement between men was easily overlooked and got lost in the noise made by throngs of people. The shortest man roughly grabbed the man's right shoulder; the other thug latched onto his left shoulder and pinched it hard enough to cause the man to wince. The tallest man, wearing the hat, stood directly in front of him, blocking his escape.

"Mr. Ballantyne," hissed the man. His crooked nose, that of a retired boxer, wrinkled as he pronounced the words. "We are delivering a message to you from our employer, Mr. McIntyre. You have exactly two weeks to come up with the twenty-five pounds that you owe him," he lowered his voice ominously, "else it won't just be the gaming hall you're banned from." The glint of a knife blade caught the afternoon sun. The thug placed the knife beneath the man's throat, causing a slight drop of blood to appear beneath the blade. "This is your third and final warning. Understood?"

"Y-y-y-y-yes," he stammered. The whites of Duff Ballantyne's eyes flashed. The thug patted Duff's chest and retrieved his billfold. He opened it and counted its contents, then pocketed the money.

"Make that thirteen pounds. Two weeks," growled the thug, holding two fingers in front of Duff's nose. He tossed Duff's now-empty billfold on the street, where it was quickly snatched up by a nearby beggar, who tucked it into his basket and scurried into the alleyway. The three thugs laughed. They released their grip on Duff's shoulders, fell back into the crowds slithering along the street and disappeared.

He watched until he was sure they were gone before he dared breathe again. He wiped his sweaty brow with his handkerchief and dabbed the blood from his throat. All he had left were the few shillings in his pocket. Ahead, he saw the dark-haired woman from the bank with her boy stopped at a street vendor, where she was purchasing salted taffy. He followed her into the market, where she entered a general mercantile. Trying to remain inconspicuous, he furtively watched as she purchased flour, sugar, salt, and butter. The shop owner seemed to know the woman and welcomed her with a bright greeting.

"Hello, Mrs. Dacosta."

"Hello, Mr. Warren. Fine day, isn't it?"

"Yes, ma'am. Lots of supplies to fill up your pantry, I see?"

"They won't be in my pantry for long. I'm baking for the church bazaar," she replied. "Will I see you there?"

"I know my wife will be going, but I'll be here in the shop. It's on Saturday, if I'm not mistaken?" he asked.

"Yes," she said. "Everyone will be there."

In his head, Duff Ballantyne made a note to cancel his plans for next Saturday.

❧

Eliza had spent all day Friday baking her famous lemon tarts for the St. Paul's Cathedral bazaar. She and Ellwyne had carefully selected the lemons from their garden, and zested them together. Eliza knew from experience which lemons were the best for baking, and she was certain that her tarts would sell out quickly. She carefully loaded her baking into a picnic basket, and summoned a carriage to take her to St. Paul's Cathedral. In British India, Christian churches had been erected since colonization to accommodate the growing European population, but this was the largest and, some would say, most beautiful of its kind. Eliza found herself admiring the Gothic architecture from a distance as they approached. Its tall, magnificent spire reached two hundred feet towards the sky. The clock tower chimed eleven times as Eliza stepped onto the cobbles, gathered her basket, and headed towards the hall.

The sale was to start in thirty minutes, so all the bakers were setting up and getting ready for the opening. Her friend Helen Gardiner had already set out her Scottish shortbread and was across the hall, speaking with another parishioner. As she laid out tarts on the table in an attractive pattern on the plate, she noticed a man she had never seen before standing close to the neighbouring table. Although well-dressed and coiffed, he was out of place and was scanning the room as if doing surveillance. "I think we're going to have a big crowd," said Mrs. Jenkins, the sale organizer, as she passed Eliza's table.

"I believe so." replied Eliza. Out of the corner of her eye, Eliza noticed movement at Helen Gardiner's table. She turned in time to see the man rifling through Helen's change box and pocketing it.

"Stop! Thief!" Eliza instinctively cried out. Her shriek pierced the air, and everyone stopped talking and looked towards the sound. The man bolted towards the door. From out of the crowd, a taller man tackled the thief and knocked him to the ground. A flurry of punches flew between the two men as they rolled about on the floor. The tall man, once he gained the advantage of being on top, punched the thief in the face, which subdued him and ended the struggle. The tall man stood, grabbed the thief by the collar, and yelled, "Go on, get outta here, ya piece of filth." Then he held the thief's arms behind his back and frogmarched him out of the hall. As he tossed him onto the street, he shouted, "And stay out!"

The tall man re-entered the hall, dusted himself off, and smiled and nodded as people clapped and shouted, "Well done," and "Thank you."

Mrs. Gardiner scurried back to her table.

"What in heaven's name is going on?" she asked Eliza, a look of alarm clouding her face.

"That man was stealing from your change box. All I could think to do was yell." Eliza now wondered what other action she could have taken. Ever since her husband died, Eliza had found herself jumpier than normal when out in public, and especially when sums of money were involved. She often felt vulnerable and unprotected on the streets, where she worried about being mugged or harassed.

"Thank heavens you were watching. And thank goodness he was stopped. How fortunate that I invited Mr. Ballantyne to the sale, or else he might not have been apprehended."

"What do you mean? Do you know the man who stopped him?" Eliza's face froze with shock.

"Oh yes. That's an old family friend of mine. Duff Ballantyne. He's just moved here from Scotland," she explained. "He contacted me the other day, and I thought this would be a good chance for him to meet some new people. Let me introduce him to you."

Mrs. Gardiner excused herself to go see the tall man she had described as a family friend. Eliza watched as Mrs. Gardiner motioned towards her table and walked across the hall accompanied by the tall, handsome man.

"Mr. Ballantyne, I'd like to introduce you to my dear friend, Mrs. Dacosta."

Although careful not to stare, Eliza couldn't help but notice he had dark wavy hair, combed back with pomade, and a neatly twirled moustache. His eyes locked with Eliza's.

"Mrs. Dacosta, I am pleased to meet you," he said with a velvety voice.

"The pleasure is all mine. Won't you please have a lemon tart?" Eliza offered him the plate. "No charge."

Mrs. Gardiner smiled knowingly and nodded. She knew that both Eliza and Duff needed someone in their lives. *Life is a lonely road to travel alone,* she thought. The suave gentleman from Scotland, with his abundant charm and good looks, would make a suitable partner for Eliza, who had been alone for several years. "No one can resist Eliza's lemon tarts," she said.

Although money was tight, Duff Ballantyne considered his little ruse an investment in his future, a self-devised method to extract himself from his current dilemma. He ascended the wooden steps into the pub. Through the thick cigar smoke, he spotted Hugh McEwan sitting at the bar.

"Nice work. Very convincing," said Duff with a slight laugh.

"Just give me the damn shilling," he growled. He had a large gash over his left eye, and his coat was ripped at the seam. "And don't ask for any more favours, either."

3

CALCUTTA, INDIA

ELLWYNE WAS SEATED at the grand dining room table, his papers spread out all around its surface. His mother permitted him to do schoolwork at the table if he padded the writing paper and didn't press his pencil into the wood surface and leave a mark behind. He was practising his printing in the primer book, with its ruled pages spaced to accommodate his clumsy block letters. The pencil he gripped was shaking as he moved it across the page. Although only seven, he wanted to become proficient at printing so that he could some-day write the letters he often saw his mother and grandmother composing to family still in Scotland. When the front door slammed shut, he jumped.

"What are you doing, Mother?" Eliza, carrying a basket, headed to the kitchen. Ellwyne had to trot behind her to keep up with her pace.

"Pass me the lemon tarts, please," she told him. They were just made, and the aroma was still fresh in the kitchen. She placed them into the basket. "I'm putting together a package for Mrs. Stewart." Margaret Stewart was a frail, elderly woman they knew from church who patted Ellwyne on the head each time they met.

"What happened?" Ellwyne recognized that baskets of food often meant a death in the family, but he recalled that Mrs. Stewart's husband had died earlier in the year.

Eliza stopped what she was doing, and as she turned to face Ellwyne, a serious look washed over her face. "Something terrible happened, I'm afraid. I don't want to frighten you, but it's better that you learn that bad things sometimes happen."

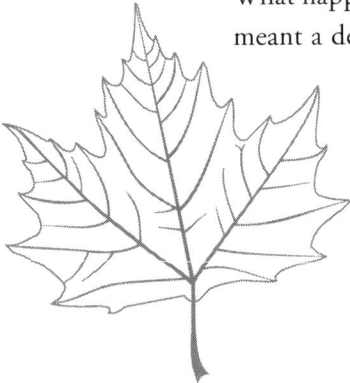

"What is it?"

"Mrs. Stewart was robbed. Thieves broke into her house and took things while she wasn't there."

"Is she okay?"

"She'll be fine, but she's frightened now. We're trying to make her feel better by letting her know that she has people who care about her," Eliza explained. "When people need help, it's our duty to step in and do something. Do you understand?"

"Yes, Momma." Ellwyne ran out of the kitchen and into the garden. When he returned, he had a pink dahlia bloom in his hand. "Maybe this would help Mrs. Stewart feel better?"

"Yes, I think you're right." Eliza was torn. She was proud that her son understood the need to care about others, but once again, she was reminded of how alone they were in a city as large as Calcutta.

⁂

"I have some news to share with you, Ell," Eliza said as she pulled Ellwyne into her lap when he returned from a visit with his grandmother. He straddled his mother's legs and grasped the arms of the velvet chair to keep his balance. He especially liked the quiet times that they spent together in the afternoons, just the two of them. That's when his mother would announce it was story time, and they would flip through the newspapers together. At first, he was only interested in pictures, but soon he was learning to read the stories about the bridges, trains, and roads starting to connect British India.

"What is it, Momma?"

"Do you remember the stories that I told you about your papa?" Eliza's soft voice, from a distance, sounded like the purring of a cat, which Ellwyne found soothing.

"Yes, Momma. He wanted to help fix a problem with the big river so that people could cross it."

"That's right. You won't ever forget that, will you?" The little boy shook his head in response.

"Good boy." Eliza took a long pause as she pressed her hands against her skirt to smooth out the wrinkles. "I can never replace your father, but you know that I have been lonely without him since he died?"

Ellwyne did not, in fact, know that. He thought that his mother was content with the way things were. His eyes widened slightly, preparing himself for what was coming next.

"Do you remember the Gardiners? They're the family we sat with at Christmas service last year." Ellwyne nodded. He remembered them because Mr. Gardiner smelled like stale cigars and Mrs. Gardiner had mints in her purse that she passed to him during the long sermon.

"They introduced me to a friend of theirs at the cathedral bazaar. He is a nice gentleman who has moved here from Scotland." Eliza watched Ellwyne's eyes. He was now staring at the floor, refusing to look back at her. She continued despite Ellwyne's obvious discomfort. "I have decided to marry this gentleman. His name is Duff Ballantyne. We're getting married in three weeks." Her words dropped like a sudden burst of unwelcome rain on a summer picnic.

Ellwyne pushed himself back from Eliza and hopped onto the floor. Landing with a thud, he didn't hear his mother's gentle voice pleading, "Ellwyne. Please, listen to me," as he ran out of the room and into the garden, where he plopped himself behind an azalea bush in full flower. Hurt and confused by his mother's shocking news, he wanted desperately to hide from the disruption being thrust upon him. He pounded his fist into the dirt and let out a little grunt of pain. Why did his world suddenly need to change?

Later that evening, after Ellwyne had taken a bath to wash the garden dirt from beneath his fingernails, he awaited the arrival of their invited guest. Dressed in his Sunday clothes, he sat stiffly on the settee with his legs dangling above the floor. He saw a tall man in a three-piece suit step into the hallway and preen himself in the mirror when he thought no one was watching. His mother came into the hallway and led the man into the parlour. The man reminded Ellwyne of the peacocks prancing in his grandmother's garden.

"Ellwyne, this is Mr. Ballantyne."

Duff Ballantyne stood with his chest puffed out and head held high.

"Hello, Mr. Ballantyne," Ellwyne muttered, feeling overwhelmed and a bit frightened. Few people, other than his grandmother and the servants, had entered their home. After she was widowed, Eliza stopped entertaining almost completely. As a result, her son was not used to having visitors, and it made him uneasy.

"Oh, so formal," cooed Duff as he stared at Ellwyne. "Please. Call me Father," said Duff, proffering his hand in a rushed attempt to seal a mutual agreement between himself and the boy.

Ellwyne continued to sit as if he had a metal rod holding his back straight. Eliza, sensing the tension between the two, interjected with an offer to get tea and biscuits, and excused herself from the room. Duff strode to the velvet chair and took a seat, exhaling as he sat with a plop, in the chair Ellwyne shared with his mother when she read newspaper articles aloud about the latest engineering inventions.

"Wait," exclaimed Ellwyne, his voice cutting through the quiet of the room. "You can't sit there." His brows furrowed.

"And why not?" A smirk appeared on Duff's face. His dark eyes turned a shade darker as he turned to focus on Ellwyne.

"That's where Momma and I sit together for story time." Ellwyne made a tight fist and gripped his fingernails into his palm. "It's *our* chair. *We* sit there." A tidy pile of newspapers was stacked next to the chair in a rattan rack.

The atmosphere in the room darkened as if a summer storm had rolled in. Duff Ballantyne narrowed his eyes and leaned forward in the chair. A prominent wrinkle appeared on his forehead. "Listen up, little boy," he snarled in a voice barely above a whisper. "*You* are not about to tell me what I can and cannot do in this home. *You* will not express your opinions." The words lashed Ellwyne like a whip. Duff's voice softened, though the boy sensed he was still capable of spewing venom at any time. "In fact, *you* will not *have* opinions at all." His words punctuated the air. Ellwyne kicked his legs, expressing his frustration in the only way he could.

Eliza re-entered the parlour, followed by a servant pushing a tea trolley containing her finest china and a plate overflowing with freshly baked tea biscuits. "Well, it looks like you two are starting to get to know one another?" Her tone was filled with hope.

In an instant, Duff Ballantyne's face lit up with a smile. "Yes, dear. Ellwyne was telling me about the chair and how he cannot wait to listen to my stories of Scotland." He turned to face Ellwyne. "Isn't that right, Ellwyne?"

Ellwyne pictured himself back in the garden. He was digging a hole large enough to crawl into. "Yes," he whispered.

"What's that?" Duff asked. "We cannot hear you. Speak up."

"Yes, *Mr. Ballantyne.*" Ellwyne replied in a defiant tone, clenching his teeth and only slightly more audible than before. In his mind's eye, he had thrown a handful of dirt from the garden onto Duff Ballantyne's crisp, white shirt.

The next day, upon hearing that Mr. Ballantyne was to arrive, Ellwyne had excused himself to his room. Though he was just a boy, Bessie Smyth trusted Ellwyne's instincts about Duff Ballantyne. Bessie was seated in her daughter's parlour in the favourite velvet chair. She stood to greet her daughter and her future son-in-law, her lips pursed. Something about this sudden arrangement didn't smell right. Why the big rush to get married? Bessie knew Eliza was well-positioned financially following Edward's death, but she also feared that her daughter's wealth made her vulnerable to attract the wrong types of men. When she had learned of Eliza's intention to marry Duff Ballantyne, she felt a sick, twisting feeling in her gut. Was he the wrong type of man? Something was not right about him, but she couldn't put her finger on exactly what bothered her most. Was it his arrogance or his crass manner that put her off? Either would be a negative trait, but Duff had both in spades. Or was he just hunting for easy money?

"Hello, Mr. Ballantyne," she said, in a tone she reserved for only the most formal of occasions. "Welcome to my home." Bessie purposely referred to Eliza's home as her own to test the reaction she would receive from the man she viewed as an unwelcome intruder. She had a suspicion and wanted to see if she was correct.

He paused, unsure how to continue. "Thank you, madam." He waited for her to indicate how she preferred to be addressed and to correct herself on its being her home. Silence was the only response he received. He noticed the intense way Bessie was examining him, which prompted him to puff out his chest even more. "I believe you mean, 'Welcome to *Eliza's* home,'" he said with an arrogant chuckle. Although Bessie had a youthful appearance, he assumed she was old enough to have a faulty memory. He sneered at her as if he had stepped into a muddy puddle.

Bessie's eyes flashed with reproach. She straightened. "We are taught to believe many things in this world, aren't we, Mr. Ballantyne," she replied, her tone rising. "I, for example, believe that it's important for people to have good manners." She gave her head a slight toss. "Please do have a seat."

Duff and Eliza seated themselves on the settee, close enough to almost be touching. Now seated closer to him, Bessie noticed the smell of alcohol wafting from his breath. Another mark against him was tallied on her scorecard.

"Mother, Mr. Ballantyne came to India from Scotland. He's an industrialist who sets up paper manufacturing facilities." Duff's chest swelled even further as Eliza spoke about him. After conversing politely for thirty minutes, Eliza excused herself from the room to prepare tea.

"I've a big day ahead of me tomorrow. I'm meeting with some investors from Britain who want to see the production facility up-and-running. Please give my apologies to Eliza, but I must go." As Duff rose from the settee, something shiny fell to the floor and made a rattle as it rolled before stopping at Bessie's foot with a soft clang. Without moving her head, she peered over to examine the object. It was Eliza's gold band, given to her by Edward Dacosta, easily identifiable by the diamonds and rubies encrusted with intricate filigree.

Duff leapt towards the ring, trying to pocket it before Eliza returned. On hands and knees, he swooped his left hand towards the ring in a scooping motion. Bessie stomped on the ring with her foot before his hand could reach it.

"As I said, Mr. Ballantyne," she stated frostily, "We are led to believe many things in this world. And I believe this is my daughter's ring, not yours to take."

He stammered, "Eliza asked me to take it to the jeweller to be cleaned. I have not had a chance to return it yet." He was still on all fours, looking like a dog begging for a bone from its owner.

"Fair enough, Mr. Ballantyne." She moved her foot and allowed him to retrieve the ring. "But," she snapped, to remind him he was not absolved of suspicion, "I will be watching you closely." She narrowed her eyes to slits.

And with her final statement, she stood and strode across the parlour and up the stairs to the study.

In that brief encounter, Bessie's opinion of the tall, handsome stranger was fixed. He had a taste for extravagant things and had been caught in a lie.

Perhaps Eliza had known Bessie would protest her daughter marrying Duff Ballantyne, because she hadn't given her an opportunity to speak up or object. She had introduced him toward the end of their whirlwind courtship and only days before they were set to marry.

Bessie felt it was a mismatch not only of personality but also of moral fibre. Eliza was kind and trusting. Duff was untrustworthy. The two were a bad fit. And then there was the matter of the little boy who came along with Eliza. She doubted that Duff, the loud and boorish braggart, cared to raise another man's child. He was too wrapped up in his own interests to bother with the well-being of a child.

*

His mother's remarriage to Duff Ballantyne changed the course of Ellwyne's life dramatically.

The initial modest ripples it produced in his life led to larger swells with far-reaching impacts, not just on the boy but also on a family a continent away, whom he had not yet met. And on that same continent, in a corner woodlot, a stand of trees huddled tightly, the remnant of what had been a huge forest a few decades earlier. The mature trees welcomed the newest seed, now cushioned in the loamy soil beneath. The lone buttonwood seed waited.

4

CALCUTTA, INDIA

TEN MONTHS AFTER marrying Duff Ballantyne, Eliza gave birth to a baby girl, Ellwyne's half-sister, Valetta. She was a blond-haired baby with ringlets and dancing eyes. As soon as she could walk, she began to follow her older sibling everywhere, sometimes to his great frustration.

"She's always following me," he would exclaim as the little girl clung to his trouser legs, making it difficult for him to walk.

"It's simply because she admires you, Ellwyne," Eliza explained with a smile. "Imitation is the sincerest form of flattery, after all." Mostly, Ellwyne appreciated the company of his younger sister and spent time playing with her in the garden. On the streets of Calcutta, they walked hand-in-hand, the older brother guiding his younger sister safely through the throngs.

"Stay close to my side, Valetta," he would tell her as they left the house. Valetta never disobeyed him and clamped his hand as they walked.

Ellwyne returned from his grandmother's after a Tuesday visit and bounded into the hallway, eager to present his mother with the delicate rose bloom he had selected especially for her from Bessie's garden.

"Momma?" he yelled as he entered the house.

No response.

"Momma where are you?" he yelled again, running into the hallway.

"Keep your voice down, boy." The grumbled reply came from the parlour, as if from a bear that had been awakened from its hibernation a few weeks early.

Ellwyne smelled the pungent aroma of cigar smoke emanating from the parlour that, in addition to the growling voice, signalled that his stepfather was present. Ellwyne edged into the room. "Do you know where my mother is?" he asked in a much quieter voice.

His stepfather was seated in the red velvet chair, his large frame filling the entire space that he and his mother shared for story time. "She's sleeping." Duff continued to puff on his cigar.

Ellwyne stared at his stepfather. Without thinking, he blurted, "That's our chair."

Duff Ballantyne inhaled the cigar, looking straight at the boy. The lit end of the cigar glowed like a demon's eye as he took the cigar and butted it into the red velvet fabric, twisting it back and forth, until it was extinguished. The scent of smouldering fabric soon replaced the pungent smell of cigar smoke. "This isn't *your* chair. And, as I've told you before, you will not have opinions." He stood and strode across the parlour and up the stairs to the bedroom.

After ensuring he was gone, Ellwyne tiptoed across the parlour to examine the damage done to the beloved velvet chair. His fist still clenched the rose bloom that he had picked for his mother. He placed it into the hole left behind in the fabric. "It's our chair."

Eliza was not just sleeping.

She had come down with a fever. And with few medical interventions available, such fevers often proved deadly. She quickly deteriorated, and from what eleven-year-old Ellwyne could surmise, her condition was grave. After five days with no information about her condition, Ellwyne could only conclude that things were serious. Outside his mother's bedroom door, Ellwyne shrank to the floor and pulled his knees to his chest, wrapping his arms around them. He was prepared to stay put until he received any morsel of information about Eliza's condition. He needed to know what was happening with her.

Approaching footsteps awakened the boy. He wasn't sure how long he had been dozing. He stretched his stiff legs and rubbed the sleep from his eyes.

"Excuse me, sir." Ellwyne looked up at the doctor. "Can you please tell me what's going on with my mother?"

The doctor looked at him and paused. "I'm sorry, son. I must attend to the patient."

"I know, but I need to know what's happening."

"I suggest you ask your father about that." And with that, he opened the door and slipped inside his mother's room. Unable to contain his growing frustration, Ellwyne pounded his fist on the plaster wall. "He is *not* my father," he said under his breath.

He tried listening to the muffled conversations inside between Eliza, his stepfather, and the doctor, but he couldn't make out any of their words.

"What's going on with my mother?" Ellwyne asked his stepfather as he exited the bedroom more than a half-hour later.

"Your mother is very sick," Duff continued to walk away.

"Can I see her?" he asked, hopeful for an affirmative answer. The only constant in Ellwyne's life had been his mother. She was his protector, his teacher, and the person he admired the most. He was afraid to even to consider the idea of losing her, especially since he had already lost his father in a similar manner.

"She's resting. I think you'd better wait," his stepfather answered over his shoulder without stopping.

Ellwyne waited until Duff had left, quietly opened the door, and shuffled to his mother's bedside. What he saw shocked him. His mother, who had appeared perfectly healthy just a few days earlier, now looked to have shrunk two sizes. Her black hair was pasted across her forehead, and the sheets were drenched in sweat. She was whimpering and writhing in pain.

"Momma, can you hear me?" A fly landed on her forehead, which he quickly whisked away.

No answer.

Eliza's eyes were fluttering open and closed and she struggled to focus.

"Momma, it's me. Ellwyne. Please let me know if you can hear me."

No response.

He knelt beside her bed and gently took her hand in his. It was clammy and hot. He could feel her pulse at her wrist; her heart was beating wildly.

"Momma, please don't leave me." Tears streamed down his cheeks. At that moment, though no one had told him, he knew his mother was dying.

Suddenly, Eliza's parched lips began to move. Ellwyne could tell that she was attempting to speak, but it was taking all her energy to muster the strength. He rested his head on the side of her bed, listened to her uneven breathing, and watched her chest heave up and down with each breath. He closed his eyes and tried to picture happier times. After several minutes, he heard his mother finally whisper the words she had been struggling to say: "I love you. I don't want to leave you." Her voice was barely above a whisper, and Ellwyne had to struggle to hear her. She continued, "But ... I'm being," she gasped for air, "called home."

Tears cascading down his cheeks, Ellwyne squeezed his mother's hand. "I love you back, Momma." In his mind, he pleaded with her not to go, but he knew she had no authority over when it was her time to leave. She squeezed his hand. It was nearly imperceptible, but Ellwyne felt it. Eliza closed her eyes and fell back into a restless state of semi-consciousness.

"Ellwyne?" He had drifted off to sleep beside his mother, oblivious to the passage of time. His grandmother stood at Eliza's bedside; concern washed over her face. "You should sleep in your own bed."

"No, I'm not leaving my mother. You can send me away, but I'll sneak back here."

She sighed. It wasn't worth arguing with him. "Fine then, dear. I'll be in the guest room. Come get me if you need to." She reached and held Eliza's hand, stroking it. "Rest well, my girl. The doctor is coming to see you tomorrow."

Ellwyne stayed next to his mother's side for the remainder of the evening, dabbing her forehead with damp cloths to try to keep her cool. He offered her sips of water. He held her hand. He told her over and over that he was with her. From the parlour below, he heard the clock chime eleven times, crawled into the bed beside Eliza, nuzzled next to her while holding onto her hand, and fell asleep. He dreamed, vividly, of his mother, resplendent in a light blue dress with puff sleeves, walking across the Hooghly River Bridge. A beam of light radiated around her as she strolled along the empty structure. At the far side of the bridge, a handsome black-haired man wearing a dark grey suit and top hat awaited her with open arms. As Eliza approached him, she said, "Am I finally home, Edward?" Ellwyne's father nodded, his eyes brimming with tears. Eliza fell into his embrace, and they stood locked together while the beam of light enveloped both of them. They turned and walked the rest of the way across the bridge together, hand in hand. The beam of light faded, and his parents disappeared into the darkness on the other side of the bridge.

"Noooooooo! Please don't go!" he yelled towards them.

It was early morning. He awoke to find that he was still holding his mother's hand, which was now cold and damp. Her forehead was cool to his touch.

Without him, Eliza had gone home.

5

MOSA TOWNSHIP, ONTARIO, CANADA, 1902

THOUSANDS OF MILES away from India, in a small farming community at the southwestern tip of Ontario, Canada, Betsy Jane McAlpine finished hoeing the final row of her vegetable garden and wiped the salty sweat from her brow. She had worked in the thick, fertile soil of Mosa Township her entire life. The vegetable garden was vital to her family's survival, and it fed them all year long, whether as fresh vegetables in the spring, summer, and fall, or as canned ones in the dark of winter. As she stood and stretched her weary back, she reflected on her years of tending the garden.

"There, that should do it," she said to the collie sprawled out on the grass, his tongue draped out the side of his mouth. The crop of carrots and beets was bountiful this year, and she would have many vegetables to put up in jars. She had won the ongoing battle with the rabbits and had kept them mostly out of her vegetable bed by erecting a small fence around its perimeter. The secret, she had discovered long ago, was to outwork the opponent. Even though the rabbits were hungry and appreciated an easy meal, they couldn't be bothered to jump the fence and earn the price of admission.

For her, the work never finished. It often felt like she had been working hard her entire life, which had been strung together from one chore after another. She picked up the hoe and brought it back to the barn and hung it on the hook on the wall.

Betsy Jane was a tall, slender young woman with long, chestnut-coloured hair that she kept loosely tied in a bun at the nape of her neck. Hard

work came naturally to her. Her ancestors were Scottish settlers, the hardy people who toiled to clear the land to make it suitable for farming. By age fourteen, she had already developed red and rough hands from a life spent farming, cooking, and scrubbing with lye soap. In her township and in neighbouring Ekfrid, most families were descended from Gaelic-speaking Scottish settlers who came from the Highlands and the Lowlands, lured to the New World by the promise of "free" land. Starting in the 1820s, the English Colonel Thomas Talbot, the administrator in the region, had given out land grants consisting of one or two hundred acres with the proviso that the settlers had to clear a certain percentage of their parcel for farming. The land was thick with the deeply rooted deciduous trees of the Carolinian Forest. Although free land was a generous offer, clearing it for farming was a daunting task, undertaken only by the most persistent of souls.

Betsy Jane grew up listening to the stories of the previous generation describing the battle they had fought to turn pristine Canadian bush into workable acreage. They were armed only with saws and axes, the will of men, the brute force of heavy draft horses, and the assistance of women and children. First, they felled the smallest trees, carrying them to a pile where they dried them out before burning them in massive bonfires. They girdled the trunks of the giant trees, chopped them down and burned them, too. Removing the stumps was nearly impossible, given their tools, and most crops in the early years of settlement were planted amid the remaining large stumps. The effort required to make the land arable was backbreaking but, unlike the rabbit reluctant to hop over the garden fence for an easy meal, the Scottish settlers did not give up on something freely offered, even if it was difficult to obtain.

On her way back to the house, Betsy Jane stopped at the mulberry tree. Although her ancestors had spilled their blood and sweat removing trees from the land, she felt a natural affinity to trees and appreciated seeing new ones take hold. She had planted the mulberry from a seed several years before and had been watching, in awe, as it first became a sapling and matured into a stout tree. She fussed over it, protecting it from the hungry appetites of rabbits.

"How are you today, Mr. Mulberry?" She stroked its lowest branch. She believed trees grew better if you spoke to them. "You're looking mighty strong."

"Betsy Jane McAlpine!" The yell came from the wooden farmhouse where she lived with her mother, stepfather, and three half-siblings. Her mother only used her full name when she needed something urgently. "Betsy Jane, I need you here."

She sighed. "Coming, Mother," she yelled back. As the eldest daughter, Betsy Jane's services were constantly in demand. She was required to help with gardening, cooking, baking, cleaning, and, of course, child rearing. "Come on, Shep." she said to the black and white collie that had followed her to the barn and was at her heels now as she responded to her mother. "We're needed at the house."

"Oh good, you're back," Nancy said as she entered through the creaky screen door. "The Campbells are coming over for tea later, and I need you to whip up a sourdough bread." They kept a sourdough starter in the pantry, so it was easy enough to bake bread, but it was a task that Betsy Jane didn't particularly feel like doing after a hard day's work in the garden. Her arms were aching, and her back was sore.

"Yes, Mother."

"And please keep an ear out for Maggie Belle. She has been sleeping, but I suspect she'll wake up any time and then will be cranky. I'm going to lie down before the Campbells arrive." Conveniently, Nancy needed to lie down before company came, meaning that Betsy Jane was left to do the work on her own. Betsy Jane sighed deeply. Having company meant extra preparation and clean-up work for her. She would much rather spend her time caring for her younger siblings than pumping water and washing dishes in the basin. Life's most important job, mothering, came effortlessly to her. She had had the mothering instinct from an early age and dreamed about the day she would have her own house and would fill it with children.

"When I'm in charge, I certainly won't spend my life washing dishes in a basin for the company," she said to no one. She headed to the kitchen and began preparing the ingredients for the sourdough bread. From a young age, Betsy Jane had been a no-nonsense person who didn't believe in putting on airs for company. Unlike her mother, she wasn't interested in trying to impress or outdo others.

"What'cha doing, Betsy Jane?" A small voice came from behind her as she kneaded the sticky dough on the countertop, adding more flour to keep it moving in her hands. It was her twelve-year-old half-brother, Duncan Alexander, whom everyone simply called "DA." His reddish cheeks were covered by smudges of dirt, which he would soon be asked to scrub away at the pump, with the icy cold water and a clean cloth. The groundwater was thick with minerals, often giving it a rusty tinge and a sulphur smell, like rotten eggs.

"I'm making bread for the company. The Campbells are coming over soon. Did you finish your schoolwork for tomorrow?" she asked him. DA was not fond of school, so Betsy Jane often spent time helping him finish his exercises.

"No. Could you help me?"

"Of course. Let me get this in the cookstove first. Get your primer and we'll sit at the table together."

"Okay."

"Watch the mat." she said. The brown-haired boy ran off to get his workbook and pencil, tripping over the mat as he ran out of the kitchen.

With the bread baking in the cookstove, Betsy Jane removed her apron and sat in the chair beside DA, who had already opened his workbook and was waiting for her instructions.

"Let's complete the alphabet first," she advised the young boy, who was holding his pencil improperly and struggling to move it across the brown paper. DA was learning how to write in cursive. "Hold your pencil like this," she advised, showing him the proper technique. She was known for her own beautiful handwriting. In her primary school scribbler, she had practised her cursive script, filling the lines of the pages in a beautiful, swirling hand. She had soon become expert at producing such a uniform script that it looked as though it came from a typesetter instead of being guided by a human hand.

As she watched DA's tiny hand trembling as he exerted pressure on the pencil, her thoughts drifted back to her own days in school. Although she now rarely used it, she had grown up surrounded by Gaelic, which she had spoken routinely until she enrolled in primary school. Under British authority, Mosa Township had strict regulations enforcing English-only within one-quarter mile of the schoolhouse. Betsy Jane and her classmates soon learned at what point they had to start speaking English when they approached in the morning and at what point they could revert to speaking

Gaelic when they were walking home from school. Despite being forced to learn in a language that wasn't her mother tongue, Betsy Jane was an excellent student and keen to learn.

"You're doing so much better," she told DA as he finished the fourteenth letter of the alphabet. He grinned and continued. With the wise head of a farmer and the tender heart of a mother, Betsy Jane knew that encouragement, above all else, helped things grow.

6

THE CORNER WOODLOT, EKFRID TOWNSHIP, ONTARIO, CANADA

THE GROWTH OF a tree is one of nature's extraordinary events. To overcome the odds against survival when sprouting from a seed defies comprehension. Vying for the resources of soil, light, and water, while avoiding the threat from herbivores, insects, and bacteria, a seed must fight to survive.

In the spring, a buttonwood seed was propelled from a doe's coat as she ran through a wooded corner of a farmer's field about ten miles from the winding river. This seed had travelled far from the riverbed: through fields, across roads, and over fences. Although much of the land had already been cleared for farming, patches of its natural ecosystem, thick with leafy deciduous trees, remained as unspoiled as they had been for centuries. The field's heavy clay soil, with its poor drainage and distance from the river, was not hospitable to a buttonwood tree.

Human eyes cannot see the cooperation between trees. Human ears cannot detect the sound frequencies and vibrations that all trees make, a hum that reflects feelings of stress or contentment. The forest appears a competitive environment, but it is actually a community, one that helps younger members take hold and weaker members survive. The network beneath the ground, like

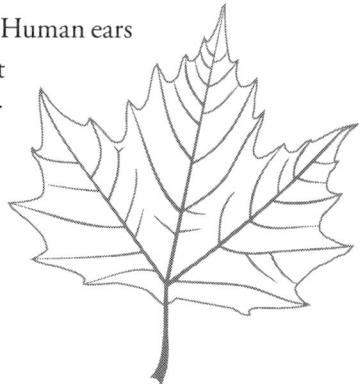

an intricate tangle of arms and fingers, interconnects one tree with another. Like a team working in harmony, the trees of the forest pass nutrients and information key to survival back and forth.

After the seed was pushed into the ground under the hoof of a wandering deer, its casing opened when a heavy rain moistened the soil. It began sending tiny roots into the soil, fingerlings looking for something to grasp. Now, all it needed was time.

Time.

Luck.

Protection.

And a source of nourishment. All things grow, with nourishment.

7

MOSA TOWNSHIP, ONTARIO, CANADA

"ARE YOU ALMOST ready?" Betsy Jane eyed her mother, who was scurrying around the house looking for her plaid handkerchief made from the bright red and green Walker clan tartan. Betsy Jane was dressed in her freshly laundered green dress with puff sleeves. On it, she had pinned her precious cameo brooch at her throat. It was her finest outfit and a departure from her usual work clothes, which bore dirt stains and patches hiding the many rips and tears in the fabric. At twenty-three, Betsy Jane had matured into a tall, long-haired beauty with piercing hazel eyes that could instantly detect even the slightest degree of insincerity or dishonesty.

"Nearly ready."

Betsy Jane sighed. She knew that her mother's version of "nearly ready" meant "*not* nearly ready." She could already feel her toes begin to tap. "I'll go harness the horse." Wearing her best dress to the barn, she risked attracting unwanted stains.

They were on their way to the annual fall fair. Each year since 1877, Glencoe had held a fair. By 1905, it had grown to become a much-anticipated tradition that celebrated the local harvest and brought people together in a myriad of friendly competitions, showcasing local excellence in cultivation of crops, herds, and flocks, and prowess in baking, gardening, and flower arrangement. People prepared weeks in advance, selecting the finest things from their field, garden, or kitchen to exhibit in the hopes of bringing home a ribbon or two, and more important, the admiration of their peers for their efforts.

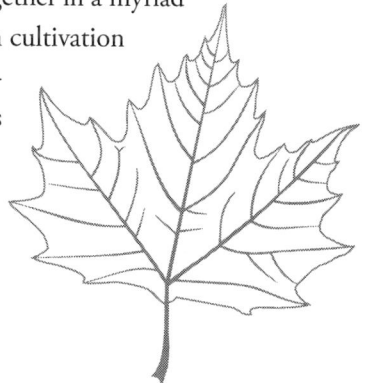

Betsy Jane's particular interest was the baking competition. For three whole days, she toiled in the kitchen, whipping up apple pie with juicy, tart apples selected from her own orchard, as well as pumpkin pie and carrot cake—all of which were now safely tucked into a basket. She had also selected her finest jars of strawberry jam, preserved plums, and grape jelly to enter in the preserves category. But this year, she was particularly anxious to debut her new cabbage and beet relish in the fair's preserves competition. It was a recipe she had created from scratch, and she hoped that it would win her recognition for her ingenuity. She had had an overwhelming harvest of red beets from the garden that summer and had stumbled upon the idea of mixing them with cabbage and vinegar to come up with a relish that didn't require canning. This cut down on her work significantly but did not sacrifice the taste, and everyone who tried it, loved it.

The twenty-minute ride to Glencoe was filled with chatter about who they would see and what they would do at the fair, a welcome break from the usual hard work and routines involved with maintaining a farm. Betsy Jane clucked at the horse to keep her moving along at a steady pace. She listened to her half-siblings, seated behind her, discussing who they might run into and what candy they might be able to buy at the midway.

They pulled into the main street of Glencoe and headed towards the fairgrounds. On that sunny Saturday in September, all roads led to the fairground, and they fell behind a stream of carriages and wagons heading down Mill Street. Betsy Jane turned the democrat into the fairgrounds, hitched the horse to the rail, and secured a feed bag. "There you go, Clara. Eat up. We'll be back in a few hours." She patted the horse, still sweaty from the exertion, on its neck.

Betsy Jane and her mother said goodbye to the younger boys and watched as DA and Archie took off at a gallop to go exploring the grounds together.

"No horseplay!" their mother yelled after them as they disappeared into the crowd.

Betsy Jane shook her head. "Let them be, Mother. They can kick up their heels as long as no one gets hurt."

Maggie Belle wanted to stay with her mother and older sister instead of running off to explore the fair with her more boisterous brothers. Betsy Jane grabbed her basket full of baked goods and headed towards the exhibitor's hall. Glencoe's main fairground building was known to everyone as the "crystal palace," although many of the farmers referred to it by a simpler moniker: the "cow palace." This octagonal-shaped wooden building had a main floor for exhibiting produce, baking, flowers, and smaller livestock like fowl and rabbits. The hall was lit largely by natural light that spilled in through the skylights in the roof. The upper floor was reserved for prize-winning entries in the baking categories, and the goal in each competitor's mind was for their entries to reach the second floor for showcasing. After registering for the competition, Betsy Jane was given a numbered table where she needed to go set up her wares. She headed towards the corner of the hall, wrestling her way through the crowds that were already milling about, waiting for the judges to begin tasting the baking and rendering their decisions. The basket became heavier in her hand the longer she held it, and she was eager to finally set it down.

"Here's my table," she said to her mother. She began setting out her pies and her jars of jams, plums, and relish. Like all accidents, it happened before she even realized what was going on. She felt a brush against her leg and gasped, watching helplessly while her table, and its contents, collapsed on the floor with a crash. Her pumpkin pie landed filling-side down on top of the apple pie, and her jars shattered into pieces as they hit the cement floor, causing the crowd to go silent at the sound of breaking glass. The delicious smell of pumpkin pie and cinnamon wafted and filled the air. She saw two older boys running away from the scene, laughing like hyenas as they escaped.

A smaller boy was splayed out on the floor on his stomach beside her knocked-over table, whimpering slightly.

"All your baking is ruined," cried her mother. "All that effort, gone." She made a tsk-tsk sound and shook her head.

Betsy Jane knelt and reached out to the boy, who was now attempting to get up. His face was dirty, and his nose was bleeding. She noticed that his trousers were not mended. "Are you okay?" she asked him.

The boy nodded, trying to suck back his tears, but one streamed down his dirtied cheek, leaving a trail across his face.

"What's going on?"

"He's acting like a fool, that's what's going on," said Nancy. Betsy Jane shot her mother a stern look and turned her attention back to the boy.

With his eyes cast downward and his bottom lip jutted out, the frowning boy did not respond. Betsy Jane offered him a hand and helped him get up. "Come on, let's get you cleaned up."

"I'm sorry about your pies, miss," he finally whispered. "The boys said they were gonna lock me in with the pigs. That's why I was running."

"Oh, they did, did they?" She felt her voice rising along with her temper.

"Yeah. They said I was a runt. Just like a pig." Betsy Jane noticed at that instant that he was awfully small. "They pushed me into the table, you know."

"I figured as much. Well, it's all done with now. No use crying over spilt milk." She paused. "Or spilt pies." From her vantage point, she could tell that the golden crusts were flaked to perfection and might have won a ribbon. "What's your name, anyway?"

The boy finally smiled, half-heartedly. "I'm Thomas."

Just then, a taller man approached and nodded his head at Betsy Jane. "Excuse me, is this yours?" He was holding a jar of beet and cabbage relish that had somehow miraculously survived the calamity. Although it was dusty from having rolled across the floor, the seal of the jar was not broken. By divine intervention, Betsy Jane had one remaining unbroken jar.

"Oh my, it is mine. I would recognize those red beets anywhere. I think my hands are still stained from slicing them," she said, glancing at her palms.

"I think you can still enter this jar if you wanted to. It's not broken."

"Nope, the jar's not broken, but my heart is. Thank you for retrieving it," she said, taking the jar from his large, weathered hands. He had the hands of a farmer. She noticed that he had a gentle face with kind eyes. "Betsy Jane McAlpine," she said with an extended hand. "But you can call me Betsy Jane."

He took her hand in his. "Nice to meet you, Betsy Jane. I'm James Andrew Carruthers, but everyone calls me 'James Andrew.' Well, some friends call me Jim, but please call me James A." In the Scottish settlements of Mosa and Ekfrid Townships, the first names John, Robert, Alexander, and James were extremely common, forcing neighbours and families to come up with ways to distinguish between the multitude of men with the same first (and sometimes last) name. People relied on middle names, initials, or nicknames based on appearance or personality to identify them.

"Will you excuse me while I take care of my new friend?" she asked the handsome farmer.

The man nodded. "Certainly." James A. watched as Betsy Jane led Thomas towards the exit. At the hand pump outside the crystal palace, Betsy Jane pumped some cold water and washed off his face with her dampened handkerchief. She noticed his bright blue eyes were less red now that his tears had dried. He looked at her. "Thanks, miss."

"Off with you, then, Thomas. If the bigger boys bother you again, you know where to find me," she said. "Run to me, and I'll deal with them."

He launched himself as if propelled by wings and disappeared into the crowds forming near the paddock, where the beef and dairy cattle were being shown. When she walked back to find her mother and her table, she was amazed to see that the table and its smashed contents had already been cleaned up. No evidence remained of the disaster that preceded.

"Thanks for taking care of that mess, Mother."

"It wasn't me. It was him," her mother motioned towards James A., who was now leaning against the wall, whistling a joyful tune that she recognized as a popular Scottish reel.

Betsy Jane walked towards him. She noticed that he had a bushy moustache and sharply carved features. Most of all, he had gentle eyes, and when he looked at her, she felt a flurry of energy tumbling about in her stomach. "Thank you for helping clean up the mess. That was kind of you, James A."

"It was the least I could do, especially because you lost all your entries."

"Not all of them." She held out the jar of beet and cabbage relish. "My thanks to you for helping out. Enjoy."

He was touched by the offer of her lone remaining item. "Most women I know would have taken it out on the boy."

"But he'd already been picked on once by the boys. No need to make it worse. Maybe it comes from my experience with my chickens. I never let the weak ones get pecked to death."

"That's the way it should be."

She smiled. "It's like the Good Book says, 'Treat others as you would have done unto you.' Anyway, would you like to try my beet relish? It could have been a prize winner after all. I guess we'll never know."

James A. smiled. "It's already a winner to me," he said with a wink.

That day in 1905 at the Glencoe Fair, Betsy Jane might have lost the contest for her baking entries and her relish, but she won the heart and admiration of James A. Carruthers.

James A. was smitten. From their first meeting, he made up his mind that he wanted to start a life with Betsy Jane McAlpine and set out to do his best to make sure that it happened. He asked around and found out in what area of Mosa Township she lived and planned to attend the next community social held at the schoolhouse in her area. He knew that the social was his best chance to see her again without being too pushy about it.

On a Saturday evening in November, James A. and his brother Neil travelled to schoolhouse Number 9 in Mosa Township, armed with a fried cabbage dish to add to the potluck. As soon as he spotted her, James A. nodded, and headed in her direction.

"Betsy Jane, it's wonderful to see you again," he said.

She had spied him coming towards her and hoped that her face wasn't too pink, though she could feel her stomach fluttering and her cheeks burning. "Why James A. What a lovely surprise."

"Here you go," he said. "I'm returning your jar, you know, from the fair." He handed her the canning jar that had once contained her beet and cabbage relish, retrieved from the dusty floor of the cow palace at the Glencoe Fair. A plaid bow, which she assumed was the Carruthers clan tartan, was tied around the neck of it.

"Oh, I never expected to get it back. Thank you."

"The relish was delicious. Truth be told, I ate most of it in one sitting, straight out of the jar."

"I bet you wished you found a bigger jar, then." Betsy Jane well knew that farmers worked up big appetites from their hours of hard work each day, tending to animals and fields and other countless chores, so his admission neither alarmed nor offended her.

"No, I just need a smaller appetite. And maybe better willpower." *He has the most charming smile,* she thought.

Betsy Jane held up the jar, noticing it was now filled with hard-looking brown nuts that resembled walnuts. She didn't recognize the species. "Thank you for returning the jar, but what's inside?" she asked, her curiosity genuinely piqued.

"Those are hickory tree seeds."

"I love trees."

He smiled. "I heard that you did."

"Curious," she said, as a smile curled the corners of her lips and her face flushed.

"I thought we could plant them." He paused and gazed into Betsy Jane's hazel eyes. "Together."

Her heart soared. "Oh? And where would you suggest planting them?"

"How about at my farm."

"And where's that?"

"Carruthers Corners, in Ekfrid Township. You heard of it?"

She hadn't. James A. explained the history of the "dot on the map" where he lived and that it was so-named because three of four farms at the intersection were inhabited by Carruthers clan members: in addition to James A.'s property was one farmed by both his father, Christopher (known as 'Kersty') and half-brother Neil and another occupied by Kersty's other son, Robert. James A.'s eldest brother, William Carruthers, also owned a farm located down the road from the Corners.

"It sounds like a grand place to plant trees," she said. "When do I get to see it?"

"I can take you out next Sunday after church. How does that sound?"

"I'd like that very much." She felt her face go hot, blushing pink at the thought of spending time alone with her handsome suitor.

The fiddle music began, and the magnetic lure of a Scottish reel filled the schoolhouse. The crowd began excited calls of "Hya!" and "Yip!" as the catchy rhythm of the music reached out and pulled them onto the wooden dance floor. After sharing a meal, the community usually pushed aside the tables to make way for dancing to end the evening's festivities. To prepare the floor, two young girls swept the dust and sprinkled it with cornmeal to give it a more slippery surface conducive to step dancing.

Carruthers Corner, circa 1911

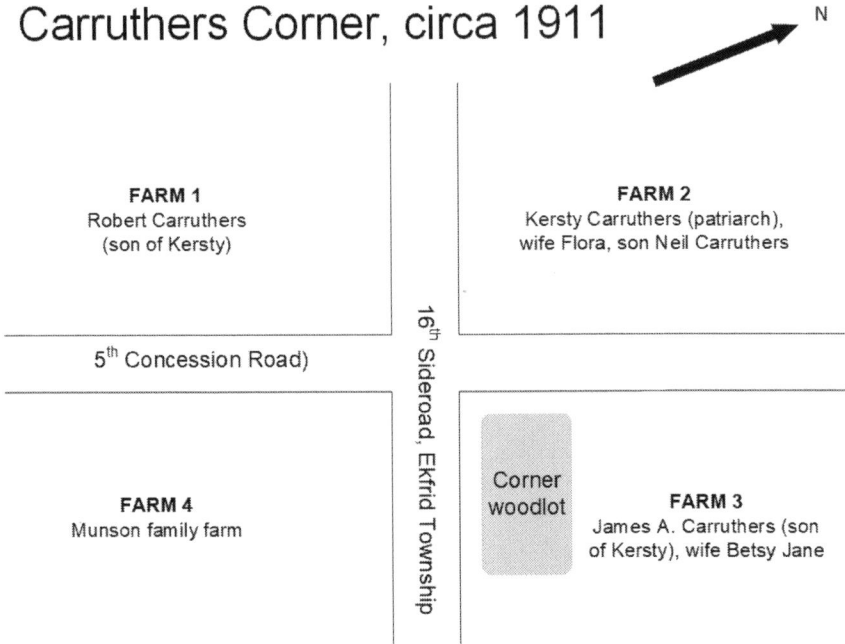

N

FARM 1
Robert Carruthers
(son of Kersty)

FARM 2
Kersty Carruthers (patriarch),
wife Flora, son Neil Carruthers

5th Concession Road)

16th Sideroad, Ekfrid Township

FARM 4
Munson family farm

Corner
woodlot

FARM 3
James A. Carruthers (son
of Kersty), wife Betsy Jane

"Will you join me in a dance, Betsy Jane?" he asked as he extended his hand to her.

She shook her head no. "Dancing isn't really my strength, but I'll certainly enjoy watching you from the sidelines, if that's okay." Betsy Jane exuded confidence in most areas of life, except this one. She did not have confidence in her dancing abilities and usually ducked out of opportunities to take the floor. Not one to pester or prod, James A. nodded, masking his disappointment, and headed towards the dance floor alone. Betsy Jane stood against the wall and fixed her gaze on James A., who blended in with a mob of others, mostly men, who also wanted to step-dance the traditional reel. The hardwood floor provided the perfect acoustics for step-dancing, echoing the tap-tap-tap of the dancer's feet. The fiddler opened at a slow pace, which meant that most dancers were able to keep up with his rhythm. But as sure as the sun rises, the fiddler switched to a speedier rhythm, prompting most of the dancers to drop out and retire from the floor, glistening in sweat from the effort. Betsy Jane watched intently, her toe tapping in time and clapping to the beat, as James A. expertly kept up with the faster rhythm, his feet tapping and moving in perfect coordination with the fiddle music. She noticed that he beamed the entire time he was dancing and kept his hands on his waist, looking effortless as he glided up and down the dance floor.

"If I tried that, I'd be a heap on the floor," said Anne McLean, a golden-haired girl from Mosa Township, as she rested against the wall beside Betsy Jane, likewise admiring the dancers keeping up with the fiddler's pace.

"I know what you mean. I can't do it either," said Betsy Jane. "My legs would end up twisted in a knot if I even tried." They both laughed at that image without taking their eyes off the dancers.

The fiddler switched to an even more frenetic pace, and now only three men remained on the floor to step it off. James A. was flanked by his younger brother, Neil Carruthers, and John Livingston, a neighbour who lived near Betsy Jane. The crowd hooted and hollered as the men, one by one, took turns showing off their best steps to the crowd, which urged them on, yelling out their names as they stepped. James A. was drenched in sweat by this time but didn't move his hands from his waist to wipe his brow. When it was his turn, he danced towards the corner where Betsy Jane stood with Anne and winked at her as he flew across the floor.

"Do you know him?" asked Anne, her eyes wide with astonishment and a touch of envy.

"Yes, I've met him. He's James A. Carruthers. He lives over in Ekfrid Township."

"How do you know him?"

"We met at the Glencoe Fair in September." Betsy Jane looked at the canning jar and the hickory tree seeds and felt a spark of electricity shoot from the jar into her hands.

"Well, I think he's the best," Anne said, swooning.

"Me too." Betsy Jane did not let attraction cloud her judgement. She really did think that he was the best dancer.

When the fiddler stopped playing, the three remaining men faced one another and bowed deeply from the waist before walking off the floor amid applause and cheers. James A. headed toward where Betsy Jane was standing with Anne. He removed a handkerchief from his pocket and wiped his brow, which was dripping with sweat.

"What did you think?" He smiled as he spoke.

"I think it wasn't your first try."

"You're right. I can't resist dancing to a reel."

After six months of courting, James A. was certain that his initial instincts from the Glencoe Fair were spot-on. He knew he had found the perfect lid to his pot in Betsy Jane McAlpine, and he intended to ask her to marry him. They were compatible on most of the important levels, and James A. was willing to accept that Betsy Jane had strong opinions of her own and was not shy about expressing them. He proposed to her when driving her home from the Kilmartin Presbyterian Church on a Sunday in May. With delight, she accepted his proposal, along with the garnet and opal engagement ring he offered. Perched on her weathered hand—one so often covered with dirt from the garden or dough from kneaded bread—the ring brought an element of sophistication to Betsy Jane's drab wardrobe.

On a crisp, sunny day in early June, Nancy Walker's home was buzzing with activity in preparation for the wedding ceremony scheduled in the afternoon. Although only close family were invited, Nancy still wanted the day to go without a hitch. This was the most important event she would ever host, and she wanted it to go smoothly. Mother and daughter had spent the previous week making the three-tiered wedding cake together, which was a complex, involved process of baking, drying, and layering, and finally topping it with an almond paste icing. The fruit and nut recipe had been passed down through the generations, and it made Nancy proud to teach her own daughter how to master it.

Standing in the largest bedroom, she beamed with pride as she focused on dressing her eldest daughter in the finest gown she would ever wear. "It's the perfect day for my daughter's wedding," said Nancy as she held out the sleeves of the delicate, cream-coloured silk gown. It had a full skirt and frilly high collar that Nancy had sewn especially for the occasion. She had begun this sewing project even before the proposal came, in faith that marriage was soon coming for her daughter. For the past four months, every spare moment had gone into stitching the gown together from a bolt of silk she purchased at the mercantile in Glencoe. She wanted her daughter to radiate the happiness she felt in having chosen a mate to share her life with. Although he was eleven years Betsy Jane's senior, Nancy felt they were perfectly matched in personality and upbringing.

"I never thought this day would arrive. Can you believe I'm getting married today?" Betsy Jane stepped into the gown and pulled it over her shoulders. She turned so that her mother could begin buttoning the back of it. Nancy had spent an hour twirling Betsy Jane's chestnut hair into an intricate knot on the top of her head while braiding purple thistle flowers gathered from the field into the plaits. The style accentuated her daughter's high cheekbones.

"I think you have found yourself a fine man in James A. Carruthers."

"He actually found me, not the other way around." They both laughed at the memory of Betsy Jane's calamity at the fair, where James A. had intervened to clean up after the loss of nearly all her fall fair entries.

"Regardless, he's a fine man and you're lucky to have him. He's both charming and responsible. In many ways, he reminds me of your own father, you know."

Betsy Jane sighed. Special occasions were when she most missed having her father around. "I only wish that he could be here to celebrate with us on this special day." Her father, Archibald McAlpine, had died when she was eighteen months old. She knew him only through the framed photograph her mother kept of him.

"When you close your eyes, picture him, and he'll be with you in your heart, dear," said her mother.

Betsy Jane looked down and closed her eyes and pictured her father from the photograph. He had a prominent black beard, and they shared the same sharp facial features. She felt a sudden warmth encircle her shoulders. When she opened her eyes, her mother was holding out an ornate framed plate. It was common practice to inscribe a newly deceased person's name and date of death on a silver plate, which was attached to the coffin. Nancy had removed this one before her husband's coffin was laid in the ground, as a keepsake by which to remember him.

"I wanted you to have this."

"Thank you, Mother," Betsy Jane said, holding back a sob that was about to be unleashed at the back of her throat.

"No crying before the wedding, but I want you to take it with you. It's now yours." Betsy Jane grasped the plate to her chest, imagining that her father was present. She placed it on the table for safekeeping until after the ceremony was concluded.

Inhaling slowly, she composed herself. "How do I look?" She twirled in front of her mother, who thought the cream gown made her already towering daughter appear even taller.

"You look as beautiful as anything I have ever seen."

Maggie Belle peeked her head into the bedroom. "Reverend McDonald says that everyone is now ready and they're waiting for the bride, Betsy Jane."

"Are you ready?" Her mother looked on the verge of tears but was choking her emotions back. Betsy Jane breathed in again and nodded. Maggie Belle handed her a bouquet of the white irises and red roses she had picked from the garden.

Betsy Jane inhaled and pushed her shoulders back, making herself appear taller. "Let's go."

As she entered the parlour, Betsy Jane was struck by two things: the scent of the flowers from her mother's garden that filled the room, and the sound of her own breathing as her chest expanded and contracted with a mix of jittery nerves and pure excitement. The Reverend McDonald stood waiting in the parlour, along with James A., and his father and stepmother, and Betsy Jane's stepfather and her half-siblings. As soon as the reverend began speaking, her nerves disappeared, and she relaxed.

After the ceremony, James A. pulled his new bride aside and embraced her. "I couldn't wait to give you this," he said, handing her a velvet-covered box.

Betsy Jane opened the lid, revealing a brooch—a solid gold horseshoe. "Oh, my. It's beautiful, but you really shouldn't have."

"Of course I should have. We'll only ever have this chance once. Would you like to wear it now?"

She nodded with enthusiasm. "Can you pin it on me?"

James A. released the clasp and pushed the pin through the silk collar of Betsy Jane's gown. "It's for good luck. I hope that we'll always have it. Together."

"*Guh gir'uh d'eeuh uhn tah ort,*" she whispered into James A.'s ear.

He widened his eyes in surprise. "What does that mean?" Despite being raised by Scottish settlers, James A. had never learned much Gaelic and wasn't fluent in it.

"It means *May God put luck on you,*" she explained.

"I hope that our path is paved with only good luck for the rest of our days," he said.

"I'd prefer to hope that we'll be shown God's blessings, instead of relying on good fortune. But to think that we met because of a jar of relish and some bad luck with my baking."

"That's the finest relish I've ever tasted," he exclaimed.

Betsy Jane blushed. "Thank you, husband." It felt funny saying that for the first time.

"They're waiting for us. Let's join the others. I hear that they have cake."

"Not just any cake. It's one that took a week to make."

"Well, in the future, you don't have to spend a week making a cake that will be gobbled up within an hour." He beamed and squeezed her hand.

First with cabbage and beet relish, and now with cake, Betsy Jane checked off in her mind two sure-fire ways to her new husband's heart.

The next morning, on their first full day of being husband and wife, Betsy Jane and James A. had plans to attend to. They donned their fine wedding garb again and travelled to town by carriage to sit for the photographer in Glencoe for their wedding picture. This time, James A. helped fasten the buttons on her cream silk gown and helped her straighten out the hairstyle that her mother had so delicately designed the day before.

"Please make sure that the back isn't flat."

"You look so beautiful. When I saw you yesterday, I knew I was the luckiest man in the world." He looked at her as if she were the only thing in the room.

"I need you to help me with the horseshoe brooch again. It's our lucky charm, and I want it to be in the photograph."

James A. again pinned the brooch through the silk of her collar. Good luck was now resting with them as they headed towards the town. After returning from Glencoe, Betsy Jane retired into the homestead, her new home, and changed into a more modest cotton house dress.

"Are you ready, then?" James A. asked her as she entered the kitchen.

"Ready for what?"

"We have some planting to do." He held up the relish jar with the hickory seeds and shook it in the air. "Remember these?"

"Of course. Where do you think we should plant them?"

"I have the ideal spot. Follow me."

James A. led his new bride to the woodlot on his property. It was the one corner of his acreage that was still thick with the trees of the Carolinian Forest that had dominated Ekfrid Township before it was settled. He opened the jar and handed Betsy Jane a handful of seeds.

"Push these into the ground, and with any luck, they'll take hold and start a new tree."

Together, they planted the full jar of hickory tree seeds.

A faint hum floated through the corner woodlot, encircling the saplings and seedlings.

8

CALCUTTA, INDIA

BY EARLY 1908, his excesses had caught up to him. After running his paper business into the ground and accruing a substantial gambling debt, Duff Ballantyne decided to leave India and return to his native Scotland for a fresh start, where no one knew his ways or would hold him to account for previous misdeeds. But first, he had to deal with the uncomfortable matter of the children and their doting grandmother.

Bessie Smyth had stopped by the house to visit with the children when Duff broke the news about the family's impending departure.

"I've decided that I'm heading back to Scotland soon. We'll be leaving in a few weeks," he said as Bessie was readying to leave.

"I beg your pardon?" she said, her jaw agape. "What about the children?"

"I'm leaving India. I'm going back to where conditions are more favourable to my way of doing business." He ignored her question about the children.

She refused to let it go. "If you're focused on your business endeavours, they can both stay with me," Bessie stammered, referring to Ellwyne and his blond-haired sister, Valetta, who by this time was seven years old.

"You know as well as I do that children belong with their father."

"But you aren't *his* father," she snapped, and looked towards Ellwyne, who was reading a book by himself on the red velvet chair he had once shared with his mother when he was a much younger boy.

"And neither are you," he said, eyes flashing. "I have as much right to raise him as you do," he said,

pausing to glance at himself in the hallway mirror. "Besides, Eliza told me she wanted it this way."

She stood outside in her garden, looking up at the sky that stretched above Calcutta. Like her own mood, it was grey and dreary. She didn't expect it to change any time soon. It had been only a few months since Bessie Smyth had lost her daughter to a sudden, ferocious fever, and now she was also losing her grandchildren. She was devastated by Duff Ballantyne's insistence on taking them with him. She well understood that a fly is drawn to honey and suspected that his interest in Ellwyne was not genuine. Though still a child, Ellwyne had inherited a tidy sum from his father's estate, and that money was what Duff Ballantyne desperately needed.

The next day, she headed back to Eliza's home at a time she knew Duff would not be present.

"Ellwyne, darling. Mr. Ballantyne informed me of his plans to take you and Valetta with him to Scotland."

Ellwyne nodded. "Yes, I heard." He looked at his feet. "I don't want to leave India. Or you." He looked at his grandmother, his dark eyes pleading with her to do something.

"I know, dear. I wish you could stay, too. Believe me." Bessie removed an envelope from the front pocket in her long skirt and placed it in her grandson's hand. "This is very important."

"What is it?" Ellwyne could still feel the warmth from her body on the envelope.

"It's my address. Keep this information with you. Write to me as soon as you arrive, so that I know how to contact you," she said. "This is a lifeline to keep us connected."

"I understand." He looked solemn.

"Good. Now go put that someplace safe. And don't lose it."

Ellwyne stuffed the envelope into his pocket. "You have my word."

Bessie lowered her voice, though there was no one within earshot. "I also put some money inside for postage and any other incidentals you might need, so guard it carefully," she whispered.

🍁

The steamer trunk in his room was filling with the few possessions he would be allowed to take with him on the voyage to Scotland. Beneath two layers of folded clothing, Ellwyne had placed the framed photograph of his mother on top of the only photo he had of his father. He removed the envelope he received from his grandmother from his pocket and tucked it into the back of the picture frame. The most valuable things he had were now stowed together. They were his lifelines to his past, his identity, his roots.

🍁

Duff Ballantyne climbed the stone steps to the consulate, trying to ignore the butterflies swirling in his stomach. *This had better work*, he thought.

The clerk behind the desk wore glasses perched on the tip of his nose.

"What can I help you with today?" he asked.

"My wife has recently passed away, and I need to file this death certificate." He passed the paperwork across the desk.

"My condolences for your loss, sir." The clerk squinted as he read the form. He took out another form and began writing information on it. "Any minor children involved? For our records, we like to track these sorts of things."

"Yes, two minor children. My daughter is six years old and, uhhh." He paused and took a deep breath. "My son is eleven."

"I see. And their names?"

"Valetta Ballantyne is my daughter and Ellwyne Ballantyne is my son." He had practiced it in his head, but it was the first time he had said it out loud, and it sounded strange to him.

After spelling both names aloud, the clerk updated the records and stamped it. "Is there anything else?"

"Yes, how would I get a birth certificate for my son?"

🍁

At the bank, Duff Ballantyne sauntered up to the teller window with renewed confidence. "My wife has recently died, and I need to transfer the funds in her bank account into my name. I have all the required documents."

Under colonial law, as a man, Ballantyne had the upper hand against Bessie, who had little leverage to use against him. Despite his grandmother's resistance, Ellwyne was forced to go with his stepfather to another continent, leaving the only home he had ever known. Eliza had long ago lost touch with Edward Dacosta's family after his death, so even they, a wealthy Portuguese family, were not able to intervene or campaign to keep Ellwyne in India, where he belonged.

It was hopeless; the boy was going to Scotland with his stepfather.

Ellwyne arrived in a new land, where he knew no one and no one knew him or cared how vulnerable he was. Despite being born as Edward Dacosta's son, Ellwyne's surname was changed to Ballantyne. Ellwyne's ties to his past began to disappear.

Chopped.

Like the swing of an axe to a delicate branch.

9

PENICUIK ("PENTYCOOK"), SCOTLAND

INDIA WAS A faint memory as soon as Duff Ballantyne returned to his native Scotland, but for two nagging problems that hung over his head. He was desperate not only for a steady source of money but also for someone to take care of the two children he had found himself saddled with now that he was a widower. Caring for his own daughter was one matter, but the additional weight of Eliza's son burdened him. Children had constant needs that he was neither fond of nor even capable of fulfilling: food, clothing, and hardest of all, attention.

Through mutual contacts, he managed to find a willing partner in Donalda Elliot, a younger woman with pale tissue-paper skin, long, chestnut-coloured hair that she piled atop her head in a massive knot, and a shrill voice. Although nowhere near as attractive as Ellwyne's mother, Eliza, she would have to do. Unlike Eliza, Donalda was prone to screaming at the top of her lungs when aggravated or annoyed. With two stepchildren now under her charge, she often found herself aggravated and annoyed. Fulfilling the needs of children was not Donalda's lifelong ambition. She did it out of duty rather than genuine affection.

Within a few months of being married, Duff and Donalda Ballantyne had a child of their own, a little girl they named Loretta. Their blended family was now five in number: a biological child, one half-sibling, and an orphan. And Duff still had a nagging problem. He needed a source of income. Ellwyne's money was disappearing as fast as he could get his hands on

it. This eventually caused friction with Donalda, who was becoming accustomed to having the finer things in life, following her husband's example.

"We don't have enough for the hat you purchased," Duff complained, annoyed at his new wife's spending habits. He had not yet shared with her the gravity of their financial situation. "Return it immediately," he demanded. His voice bellowed through their rented flat.

"But you said that I should have a new hat for Sunday service," whined Donalda as she ran her fingers over the feathers attached to the hat's velvet brim. She peered over at her husband, hoping he could see her lower lip starting to quiver.

"Unless we can comfortably *live* in your hat next month, then you must return it." He pounded the table, its rickety legs rattling with the force of his fist. With the verdict rendered, the hat was returned.

Duff Ballantyne hatched an idea. He knew that Donalda had an uncle who had emigrated from Scotland and gone to Canada many years before. Although he was a farmer, he had land—and to Duff, having land meant having money. What did they have to lose?

"Donalda, who's that uncle you once mentioned who now lives in Canada?" He used the gentle, soothing tone he adopted only when he wanted to ensure that he got his way.

"It's my Uncle Kersty. Why do you ask?"

Donalda was referring to her mother's older brother, Christopher Carruthers. He was a "first footer" for the Carruthers clan, meaning the first of the family to uproot and immigrate to North America as a young, single man.

"I think it's time for you to write him a letter and let him know that we're coming to visit," he cooed.

Donalda spared no time and scribbled a hasty letter to her uncle.

January, 1908
Mr. Christopher Carruthers
R.R. #4
Glencoe, Ontario
Canada

Dear Uncle Kersty:

This is your niece, Donalda Elliot. It's been many years since we've been in contact since you left Scotland, but I figured it was a good time to write and catch up with you. We have all missed you and wondered how you have fared in Canada. I now have a husband and a child of our own. We, too, will be making our way to Canada in a few weeks' time and want to settle in your area to make a new start. We will see you upon our arrival in Glencoe.

We're looking forward to spending time with you and your family and getting reacquainted. Until then,

Donalda Elliot Ballantyne

Using a large portion of the remaining money, Duff Ballantyne purchased five tickets in first class on a ship departing from Liverpool, England, bound for New York City. He hoped that their plan would work. It had to.

The wind whistled like a freight train as a wicked winter storm rolled into the Scottish Lowlands, making the thin window frames of the cottage rattle. The unsettling sound of winter attempting to penetrate the comfort of indoors was keeping Ellwyne awake. He pulled the covers up over his chin, but this didn't stop him from overhearing the hushed discussion between Donalda and his stepfather in the next room.

"You've sent the letter, haven't you?" his stepfather's voice growled like a dog preparing to bite.

"Of course I have." Donalda responded. "You asked and I did it. I'm not a child." Despite her protests to the contrary, Ellwyne thought Donalda did sound like a child.

"Fine. Our tickets are purchased. We set sail in two weeks." On Duff's mind was the fact that they needed to vacate the cottage before the next rent payment came due.

"I do love this cottage," Donalda gushed. The stone structure was an old pump house that had been converted into living quarters. It was available for rent by the week for a modest sum.

Ellwyne felt his stomach twist into a painful knot. More uprooting lay ahead, though they had arrived in Scotland less than a year ago. He crawled out of his bed and crept to his steamer trunk, which was taking up one corner of the room he shared with Valetta. The framed photograph of his mother was carefully stowed, wrapped in a shirt to prevent it from breaking. Peeling back the frame, he checked that the money his grandmother had given him was still there.

Phew, he thought. The money hadn't gone missing. Not yet at least. He knew that he had to protect it from his stepfather's greedy grasp.

The next morning, Ellwyne sat on his bed and, using messy block letters, scrawled a letter to his grandmother.

April 6, 1908
Mrs. Bessie Smyth
Howrah, India
Dear Grandmother:

How lucky you gave me money so that we could keep in touch. You would have a hard time finding me otherwise. Turns out that by the time you receive this letter, we will already have left Scotland. Ballantyne has a new wife named Donalda. He's taking all of us to her uncle's farm somewhere in Canada. I will write you when we arrive so you'll know how to reach me.

Valetta is growing taller, and so am I. I bet I could reach the mangoes from the tallest branches now. Pick one for me. And be careful of the peacocks.

I miss you very, <u>very</u> much.
Love,
Ell

He dipped into the stash of money his grandmother had given him for postage, walked to the village, and mailed the letter to his grandmother in India. He needed her to know that he was making another voyage with the Ballantynes, taking him yet farther afield from India. The scent of mangoes was growing faint in his memory. His nostrils were filled with the cold Scottish air that had replaced the fragrant warmth of his beloved Indian home.

10

CARRUTHERS CORNERS, ONTARIO, CANADA

"THIS IS WHERE it belongs," Betsy Jane said as she pointed to a blank area on the wall of her new home. James A.'s farm property contained a modest one-and-a-half storey, wood-framed house that had been built by the McEacherns, the family that had settled and cleared the land before James A. purchased it from them.

"Looks like the perfect spot to me," he said. Betsy Jane passed him the frame, dusting it off before she handed it to him. Her mother had given it to her at her wedding, and it held enormous sentimental value for her. The framed silver plate removed from her father's coffin was engraved with the phrase "NO CROSS, NO CROWN." Archibald McAlpine had been a devout man with a prominent black beard, who was studying to become a Presbyterian minister when his appendix ruptured. He suffered in agony against all efforts to save his life until he died from peritonitis at the age of thirty-one. Betsy Jane kept two elements of him in her consciousness. The first was this silver coffin plate; the second, his faith in the teachings of Christ. Betsy Jane was a believer, and her faith guided her decisions like a compass. She believed in knowing right from wrong and in the promise of life after death. She was a God-fearing person who lived her faith in the choices she made and how she treated others. That was another reason why she and James A. had been drawn to each other. They shared a similar upbringing and morals.

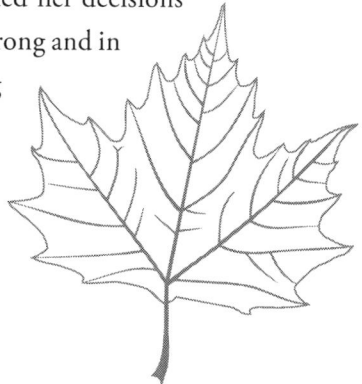

"I can't wait for our little ones to arrive," James A. said as he took Betsy Jane's arm. He was thirty-five years old and more than ready to become a father. The tiny homestead sat like a nest waiting to be filled. When she was a young girl, Betsy Jane had discovered a fledgling on the ground that had fallen from the safety of its nest. The bird cowered as it awaited sure death without the protection of its mother or the ability to fly. She cradled the fragile bird in her palm and carried it to the loft of the barn. In the haymow, she tucked the bird into a corner far from the bustle of the cattle and horses housed below. Using her hands, she weaved some straw and hay into a small cup shape and placed the bird into it, which easily hid it from view. For days, she fed it water and fresh milk from a spoon until it gained strength, and she began offering it worms and insects, like its mother would have. Although she had long tended flocks of chickens, turkeys, and ducks, from that day forward, she saw the nest as a safe spot, a place where weaker ones could gain strength before taking their first flight. It's how she envisioned her new home.

"I've been taking care of children my whole life. I'd like them to finally be my own," she said with a slight laugh. However, for the woman who longed to be a mother, having children didn't come readily to Betsy Jane. Many times, she thought she might be pregnant, only to have her hopes dashed. Although she and James A. had difficulty conceiving a child, Betsy Jane never lost faith that, someday, her wish would be fulfilled, and she would finally start filling her nest.

In 1909, when she made it past a fourth month of pregnancy, Betsy Jane began to feel more confident that she was finally on her way to having her first baby. The excitement and anxiety worked in opposition, but she tried not to dwell on the outcome after so many prior disappointments. "Whatever will be will be," she would tell herself, and get on with her day, tending to her flock and vegetable garden.

In the fall of 1909, after a few years of crushing disappointments, Betsy Jane's dream finally came true when she gave birth to her first child, a little boy with light hair, round cheeks, and bright blue eyes. The baby arrived on October 17th, the day after James A.'s own birthday.

"So close to being born on my birthday," he joked. "But he needed to make a splash with his arrival."

"Well, we waited for him for so long, I guess he needed his own day," Betsy Jane said as she tucked the baby into the hand-carved wooden cradle at the foot of their double bed. "What are your thoughts on his name? I'd like to name him after my father," she said.

"I think that's a fine idea," he said. Usually, Scottish families named firstborn sons after the father's father, but James A. was always willing to compromise with his wife. "Any ideas on a middle name?"

"I was thinking 'Alpin.' What do you think?" she asked, her hazel eyes glowing with Scottish pride.

"Alpin? What kind of a name is that?"

"It's a Scottish king, I'll have you know." Betsy Jane was an avid reader, and she dove into historical texts about her ancestral homeland whenever she was allowed some time away from gardening, canning, and tending her flock.

"Nah. Don't think so," he said, shaking his head stubbornly.

He rarely dug in, but she could tell that he was not going to compromise on that. Because they couldn't agree on a middle name, they settled on Archibald A., or "Archie" for short.

With his swirl of blond hair, Archie was a healthy, gregarious baby who clung to his mother's fingers and watched her as she darted around the house and barnyard tending to her chores. He giggled to himself as if he were the only one in the room who understood the joke. Having a new baby in the house gave Betsy Jane affirmation of her higher calling: to nurture and to guide children. Although she managed to keep up with her canning, cooking, and baking chores after she became a new mother, she enjoyed child-rearing the most and looked forward to adding many more children to her nest.

11

THE NORTH ATLANTIC OCEAN

A JOURNEY ACROSS the North Atlantic was undertaken in winter only by those most desperate to run to better circumstances. Icy, choppy seas made for a bumpy voyage, and the risk of icebergs and vicious storms was a constant concern to crew and passengers alike. In February 1909, Duff Ballantyne, eager to run from a growing pile of debts accrued, had decided to gamble once again in taking this voyage with his mismatched family. It promised a clean start for Ellwyne, but he missed his mother and grandmother terribly, and more than ever. He was being taken even farther from his Indian roots.

Ellwyne stood outside the cabin door and leaned in, his hands cupped over his ears to hear the conversation between his stepfather and his new wife. Her high-pitched voice grated on his nerves, but it did make it easier to hear what he was not meant to hear, even through doors and walls.

"But if we only had *two* mouths to feed, we'd be better off," she said in a whispered voice.

"Clearly, but what was I supposed to do? Dump him in Scotland and run?" His stepfather's voice rose in volume with each word he sputtered out. Ellwyne imagined him as a circus tiger, pacing in circles, his frustration growing at the limitations of his shortened chain.

"Well, It's not like it hasn't been done before," she hissed. "Remember the 'hunting accident' I told you about?"

Without hearing any names, Ellwyne knew they were speaking about him. He often felt alone and unwanted, always an afterthought. Sometimes,

when he allowed himself to drift into daydreams, he heard his mother's voice echoing in his mind, reassuring him that she loved him. He longed for her hugs and kindness. With her, he had never wondered whether he mattered. He longed for those carefree days in India, of that assurance. When he closed his eyes, he could picture himself in his grandmother's garden, walking amongst the flowers and fruit trees. Carefree. Effortless.

The ship rocked, making Ellwyne stumble as he turned the handle and entered the cabin. Immediately, all conversation stopped.

Donalda pasted a smile over her familiar scowl. "Ellwyne, dear. You should knock before you enter a room."

"Yes, boy. What have we discussed with you before about making yourself less conspicuous? We're already living in crowded quarters, so you need to be more mindful about other people's space. Make yourself *smaller*." Duff clasped his hands together.

He despised being called "boy," especially by him. Ellwyne was used to being referred to by pet names or diminutives. His grandmother had called him "Ell," and he missed that. He took a seat on the cot that he was sharing with Valetta and stared at his feet, noticing for the first time that his big toe was starting to protrude through the tip of his shoe. He wiggled his toe, and it broke right through the weakened brown leather. His grey woollen sock made an unintended appearance in the already crowded room.

"Uh-oh," he said, under his breath.

Donalda snarled and unleashed a flurry of questions. "How did that happen? Did you do that on purpose? Don't you know the cost of shoes? Do you think they grow on trees?"

Ellwyne didn't look up but continued to wiggle his toe, freeing it from its captivity. He thought about the mango tree in his grandmother's garden and imagined a pair of black leather shoes hanging from the lowest branch, which made him smile. It was the wrong reaction.

"I hope you'll enjoy having cold, wet feet, because we won't have the chance to get you new ones for several weeks," said his stepfather.

"Weeks? Just how long is this voyage?" Donalda stood with her hands on her hips.

"Longer than anything I'd hoped for," Duff snarled.

"So what are you saying? You don't want to be here with me?" Donalda stood over top of Duff and leaned into her husband as she spoke.

"I'm saying it's longer than any man should have to sit here and listen to you." The glass ashtray on the cabin's dresser rattled as his voice bounced off the four walls.

Ellwyne froze, unable to move but relieved that their focus had turned from him back to each other. Chaos and noise accompanied his stepfather and his new wife everywhere they travelled. Ellwyne found his stepfather's booming voice discomforting and sometimes frightening, a sharp contrast with the gentle and soft-spoken ways of his mother. As his stepfather roared, Ellwyne snuck across the cabin and opened the door without making a sound. He felt a pull on the back of his trousers and turned to see Valetta trying to follow him out of the cabin. "No, Valetta. You gotta stay here. It's freezing out there, and you'll catch a cold." Valetta looked up to her older brother, frowning, yearning to escape the chaos with him. But she obeyed her big brother's words.

Having a first-class ticket meant Ellwyne had some access to the lounges where gentlemen sat at tables smoking cigars and sipping on brandy and liquors. Although children weren't allowed in the lounges, Ellwyne had figured out how to sneak in and out without being noticed.

He darted to an abandoned table, where a discarded newspaper from January 1909 had been left behind by a previous occupant. He tucked it under his arm and headed out to the ship's deck. After finding a bench that was shielded from the wind behind a screen, he opened the newspaper and scanned the articles. Politics. Conflicts. Labour movements. Unrest. Nothing caught his eye until he reached the third page, where he noticed an advertisement offering a £1,000 prize to anyone brave or daring enough to attempt to pilot an aeroplane across the English Channel. Ellwyne was fascinated by flight and had envisioned what it would be like to soar above the clouds. His mother had stoked this passion by reading newspaper articles to him about flying machines. As he read about the contest, he drifted back to a memory from five years ago. He and his mother were seated together in the red velvet chair where she read stories to him. Instead of a book, she held a newspaper.

"Look at this, Ellwyne," she said as she pointed to the photo on the front page. It showed a skeletal machine with long wings, a tail, and a propeller that rotated. She read to him about the first powered aeroplane flight by two American inventors over a windswept beach in a faraway place called North Carolina. She explained that they were brothers who worked together to solve a problem and that many people had tried to make a machine that could fly, but Orville and Wilbur Wright were the first ever to do it successfully. Ever since that day, Ellwyne had dreamt about one day taking a flight.

To pass time, Ellwyne remained on the deck, staring at the lifeboats hanging from the railing. He memorized their shape and size. He admired their stark white hulls, which contrasted with the blue sky on sunny days and blended in with the scudding clouds on grey days. He imagined running his hands across the surface of the boats. The painted wood was smooth and glossy. He thought about what kind of tree the wood came from, probably a once-majestic elm or oak. The tree had been destroyed and changed into an object so that people could be saved. The tree didn't get to choose its fate. It had been transformed into something else, yanked away from where it had once grown, forced to become something else.

The tree didn't have choices.

For the first time, Ellwyne realized that neither did he.

12

THE CORNER WOODLOT, EKFRID TOWNSHIP, ONTARIO, CANADA

TWO BROAD LEAVES on the buttonwood sapling glistened with morning dew. A hawk's piercing cry broke the stillness of the morning. Below it, a tiny mouse scurried in the weeds. Sensing its chance, the hawk launched itself off the branch it was resting on and dove downward, wings folded, and talons outstretched, hopeful for its next meal. The mouse sensed impending danger and instinctively slipped into the taller grass, narrowly avoiding the hawk's crushing grasp. The mouse brushed against the buttonwood sapling as it rushed past it, causing a drop of dew to spill to the hardened clay soil. The hawk took two jumps, propelling itself forward, and launched into flight once again. It rose skyward and took its perch on a hickory branch. Watching, waiting.

The mouse kept still. Listening. Waiting.

The buttonwood sapling was also watching, waiting.

13

NEW YORK CITY, USA, AND EKFRID TOWNSHIP, ONTARIO, CANADA

IT WAS THE longest two weeks of Ellwyne's short life, but the ocean voyage was finally over. The ship docked in New York City on a frigid February morning in 1909. Grey smoke rose from building chimneys like streamers and hoar frost clung to each tree branch like lacy white icing. To celebrate their safe arrival on the shores of a new continent, Duff Ballantyne tossed a handful of gold coins overboard into the harbour water, hoping to impress his fellow passengers with his importance and apparent wealth. Although they had experienced a taste of winter in Europe, the Ballantynes were met with a different level of cold weather upon arriving in North America. Taking a deep breath made their lungs ache and their nostrils temporarily stick together. Though they wrapped themselves in multiple layers of clothing, they still felt the sting of winter's bite each time they ventured outside.

Compared with Calcutta, Ellwyne found New York City in February to be a cold, dreary, sooty place with hordes of people walking the streets as if on a tremendous conveyor belt. The crowds elbowed him as he walked along the street and he learned to be vigilant, ready to jump out of the way lest he get run over by pedestrians or carriages. He was fascinated by the abundance of motorized vehicles on the streets of New York. Their blaring horns made him jump in fright each time one sounded. Although he had grown up in a large city, he didn't feel at ease in this one. In crowded Calcutta, people were more relaxed and willing to give way. In New York, people were in a

constant rush, their destination top of mind. Other pedestrians were obstacles to overcome, even if it meant pushing someone out of the way. Ellwyne was relieved when they finally boarded a train and left for Canada.

The Ballantynes took a series of long train rides, each one longer than the previous. They eventually arrived in Glencoe, Ontario, in the heart of Ekfrid Township on a wintry night. Compared with the hustle and bustle of the large cities they had experienced in India, the United Kingdom and America, the tiny hamlet of Glencoe looked uncomplicated, but had a calmness that seeped from its pores. It had one main street only about a mile long. The town had a feed mill, a few shops, a post office, and a train station. The railway line was the true artery, bringing in people and supplies and taking away the wheat and corn that the farmers all around the town produced. Arriving in Glencoe felt like sitting to rest after being on one's feet for days. Donalda Elliot's uncle lived several miles from Glencoe, which was much too far to walk, what with all their worldly belongings packed up in several steamer trunks. So, on their arrival at the train station, Duff Ballantyne found a livery carriage to hire.

"Take us to the farm of Christopher Carruthers, in Ekfrid Township at Carruthers Corners," he told the driver. Donalda's uncle's farm was at the intersection of 5th Concession and Sideroad 16.

Snowflakes were floating down to build a layer of snow atop the steamer trunks, which sat on the road exactly where they had been unloaded from the train. It was well after midnight when the trunks were finally loaded into the carriage, which had sleigh runners instead of wheels. The horses themselves were also equipped for winter weather with spiked shoes to give them extra grip as they jogged across snow and ice.

They set off for the farm filled with expectation about their new lives, flying through the darkness of open fields to avoid the large drifts that impeded clear passage on the road. Like the wake that had trailed their ship as it navigated the ocean waves, huge plumes of snow sprayed out from behind the carriage as it cut through the considerable drifts. Ellwyne listened to the brass bells fastened on the horses' harnesses as they jingled a joyful melody, similar to the peal of church bells he had heard in Calcutta. It was like being accompanied by an orchestra, and he thought it surely must be part magic. He expected the horses to take flight as they pulled their heavy load with ease. He listened as the driver clucked to the horses, which he called Belle and Bonnie.

The carriage arrived at Carruthers Corners within an hour. Duff and

Donalda waited until their luggage was unloaded, the driver was paid, and the carriage had left before walking up to the door of the darkened farmhouse with the children in tow. They had to rap on the door several times, each time with increased intensity, before a dim light finally appeared and noise came from within the house.

As Kersty pried open the door, a shrill voice filled the empty air.

"Uncle Kersty. It's me, your niece Donalda. Did you get my letter?"

Of course he had received her letter, but Kersty hadn't imagined that the family would arrive on his doorstep in the dark of night, without warning. Kersty scanned the brood standing on his verandah. His eyes were drawn to a black-haired boy standing off to the side, apart from the others, head bowed, his eyes focused on his feet. The boy looked shy and unsure, and given the way that Donalda clutched the other two children, it struck Kersty that he didn't quite belong with them.

Kersty cleared his throat. "Donalda, how nice of you to visit," he replied, a rough edge to his voice after being pulled out of a deep sleep. "Do come in, lass."

"Thank you, Uncle Kersty." She motioned to the others to follow her inside.

The Ballantynes huddled around the woodstove to warm their ruddy cheeks and hands.

"I didn't come to the door right away because I didn't recognize the bells," said Kersty. The Carruthers clan and their neighbours all fastened sleigh bells to their harnesses in winter. Each family's rig had a different size and number of bells, which rang out unique melodies as the horses jogged along, making it possible to know who was passing by without having to look.

"What a curious thing. Being able to tell who's outside based on the sound of ringing bells," scoffed Duff, causing Donalda to poke him in the ribs.

"We've had such a long journey to finally make it here," said Donalda, as her eyes scanned the quaint room, with its low ceiling and solid, but modest, furnishings. She began to wonder if perhaps her uncle did not have as much wealth as she had imagined.

14

CARRUTHERS CORNERS, ONTARIO, CANADA

THE UNEXPECTED ARRIVAL of the Ballantynes in the close-knit Carruthers Corners settlement came like a sudden gust of wind, raising eyebrows
and many questions. Who were these people? Why had they come? How long
did they intend to stay?

James A. Carruthers tolerated change, reluctantly. Like all farmers, he
was at the mercy of weather, so he had little choice but to accept the things
he could not control. "Did you know about the new family we have at
the Corners?" James A. asked Betsy Jane the morning after the Ballantynes
arrived, as they sat to eat breakfast at the oak dining table. Newcomers were
rare in Ekfrid Township, though generally welcomed.

"No, I haven't." Betsy Jane felt a stir of excitement, coupled with uncertainty, as she passed James A. the butter. He slathered some on his toast and
dipped it into the soft egg yolk.

"Far as I heard from Neil this morning, they're a married couple with
some kids in tow. The wife is dad's niece, so she's a distant cousin of mine
though I've never heard of her til now. They're here all the way from
Scotland. I think they arrived kind of unexpectedly. At least they
seem to have taken dad by surprise last night."

Betsy Jane raised her eyebrows. She wondered if
this might give her a longed-for opportunity to let
some Gaelic fly with another native speaker. "Oh
really? So, they're proper Scots?"

James A. continued. "Yes and no. Donalda Bal-

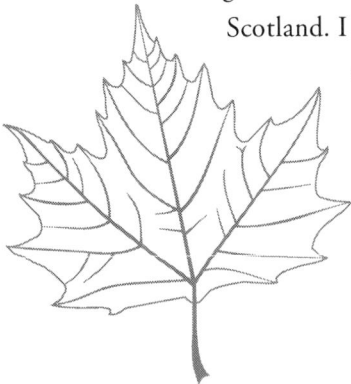

lantyne, dad's niece, is. Her husband, Duff, is Scottish by birth, but he lived in India for a spell."

"India?" Betsy Jane's eyes widened.

"Yeah. It's a complicated situation. Duff and Donalda have one child of their own, a baby. Then, there's a little girl with long blond hair that belongs to Duff and his late wife. The girl's mother died a few years back, while he was living in India. And then,"—he paused to take a sip of tea—"there's a young boy with them."

"Oh my. That's quite the knotted ball of yarn."

"The boy is a half-brother to the blond-haired girl." James A. paused. "But he's an orphan. He doesn't belong to either Duff or Donalda."

"An orphan? How terrible." Betsy Jane's brow wrinkled with concern.

"Yeah, his mother died a few years back, after marrying Duff Ballantyne. His mother was a widow. She was Scottish but born and lived in India her whole life."

"I'm going to need crib notes to keep that straight." Betsy Jane felt a stab travel through her chest. The sting of losing her own father felt fresh and remembering that pain made her empathetic to the struggle of a child left alone in the world without guidance. "That's remarkable. A young boy who's already stepped foot on three continents, when most of us don't even leave this township."

"Three continents?" asked James A.

"India is in Asia, so that's one. Scotland is in Europe, so that's two. And now Canada in North America makes three," she explained, pleased to have a chance to show off her knowledge of geography.

"Neil says you'll recognize him as soon as you see him. He doesn't look like the others at all. He's dark-haired, kind of olive-skinned. And he doesn't say much."

Betsy Jane shook her head with a look of both curiosity and concern. "And what's his name, dear?"

"Ellwyne."

"Ellwyne," she repeated. "What an unusual name." She repeated it again in her head, committing it to memory.

"It's not one I've ever heard before, either."

"I like unusual things. We can't all be cookie-cutters, or else the world would be a boring place, don't you think?"

James A. nodded. "Ellwyne. It kind of makes me think of an elm tree. And I sure do love elm trees."

After breakfast was finished and James A. headed out to the barn to continue the morning chores, Betsy Jane set herself to welcoming the new family, so she could learn as much as possible about them. She couldn't shake the thought of the dark-haired boy from her mind. She pulled her trusted sourdough starter from the pantry, added wood to the stove, and began creating one of her famous breads. Visitors deserved a proper welcome, and food was the quickest way to forge a new friendship.

With the still-warm sourdough bread wrapped in a plain tea towel, Betsy Jane set out down the laneway and headed towards Kersty's farm. Her younger half-sister, Maggie Belle, had stopped by and offered to watch her baby, so she knew she had a good amount of time to visit without worrying about her responsibilities at home. The sharp February wind ripped through her woollen coat and pierced her chest. She hunched her shoulders up to protect her ears and blinked hard to keep her lids from freezing. She clung to the sourdough bread as if it would prevent her from feeling the snap of the cold. "Well, here goes nothing," she said to herself as she stepped onto her father in-law's step, rapped at the door, and stood back, waiting for it to open.

"Betsy Jane, what a nice surprise," said Flora, Kersty's second wife, whom he had married following the death of his first, Elizabeth, several years before. A blast of warm air from the woodstove hit Betsy Jane's face and she could feel her skin warming. "What brings you this direction on such a cold morning?"

"I'm here to welcome our guests." Betsy Jane handed Flora the sourdough loaf and unbuttoned her coat. "I heard about their arrival from James and wanted to meet them in person." She glanced around the empty parlour. "Where are they?"

Flora smiled. "Just a moment." She turned her back to Betsy Jane and bellowed, "Duff! Donalda! Come down. You have a visitor." Her voice made the doorjamb rattle. Betsy Jane removed her coat and offered it to Flora, who hung it on the back of a chair in the kitchen.

Within minutes, the guests had shuffled down the narrow staircase and appeared in the parlour: the man, his wife, who was cuddling a baby wrapped up in blankets much like Betsy Jane's sourdough bread, and a young girl with long blond hair tied with a white ribbon.

"You must be the Ballantynes," said Betsy Jane. "So nice to meet you. I'm Betsy Jane Carruthers, Kersty's daughter-in-law. I live at Carruthers Corners with Kersty's son, James Andrew."

"Mrs. Carruthers," said Duff, "I'm Duff Ballantyne. How nice of you to stop by to welcome us to your," he paused, "humble settlement among the many, many trees."

She noticed that his moustache and hair were slicked back in a style not common to the area. In his words, Betsy Jane detected an air of disrespect, if not towards her then at least towards Carruthers Corners. She straightened her shoulders and stood even taller. "Well, it may not be much, especially to city dwellers, but it's our home. And we love it." She turned her eyes towards Donalda Ballantyne, dismissing any further conversation with Duff.

"Hello there, you must be Donalda?"

"Yes. How nice to meet you, Mrs. Carruthers," said Donalda as she extended her free hand towards Betsy Jane. As Betsy Jane's hand touched hers, Donalda withdrew it and proclaimed, "My goodness, your hand is frozen. It's like a corpse."

At that moment, Betsy Jane noticed a dark-haired boy standing halfway down the staircase, holding onto the railing. She smiled at him, and he shyly smiled back. "Well, I've walked here and the wind's quite brisk, so I'm still warming up from the cold."

"Right then," Donalda said without much further concern. "This is our daughter, Loretta," she said, holding up the baby for Betsy Jane to inspect, like a newborn calf at the fall fair.

"She's lovely," said Betsy Jane. "And who's this?" she said as she leaned to greet the blond-haired girl.

"This is Duff's daughter, Valetta," said Donalda. "Valetta, say hello to Mrs. Carruthers."

"Hello, Mrs. Cr-cr-others," said the girl. Betsy Jane smiled at her botched pronunciation, which closely imitated the Gaelic origins of the surname.

"And aren't we missing one?" asked Betsy Jane, looking towards the staircase to see if the dark-haired boy had reappeared.

"Oh, him? Even we sometimes forget that he's here," said Duff with a scoff.

Betsy Jane felt blood rising in her temples. "How do you forget about a *person*?"

Duff stammered and averted his eyes, busying himself with straightening his cuffs. Betsy Jane continued to look at him, not letting him escape the question, which he didn't answer, until she noticed the dark-haired boy slinking down the stairs. He was carrying a folded-up quilted blanket.

"Here you go, Mrs. Carruthers." The dark-haired boy stretched his arms out, proffering the quilt. Betsy Jane noted his now perfect pronunciation of her last name. "I heard you were cold. Would you like me to put this around your shoulders?"

Betsy Jane smiled with appreciation and nodded. "Thanks very much, dear."

"When we arrived, I was frozen to my bones until I got beneath this quilt," he explained.

"You must be Ellwyne, I suppose?"

"I am. I'm E-E-Ellwyne Ballantyne. Pleased to make your acquaintance, ma'am."

"It's nice to meet you, Ellwyne Ballantyne." Betsy Jane turned and crouched to allow the boy to wrap the quilt around her shoulders like a shawl. With an extra layer of fabric, Betsy Jane felt the warmth returning to her body. "I'm feeling better already," she said, turning back to Ellwyne. "I should be warm in no time at all."

Duff snickered. "We don't normally offer up our used bedding for guests to wear as housecoats," said Duff. "You'll have to excuse the boy and his somewhat rustic manners." He emphasized *rustic* so that it hung in the air like a cuss word.

With that gibe, Ellwyne lowered his eyes to the floor and kicked at an imaginary stone. Betsy Jane sensed a change in the boy's mood.

"That's well and fine." Betsy Jane glared at Duff. "We tend to do things differently in our *humble* settlement among the many, many trees." She turned to Ellwyne, "Thank you for your concern about my well-being, Ellwyne. I can feel myself warming up already, thanks to your generosity." She pursed her lips and looked again at Duff, who was still fiddling with his cuffs. "Now, shall we enjoy some of my sourdough bread with a warm cup of tea?"

James A. slammed the door shut behind him as if locking out a ferocious predator on the other side. "That wind. She's a sharp one." He shivered his shoulders to dramatize the cold. "How was your day?" he asked Betsy Jane, who was bringing steaming bowls of potatoes and carrots to the table for supper.

"If you can believe it, I took a stroll in this weather."

"Must've been something pretty important to make you venture out on a day like this. I was only out in it because I had to be."

"Yes, it was important. I wanted to meet the Ballantynes at your father's place."

"Oh. And what did you think?"

"I'm not sure. I think there's more going on than meets the eye. Duff Ballantyne seems to think he might be better than the rest of us. It's a feeling that I got from him, kind of like he's too big for his britches. He wants to present himself as a gentleman of the house, but honestly, someone else had far better manners than he did."

"Donalda?"

"No, not Donalda. It was Ellwyne. The lad offered me the quilt from his bed after overhearing that I was cold from being outside."

"That's awfully kind."

"Yes, it was," said Betsy Jane, recalling the soft-hearted look on Ellwyne's face as he handed her the quilt. "I think he would have let me leave with it if I'd needed to. Imagine giving up your warmest blanket to a stranger? But then, Duff tried to shame him by suggesting it was rude to share one's dirty bedding with a guest." Betsy Jane shook her head in disapproval. "He's a well-brought up boy. And I, for one, can't wait to learn more about him."

"I'm sure we'll get that chance," said James.

"Depending on how long they stay."

Betsy Jane picked up her Bible as she sat for her evening read. Still fresh on her mind was the well-mannered boy who had thought about her comfort before his own with his thoughtful gesture. She opened the book to a well-thumbed chapter from the Book of John and read it to herself.

This is my commandment. That ye love one another, just as I have loved you. Greater love hath no man than this, that a man lay down his life for his friends. (John 15:12-13, King James Version)

"Amen," she said, caressing her book and closing her eyes. "And very nice to meet you, Ellwyne Ballantyne."

15

CARRUTHERS CORNERS, ONTARIO, CANADA

THE BALLANTYNES STAYED for many months with Kersty Carruthers and his family in their modest farmhouse. To make up for the extra mouths to feed, each morning, well before the sun rose, Duff Ballantyne was expected to participate in the farm chores alongside the Carruthers clan. But as they all soon discovered, hard physical work did not suit him. In India, he had ordered others around and had servants who catered to his every whim. In India, he was important. He mattered. He commanded respect. Duff Ballantyne much preferred directing things and people, rather than having to do what he was told.

The rooster crowed when the sky was still dark. The sound forced Duff to open his eyes, which immediately rolled back into his head. He was laden with a heavy sense of dread.

Why must I do such belittling work? Without moving, he could tell his muscles were still aching from yesterday's work stooking sheaves of wheat. Although not heavy, the sheaves were dusty, and he'd had to bend over hundreds of times as he walked up and down the field, placing them into tepee-like formations. Farming was monotonous, dirty, difficult work that he despised. His lower back twinged in protest, locking itself in place as he tried to move. With a groan, he forced one leg over the edge of the bed, then the other. His feet hit the hard wooden floor with a thud, causing Donalda to stir in the bed beside him.

"What is it?"

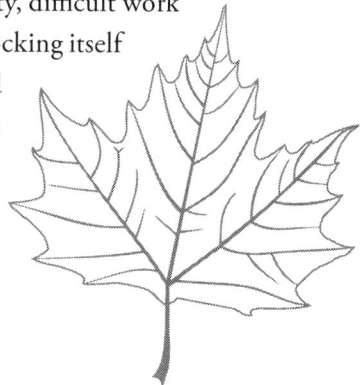

"It's time to get up," he growled, irritated that he could not at least sleep in until daylight.

"Maybe for you, not for me." She closed her eyes and fell back to sleep.

Duff snorted derisively. He fumbled around in the dark until he found the overalls he had worn the day prior and had carelessly flung over the bedpost. He plugged his nose as he picked up the soiled work clothing, stepped into the legs, and fastened the shoulder straps. "I smell like a horse," he said quietly. He felt his way in the dark along the wall to the door, opened it, and closed it behind him with a slam. Below, Duff could hear the Carruthers family readying for their day with the clang of plates and cutlery and the tumbling sound of logs being thrown into the stove. He overheard their voices talking about the day's tasks and the meals that would be served to the men.

Who are these people? Do they never rest? He couldn't imagine a lifetime of doing the same tasks, day in and day out. Keeping the homestead running was one chore after another, dawn to dusk, day in and day out, the only variation happening with the change of seasons. *That's what servants are for.*

As he stepped into the kitchen, Kersty Carruthers said brightly, "G'mornin' to ya, lad."

Duff simply nodded and took a seat at the table. He placed his head in his hands and waited for his breakfast to arrive in front of him.

"We need a few more eggs. Duff, can you go out and fetch us a few from the coop?" asked Kersty.

Duff pushed his chair back from the table without saying a word, opened the screen door, and stumbled across the verandah. It was still too dark to see, so he headed back to the house to get a lantern.

"Did ya forget this?" Kersty offered him a lit lantern.

Duff grabbed the lantern from Kersty's hand and headed back out, grumbling under his breath, "This is what servants are for."

He knelt and crawled into the coop through the small door. The dewy ground soaked his knees, making his joints seize and his shoulders shiver. Inside the coop, Duff clumsily checked the nests for eggs as the hens clucked and squawked in protest, pecking at his arms and hands.

"Get back, ya heathens," he snapped at the chickens. Ignoring him, they continued to squawk and peck. After collecting the second egg, he realized he hadn't brought anything to put them in to carry them back to the house. Exhaling heavily, he headed inside again, still guided by the lantern light. As he opened the door, he was met by Flora Carruthers holding the wire basket. "Looking for this?" she asked happily.

Duff grabbed the basket from her hand and headed out again, grumbling, "Why am I doing this? Isn't this what servants are for?" Back in the coop, he scooped up the eggs he had already gathered and with mounting frustration, threw them into the basket, breaking two in the process, which splattered their yolks and whites on his pants. As he crawled out of the coop, the farm collie stood waiting for him to emerge, barking joyfully. "Shut up, you mutt," Duff cussed. He stood and turned to head to the house. The collie jumped up on his chest, leaving two muddy pawprints on the bib of his overalls. "Now I smell like a horse and look like a pig," he said aloud, scowling.

He gingerly opened the door, hoping to enter unnoticed, given his dishevelled appearance. The family was gathered round the table. It was impossible to overlook Duff's filthy clothing, but no one said a word. Flora thanked him for the eggs and hurried back to the kitchen to fry them up in the cast-iron pan. With scrambled eggs on the plate and scrambled eggs on his shirt, Duff's day was shaping up to be another disaster on the farm.

🍁

He was going to have to find something else to do soon.

Duff and Donalda had been living at Carruthers Corners for many months, but like food left out in the sun for too long at a picnic, the Ballantyne family's presence at the quaint farmhouse was beginning to cause a noticeable stench. After it became clear the Ballantynes had outstayed their welcome with Kersty, they moved in with Robert Carruthers and his family, to the farm located several hundred feet across the road. But a tiger doesn't change its stripes, and the same issues that emerged with Kersty also arose with Robert. Duff Ballantyne was expected to help with the farm chores, but he was neither proficient nor enthusiastic about his expected tasks. Clearly, something was going to have to change.

🍁

"What are we going to do about Ballantyne?" asked Robert Carruthers. He and his father and brothers Neil and James A. were seated at Kersty's sprawling dining table, where they often convened after Sunday service to discuss matters of the upcoming week.

"What do you mean?" asked Neil.

"Well, the man isn't happy. He can barely muster the strength to get himself out of bed in the morning, let alone work all day. He doesn't have the heart for the work we need to do. And he's weighing us down like a lame horse in the harness."

"Aye, then let's get him out of your hair, Robert. We could build them a small cottage on your farm. If you buy the lumber, we'll help raise it. Even though winter's here, we can use our spare time to start on it. Shouldn't take us too long if we work together." As usual, the clan worked together on most every project that took place at the Corners.

And so, in the dead of winter, the Carruthers clan decided to build the Ballantynes a home of their own on Robert Carruthers's farm, in hopes that it would provide the family with a place where they could feel more comfortable and give some breathing room to Robert Carruthers and his brood. They had raised other buildings before and felt confident in their ability to complete this project quickly, despite the challenges of the winter weather. The land in that part of Ekfrid Township was too close to the water table to dig basements, which meant this was an ideal winter project. After the lumber was delivered, the structure itself was built within a few weeks. A cold snap hit, right as they were nailing the shingles on the roof.

"I can't nail with my gloves on," Robert lamented. "But my bare fingers are frozen to the bone within a few pounds of the hammer. We need another way."

"Yeah, it's gonna take a lot longer to do the roof if we have to keep pausing to warm up our hands," said Neil, rubbing his hands together to generate heat.

"I have an idea," said Kersty. Without another word, he dropped his hammer and headed to Robert's farmhouse. In a few minutes, he returned, with Donalda Ballantyne tagging along behind.

"This had better be important," she muttered as she shivered and huddled behind Kersty, which blocked the wind. She had been in the midst of bread-baking when Kersty had asked her to join him outside.

"What's your idea?" asked Robert.

"Load up all your roofing nails into this sack." He unfurled a burlap flour sack. "Donalda here has generously agreed to take them to the house and warm them in the woodstove for us." With that, he grinned and motioned to Donalda as he handed her the sack.

"That's bloody brilliant," exclaimed Robert.

The men gathered the nails and dropped them into the sack, which became heavier with every handful of nails they dropped into it, lowering Donalda's arms. She groaned with the effort of hanging onto it.

"Now, off you go, lass. Put small batches of these nails in the woodstove and heat them up for our frozen hands."

"Yes, Uncle," she muttered as she began to trudge back towards the farmhouse.

"And remember to bring them back out to us when they're warmed up."

With that innovation, the work proceeded without another hitch, and the Ballantynes soon had their own cottage on Robert's farm. When it was completed, all that remained was to move the family into it and discuss the matter of rent. Because Robert Carruthers had fronted the money for the softwood lumber needed to construct it, the clan agreed that he should charge the Ballantynes a modest monthly fee to recoup some of his costs.

"How will he pay me for rent?" wondered Robert aloud.

"Well, they arrived with money, so I assume that they have some funds to put towards living expenses," Kersty replied. "Plus, you're paying Ballantyne for his work, so he should be flush."

"We're all pleased to help you move into the cottage," said Robert. "I know you've been itching to have a place to call your own since you arrived in Canada. Let us know when you'd like a hand moving your things."

"We're ready any time," replied Duff, who was as eager to get out of Robert's house as Robert was to help them move. Duff wasn't used to such crowded living spaces; his home in India had been spacious and filled with fine furnishings. Here, the farmhouse had simple wooden chairs and tables, none upholstered, and each room had at least one occupant.

The next clear day, a group of Carruthers clan members showed up to help move the Ballantynes' scant belongings into their newly built cottage. The farmhouse itself breathed a sigh of relief as their belongings were carted out and carried across the yard to the smaller cottage. Like a spring purging, this moment promised new beginnings.

"You'll need to start stacking wood for the woodstove to keep you fed and warm," explained Robert. "You can pull some from my pile for now, but in the spring, you'll need to look for a source of your own." In an odd way, trees had both impeded and accelerated Scottish settlement in the area. The land was still clogged with the roots of the Carolinian Forest from the chopped down trees, but those fallen were burned in woodstoves, which kept the settlers warm and fed.

These words sent a flurry of anxiety through Duff's bones. As he feared, more work was headed in his direction. It simply never stopped on the farm. From morning till night, the farmers took care of one task after another to keep the wheels in motion, and the big machine never slowed, let alone stopped. And not a servant in sight to assist. *I wasn't cut out for this life.*

"To keep things square, I'll need to charge you rent on the cottage," said Robert. "It cost me quite a sum to buy the lumber, so I'm recouping my costs."

Duff immediately felt the heat rise from his neck to his face. "How much were you figuring?" he asked. "For rent?"

"Eight dollars a month. You can pay me on the first."

"Not a problem," said Duff Ballantyne, a cocky smirk on his face.

In the pit of his stomach, however, he knew it was a problem. Although Robert was paying him some money for his labour on the farm, it wasn't enough to live on, not with a wife and children to feed and clothe. Months ago, he and Donalda had burned through the bulk of the money, spending large amounts to pay off gambling debts, business debts, and paying the fare for the voyage across the Atlantic. As it had been in Scotland, paying monthly rent was going to become a problem.

16

CARRUTHERS CORNERS, ONTARIO, CANADA

COMPARED WITH HIS stepfather, Ellwyne had adjusted easily to farm life in Southwestern Ontario. He enjoyed breathing in the fresh air, walking through the green fields, and visiting and tending to the animals, especially the horses. Most of all, he enjoyed being around the Carruthers clan. They were talkative and friendly. Their voices were raised only in frivolity, not in the thunderous, frightening way he had heard Duff Ballantyne raise his voice, first towards his mother and now towards Donalda, and increasingly towards him. Compared with the Ballantyne family, the Carrutherses were easy to be around. Conversation came naturally with them, and Ellwyne began to relax and open up. For the first time since his mother died, he was feeling more secure. For the first time since he left his grandmother, he felt as though someone actually *saw* him. For the first time since he left India, he felt he had a real home.

Ellwyne was especially drawn to the family of James A. and Betsy Jane Carruthers. Soft-spoken James A. had a bushy moustache and large hands roughened by years of manual labour. He usually wore overalls, a button-up long-sleeved shirt, and a wide-brimmed straw hat to keep the sun out of his eyes. He had an irrepressibly positive outlook on life that was contagious, especially to Ellwyne. The couple had an adorable baby named Archie, a collie dog named Fanny, and several draft and carriage horses that were treated more like pets than livestock. Their farm-house, although much smaller than the places he had known in India, reminded Ellwyne of a ginger-

bread cookie creation, with its scalloped eaves and gable roof. It exuded warmth, and those invited inside were soon treated to hospitality and kindness.

"I'm going to be ploughing fields tomorrow, Ellwyne," said James A. "Any chance you'd like to join me?"

"Sure, Mr. Carruthers." Ellwyne was now almost fifteen and going through a growth spurt. James A. knew he could help by walking alongside the plough with the horse to make sure the lines were straight.

"Fine, then. Be here tomorrow around daylight, and we'll head out into the field and see what trouble we can dig up," he said with a chuckle.

The next morning, James A. stepped onto the verandah and found Ellwyne waiting for him on the step. "You're early."

"I wanted to learn how to harness the horse, if you'll show me."

"Well, we have to go get her from the field first."

"I already did, Mr. Carruthers. She's waiting in the stall." James A. was impressed. Unlike his recalcitrant stepfather, Ellwyne was industrious, eager to help, and keen to learn. Not only that, he had a real knack with the horses on the farm. Horses, by nature, are suspicious of newcomers until they get to know them. To catch a horse from a field, you had to earn its trust first, sometimes with carrots, but mostly through kindness and reliability. James A. knew that having a strong relationship with the workhorses was an important element of successful farming, and he was proud to see Ellwyne already figuring that out for himself.

From that day forward, James A. began inviting the young lad to join him as he ploughed fields, fixed machinery, cleared trees, fed animals, or ventured into town to pick up supplies. James A. valued the company, and he sensed that Ellwyne soaked up the extra attention. Instead of being made to feel he was in the way, Ellwyne began to feel welcome, not a nuisance to be dealt with. He felt that he had found a place with James A. and Betsy Jane. Soon, instead of waiting to be asked whether he wanted to join James A., Ellwyne assumed that he would do so. Each morning, he was waiting outside, ready to take on whatever task awaited them.

"Good mornin', Mr. Carruthers," Ellwyne said as James A. opened the door and stepped onto the verandah. "What do you have in store for us today?"

"Well, it's not one of the more pleasant jobs around here, but it's one we gotta do."

"I'm ready." Ellwyne rubbed his hands together in anticipation.

"We have to draw out the horse and cattle manure, to get ready to spread it on the fields as fertilizer. The good thing is that everyone will know what we've been up to," James A. added with a grin. "Oh, and I've already started logging your work hours in a ledger. We've all discussed it. From this point forward, Neil and I will be paying you for your work."

Ellwyne felt like the wind had been sucked out of his chest. He wasn't sure how to respond. "Thank you, Mr. Caruthers. I promise that I'll work hard. I won't let you down."

"I know that. You've already shown us that you're a hard worker. I'm not even a tiny bit worried." A smile crept from beneath his moustache.

"Thank you, Mr. Carruthers. That means a lot to me."

James A. paused. "How about you call me James A. from now on, okay?"

The pause between them lasted for what felt like minutes. "Okay … James A." It felt awkward for him to use his mentor's first name, but he was thrilled that they had crossed this point in their burgeoning relationship.

James A. put a weathered hand on Ellwyne's shoulder. "Then, let's go raise a stink." They laughed as they walked off together to the barn.

Slowly, like a root taking hold in the soil, the boy was becoming part of a new family.

17

CARRUTHERS CORNERS, ONTARIO, CANADA

ELLWYNE SLID HIS legs over the side of his bed and put his feet on the cold floor of his crowded bedroom in the Ballantynes' cottage, wanting to make his way over to James A.'s farm before sunrise without awakening anyone. He hoped to slip away without being asked about his day's plans. He dressed as quietly as he could and opened the bedroom door without making the usual creak that might alert Donalda or Duff that he was leaving. Ellwyne had learned that the less time he spent with the Ballantynes, the better off he was. *Almost out the door*, he thought as he grabbed a chunk of soda bread from the kitchen before silently opening the door and exiting onto the verandah.

As he sat and tied up his boots, he heard the tell-tale creak behind him. Ellwyne shuddered. Evidently, he hadn't been silent nor speedy enough.

"Where the hell do you think you're going, boy?" His stepfather's familiar growl made his shoulders tighten and his stomach twist.

Without turning to face him, Ellwyne replied, "I'm, uh—"

"You're, uh … what?" His stepfather's impatience interrupted him. "You have a mouth, so use it. SPEAK!"

"I'm heading over to the other farm to work with Mr. Carruthers today."

"Haven't you thought that maybe we need you here today? You have work to do around this place, too. Do you think we want you around for your pleasant company?" Duff's eyes blazed with smouldering fury, practically burning a hole in Ellwyne's neck.

"I just thought—" Ellwyne stammered.

"You just thought what? You just thought you'd just do what you wanted to do?"

Silence.

"Answer me. What did you think?" Ellwyne could feel the rage barrelling towards him like an angry bull. He braced himself for impact.

"I thought I could help out the Carrutherses today. They've been so good to us, and I thought they'd appreciate my help."

"Your help?"

"Yeah …"

"You're a big help to them, are you?"

Silence.

"TURN AND LOOK AT ME WHEN I'M SPEAKING TO YOU!" In the distance, Ellwyne heard a horse whinny. He wished he could transport himself to the field with the horses. He wished he could melt into the ground and disappear. He wanted to be anywhere else but sitting on the verandah in front of an enraged Duff Ballantyne. Ellwyne turned his head to look at his stepfather, figuring that if he complied, he could soon end the discussion and escape.

He wasn't prepared for what happened next.

THWACK!

The open hand slapped across his face, so sharply that the sound of it echoed off the wall behind him. A songbird in the nearby tree stopped chirping and flew away. The sting of it prickled through his face and filtered into his body. Within seconds, his face was throbbing. He winced but didn't dare touch his cheek, lest he give Ballantyne the satisfaction of knowing that it had hurt.

Ellwyne finished tying his boot and stood. Duff Ballantyne was still in his underclothes, which were sweat-stained and torn, and carried the pungent odour of salty sweat. He recalled the man's proud strut the first time he had met him in his mother's house in India. Time had not been kind to Ballantyne. Ellwyne shook his head as he took in the sight, and smell, before him.

"If that's all, I'll be going." He knew that speed and fitness were his only defences. If he made it to the Carruthers homestead, his stepfather would never go there seeking him. He might be a boy, but he knew that Ballantyne was intimidated not only by the taller and stronger James A. but also by Betsy Jane, with her sharp wit, penetrating eyes, and abundant confidence.

Ellwyne turned and headed for his safe spot, rubbing his face, and hoping that the mark wouldn't still be showing by the time he arrived at the homestead.

18

CARRUTHERS CORNERS, ONTARIO, CANADA

IT WAS A typical April morning on the homestead. Betsy Jane awoke before sunrise and was out in the coop, tending to her large flock of chickens and ducks, before she headed back to prepare breakfast for her husband and baby. She had long, dark brown hair that she kept piled in a severe topknot, but she put it up only after she had fed her chickens and gathered the eggs. The topknot kept her hair out of her way while she cooked and did indoor chores, but she liked how it flowed around her shoulders as she tossed feed and scraps to her flock. Her high cheekbones gave her a somewhat stern look, which she could use to her advantage when she needed to.

Later in the day, she headed back to the coop to set up the eggs for hatching in the rickety old incubator heated by a coal oil lamp. The hatchlings would provide the next crop of fowl for her flock: pullets (the females) for laying eggs, and cockerels (the males) for meat. The eggs gathered from the coop each morning made up an important part of the Carruthers clan's diet. This vital protein source fuelled the hard manual labour that went into keeping up the rest of the farm.

She had been thinking a lot lately about Ellwyne and his mysterious, unexpected arrival at Carruthers Corners. She and James A. were impressed with his good manners and how willing he was to pitch in and work. Farm life requires that all available hands, no matter how small, do their part to keep the machine rolling, and she marvelled at how fervently Ellwyne tried to do his part, even though he was still just a boy. She also noticed that

he was drawn towards James A. and spent as much time with him as he could. The man who had waited so long to become a father was now fathering not one, but two boys.

Although he was content in the company of James A., Betsy Jane sensed that Ellwyne was holding something back. He drew in a deep breath at any mention of the Ballantynes, and his mood darkened considerably when the topic of his stepfather came up. Something was not right, and Betsy Jane, ever the nurturer, knew that the boy needed to release the pressure so that he could feel safe and protected.

That evening at the supper table, after Ellwyne and James A. had returned from the field, Betsy Jane hatched an idea.

"Tonight is correspondence night," she proclaimed.

James A. clapped his hands together. "And here I thought it was just another Tuesday." Betsy Jane ignored her husband and carried on. He pushed back from the table and busied himself in the kitchen.

"I'm going to write a letter to my mother. She's living in Saskatchewan with her two sons, my half-brothers."

"What is Sass-catch-a-wand?" asked Ellwyne.

Betsy Jane smiled at the bungled attempt. "*Sas-kat-che-wan* is a province in Canada northwest of here. It's on the prairies. Lots of tall grass and openness, blue sky for miles."

"I'd like to see that someday."

"Maybe you shall. Would you like to join me and write a letter to your grandmother in India?" she asked Ellwyne. The boy's eyes widened, and he nodded his head in quick agreement.

After the table was cleared and the dishes washed, Betsy Jane invited Ellwyne to sit at the table in the chair beside her. She handed him a piece of paper and a pencil that had been sharpened with a jack-knife. She watched him cautiously pick up the pencil and slowly begin to form letters on the page.

"Do you know how to write in cursive?" she asked him. "It's quicker."

"I started to learn, but I haven't had much practice with it lately," he replied, pausing to see if he sensed disappointment in her. His writing skills were weak, and he mostly relied on clumsy block printing when composing his letters to India.

Betsy Jane found a ruler and drew a series of lines on her piece of paper.

She carefully wrote out the alphabet in her beautiful, curled writing. She pushed the paper towards Ellwyne and instructed him to trace over top of her elegant letters. As he attempted to form an A, he glanced at Betsy Jane, who encouraged him with a slight nod. He continued to the next letter. He pressed the pencil to the paper and slipped as he was making the bottom curve of the B. The pencil lead broke, and Ellwyne frowned.

"Don't hold your pencil so tight and try not to press so hard on the paper," she advised him and again gave him a nod of encouragement. "Let the pencil dance across the page, kind of like a feather that blows in the wind." She mimicked the action using her own pen. Ellwyne copied her gestures and beamed as he worked his way through the alphabet without breaking the lead again.

"I think you can start your letter now," she told him.

"I want to tell my grandmother about all the work I've been doing," he said. He also thought about all the hard work that Duff Ballantyne *hadn't* been doing. His grandmother would also want to know about that.

"She'd be proud of you, I'm sure," said Betsy Jane.

"Yeah. She wanted me to become an engineer like my father."

"Really? Your father was an engineer?"

"He designed bridges. Brilliant ones. The one that connected Howrah to Calcutta floated on pontoons so that it wouldn't get washed out in the rainy season." Ellwyne felt his chest puff up with pride as he thought about his father's accomplishments.

"That's something. We don't have things like that here. Do you miss it? India, I mean?" she asked him, realizing that she might be picking at a thinly healed wound.

"Sometimes." Betsy Jane felt the air in the room change. She watched him write a few words. With the moment lost, he didn't offer any further comments about his former circumstances. She knew not to pick at the scab.

"Much better," she said in a softened voice. "Keep practising and you'll soon be able to do it without thinking. Now, let's finish our letters."

They sat together in silence, the only sound coming from his pencil as it moved across his paper and the rhythmic ticking of the gingerbread clock hanging on the wall behind them. After several minutes had passed, Betsy Jane peered over at Ellwyne's letter. The words *afraid* and *sad* jumped off the page, which sent a stabbing pain through Betsy Jane's chest as she felt her heart begin to beat more quickly. Closing her eyes tight, she felt her lids moisten as tears formed in her eyes. Her fists clenched and she bit her lip until the pain made her stop. Opening her eyes, she continued to write. The next time she stole another glance at his letter, she watched his pencil finish the *s* on *friends*. The gingerbread clock chimed seven times, as if to punctuate the end of Ellwyne's sentence.

After he had folded and pressed his paper, Betsy Jane asked, "Would you like to stay at our house tonight?" She cocked her head to one side as she continued. "James A. is going to be working in the corner field tomorrow, and I am sure he would appreciate your help and an early start."

Before Ellwyne could reply, Betsy Jane had pushed her chair back from the table and was off to ready a room upstairs for him.

She already knew the answer.

So did Ellwyne.

19

CARRUTHERS CORNERS, ONTARIO, CANADA

"I SAW THE welt on his face, James," Betsy Jane said to her husband as they lay awake in bed. "It was as clear as day. He's been struck." They both had noticed the red mark on Ellwyne's face when he showed up that morning. They also noticed how jumpy and tense the boy acted. The slightest noise startled him.

"Yeah, I saw it, too. I asked him what happened, and he told me that he hit his head on a tree branch when he was walking over to our house. That didn't seem likely, but I didn't press him on it."

"Hmmm. Well, I saw some of what he wrote to his grandmother in his letter a while back, and he says he's afraid of Ballantyne." Betsy Jane wrung her hands, trying to think of what to do next. "I think we ought to write to his grandmother and let her know our concerns and also that we'll look out for him."

"That's a sensible plan. I'll do it tomorrow." Betsy Jane was more than capable of writing the letter herself, but they both agreed that it would have greater impact if the initial contact came from him.

In the morning, James A. sat at the oak dining table before breakfast and wrote a letter to Ellwyne's grandmother, copying the address Betsy Jane had written on Ellwyne's envelope.

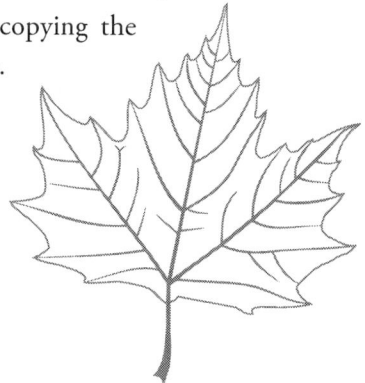

October 5th, 1910
Mrs. Bessie Smyth
Howrah, India

Dear Mrs. Smyth:

Me and my wife Betsy Jane live at Carruthers Corners in Ekfrid Township, Canada. We have been fortunate enough to meet and make friends with your grandson, Ellwyne.

We don't mean to alarm you, but we believe that Ellwyne is being mistreated by Duff Ballantyne. Ellwyne hasn't said anything to us directly, it's just observations we've made. We want to assure you that we'll look out for Ellwyne and make sure that no further harm comes to him. We've asked Ellwyne if he wants to stay at our house, because he seems to enjoy it here. We can keep a close watch on the situation this way. Ballantyne won't try anything while we're around.

Ellwyne is a pure joy to know. We're sure you miss him greatly.

Yours truly,

James Andrew Carruthers

PART 2
GERMINATION
1911–1913

"The true meaning of life is to plant trees under whose shade you do not expect to sit."

—Nelson Henderson

20

THE CORNER WOODLOT, EKFRID TOWNSHIP, ONTARIO, CANADA

THE TINY BUTTONWOOD sapling had nestled itself amongst the stand of other trees. Maple, elm, oak, and hickory trees surrounded it, but there were no other saplings like it.

It was out of place.

And it was jockeying with other saplings for its survival.

But miracles happen in nature all the time. The sapling had a secret. To thrive, it needed a ready water source. In the heavy clay at the edge of the farmer's field, no water source was visible, at least not to the naked eye. But the buttonwood's root system had reached down and tapped into an underground aquifer. As if working in tandem, it had intertwined itself with the root system of a neighbouring maple sapling, which led it to the secret water source. As if guided by the hand of a higher being, it had rooted itself in exactly the right place and, with abundant fortune, found the essential element it needed to survive: nourishment.

All things grow with nourishment, after all.

21

CARRUTHERS CORNERS, ONTARIO, CANADA

"LOOK AT ME, Donalda," Duff Ballantyne said with a moan while the corners of his mouth turned into a deep frown. He was dressed in his farming clothes, consisting of canvas trousers with a multitude of rips (all patched) and unknown stains, and a plaid flannel button-up shirt with patches on the elbows and a repaired pocket. Ballantyne was used to wearing three-piece suits with starched collars and a shiny pocket watch on a dangling chain. He despised farming life, with its dirt, sweat, and monotony. He longed for the days when he wore "proper" clothing each day instead of the ragged, sweat-stained, stinky hand-me-downs that became ripped and shredded as he worked alongside the humble farmers. Sweating was for workers, not for thinkers like him.

"I think you look nice, dear," Donalda said. Since arriving in Ekfrid, her customary clothing style, long skirts with long-sleeved blouses, hadn't changed as radically as her husband's, so she had little sympathy for his constant complaints about new attire.

Ellwyne's affinity for the Carruthers clan did not go unnoticed. In contrast, Duff Ballantyne simply couldn't understand why Ellwyne found the fields of Ekfrid Township so inviting, nor how he could find the people here so appealing. What about this place drew him in? More importantly, what secrets would he spill? Though nothing was said aloud (at least not in front of others), disapproving eyes watched him, wanting to control what he said and what he did. The boy's obvious preference for James A. Carruthers got under his stepfather's skin. It bothered him like an

itch that couldn't be scratched. It sometimes kept him awake at night. On the increasingly rare occasions that Ellwyne did spend time with the Ballantynes, it usually ended in arguments punctuated by loud outbursts from his stepfather.

"Why must you spend all your time with them?"

or

"Don't you know that I am your father?"

or

"You will do as I say."

By instinct, Ellwyne understood that answering any of those statements was useless and would only cause more conflict and despair. Each time rage spilled over him, Ellwyne withdrew into his protective shell of silence, where he felt safe. He needed shelter from the storm. Over the months, he wrote multiple letters to his beloved grandmother in India, describing his melancholy and distress with his living situation.

January 7, 1911
Mrs. Bessie Smyth
Howrah, India

Dear Grandmother:

The money you gave me for keeping in touch was spent long ago, but I'm earning my own money so I can continue to write letters to you. I am enjoying life on the Canadian farm. Can you believe it? I'm a farmer now.

The life here is unlike anything we had or saw in India. The days are filled with sweat and hard work, but it is made more pleasant by teamwork. Even though the Carruthers families have separate farms, they rotate work so that everyone's crops and livestock are taken care of.

I guess it wouldn't be a surprise for you to hear that the only person who doesn't take part is Ballantyne. I think he has shown his true colours to the Carrutherses and they realize that he's as lazy as an old mongoose. He is plain miserable to me. I cannot stand up to him because he knows he can beat me, but I am desperately unhappy here with him and Donalda. Luckily, I can escape the nonsense by working with James A. Carruthers and his brother Neil. Betsy Jane also watches out for me. She isn't afraid of Ballantyne and he knows enough not to try anything while she's around. So I'm safe as long as I'm with them. You'd like Betsy Jane. She can control people with her eyes. People respect her.

I smiled the other day, the first time in a long while. I must remember to smile more often. James A. told me that even if you don't feel happy on the inside, if you act happy on the outside, soon your insides will catch up. James A. is wise.

Write again soon. I miss you.
Your loving Ell

He didn't know how much longer he could survive living with the Ballantynes.

22

CALCUTTA, INDIA

WITH EACH LETTER received from Ellwyne, his grandmother became more and more convinced that she was correct to have protested his departure from India with Duff Ballantyne so long ago. It was clear that the boy needed guidance and a gentle hand. But Bessie was also encouraged by his repeated mention of the couple at Carruthers Corners who had taken a genuine interest in him, and vice versa. It gave her renewed cause for optimism in a situation where she now had little influence.

She was concerned for Ellwyne's welfare, and she knew whom to contact. She opened her writing desk, took out a piece of paper, picked up her pen, and began to write.

February 7, 1911
Mr. and Mrs. James Andrew Carruthers
Ekfrid Township
R.R. #4
Glencoe, Ontario
Canada

Dear Mr and Mrs. Carruthers:

*I thought it best to let you know directly what's
happening with Ellwyne. He tells me that he is very
unhappy with the Ballantynes, and that he is being
bullied by Duff Ballantyne. It's important for
you to know what kind of person Ballantyne is. His*

mother received a significant inheritance from her husband after he died. With the passing of his mother, the money went to Ellwyne. Ballantyne intercepted it and has spent almost all of it on himself. His boorish behaviour basically killed my darling daughter. I don't want him to have the same effect on my grandson.

I thank you for interceding and taking care of my dear Ellwyne.

Yours truly,
Mrs. Bessie Smyth
Howrah, India

She folded the paper and put it into an envelope. Next, she took another piece of paper and began to pen a letter to Ellwyne.

February 7, 1911
Ellwyne Ballantyne
Ekfrid Township
R.R. #4
Glencoe, Ontario
Canada

My dearest Ell:

It is a long while since I've had a letter from you, but I hope that you are well. Ell dear, do not trouble yourself about Ballantyne. Take no notice of him, he is a big coward. Tell him to go work and be a man, which he is not. Do not be frightened of him, he can do you no harm. Mr. Carruthers wrote and told me that he would look after you. So, if he worries you, tell Mr. Carruthers and he will take it up with Ballantyne. What made him go to Canada and settle down was he was frightened after owing all the money he does. I intended to send you some money on your last birthday but did not know how to send it and was afraid Ballantyne would get hold of it.

will end here. Know that I love you and miss you.
Your loving grandmother

She folded the paper, placed it in an envelope, and kissed it.

23

CARRUTHERS CORNERS, ONTARIO, CANADA

FARMERS ARE MASTERS of observation. They learn to notice minute changes in their crops that mean it's time to harvest. They learn to notice slight changes in a cow's udder that means she's about to give birth. They learn to notice the subtle changes in a horse's gait that mean it's lame and too sore to pull the plough. James A., although quiet by nature, had developed a keen sense of observation, and he learned to notice the small changes in Ellwyne. He sensed the boy's misery at his living arrangements with the Ballantynes, and he could tell when a fight had occurred. Ellwyne's shoulders slumped forward, he kept his eyes downcast, and his lips turned down at the edges instead of bursting into his usual smile.

Ellwyne had been at Carruthers Corners for months. One September morning, James A. found Ellwyne alone, sitting on the veranda, whittling a piece of discarded maple from the woodpile. Ellwyne had already filled up the woodbox with the day's firewood. His slumped shoulders were a tell-tale sign of another angry outburst from his stepfather.

"Good mornin', Ellwyne."

"Hello, James A." He did not meet James A.'s eyes when he said hello. Ellwyne had already created the elongated shape of a boat out of the wood and was concentrating on refining the inner details.

"What are you carving?" asked James A., peering with curiosity at Ellwyne's creation.

"It's a lifeboat."

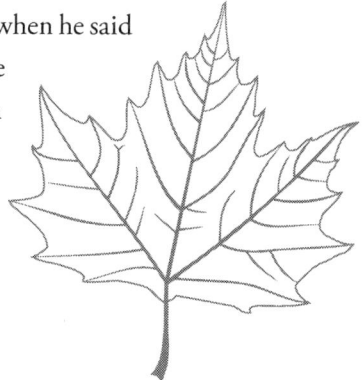

"Say now, that's interesting. What made you choose that?"

"I spent a lot of time sitting on the deck when we were on the ship coming across the Atlantic." He kept his eyes focused on the ground.

"But you took a winter crossing in February. Wasn't it cold on deck?"

Ellwyne laughed. "I considered it training for my life in Canada." James A. laughed as well. Ellwyne's mood darkened. "I found it quieter on deck. And when I was out there, I passed time by sitting on a bench. And hanging above it was a lifeboat. I would focus on trying to memorize the details of how it looked, to keep my mind busy. There wasn't a whole lot else to do, so I focused on that."

"Well, I think it's a mighty fine carving." James A. expelled a low whistle.

Ellwyne paused from his carving and looked at his friend. He basked in James A.'s positive outlook on life. James A. had a knack for bringing lightness to darkness. He could feel his own darkness lifting.

"That piece of wood was probably too small to burn in the woodstove anyway," James A. said, adding, "If it had been burned, no one would have known about it, but now you've gone and made something from it. Years from now, I bet that people will still be able to look at that piece of maple and realize that it became something else."

The smile returned to Ellwyne's face. He continued to whittle and carve, this time with more enthusiasm in his motions.

"When you're done with that carving, why don't you come with me to check on the old grey mare? She's ready to foal."

The gentle draft horse that they called Old Grey had been left in a stall for the past week in preparation for the birth of her latest foal. James A. turned away from Ellwyne and headed to the barn, whistling a jolly tune as he walked.

He found Old Grey standing up, chewing on some hay with a peaceful look on her face. She nickered her greeting and turned back to her breakfast.

"Hey, Old Grey girl. How are you feeling today?" he asked the mare, almost expecting her to reply. James A. wondered when, if ever, she was going to give birth. Because of her age, he wanted to make sure that things were still progressing well with her. He opened the stall door and from behind Old Grey's massive hindquarters, a tiny set of eyes peered back at him, blinking wildly as if trying to focus. The foal was still wet with afterbirth and was taking its first tentative steps in the deep straw that Old Grey had been lying on only moments before. James A. was certain he had missed the birth by only a few minutes. As a rule, new foals need to stand up within one hour of birth, and James A. was thrilled that this one was already ticking off the checkmarks of good health.

"Couldn't wait for me, could you?" he mused to the mare. The foal was teetering on its ridiculously long legs, attempting to stand without wobbling or toppling over. The foal edged towards Old Grey's udder and began its first attempts at nursing. James A. had been too focused on the mare and her new foal to hear Ellwyne enter the barn, but he turned his head when he heard footsteps echoing on the concrete floor of the stable. He signalled for Ellwyne to stand beside him and peer into the stall. The mare nickered again upon seeing Ellwyne, like greeting a good friend.

"Old Grey already had her foal. The hard work is done," said James A. quietly, not wanting to break the magic of the moment. He marvelled that a new life had entered the world. The little foal latched and began sucking in its first mouthfuls of mother's milk.

Old Grey exhaled a contented sigh as if agreeing with him.

"What do you think we should call him?"

"Well, what about Billy? He looks like a 'Billy' to me."

"Then, Billy it is," James A. was pleased with the arrival of the new foal and its newly anointed name, one he would surely somehow grow into.

Ellwyne (front), James A. (behind), a draft mare and her new foal

"Now Old Grey can show us what a terrific mother she is."

"I think she already has."

Ellwyne swallowed, trying to ignore the lump in his throat, but he couldn't. He thought about his mother and when he last saw her. How long ago it seemed. He tried to remember the sound of her voice, the scent of the perfume she wore when she dressed up in her finest clothes. But some of those memories were fading, becoming fuzzy. He wondered why his mother had died and why he had been left alone. He watched the foal on its wobbly legs, struggling to stand.

"You'll be okay, little fella," Ellwyne whispered to the foal. "Stay close to your mom, Billy. She'll take care of you." Ellwyne thought again about his own mother. He had never stopped missing her. On the days that he spent with James A. and Betsy Jane, he missed her both less and more, because he was reminded what it was like to be surrounded by a family, to love and be loved.

Overcome by emotion, he steadied himself on the wooden post of the birthing stall. The trembling in his legs stopped. As if in solidarity, the foal's legs also stopped wobbling momentarily.

24

CARRUTHERS CORNERS, ONTARIO, CANADA

SHE AWOKE WITH a startle. As Betsy Jane opened her eyes, she had a feeling something had changed in the homestead. Her little family, made up of her hard-working husband and little boy, seemed to have expanded by one. It was inexplicable, though. It wasn't like having an overnight guest in the house. Betsy Jane had never been one for the idea of hosting guests. In her eyes, either you belonged somewhere, or you didn't. You fell in step with the routines of the house, not the other way around. With Ellwyne there, it was different. He had been staying with them for several weeks now, and everything was different with him around, but only in remarkably good ways. It felt right, and she found herself grinning as she rose from the bed and readied herself to face the day with a renewed hop in her step.

"What are you up to today, James A.?" she asked her husband as he sat down to dive into his morning breakfast of freshly gathered eggs, bacon, and toast thick with creamy churned butter.

He paused with his fork in hand and smiled. "That last windstorm did some damage. William's got some holes in the barn roof that need fixing before the next rain. Neil and I are going over to help him patch it."

Betsy Jane sighed, loudly enough for everyone else at the table to hear. Although she understood that the Carruthers clan stuck together and did most everything as a team, she sometimes found it annoying that the brothers put everything on pause to help William, often at the drop of a hat.

Ellwyne Ballantyne, Nancy Walker, James A. and Betsy Jane Carruthers,
and the farm dog in front of the homestead.

"But what about the ploughing? That needs to get done here ..."

"Don't worry. As soon as we're done at William's, I'll come back and continue with the ploughing. We'll get it done." He knew that Betsy Jane grew a little irritated when he paid more attention to William's farm than his own, but he had valid reasons for it. William, Kersty's oldest son, had given up his chance to go to school after their mother died, so that his younger brothers, Robert and James A., could get an education. To repay him for his sacrifice, the Carruthers brothers always prioritized the upkeep of William's farm. It's how they did it. They worked together and recognized the contributions that all members made.

Ellwyne had been sitting quietly to the right of James A., nibbling on his breakfast eggs as he listened to the conversation evolve between James A. and Betsy Jane. In the pit of his stomach, he worried that the discussion was going to explode and turn into an argument, like the ones he had witnessed between his stepfather and Donalda Ballantyne. He focused on his plate and didn't look up at either James A. or Betsy Jane as they continued to discuss the matter at hand.

"That's fine, then. I'm heading over to my old neck-of-the-woods in Mosa to gather up a load of hickory nuts and walnuts. I'll take Archie with me and make a day of it." Betsy Jane needed several bushels of walnuts and hickory nuts for her baking, and she was running low. The best of the new crop was lying on the ground at the foot of towering roadside trees on the seventh and eighth concessions, and she knew exactly where to go hunting for them.

"Those bushels are heavy." Then he turned his focus to Ellwyne. "Do you mind going with Betsy Jane to help her out? Many hands make lighter work. And I promise you that the payoff will be worth it." He chuckled.

The smile returned to Betsy Jane's face. "Ellwyne, I'd love your help. It'd make it go so much faster."

"Glad to help," said Ellwyne. "Sounds like fun, actually."

"Perfect. If you come with me for the morning, then you can join up with James A. and Neil after lunch as they start ploughing. How does that sound?" Betsy Jane was waiting for Ellwyne's response.

"Count me in."

As he stood to leave the breakfast table, James A. cleared his throat. "Ahem." He cleared his throat again, louder this time. "Aren't you forgetting something?"

Ellwyne cringed. *What have I neglected to do?* he wondered. Worried that James A. was going to scold him, he bowed his head in preparation, certain that this was like the arguments between Duff and Donalda Ballantyne after all.

"I'm sorry. Did I do something wrong?" he asked, looking up at his mentor.

"Nothing at all, but don't you even want to know what the payoff is?"

Ellwyne's shoulders fell as the tension melted away from his body. He smiled and nodded, looking at James A. and waiting for the explanation.

"The payoff is ..." James A. felt himself begin to salivate in anticipation. "... only the best hickory nut tarts you've ever tasted in your life." He rubbed his stomach in excitement.

"You don't have to flatter me. You know you'll be getting your share," said Betsy Jane as she pretended to swat James A.'s arm with her tea towel. They laughed together, the disagreement resolved, and the day's plans settled. Betsy Jane turned her focus to Ellwyne. "James A. here has a sweet tooth. He loves my hickory nut tarts. Have you ever had something like that?"

"No, but my mother used to enjoy baking as well. We didn't have a lot of nuts in our pantry, though. She would make lemon tarts using the lemons that grew in the trees in our garden in India." Thoughts of Eliza flooded back into his mind as he recalled his dark-haired mother and her gentle voice that guided him even in his memories.

"We don't get too many lemons here. They're a bit of a rarity, and very costly. But I'd love to hear more about your mother and your life in India sometime," said Betsy Jane. Since her schooldays, she'd been curious about faraway places that she had only ever read about.

Now everyone could go about their tasks. Unlike the loud, messy arguments he had witnessed between his stepfather and Donalda Ballantyne, which tended to derail the entire day and ended with slammed doors or broken plates, the Carrutherses simply discussed the matter and got on with it and continued about their business.

The harmonious simplicity of life at Carruthers Corners suited Ellwyne just fine.

Ellwyne watched as Betsy Jane opened the paddock gate and exited the field with her road horse, a pretty bay mare with three white pasterns, called Holly. She preferred driving a lighter horse on the road because it required less strength than the heavier draft horses, which could be hard-mouthed with steering and stopping. Although she was much smaller than James A. or any of the men at the Corner, Ellwyne sensed that Betsy Jane was as capable of handling the horses as any man he had seen. She moved with ease and confidence around the horse, and in response, the horse respected and trusted her. From his time in Ekfrid Township, Ellwyne had learned that horses were the farmer's partner, relied upon for transportation, muscle-power, and companionship in the fields.

While she harnessed the horse and backed the mare into the shafts and fastened the straps, Ellwyne kept his eyes on Archie as the young boy sat on the milking stool in the barn, humming a nursery rhyme tune that he had recently learned.

"Where did you learn that tune, Archie?" Ellwyne thought of the velvet chair from so long ago.

The young boy's blue eyes brightened, and his rosy cheeks burst into a smile. "Momma taught me."

"Okay, Ellwyne, we're ready to go," said Betsy Jane as she led the horse by its bridle and asked her to whoa so that the passengers could load into the democrat.

"Come on, Archie!" Ellwyne yelled towards the barn and the little boy trotted to the democrat and held out his arms, waiting for Ellwyne to lift him onto the seat. Ellwyne scrambled up to take a seat beside Archie and patted the boy on his head. "All set?"

"Take up the reins, please," said Betsy Jane, who hopped up onto the seat, clucked, and jiggled the reins. The horse began walking and they headed out of the laneway, west towards the hilly roads of Mosa Township. "I have a couple of spots where I know there are good trees that should have plenty of nuts waiting for us."

The first spot she stopped was on the Eighth Concession, beyond a bend in the road, where there was a stand of trees. "See that tree? That's one that usually has lots of walnuts. I've been coming to this tree since I was a young girl." Betsy Jane knew it well because it was one concession road away from her childhood farm. She stopped the horse and pulled up the brake. "You get the bushel baskets from the back, and I'll start picking." In a flash, Betsy Jane had hopped off and was bent over, scooping nuts into her apron.

They spent the next half-hour harvesting fallen walnuts from the ground beneath the towering black walnut tree by the roadside. The hard, light-green orbs were about the size of a small crab-apple. "These look more like limes to me than walnuts," Ellwyne said.

"Deceiving, isn't it?"

"Yeah. What do you do with them?"

"The thick green skin is like a leather casing that protects the nut. We'll gather these today, but they won't be ready for me to use in baking until September or October. I have to tear open the green leathery part to get to the nut inside. After they've dried out for a few weeks, I have to smash the nut open with a hammer to get the jewel inside. They're like the pearl of the forest."

"Seems like a lot of work."

"Well, it is, but most things in this life are, aren't they? James A. is right. The payoff is worth it in the end."

After they had gathered four bushels of black walnuts and loaded them into the back of the democrat, they made their way to the Seventh Concession, to visit the hickory tree Betsy Jane anticipated would also have a bounty of nuts. Ellwyne let himself daydream as he listened to the rhythmic clip-clop of the horse's hooves on the hardened road. From out of nowhere, a white-tailed deer darted in front of the horse and sailed across the road, leaping over the fence and dashing across the field to the safety of the bush. The horse was wearing blinders to block her peripheral vision, but when the deer crossed in front of her, she spooked and jumped to the side, making the shafts of the democrat twist. The horse reared up and collapsed sideways into the ditch, which made the democrat career sideways and tip over too. All three passengers were thrown from their seat into the ditch. With the crash of wood hitting the hardened ground ringing over and over in his head, a dazed Ellwyne blinked hard. He realized that he was now lying on his stomach, face down and breathing in dirt.

"Ellwyne! Get Archie!" Betsy Jane yelled, but he could not see her.

Ellwyne reached out and felt a soft arm beside him. "Archie, is that you?"

The little boy murmured a quiet "Yes."

The sounds of the horse kicking and thrashing echoed in his throbbing skull. Still attached to the democrat, the horse, lying on its side, was panicking, trying to get up and flee. This threatened to pull the democrat, now lying on its side, over top of Archie and Ellwyne lying in the ditch. Ellwyne blinked hard again, wetting his eyes that now stung with dirt, focusing on the sound of the horse's struggle.

"Hey now, quiet, girl. You're okay. Whoa girl. Easy girl." To his amazement, Betsy Jane had plopped herself down on the horse's neck, just behind the mare's head, and was stroking her neck as she soothed the horse in a reassuring tone. By placing her full body weight on Holly's neck, Betsy Jane was preventing the horse from rising and bolting. Calmly, Betsy Jane said, "Ellwyne, move Archie to the other side of the road, and come back here. I need your help."

"Yes, ma'am." Ellwyne raised himself to his feet, took Archie's pudgy hand in his own and whisked him across the road. He seated him on the grass and said, "Stay here until we come back for you. Count blades of grass as high as you can. I'll be right back."

"Okay," replied Archie. The boy, probably in shock, was stoic in silence.

Ellwyne, now coming out of his own shock, raced back across the road, slowing as he approached the horse, which had finally stopped thrashing and struggling. Betsy Jane continued to use her weight to keep the horse down, stroking her neck. "Atta girl. We'll help you. Just wait a bit longer," she cooed to the terrified horse. She turned to Ellwyne and said, "Carefully release the harness from the shafts. There are two buckles to undo and you have to untwist them from the shaft. When you're done, we can let Holly stand up and see if she's hurt."

Ellwyne kneeled at the shafts and undid the harness buckles as quickly as he could. "Okay, she's free," he said as he shook the reins.

Betsy Jane stood. The horse, still lying on her side, snorted to expel dirt from her nostrils. She raised her head and pushed off from the ground with her front legs and lifted herself to a standing position. She shook her entire body, as if releasing the bad energy that had caused her to spook in the first place. Betsy Jane led the horse in a few small circles and cooed to her as she walked, reassuring the horse that all was well.

"Attagirl, you're okay," she said to the horse as she studied her gait and movement while walking. She turned to Ellwyne. "Well, it looks like Holly is fine. That frightened her to high heavens. How's Archie?"

"Other than dirtying his shirt, I think he's perfectly fine. You?"

"Not a hair out of place. We got real lucky."

"How did you know to do that? It happened so quickly ..." Ellwyne was in awe of Betsy Jane's lightning-speed reactions in a dangerous situation.

"I'm a farm girl, Ellwyne. It's what we do. We don't scare easy." She handed the reins to Ellwyne. "Can you wait with Holly? I want to check on Archie."

Ellwyne watched as Betsy Jane scurried across the road, dusted off Archie, and lifted him into her arms. "Attaboy," she said. "Your father will be so proud of you, you brave boy."

"What do we do about the democrat?"

"If you and Archie wait here with the horse, I'll walk to the Livingston place and get them to help us right it." And with a wave, Betsy Jane set off to get help.

Within half an hour, with the help of the neighbours, the democrat was turned upright, the horse was again hitched to the shafts, and they were able to finish the nut-gathering expedition, hardly any the worse for wear.

"You did well today, Ellwyne," Betsy Jane said to him as they drove back to the homestead. "You kept your wits about you."

"Perhaps, but not like you did."

"Maybe not, but you didn't panic, and that's the most important thing. Your calmness will serve you well later in life. I know it."

"Inside, I felt like panicking," he admitted.

"And that's okay. Everyone feels fear sometimes."

"I guess so."

"I know so. Without fear, courage can't exist." Betsy Jane put her hand on Ellwyne's leg and gave him a pat. "Courage isn't the absence of fear, it's knowing that you've put your trust in God's hands. Always remember that when you feel afraid."

Several minutes passed before Ellwyne finally spoke again. "I was afraid when my mother died."

"I'm sure you were. Anyone in that situation would feel afraid. What did you do to overcome your fear?"

"Well, like you said, I never lost my faith that things would somehow get better. And they finally did." He held Betsy Jane's stare. And in that moment, she knew with absolute certainty that he belonged with them. He was home.

25

CARRUTHERS CORNERS, ONTARIO, CANADA

JUNE WAS TYPICALLY one of the warmest and most uncomfortable months in Southwestern Ontario, but June of 1912 was particularly oppressive. The heat of the sun, coupled with the staggering humidity, could flatten even the strongest if they overexerted themselves. June, unfortunately, was also the month for one of the most strenuous farm tasks: haying season. Overexertion was almost assuredly a part of the deal. Each farm required enough forage to keep their cattle, sheep, and horses fed over the fall and winter. After cutting the hay in the field, it needed a few days to dry out before being gathered into wagons and moved back to the barn for storage until needed. Haying season summoned "all hands on deck," the Carruthers clan worked as a team, as they did with most tasks, to ensure that it got done. The men worked out in the fields, the horses pulled the hay wagons, the boys took care of the livestock chores, and the women made sure that everyone was fed and hydrated.

It was Ellwyne's first time working with the men in the hay field, and he was eager to show both James A. and Neil that he belonged beside them. He felt like he had something to prove, even though they put no pressure on him. They were getting ready to head out to the field to load up the dried hay when Neil noticed that someone was missing.

"Where is Duff?" Neil asked Robert Carruthers, referring to Ellwyne's stepfather. "I thought he was going to help today."

"The last time I saw him, he was sitting underneath the apple tree near his house smoking a cigar," said Robert with a shrug. "I haven't seen him since."

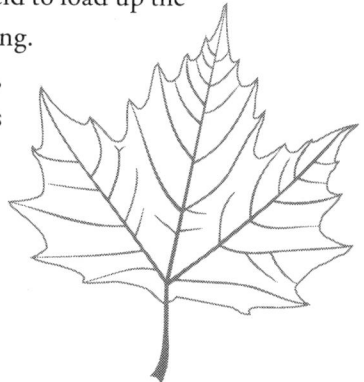

"Well, I guess he'll show up when he shows up," said Neil, shaking his head with a mix of amusement and bewilderment. He wasn't accustomed to having to nag someone to do their part. He was used to having willing helpers. Even those who weren't proficient at a task, either due to lack of strength or knowledge, exerted the effort, or volunteered to take on the less enviable tasks that no one wanted to do. That's how the heavy load became lighter. That's how it worked at Carruthers Corners, so having a weak link in the chain slowed everyone down.

At the mention of Duff Ballantyne's name, Ellwyne experienced two immediate gut reactions: dread, followed by embarrassment. Dread because he did not look forward to working in proximity to him, and now embarrassment because Duff was disappointing the people who had shown him so much generosity and hospitality since their arrival. Ellwyne steeled himself to work twice as hard to make up for his stepfather's dereliction.

"Ellwyne, why don't you and Charlie hop up into the wagon," said Neil. "When we throw up the hay, you boys push it to the front so we still have lots of room at the back." Ellwyne nodded and smiled, pleased that he had been paired up with Charlie Reath, one of the neighbour boys who lived on a farm on the Fifth Concession in Ekfrid. He was about the same age as Ellwyne but had fair skin, blue eyes, and lighter hair that made him a candidate for a bad sunburn. Ellwyne had noticed Charlie's skin already starting to redden in the sun.

"Here," said Ellwyne, as he handed him his wide-brimmed straw hat. It was a perfect match to James A.'s headgear, and he never left the house without wearing it. "You might need this more than I will today."

Charlie accepted the hat like he had won the grand prize for his Aberdeen Angus steer at the fall fair. "Thanks. You sure?"

"Yup. Let's go." Ellwyne had learned early in life that not everyone was trustworthy, but he knew that when you found a friend, you should do what you can to protect him.

Witnessing the exchange, Neil leaned in towards James A. and in a hushed tone said, "Ellwyne is nothing at all like that stepfather of his, is he?"

"Nope. Nothing at all." James A. beamed with pride.

The two boys scrambled into the wagon. James A. was going to drive the wagon while Neil and Robert walked behind. Although it was an integral task in the process, driving was the least physically strenuous. The men intended to share driving duties among Neil, Robert, and James A. so that they could each take a bit of a break throughout the morning.

"Walk on, Grey." James A. jiggled the reins and clucked. The old draft mare leaned into her harness, and the wagon lurched forward. She was one of the most dependable horses on the farm and was paired with a younger horse named Jigs that was still learning the ropes of being teamed with another horse. The older, experienced horse would guide the younger one, just as the men would show the boys how it was done. That's how it worked on the farm.

When the men returned from the field after spending the morning filling three wagon loads of dusty hay, they had worked up a big thirst and an even bigger appetite. Betsy Jane and Maggie Belle, who had married Neil Carruthers the year before, had set up the two makeshift tables that they used for outdoor dining during work bees like this. The spread included roast beef sandwiches, made with thick slices of homemade wheat bread slathered in fresh butter, and a bowl of coleslaw with vinegar dressing, along with three pitchers of cold water pumped fresh from the well.

"Oh, I was hoping they would have roast beef," exclaimed James A., within earshot of the women, his face beaming.

"It's what you asked for." replied Betsy Jane, feigning surprise. James A. and Betsy Jane discussed most things, even meal planning. "Wash up before you sit at the table," said Betsy Jane, her eyes focused on Ellwyne and Charlie.

The boys headed to the pump together to clean the sweat and dirt off their hands and faces before eating. Betsy Jane had set out a bucket of water with a bar of her homemade lye soap and a soft towel.

"How are you feeling?" asked Charlie as he scrubbed his hands.

"Hungry. Tired. Very dirty. But also happy," replied Ellwyne. "I feel like we kept up with them."

"I think we did." Charlie removed the straw hat. It had shielded his face from the sun, just as intended.

The boys headed back to the table and took their seats around it. Everyone quieted. James A., at the head of the table, asked everyone to join hands. He bowed his head. "Dear Lord, we want to give You praise and thanks for

Your glory as we work today to provide sustenance for the animals that will, in turn, sustain us over the winter. We thank You for allowing us to work side-by-side in harmony. We also thank You for bringing us an extra hand in Charlie." Charlie beamed with pride at the mention of his name in the prayer. "We have now gathered to share a meal in Your honour. Thank You for this food. Bless it to fuel our bodies forward into Your will for our lives. We pray that we will be able to work for the glory of Your Kingdom. In Jesus' name, Amen."

"Amen," said everyone in harmony.

James A. lifted the sandwich plate and offered it first to Betsy Jane, seated to his left. It was passed around the table until it finally returned to James A. The sandwiches were devoured by the hungry work crew. Betsy Jane excused herself from the table and returned moments later from the kitchen, carrying a glossy cake on a white platter.

"This is the real surprise," she said, and smiled at James A. "What would haying be without a bit of burnt leather cake?"

Ellwyne nudged Charlie in the ribs. "Wait till you try this. We only get it on special occasions."

"What's the special occasion?" asked Charlie.

"We worked as a team. And the young whips kept up," said James A.

Everyone laughed.

"The first piece to you," said Betsy Jane as she passed a slice to her husband. "I know it's your favourite."

26

CARRUTHERS CORNERS, ONTARIO, CANADA

LETTERS, PACKAGES, AND newspapers from India arrived consistently over the years to Carruthers Corners. Each was addressed to "Ellwyne A. Ballantyne" at R.R.# 4, Glencoe, Ontario, Canada, which had now become his permanent mailing address and home. Their arrival sent a flurry of elation through the boy that rippled through their tiny home. Receiving mail from his grandmother meant so much to Ellwyne. Betsy Jane could readily understand how Ellwyne's spirits were lifted by knowing that a blood relative living so far away was thinking of him. She imagined that each letter and package brought him a piece of his mother across the continents and oceans that separated them. Ellwyne sometimes wondered about his father's family, but he had never known them, and they were never a part of his life. Following Edward Dacosta's death, Eliza had lost touch with the family after they returned to Portugal.

An avid reader, Betsy Jane especially relished the newspapers Ellwyne received from India. Though they were quite outdated by the time they arrived, it didn't stop her from reading them from beginning to end. Although she let Ellwyne read them first because they were, after all, intended for him, she spent hours poring over them after he had finished. It was how she learned many details about the coronation of King George V in 1910, about the formation of an organization specifically for girls called the Girl Guides, and about an expedition to explore Antarctica. Ellwyne, passing through the parlour, stopped when he noticed Betsy Jane, her face hidden behind the broadsheet pages she read so raptly.

"What have you learned about the world from those pages, Betsy Jane?"

"Oh, lots of things," Betsy Jane did not look up. "There's quite an article here on the coronation of our new King George. Did you know that, besides being our king, he is Emperor of India?"

"My mother used to tell me that my father was named after a king."

"Oh? What was your father's name?"

"Edward," said Ellwyne. "Edward Dacosta. I never knew him, though. He died when I was still a baby. And my father's family was never part of my life. I don't even know what happened to them. Maybe they returned to Portugal? Or maybe they stayed in India, but I don't know."

Betsy Jane folded the newspaper and put it in her lap. "It is a great sorrow to lose one's father at such an early age."

"Yeah …." He paused, unsure what to say next. His heart twinged with sadness at the thought of his long-dead father.

"I know, because mine died when I was young, too." She gave him a gentle nod and closed her eyes.

"I guess we're a bit alike then?"

"Maybe just a little bit." She chuckled.

One August afternoon, James A. returned from the mailbox at the corner and placed a package wrapped in brown paper on the oak dining table. He called to Ellwyne from the barnyard to tell him that a package had arrived for him. The boy dropped the shovel he was holding in its spot, pivoted, and sprinted towards the house, launching himself up the back verandah steps with the energy of a loaded spring. He burst through the door, forgetting momentarily to remove his boots, retraced his steps to the door, and stepped out of them.

"I picked it up at the post at the corner today as I drove past on my way back from Neil's," explained James A., pointing at the box. "Go ahead. Open it."

Ellwyne tore into the outer wrapping and ripped open the cardboard box with the fury of a bull. He dug around until he found an off-white cotton sack, beautifully embroidered with blue and red ornate letters that read *E.A.B.* in a swirling cursive script.

"She remembered my initials," he exclaimed, laughing.

Betsy Jane and James A. were standing behind him, waiting to see what was inside the sack. He untied the string, opened it, and removed a deck of playing cards. These were not ordinary cards, however. These were special. They were made of ivory, each one masterfully and delicately carved with the suits and numbers. Ellwyne's eyes grew large as he ran his fingertips across the ace of spades.

"These are remarkable." He met Betsy Jane's eyes and could sense her impending censure, even though she was trying to contain it (at least momentarily). Betsy Jane was vehemently opposed to gambling in any form, and playing cards was forbidden in her house, or anywhere in her sight, for that matter. But despite her strong views, she could hardly take away Ellwyne's joy at having received such an expensive and elaborate gift from his grandmother.

Finally, it came.

"Even though I know you're proud of the playing cards," she explained, "I do not want them used in my house. I do not agree with the notion of gambling. It's the devil's work, and we want to keep anything of that sort away from here."

"Yes, Betsy Jane," said Ellwyne. "I understand, and I promise that I will not play with them." He held her gaze, and looking as sincere as a fourteen-year-old boy can look. He wrapped the cards back up in the sack and tied it tightly, as if it were holding a prisoner not meant to escape. He brought the playing cards upstairs to his room and hid them from her sight in his dresser.

Instead of being heavy-handed with him and confiscating the playing cards or asking him to destroy them, Betsy Jane decided to test Ellwyne to see if he would keep his word.

She never saw the ivory playing cards in his hands again.

He was as good as his word.

Through letters addressed to them from India, James A. and Betsy Jane gained a clearer picture of the struggles that Ellwyne had been managing alone for months while living with the Ballantynes. They suspected that Duff Ballantyne did not treat Ellwyne properly, and the letters confirmed their fears and filled in some missing pieces of the puzzle.

Betsy Jane and James A. convened about the situation one night in the kitchen while Betsy Jane finished cleaning up the dinner dishes. Although James A. was the patriarch who made most of the decisions on behalf of the family, he tended to listen to Betsy Jane's views before acting on anything. And in matters of utmost importance like this, he relied on her to share her unvarnished opinion.

"Now that we know for sure what's going on, what do you think we should do about Ellwyne?" he asked Betsy Jane, still holding the letter he had finished reading for the second time. Although he had already decided what should be done, he wanted to give Betsy Jane a chance to air her thoughts, on the off-chance that they differed from his.

"As far as I'm concerned, he can stay here with us for as long as he likes. I do not trust that man to look out for his interests or well-being, not one bit."

James A. could sense that his wife was not going to shift her opinion about Duff Ballantyne. He could feel the temperature change as she fumed, like a slow-burning fire that builds strength with a gust of wind. "So, it's settled then?"

"Completely. As far as I'm concerned, he's not going anywhere." There was a streak of venom in her voice. Although she despised laziness, Betsy Jane abhorred the idea of someone mistreating a powerless person even more, and now Duff was guilty of both offences. Under her watch, like the mother goose she was, it was never going to happen to Ellwyne again. "We'll write Bessie Smyth another letter and assure her that no hair on her grandson's head will ever be touched."

Betsy Jane could feel her jaw throbbing as she clenched her teeth, sick with the thought of Ellwyne being mistreated by his stepfather. She had made a snap judgement about Duff Ballantyne when he had first arrived at Carruthers Corners, and she felt vindicated now for having not trusted him. She thought about the large flock of chickens she tended to. Ill-tempered roosters, the ones that bullied the weaker hens or dared to attack her or little Archie, were never tolerated or given second chances. Nasty roosters met their fate in her soup pot, boiling on the cookstove. Her hazel eyes flashed and narrowed as she considered Duff Ballantyne one last time, and dismissed him with a final huff.

And like that, the decision was made. The air shifted in the room as the mood changed and the tension eased. Betsy Jane smoothed her apron and turned back to her stove. James A. stood, put his straw hat back on his head, and pulled the brim over his eyes as he readied to return to the sun.

"I'll go tell Ellwyne that he might as well make himself at home then," declared James A., and he set off to go find him in the pasture, where he had left him digging post holes for a new fence.

Sweat was pouring off Ellwyne's brow when James A. returned to his side. The boy had managed to dig two more holes by himself while he was gone. Unlike his stepfather, James A. reflected again, Ellwyne was a hard worker not afraid of putting in a full day's work.

"Betsy Jane and I were wondering something," he began slowly.

"What's that?"

"Well, do you like staying with us, Ellwyne?" James A.'s face was full of genuine concern.

Ellwyne stopped what he was doing, aware that James A. was staring at him, waiting for him to hold eye contact. His shoulders tensed with dread. The Carruthers clan had never broached the subject before, and now he worried that he had overstayed his welcome.

"Of course I do." His eyes lowered, and his shoulders dropped. "But have I done something wrong?" Worry tightened his jaw.

"Not at all. You have been an immense help to me. We like having you here." James A. smiled.

Relief poured through Ellwyne's tense body. "Phew. I was afraid you were going to send me back there." He cast a gaze towards the cottage where the Ballantynes were living.

"No. Betsy Jane wanted to let you know that you should bring all your things over and make yourself at home here with us, if that's what you want," he said, waiting for Ellwyne's reaction.

Ellwyne's shoulders relaxed, and a grin broke out from ear to ear. The boy picked up the auger again and began twisting it into the thick, heavy clay. Working with this clay soil always proved a strenuous affair.

"Come on, James A.," said Ellwyne, gesturing towards the other auger. "We've got ten more to go before supper. And time's a-wastin'."

And like that, the question of whether he could or should stay at Carruthers Corners was never again mentioned.

⁂

James A. and Betsy Jane walked together to the Ballantyne cottage that the Carruthers clan had constructed for them in the dead of winter. They stepped onto the porch and rapped at the door and waited. It opened, and a waft of cigar smoke hit their nostrils.

"Hello, Donalda," said James A. "Is your husband at home?" Betsy Jane nodded, shoulders pressed back firmly, making herself appear even taller than she was.

Donalda eyed them both suspiciously, turned her head and screeched, "Duff. Come here!" The sound reminded Betsy Jane of her noisiest hen squawking before laying an egg. She smiled to herself and tried not to laugh at the image in her head.

Duff Ballantyne appeared in the doorway with dishevelled hair and an untucked shirt, with the appearance of having woken from a lengthy nap. It was the middle of the afternoon, and Betsy Jane wondered what chores he had let slide. Judging by the overgrown weeds surrounding the house, it was clear that he had not trimmed the grass regularly, which was necessary to discourage the field mice from wanting to take up residence indoors come fall.

"We wanted to let you know that Ellwyne has decided to stay with us," explained James A., to dead silence. "We've made a room up for him."

There was a long pause as Duff Ballantyne pondered this, his brows furrowed.

"Oh? Did he say why?" he asked, his expression suggesting he was wondering if some secret had been spilled. Betsy Jane smelled alcohol on his breath as soon as he spoke.

"I think he finds it easier, now that he's working nearly full-time for me and Neil." James A. gave Ballantyne the chance to save face.

Relief washed over Ballantyne's face. He assumed they hadn't noticed the red marks on Ellwyne's face, or the welts on his back. "That makes perfect sense. Is that all, then?" He rushed to end the conversation.

"There's not much more to it than that," James A. added, "Is there?" He raised a quizzical eyebrow.

Ballantyne's face reddened. "Of course not. That's it."

They nodded their polite goodbyes and turned away to walk home.

"They didn't raise a fuss about losing a family member, did they?" asked Betsy Jane when they were out of earshot. "You'd think they'd put up more of a fight if they genuinely cared."

"Now, Betsy Jane. I think we both know what's up. Ellwyne's safe, so let's just put it to bed."

"Fine by me."

James A. smiled to himself. He knew his wife would stew on it for a few days longer, muttering to herself as she stirred a pot on the stove or threw feed to her chickens. Betsy Jane tended to take the side of the underdog. The day he met her, she had defended a small boy being picked on by a group of bullies. Some things never change, and he gave thanks for that.

January 3, 1912
Mr. and Mrs. James Andrew Carruthers
Ekfrid Township
R.R. #4
Glencoe, Ontario
Canada

Dear Mr. and Mrs. Carruthers:

Ellwyne has informed me that he is staying with you now full time. Thank you for giving my grandson a home once more. He is a good boy who is dearly loved and missed by all of us here. I am so grateful he has found a safe place to weather the Ballantyne storm. His darling mother, if she were still alive, would also want you to know how much your kindness means.

Despite the thousands of miles that separate us, I feel a closeness to you. I guess we have a bond through Ellwyne now.

God bless you both.

Yours sincerely,
Bessie Smyth

Tucked into the envelope was a pressed rose petal from her garden.

27

CARRUTHERS CORNERS, ONTARIO, CANADA

ELLWYNE WAS NEARLY done filling up the water troughs for the horses and cattle. On the farm, everyone had a vital part to play to keep the operation running. He had a long list of daily tasks, but he didn't mind; he liked the routine and responsibilities, and he was good at his chores. Each day at the Carruthers farm, regardless of season, he had to make sure that the livestock were fed and watered. Water gathering was particularly strenuous, because he had to hand-pump the water from the well behind the house and carry the pails to the barn, sloshing the water as he walked, and dump the contents of the pails into the troughs. Nevertheless, he especially enjoyed taking care of the animals. They showed him their gratitude and he trusted their true motivations, which was not something he could say for his interactions with some people in his life. "There you go, Grey," he said as he emptied the final pail into the tin trough. The mare, one of his favourites, nickered her thanks as she dipped her nose and drank. He patted her muscular neck. The sound of her sucking up the fresh water brought a smile to Ellwyne's face.

"Ah, there you are." A voice from behind startled him, breaking his concentration. He would recognize that voice anywhere. He felt his shoulders rise and his stomach twist.

Without turning to look at him, Ellwyne sighed and snapped, "What do you want?"

His stepfather had walked from Robert Carruthers's farm and was sweaty from the effort, despite the short distance. He wiped his hand across his brow and exhaled.

"Now, now. Is that any way to speak to your father?"

"As I've said to you before, you're *not* my father." Ellwyne felt an equal amount of annoyance rising in his voice.

"How can you stand doing that?" Duff asked as he watched Ellwyne, covered in sweat, heading back to the pumphouse for another pail of water. "It's like being in prison." Duff trailed behind him.

"I happen to enjoy it. And that's how a farm works: Everyone pitches in to do their part."

"Well, I don't."

"Yeah, I've noticed. And so has everyone else. You didn't show up for haying. Neil and Robert were disappointed."

Duff snorted. "It doesn't matter now. We're leaving. I cannot stand it here any longer. Even the smell ..." Duff said, turning up his nose.

Ellwyne ignored the comment and cut him off. "Where are you heading?"

"To a bigger place. Donalda thinks she can find me a job in the city that's more to my liking and uses my natural talents more effectively than ... *this*," he said, waving his hand around at the barnyard and its residents. "I expect you to come back and gather your things and get ready to head out with us." Although Ballantyne did not care about Ellwyne's well-being or want him as part of his family, he knew that the lad had saved up a hefty sum of cash through his work with the Carrutherses. And that cash could soon come in handy as they tried to settle in a new city.

"No," Ellwyne said flatly. "I'm not leaving here."

Duff stepped backwards. He noted that Ellwyne, though still a boy, had grown taller and stronger. "No? Well, how will that look when *we* leave, and *you* stay behind?"

"I'm not worried about how it looks. I'm not leaving. I belong here now."

"Really? You belong here? With cattle, and horses, and pigs?" Duff was unable to hide the mocking tone.

"I'm staying here" Ellwyne stood firm and unyielding.

Seeing that he was not going to persuade Ellwyne to change his mind, Duff snapped. "Have it your way, then. I'm done with you, anyway." Duff had a habit of needing to finish arguments by stabbing his opponent. Ellwyne was used to this tactic and ignored the comment. Sensing this was another form of manipulation, Ellwyne dismissed the idea of leaving with the Ballantynes and flushed it from his mind.

At that moment, James A. emerged from the barn, adjusted his straw hat, and gave a friendly wave to both Ellwyne and Duff.

"Hi, there," he yelled, before whistling an upbeat Scottish reel that cut through the tension between Ellwyne and his stepfather, which hung in the air, like a foul odour.

"You'd best leave now. I have work to do. And time's a-wastin'." He watched as his stepfather turned away and trudged down the laneway towards his cottage at Robert Carruthers's farm. "Good riddance," Ellwyne added to no one in particular. A flurry of emotions swirled over him, but he clenched his jaw and shook his head.

"Hey, Ellwyne. What did Ballantyne want?" James A. asked as Ellwyne entered the barn.

"Nothing."

"That sure doesn't sound like him."

"I mean, he always wants *something*, but it's nothing I can help him with."

"I see." Multiple scenarios raced through James A.'s head about what the man could be pestering Ellwyne for. Was he asking to borrow money? Now that Ellwyne was being paid for working at Carruthers Corners, James A. knew he was socking away his earnings and might be easy prey for the money-hungry man. It was no secret in the Carruthers clan that Duff didn't embrace farm life. When he didn't show up for work, he didn't get paid.

"Yeah. It's complicated."

"You know, if you ever need help, you can come to me and Betsy Jane, right? We're pretty good listeners."

Ellwyne nodded. "I know you are. You've always been so good to me."

28

CARRUTHERS CORNERS, ONTARIO, CANADA

"I CANNOT STAND it here any longer," Duff Ballantyne told Donalda. He was stretched out on their bed, taking up more than his half of it. "I don't belong. The work's too hard. My body is sore, and it aches." To illustrate his point, he bent his knee, which made a loud crack as the angry joint reluctantly complied.

"And your back?"

"It's a wreck." He pouted. "And if I have to listen to one more story about crops and how they're growing or not growing, or whether Charlie's prized cow has enough milk, I might die of boredom." Duff remained shocked at how much time the Carruthers men spent talking about the weather and its impact on the growing season. To him, it was monotony. He didn't understand that to them, it was survival.

"I know, dear. You're not meant for this life," said Donalda. Although she had enjoyed being around her uncle and his family, she recognized from the start that her husband was a fish out of water. The physical work they expected of him caused him both pain and misery. And the more miserable he became, the more it affected everyone who lived under their roof.

"We're leaving tonight. Pack the children's things. One trunk for us all. If it isn't valuable, do not pack it. Just leave it here."

"And what about Ellwyne?"

"He's not coming. He'd rather stay here with …"—Duff wrinkled his nose and made a face like he'd smelled a foul odour—"*them*."

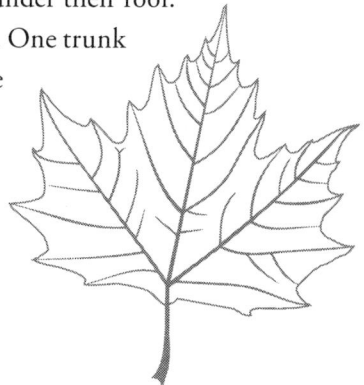

"I don't understand that boy." Secretly, Donalda was pleased Ellwyne was not joining them. It was one less mouth to feed. Plus, she had never developed a kind or meaningful relationship with the boy who had come along with her husband like so much heavy baggage. She was unaware of the stash of money that Ellwyne had saved and stuffed into his mattress at James A.'s farm, however.

"He loves it here. When I saw him earlier this week, he was drenched in sweat, hauling water, like a servant for horses. And he loves it. He doesn't have my blood in him, that's for sure."

"Clearly not." She tsked.

"I knew the moment that I met him that he had too much of his father in him." Duff had never known Edward Dacosta, but that didn't stop him from hurling insults towards his memory. Eliza had once told Duff about her late husband's design work on the Hooghly River Bridge in Calcutta, but he listened half-heartedly, perking his ears only when he heard about the fortune Edward had left behind after his death.

"What about the rent money we owe Cousin Robert?"

Duff grumbled and forced himself to rise from the bed, moaning as he did so.

"He'll get his money."

In his gut, Duff knew that Robert Carruthers was never going to see any more money from him. There was nothing left to give.

After the sun had set that evening, Duff and Donalda packed up their two children and scant belongings and rushed down Sideroad 16 on foot. They were headed to the railway line in Macksville, a tiny whistle-stop close to Carruthers Corners. They planned to catch a train that would take them eastward to Toronto, a large city with a mix of industries where Donalda felt confident that her husband could obtain non-physical work in an office. Surely there was a company in the metropolis that could use the formidable business skills he had developed in India while managing a business of his own. The Ballantynes said nothing of their moving plans to the Carruthers clan. They hoped to slip away without being detected, like a serpent slithering through grass.

Donalda pushed the baby pram with her right hand while balancing a suitcase on her left hip. The weight of it, along with the stress of being uprooted again, was making her cranky. "Hurry up!" she screeched at eight-year-old Valetta, who was carrying a small leather suitcase packed with the few things she needed. Valetta had to stop every ten steps to put down the suitcase to give her arms a rest. With her short legs, she lagged behind her stepmother, who was walking at a pace far faster than Valetta could manage. Each time she paused, Donalda yelled at the girl, "Come on, keep walking."

"I'm trying." Tears of exasperation burned Valetta's cheeks. She blinked to clear her eyes as she walked, but she didn't dare let her stepmother know she was crying. Valetta, like her half-brother, had learned by now that it was far better to keep one's disappointments cooped up inside than to air them and risk being ridiculed, or worse, called out for selfishness. Those who didn't agree with Donalda's wishes were selfish.

Once they reached the train station, the family rested on their suitcases to catch their breath. Duff was dripping with sweat from the speedy escape on foot from Carruthers Corners. As Donalda tended to the baby, he wiped his forehead with his handkerchief and heaved a heavy sigh of relief.

"To new beginnings," he said to Donalda. He looked at his dingy, torn, and patched trousers. How far he had fallen since his days in India, when he dressed up each day and looked like a respectable gentleman. He knew he wouldn't recognize himself in a mirror when he saw himself dressed in farmer's clothes. He no longer had a tidy, twisted moustache. He didn't dab behind his ears with the expensive aftershave he once used. He walked with a half-limp on account of the constant ache in his back, made sore from the hours of daily bending and lifting, throwing and stacking that had become routine since they had submerged themselves in farm life. A life of physical labour didn't agree with Duff Ballantyne. "I cannot wait to wear a suit again."

"I cannot wait to have a home again," Donalda replied. "I really liked the cottage at Carruthers Corners. I wish we could've stayed on." Her bottom lip jutted out in a familiar pout.

Duff knew that he would have to listen for several weeks to his wife's moaning at the loss of her beloved cottage. "I know, dear. But we'll find something else just as nice." And *cheaper*, he thought.

"I suppose." The pout remained fixed on her face.

When the train carried them away, Valetta stared out the window at the passing scenery, wondering when she might see the green fields of Ekfrid Township again. For the second time that day, a warm tear slipped across her cheek, which she wiped away before her stepmother noticed. She hoped that Ellwyne would be able to keep in touch with her through letters. She had made sure to get the mailing address so she could send him a letter once they settled. He was her last connection to their mother, and on days like this, she ached for her.

29

CARRUTHERS CORNERS, ONTARIO, CANADA

WHEN DUFF BALLANTYNE didn't show up for work, Robert Carruthers climbed the steps to the wood-framed cottage that he and his father and brothers had built for the Ballantynes. He rapped on the door and waited for an answer. Not a peep came from inside. After several minutes, he walked to the front window, cupped his hands on the glass, and peered inside. Through the thin curtain, he could see that the house was mostly empty, except for a few furnishings now covered in sheets.

"Ballantyne didn't show up again for chores. When I went over to check on him, I found the place empty. I think they've gone," he said later to his half-brother brother Neil as they readied for the workday.

"The Ballantynes? Gone?" asked Neil.

"Aye. It's like a storm whipped through and blew them away. Did they say anything to you about leaving?"

"Not a word. And I didn't hear any ringing bells last night from passing carriages."

"Well, maybe it's for the best. Ballantyne wasn't much of a farmer. I don't think it was in his blood."

"You could say that again," said Neil. "I remember when he first arrived, Dad once asked him to go gather eggs for breakfast. He ended up with more broken eggs *on* him than in the basket."

"Well, it's a good thing he didn't ask him to get some milk." The two men laughed, perhaps a little harder than they should have.

The next time the clan was gathered after Sunday service, the oldest Carruthers son, William, made an announcement. Their patriarch, Kersty, had passed away the year before, so the leadership duties had naturally fallen to William.

"As you all know, the Ballantynes are no longer here at Carruthers Corners," he said. "The cottage is completely empty, and it appears that they're gone for good." There was a general murmur of agreement.

"Does anybody have any idea where they've gone?" Neil finally asked. He suspected that Ellwyne might know but didn't want to put the lad on the spot in front of the others.

"They didn't say a word, as far as I know."

James A., who had been watching Ellwyne for his reaction to William's words, detected a slight smile breaking across the boy's lips. He imagined that it might be bringing a sense of relief to know that his stepfather would no longer be there to intimidate him. James A., always a keen observer, had sensed palpable tension between Ellwyne and his stepfather whenever he saw them together.

James A. stood and cleared his throat. "If I may," he said, glancing at Ellwyne before turning his focus to the larger group. "Although we're surprised to see them go, let's remember that we're lucky to have a Ballantyne still with us at Carruthers Corners. And if I had to choose which one I wanted to remain, I couldn't have chosen any better."

James A. nodded in Ellwyne's direction.

Ellwyne's smile broadened and his shoulders straightened up a little more. James A. strode over to Ellwyne's side, placed a hand on his shoulder, and squeezed. "Glad to have you here, my boy," he said quietly, so that only Ellwyne could hear.

While Ellwyne had refused to leave Carruthers Corners with Duff and Donalda Ballantyne and had rooted himself in the farm in Ekfrid Township with James A. and Betsy Jane, his refusal had repercussions weeks later. It came in the form of a single stinging letter of reproach from Donalda. Addressed to "Ellwyne Ballantyne," the envelope virtually smouldered with its flaming contents. With hesitation, Ellwyne opened it, removed the letter, and scanned the lines.

April 3, 1912
Ellwyne Ballantyne
Ekfrid Township
R.R. #4
Glencoe, Ontario
Ellwyne:

I hope you realize your mistake and know that you've made your daddy angry. He says that you've always been an ungrateful sort and that we should have left you in Scotland when we had the chance. Everything you have in this life is because of him and the sacrifices he's made for our family. He is an important businessman. He didn't want to work on the farm, but he did it because it was best for you and Valetta. You'd best remember that.

He wanted you to come with us to Toronto. What will the Carrutherses think now that you've stayed behind with them? And, in case you didn't know, you've also upset Valetta terribly. She doesn't understand what's happened and won't stop asking why you're not here with us. As a punishment for your bad behaviour, she's not to write any letters to you. And don't bother sending her any either. She won't get them. I will make sure of that.

Someday you will realize that you need your mom and daddy and what a selfish boy you've been.

Your mother,
Donalda

🍁

The word 'mother' was underlined three times and she had pressed hard enough to tear the paper when she wrote it. He absorbed each verbal swat she delivered with a deep exhale and a further drop of his shoulders. The idea that Ballantyne had performed any valuable work on the farm made him snort, but he especially did not appreciate Donalda's determined insistence that Duff Ballantyne was his "father" and she his "mother." If he knew one thing for certain, it was that he had a mother and father, and neither was named Ballantyne. His heart ached as he thought about his parents and how they had died far before their time, and how much he had missed out by not knowing them.

I miss you, Momma, he said to himself. *I hope you're still here with me.*

After reading the letter once more, Ellwyne folded it up, put it back in the envelope, and hid it in his room in the back of his dresser. He retreated to the barn, where he sat on the stall door, watching Old Grey munch on hay. The soothing sound of her crunching helped him relax and see problems through a different lens. The letter, despite its nasty tone, did serve one important purpose: it confirmed that he had made the correct decision to stay behind with James A. and Betsy Jane in Carruthers Corners.

This was where he belonged and where he wanted to stay.

This was where he felt safe.

The boy who felt he didn't fit in with the Ballantynes had carved out a place for himself in the feathered nest of Betsy Jane and James A. Carruthers. Thousands of miles away from where he was born, he found home again.

The envelope was weathered and worn, as if it had been stored in a pocket for weeks before being mailed.

"Here you go, Ellwyne. I picked this up at the mailbox. It's for you. All the way from Toronto." James A. handed it to Ellwyne, who retreated to his room before daring to open it.

June 12, 1912
Ellwyne Ballantyne
Ekfrid Township
R.R. #4
Glencoe, Ontario

Dear Ellwyne:

We have settled in Toronto. Donalda says I'm not allowed to write to you, but my teacher said I should send you a letter to let you know where I am.

She is helping me write this. Daddy is still cross with you, so maybe don't send me any letters for a few months until things settle.

I go to a school where we sing songs each morning and then practice our times tables and printing. The children teased me about my long hair, but Teacher says they're jealous.

I rode on a streetcar. We visited a flower garden filled with tulips and roses. No mangoes or peacocks, but it reminded me of Grandmother's garden. Sort of.

I miss you, dear brother.

Your loving sister,
Valetta

He trembled, knowing that Valetta had taken a great risk in writing to him against her stepmother's wishes. But he also appreciated and marvelled at her creativity in finding a way to reach out to him. Valetta was young, but she had a cunning side that he figured would serve her well. Receiving her letter had touched him, and he vowed to try to keep the connection alive despite their separation and the animosity that had developed between him and the Ballantynes. *They can't keep us apart forever.*

30

CARRUTHERS CORNERS, ONTARIO, CANADA

LIFE CHURNED ON. The weeks turned into months and slipped into years. Ellwyne settled into the routine of life at the homestead with James A., Betsy Jane, and Archie. It felt as though he had always been there, had always been a part of the Carruthers clan; at other times, it seemed like time was moving too quickly.

In the depths of January 1913, the sun disappeared from the sky by five o'clock, cloaking the homestead in darkness until it rose again at seven-thirty the following morning. After the supper dishes were cleaned and put away, the only activities left to do were reading or writing by coal oil lamplight. On evenings when neither appealed, an early bedtime was a welcome option, even for the adults of the household. One gusty winter evening, the waiting warmth of his feather bed called to Ellwyne shortly after supper.

"Well, I think I'm going to tuck in early tonight." He pushed his chair back from the oak dining table. "What do you say, Archie? You too?" He gave the boy a pat on his shoulder. Archie smiled, proud that he was going to bed at the same time as Ellwyne.

"Archie, wash up at the basin first," his mother told him. "And make sure you get behind your ears this time." She snapped her fingers at Archie and pierced him with her hazel eyes. Certain his mother's snapping fingers contained magic powers, he dashed off to the basin to scrub his face.

Ellwyne covered his mouth as he yawned. "I apologize for the lack of conversation. I'm just beat," he told James A. "You worked me too hard today."

James A. looked up from his book. "Then you best get some shut-eye. We've got more hard work waiting for us tomorrow."

"Take a brick with you to bed. The mercury is going to dip tonight," said Betsy Jane as she headed to the cookstove to retrieve a heated brick for his bed.

He remembered that, when he had first stayed overnight with them, Betsy Jane had walked him up the narrow staircase to the cramped room he shared with Archie. She guided them by the flickering lamp light and sat on the edge of the bed discussing the day's events with him. She led him and Archie in a night-time prayer and waited until Archie fell asleep. To soothe her young son into slumber, she would rub his back in rhythmic, flowing circles while telling him a story. Ellwyne listened attentively, even though the stories were intended for Archie.

At seventeen, Ellwyne was becoming a young man. It was rare that he would retire at the same time as Archie, as he was doing tonight. After inspecting Archie's scrubbed ears, Betsy Jane pulled back the quilt and smoothed out the sheet.

"Hop in, Archie."

The boy catapulted himself beneath the covers to escape the cold, bare floor that was already making his feet tingle.

"What story do you want to hear tonight?" his mother asked.

"Something I haven't heard in a while."

"An oldie. Okay. I know just the one." It had been years since Betsy Jane had told the story she had in mind, but she knew it well. Although she had many variants on her bedtime stories, the most common plotline involved a doe and her fawn. Betsy Jane recounted the story in her head and began weaving the tale.

While she left to look for food and water, the doe hid her fawn in a bush and told him to wait there until she returned and warned him not to talk to anyone while she was away. The fawn settled in and waited. He slept for a while, but when he awoke, his mother had not yet returned.

He waited and waited.

His mum had been gone a long time when he noticed a fox watching him. The talkative, friendly fox told the fawn that he should come out and play a game of tag. The fawn explained that his mother had told him to wait for her and to stay hidden in the bush. The fox said that no one would know if he moved. He was persuasive, and eventually, the fawn decided that he could probably play one game of tag with the fox without getting into trouble. Who would find out?

As he emerged from the safety of his hiding place, he felt afraid, but the fox told him to relax and that he shouldn't always listen to his mother. Mothers are boring and don't want us to have any fun, he told the fawn as he feigned boredom with a yawn. Then, the fox touched the fawn's leg and said, "Tag, you're it!" and took off running toward a field.

The fawn chased after the fox, running as quickly as his legs would allow him to move. He chased the fox through the field and over fences. He hopped over logs, and crawled through bushes, but he still couldn't catch the fox. Finally, the fox ran into a farmer's wheat field and then stopped and turned back to look at the fawn. The fawn thought he might finally catch the fox and dashed into the field after him.

At that moment, the fawn saw his mother sprinting towards him with a terrified look in her eyes. "Follow me!" she screamed at her wide-eyed fawn. The fawn obeyed his mother and kept as close to her as he could. Together, they dove into the brush at the edge of the field and hid in a thick raspberry bush. Although they were cut by the thorns of the thicket, they felt protected and safe in their hiding spot.

The air burst with the barks of dogs, and the ground shook with the pounding sound of horse's hooves on the ground. A bugle blew, and the dogs began to howl and pressed their noses to the ground. They were on the trail of something, and they were getting excited about how close they were to reaching it. The fawn squeezed his eyes shut and waited for something bad to happen and slowly counted to three.

The noise of the dogs approached their hiding spot but passed by them and headed towards the hollowed-out log. The dogs surrounded the log and began to howl and say, "We found him! We found him! He's here!" The fawn watched as a tangle of horse's hooves swirled past him and gathered around the hollowed log. "Don't watch," said the doe, "And don't say a word."

The dogs barked and barked.

The hunters laughed and cheered and drank ale from a shared stein.

The horses whinnied and neighed.

The fox was never seen again.

The fawn learned a valuable lesson that day: *Always* listen to your mother. Even when she wants you to do something that's difficult or that you might not understand, you must listen, because it's for your own protection.

"Do you remember the first time I told that one?" she said quietly, being careful not to awaken Archie, who was now fast asleep.

"Yeah, and I remember asking you what would have happened if the fawn's mother didn't come back for him."

"That's right," she said. "And do you remember my answer?"

"I sure do. But you can remind me again."

"I told you that another doe would have shown up instead, because that's how it works in nature. When a mother can't do her job, another one steps in to take her place."

"Good night, Betsy Jane."

"Sleep well, Ellwyne." She picked up the lamp and headed for the door. She remembered that, after the first time he'd heard that story, when he was younger, Ellwyne had never questioned the ending. But it had sparked a new ritual for him; he began reporting to her each time that he and James A. spotted a deer wandering the fields of Ekfrid Township.

31

CARRUTHERS CORNERS, ONTARIO, CANADA

AT SEVENTEEN, ELLWYNE had grown much stronger and taller. His arms and shoulders bulged beneath his cotton shirt, muscles built through the labour of lifting, throwing, digging, pushing, and stacking. More important, to match his strength, he had also grown in confidence. He kept his shoulders pressed back when he walked, no longer caving in at the chest like a beaten dog.

"Today, we're going to work on clearing that final corner of the field along the sideroad," said James A. It currently held a stand of trees, and he wanted to turn the remaining acreage into workable cropland. He knew it was going to be strenuous work, but Ellwyne never turned down a challenge, which was one reason he was so highly regarded by the Carruthers clan. James A. kept track of Ellwyne's work hours in a small ledger book and paid him weekly for his labour at both his farm and his half-brother Neil's. When needed, Ellwyne, like James A., also helped at William's and Robert's farms, and carried on the time-tested tradition of the clan working together. Together, they were stronger.

Despite standing only about five-foot-six, Ellwyne had proved an invaluable farmhand for James A., who was approaching forty. But their work relationship was so much deeper than that of employer and employee. They had developed a mutual respect, and Ellwyne relied on James A. for company and advice, much as a son relies upon his father.

The men gathered up their equipment, loaded it into a wagon, and headed to the corner. James A. suggested that they first take a walk through the bush and identify the easiest cuts: the dead trees and the

young trees that would put up the least resistance. He sent Ellwyne westward, while he walked eastward. They had been separated for about thirty minutes when he heard Ellwyne calling his name. James A. headed towards the shout and found Ellwyne kneeling on the ground, hands outstretched, caressing the leaves of a young tree.

"Look at this," he whispered in the muted tone of someone in a place of worship or a library. "I've never seen one quite like this one, have you?"

Ellwyne had stumbled upon an unusual-looking tree, all alone in the midst of a crowd of more common species. It was easy enough to miss unless you were paying attention, but Ellwyne was *always* paying attention. He was learning the keen observation skills of a farmer from spending time with his experienced friend. James A., too, was dazzled by the unusual shape of the leaves.

"I think this is a buttonwood, Ellwyne." The tree was about twice the height of James A. "You don't expect to see one in this area because they're a thirsty tree. I've only ever seen them next to rivers. I bet there aren't too many farms or fields around here that have a buttonwood tree." Ellwyne was rapt, listening carefully to James A., but caressing the leaves of the tree.

"I've never heard of a buttonwood tree before."

"As I recall, they're called *buttonwoods* because their wood is used to make buttons. Makes sense, right?"

Its foliage stood out from the rest, growing in an area where its species would normally struggle to thrive. He looked around but saw no other saplings like it. James A. leaned forward beside Ellwyne and reached out towards the sapling, pausing as his fingers touched the slender trunk.

"Can we leave it be? I think it deserves a chance to grow, don't you?"

James A. nodded in agreement, offered Ellwyne his hand, and pulled him to his feet. Although imperceptible to them, a melodic hum filled the woodlot as the two men paused. They walked together to a different section of the bush, far from the buttonwood, and marked other trees for clearing. They picked up the dead wood and brush they found and loaded it onto the wagon.

Spared the axe, the little buttonwood tree, growing in a place it didn't belong, had been given a second chance.

Thump-thump. Thump-thump.

The beat originated from deep within the ground. It rose, swirling in the air before dissipating.

They put in an exhausting day's work together and headed back to the farmhouse for supper. Betsy Jane was piling steaming mashed potatoes, topped with whipped butter, and turnips into bowls on the stove top before carrying them to the table.

"How did you make out?" she asked James A. as he and Ellwyne entered the kitchen.

"Gruelling. We broke our backs as usual, didn't we, Ellwyne?"

"Sure did." Ellwyne's shoulders ached.

"I have the cure for that." she said. The scent of roast beef filled the room, mixed with the delicious aroma of carrots and turnips.

"Something else kind of interesting happened," said James A.

"What's that?"

"Ellwyne came across a buttonwood tree in the northwestern corner of the field."

"Really? A buttonwood?"

"Yeah. We thought it was kind of odd, too. Not too many of those in this area. They're mostly near the Sydenham River."

"Is it firewood now?" she asked haltingly.

"Nah. We decided to leave it be."

Later, after the dishes were cleared and put away, Betsy Jane was still thinking about the buttonwood as she thumbed through her Bible for her routine evening read. She stopped at the book of Psalms, as she often did, and paused at Psalm 96:11. She read it first to herself, and then aloud.

Let the heavens rejoice, and let the earth be glad; let the sea roar, and the fulness thereof.

Let the field be joyful, and all that is therein: then shall all the trees of the wood rejoice

Before the Lord: for he cometh, for he cometh to judge the earth: he shall judge the world with righteousness, and the people with his truth. (Psalm 96 11-13, King James Version)

At that moment, everything had fallen into place in Carruthers Corners. Betsy Jane hummed James A.'s favourite hymn, "Let the Lower Lights Be Burning," closed her beloved book, and placed it back on her bedside table.

PART 3

GROWTH AND CHANGE 1914–1917

*"We stand tallest in our weaknesses.
For it's the backbone to growth."*

—Angie Weiland-Crosby

32

THE CORNER WOODLOT, EKFRID TOWNSHIP, ONTARIO, CANADA

BY 1914, HAVING reached a sizable height, the buttonwood had a solid trunk and was now strong enough to withstand the force of the wind without bending. It was no longer at risk of being devoured by a hungry rabbit or a passing deer. Its root system had been firmly established, and it was regularly drawing on the underground aquifer to quench its thirst and send nutrients to its crown.

The buttonwood tree hummed with jubilation as it reached towards the sky.

Growth was inevitable, but with growth also comes change.

The sour winds of change were blowing, sending waves of uncertainty through the wooded lot.

33

CARRUTHERS CORNERS, ONTARIO, CANADA

IN AUGUST 1914, Great Britain declared war on Germany after the expiration of an ultimatum. It all seemed so far away from the happenings in tiny Ekfrid Township, thousands of miles, and an ocean away from Europe. The Carruthers first learned about the great war from newspaper articles and the mutterings of neighbours. Even in India, the war was front-page news.

"Look at this headline," Betsy Jane said as she read through the latest batch of newspapers that came to Ellwyne from his grandmother in India. "It says 'GREAT BRITAIN DECLARES WAR ON GERMANY.' The whole world is fearful."

"I wouldn't worry too much about it. It's a long way from us," James A. said reassuringly, although in the back of his mind, he wondered about the potential impact on them.

"Still, I do wonder if we should stock up on sugar and some other supplies, just in case?"

James A. nodded. "Yeah. It's wise to prepare for bad weather ahead, isn't it?"

With the declaration of war in 1914, the mood in Ontario was one of optimism, and many felt certain that the conflict would be over swiftly, certainly by the end of the year. When it wasn't resolved by the end of the year and the conflict showed signs of being more drawn out than first thought, recruiters began to move from the urban areas, where recruits were first

plentiful but now in shorter supply, to rural areas, where persuading men to enlist proved more challenging. The farming communities needed their sons to keep food production going. Taking away a farmer's labour was not viewed favourably. A few families in the Glencoe area had sons who had enlisted to serve overseas as the conflict spread across Europe, but so far, it had not touched anyone directly in the clan at Carruthers Corners. The rhythm of life continued, mostly as it always had, dictated by the season and the needs of the farm, to keep humans and animals fed and sheltered. Chores never stopped— not for weather, not for sickness, nor when a distant war raged.

On a frosty morning in December 1915, James A. asked Ellwyne if he wanted to accompany him to Glencoe to take a load of grist to be ground at the mill.

"It'll give us a chance to see the fields of winter wheat." As a farmer, James A. enjoyed looking at other farmers' fields to see how their crops compared to his. He took mental notes about weather patterns and other trends. They harnessed up the horse to the wagon and travelled southwest towards the small town.

"I don't remember winter ever being this cold," Ellwyne felt a slight shiver travel up his spine. He had lived in Canada for almost six years and still found the winters harsh and inhospitable, but memories of life in balmy India were fading with time.

"Yeah, we've burned through a lot of our wood already." The stove provided heat for the house as well as to cook their food. The colder the winter, the more wood they burned. "Has Neil invited you to the hunt yet?"

"No, what do I need to bring?"

The annual rabbit hunt on Christmas Day was a Carruthers clan tradition. After the meal, the men joined up for a hunt using spades and axes.

"Just bring your enthusiasm," said James A. "Hopefully we'll find a few holed up."

Conversation between them flowed easily, as it always did. By now, the bond between James A. and Ellwyne was close, built on love and mutual respect.

When they arrived at the mill, Ellwyne hopped off the wagon and led Old Grey to the hitching post, tied her to the rail, and put a heavy blanket over her back to keep her warm while she stood waiting.

"I'm going to wait inside while they grind the grain," said James A.

"Why don't you take a walk through town? You deserve a break. Go ahead, treat yourself."

"I'll take that offer." Ellwyne hadn't been to town in a few weeks and was looking forward to the break.

"Be back in about two hours. I'll still be inside."

James A. entered the feed mill and took a seat on the bench set aside for customers. Through the door's frosted glass, he could see Ellwyne's silhouette departing down the road towards Main Street. He was shuffling his feet, hands shoved into his pockets for warmth, shoulders hunched to protect his ears from the cold. James A. sighed, reached into his coat pocket, and pulled out a tea biscuit wrapped in cloth that Betsy Jane had packed for him. He finished it off in three enormous bites, relaxed his back against the wall behind him, cut a chew of tobacco, and closed his eyes.

🍁

Having free time to wander the shops of the town was a rarity for Ellwyne, so he was pleased when James A. suggested it. His breath hung in the crisp air as he exhaled. It was the type of cold day that made him yearn for the warmth and humidity of Calcutta. *I miss you, Grandmother,* he thought as he hunched, walking into the bitter westerly wind.

The main street of Glencoe, Ontario circa 1914

Glencoe's Main Street was bustling with bundled-up people going in and out of shops, making purchases for the upcoming Christmas holiday. He stopped to gaze at the window at Mayhew's Mercantile and General Store. He admired the gloves laid out for display and the intricate cut-out paper snowflake decorations scattered amidst the gloves. He thought that James A. and Betsy Jane could each use a warm set of gloves and made a note to stop in on his way back down the street and buy two sets. He was still wandering west when he spotted a large sign in a window he had not yet seen. The poster had a dark khaki background and a bright red, white, and blue Union Jack flag. A serious-faced soldier in full uniform pointed a cane towards the flag.

THIS IS YOUR FLAG.

IT STANDS FOR LIBERTY.

FIGHT FOR IT.

JOIN THE OVERSEAS BATTALION.

Another poster's red writing on a mustard-yellow background screamed:

NEW NAMES IN CANADIAN HISTORY.

MORE ARE COMING. WILL YOU BE THERE?

ENLIST!

The poster next to it had a stark white background. The Union Jack and Ontario flags twisted together like two ballerinas performing a dance, and its bold blue and red lettering shouted out at him as he paused to read it:

IF YOU WERE A GERMAN AGED 18-50

YOU WOULD BE FIGHTING FOR THE KAISER!

WHAT ARE YOU DOING FOR THE KING?

Through the window glass, he spied movement. He was squinting his eyes to read the fine print at the bottom of the poster when the office's door creaked open, blasting a stream of warm air that hit him in the face, immediately warming his nose and cheeks.

"What'cha doing, lad?" the grey-haired man asked him. He was smartly dressed in a full military uniform, with polished black boots and a cap cocked over one eye. Wire-rimmed glasses perched on his bulbous nose.

"I'm interested in reading these posters you've got here."

"You look like you're exactly the someone we've been waiting all day for."

Ellwyne smiled. "Is that so?"

"Absolutely. Why don't you come inside, where it's warmer? We're serving up hot coffee and biscuits." The man smiled at him and gave him a wink.

Ellwyne was a bit hungry, and he had two hours to kill, so he followed the man inside.

"Fletcher, please get this handsome young man a coffee," said the older gentleman. A younger man, also in uniform, snapped to action from behind a desk, jumped up, and headed towards the woodstove where a coffee urn was percolating. The smell of fresh roasted coffee beans filled the office's air. Coffee was not widely available, and Ellwyne had only tasted it in India, and he remembered the aroma and taste with great fondness. He eagerly awaited this rare treat.

"One cube or two?" Fletcher asked Ellwyne as he dangled sugar cubes over the cup of steaming coffee. Ellwyne rarely enjoyed white sugar cubes at the homestead, as it was a rare and expensive commodity used only on special occasions. They used maple sugar instead, made from sap harvested from the trees in late winter. Being treated not just to coffee but the bonus of white sugar cubes made him feel like he'd won a prize.

"I'll take two." Ellwyne could hardly wait to taste the bitterness of the dark coffee balanced against the glorious sweetness of two sugar cubes. He wrapped his cold hands around the mug and immediately felt them warming up.

"I'm Officer Carl Sloane," said the older gentleman, offering Ellwyne his leather-gloved hand to shake.

"Ellwyne Ballantyne," he replied as he shook Carl's hand. His grip was firm. The black leather was soft and supple, and he could feel the heat of Carl's hand through the glove.

"Nice to make your acquaintance, Ellwyne Ballantyne," said Carl. "I bet you'd love to see the world, wouldn't you?" He raised one eyebrow expectantly.

"If you can believe it, I've already seen quite a lot of it." Sometimes, Ellwyne even amazed himself when he thought about the long journeys he had already taken in his short lifetime.

"Oh? Tell me your tale."

"Well, I was born in India, where I lived until I was twelve. After my mother died, I moved to Scotland with my stepfather and his new wife, until we came to Canada."

"That's remarkable. I bet you'd like to see more of Europe, though?"

"Not particularly. I like it here. Ontario suits me fine."

Carl changed tactics. "Well, what do you want to do for the rest of your life?" His gaze focused on Ellwyne's bare hands. "Surely not farming?" he said with an edge of dismissiveness, as if being a farmer were something to be ashamed of.

"I'm working as a farmhand." He immediately thought of James A., probably snoring as he napped at the feed mill. "But I have an interest in mechanics."

"Funny you should say that," said Carl. "I was going to tell you that you didn't look like a typical farmer. To me, you look like an engineer."

"Really? My father was a civil engineer. He designed bridges." Ellwyne thought proudly of his father and the elegant Hooghly River Bridge, resting on its pontoons. To think that someone equated him with the profession of his father sent another jolt of warmth coursing through his body. Although he had no memories of his father, he still felt a strong connection to him.

"Does that interest you?"

"Engines and mechanical things interest me."

"What about aeroplanes?" Carl pointed towards a poster with a drawing of an aeroplane. The biplane was painted the same khaki green colour as Carl's military uniform.

"The incredible flying machines?" Though he didn't mean to, Ellwyne's mouth was agape at the thought of working on new technology like aeroplanes.

"Yes. Machines that can fly. Astounding, isn't it? Humans taking flight like birds."

"Sure is," Ellwyne exclaimed, with a little more enthusiasm than he intended. "When I was a young boy, my mother read me a newspaper article about the first flight by the Wright brothers in North Carolina. I think it was a place called Kitty Hawk."

"Well, then, how would you like to work on aeroplanes and learn how to repair their engines?" Carl walked towards his oak desk. He sat down and rummaged through some papers.

"I think I would like that." Ellwyne took a long sip of his coffee and made an "Ahhh" sound as he swallowed. It was the finest cup of coffee he had ever tasted. He decided that he needed to have coffee more often and wondered how he could secure some to let Betsy Jane and James A. taste it.

"We can teach you all that and more," Carl said firmly. "Tanks, aeroplanes, trucks, you name it, we have it." He motioned to posters adorning the walls showing different types of military equipment. "It all needs fixing, and we need skilled, smart mechanics who can do it for us."

"I sure would like to learn about engines." Although Ellwyne enjoyed working on the farm with James A., he couldn't deny that he had different aspirations when he allowed himself to dream a little.

"Let us teach you. And not only that, but you'll learn from us and we'll *pay you* to do it." Ellwyne's eyes widened at the prospect of being paid to learn. "You'll get paid fifty cents a day or so. Imagine that, being paid to learn." Carl sighed. "Usually, the student has to pay the teacher, but we can teach you all you need to know to become an engineer or a mechanic, and we'll pay you to do it."

"What do I need to do?" Ellwyne was now genuinely curious.

"Volunteer a bit of your time with us, and we'll take care of the rest." He removed a file folder from beneath a pile of papers on his desk. "When the war is over, you'll have the world at your feet."

Ellwyne shifted from one foot to the other as he weighed the options in his mind. "Then I could move to a city." He loved the farm fields of Ekfrid Township, but he had never forgotten his childhood days in bustling Calcutta, where he spent his days with the two women who had first shown him love.

"You could move *anywhere* you wanted. Why limit yourself?"

Ellwyne immediately thought of his grandmother in India and how much he'd like to visit her again. It had been more than six years since he had last seen her, and he felt disconnected from her and from his past.

"Just a few preliminary questions." Carl's question snapped him back to the present. "How tall are you?" Carl felt confident that the hook was now secure in the catch's cheek.

"I'm five-six," said Ellwyne, rising a little on his toes, as if promoting himself one or two more inches in height.

"You're precisely what we're looking for," said Carl, while mentally putting another notch on his belt. *That's five new recruits today.*

Glencoe had been fertile ground for the recruitment officers of the Canadian Expeditionary Force. They were reaping a harvest of young, strong farm boys from the fields of Mosa, Ekfrid, and Metcalfe townships, whose citizens were donating their crop of healthy sons to the effort.

God save the King.

Exactly two hours later, James A. awoke to a gentle shake of his shoulder. Ellwyne was standing in front of him, looking amused.

"Did you enjoy your nap?" asked Ellwyne. "The boys said we're all done and loaded. We can head back home now."

The ride home was quieter than usual. As they approached a massive oak tree alongside the Appin Road, James A. noticed a large red-tailed hawk sitting on a branch and pointed it out to Ellwyne. The impressive bird's steely eyes were monitoring the snow below, watching and listening for any sign of movement beneath the crust of the snow. It cocked its head to one side, as if tuning in a signal. Suddenly, the hawk dived, gliding like a dart towards its target. The hawk's forceful landing thrust its body through the crust of the snow, and it flapped its wings a few times before lifting its head to reveal a mouse squirming in its beak. A speck of bright red was still visible in the snow when they passed.

"I have something to tell you."

"What's that?" James A. asked, full of curiosity.

"I stopped in at the recruiting office while I was in town, and I, uh, I enlisted." Ellwyne's voice cracked.

There was a long, awkward pause. The clip-clop of Old Grey's hooves was the only sound either man could hear.

"What does that mean exactly?" James A. was taken aback.

"It means that I've signed up for the army. I'll be heading overseas to join the action in Europe. I will be leaving soon for Niagara for basic training."

Thousands of questions swirled through James A.'s mind, but all he could muster to say was, "Are you sure that's what you want to do?"

"Yes. I want to learn about engines. The recruiter said I'd get to work on aeroplanes and tank engines if I volunteered. Lots of other boys have already volunteered. I'll get left behind if I don't go now. And they're going to pay me, so I can save up some money, maybe buy a farm of my own, or ..."

"Can you think about it first, before committing?" James A. raised his eyebrows in hope.

"No. I already signed the papers. I leave in a few weeks."

James A. swallowed the lump in his throat. "I see. That's a mighty big decision."

"I had to take a solemn oath to the King, if you can believe it," Ellwyne said, continuing to chatter about his experience at the recruitment office.

"Oh?" James A. muttered.

"Yeah. They also asked me who I wanted to be in charge of my things while I was gone. I put your name down, hope you don't mind."

In his head, James A. shouted, "Please! Don't do it!" Instead, he kept his emotions locked inside. Now was not the time for harsh words that he might regret later. He kept his shock and sadness in check. Although James A. had come to rely on Ellwyne's help on the farm, his feelings went far beyond that, and now he knew with certainty that the feeling was reciprocated. He recognized that Ellwyne wasn't just a hired hand to him. He had grown to love him like a son, and he didn't want to lose him, especially not to someone else's far-off war and for a King they would never meet.

"Well, I guess if that's what you want to do, that's your decision," he said glumly. "But you need to be the one to tell Betsy Jane. You know how she doesn't like guns."

James A. took up the reins in his right hand and placed his left on Ellwyne's knee, giving it a gentle squeeze. For the first time since knowing him, James A. felt disappointment in Ellwyne. He didn't look at him or ask any further questions.

34

CARRUTHERS CORNERS, ONTARIO, CANADA

CLANG! THE METAL spoon Betsy Jane was holding crashed to the floor, the clang reverberating through the small room. She did not think to pick it up.

"You did *what*?" Betsy Jane asked Ellwyne for the second time. The whites of her hazel eyes were penetrating even in the dim light. As James A. had correctly predicted, Betsy Jane did not receive the news of Ellwyne's enlistment in the army with an open or enthusiastic mind. The Scottish settlers had no strong allegiance towards Britain given the long history of their homeland's conflict with England. When settling the land in South-western Ontario, many Scots believed that the British Colonel in charge had purposely given them the least arable land that proved most difficult to clear, the "leftovers."

"I signed up for the army," Ellwyne said quietly.

"Why on God's green earth did you do that?"

She listened to his explanation, the same one he had given to James A. on the trip home, and turned away from him and stirred the now-boiling carrots in the pot on the cookstove, this time with a wooden spoon. Betsy Jane did not want him to see the tears streaking down her face. She couldn't bear the thought of him going so far away and putting himself in danger. And for what? He had volunteered, but the longer the war dragged on, the more the Canadian government would ask from its citizens. Although right now the recruiters were waiting for volunteers to show up, mandatory enlistment could be just around the corner. If that happened,

Ellwyne could have received an exemption easily because he was needed on the farm and James A. had no other sons old enough to help him. But that was now water under the bridge. Ellwyne had volunteered.

"Are you sure that that's what you want to do?" She repeated the question James A. had asked, her back still towards him.

He nodded. "Yes. It is what I want. They told me I'll be able to work on machines and engines, maybe even with aeroplanes or tanks," he said, stammering and with a more defensive tone than he intended. "Maybe then I can become an engineer like my father was." No turning back now.

Betsy Jane wiped the corner of her eye with her apron, turned around and faced him. "If that's what you want, we'll support you. Wouldn't he be so proud of you if you were able to follow in his footsteps?" It took every bit of her being to rally that tiny amount of enthusiasm for him. She grabbed Ellwyne and pulled him close to her, squeezing his shoulders tightly. At that precise moment, she felt the baby growing inside her move for the first time. Another tear slipped across her cheek.

Over the next few weeks, Betsy Jane tapped into her tough, hardened Scottish roots and turned to her faith in God to help her through the prospect of Ellwyne's departure. She knew the hardest part about filling the nest is knowing that the nestlings will someday leave it. She had hoped that Ellwyne would stay in the area, settle down, and marry a Scottish girl from a neighbouring family. Maybe that could still happen. He had to make it through the war. And no one knew how long it would last, or how many lives would be lost in the conflict.

35

THE CORNER WOODLOT, EKFRID TOWNSHIP, ONTARIO, CANADA

ALL TREES GO into a kind of hibernation to survive cold weather. The Canadian winter was harsh, with whipping winds that lashed the trees and large snow drifts that covered their bases and weighted their limbs with ice, causing the weaker twigs to snap off and tumble to the ground.

As expected, the buttonwood tree's inner metabolism slowed, and it commenced its dormant period to prepare for winter. The first chunks of bark dropped off, slowly at first; then the shedding accelerated.

Bit by bit, long, thin pieces of bark fell to the ground and gathered in a heap beneath the buttonwood. The tree shed bark like falling tears, until it had no more bark to shed.

36

EKFRID TOWNSHIP AND NIAGARA-ON-THE-LAKE, ONTARIO, CANADA

NEWS SPREAD RAPIDLY throughout the community, as news does in small towns, that Ellwyne Ballantyne, the now twenty-year-old man whom James A. and Betsy Jane had taken under their wing, had enlisted in the Canadian Expeditionary Force. The recruiting officers had been scouring for volunteers for months; their temporary office in Glencoe had possessed a sort of magnetic draw for some of the young men of the area. It wasn't a huge surprise that another able body was being added to the list to fight for Mother Britain.

After reporting for active duty at Wolseley Barracks in London, Ontario, Ellwyne joined the 135th Battalion of the Canadian Expeditionary Force, stationed in the picturesque town of Niagara-on-the-Lake. That's where they would train for their military exercises, at Camp Niagara. This community was located on the shores of Lake Ontario, and although Ellwyne had seen the ocean and had a grasp of its enormousness, he was fascinated by the vastness of this inland freshwater lake. The training camp had opened shortly after the war broke out, and the town had swelled in size to accommodate the soldiers who were being processed through army training in a methodical way. Boys streamed in; men flowed out. The experience of basic training was geared to transforming wide-eyed farm boys into more hardened men preparing for total uncertainty ahead.

Wolseley Barracks in London, Ontario.

The pennant from the 135th Battalion of the Canadian Expeditionary Force.

On a crisp, brilliant morning, Ellwyne watched the sun rise in the sky as he stood in a queue that snaked around the grassy field, waiting his turn to get his paperwork, camp assignment, and army-issued khaki uniform. Although the camp had a few barracks, most of the men had to sleep in large, conical canvas tents erected in tidy rows. It looked as if someone had planted tent seeds the season before and they had sprouted in plough lines.

"Name?" the gruff officer seated at the table asked Ellwyne, without looking up from his ledger. He was an older man, with his cap pulled down low enough to obscure his eyes.

"I'm Ellwyne Arthur Ballantyne."

The officer thumbed through the pages, stopping at the correct one. "Rank?" he barked. He had been processing men for hours and the names were starting to blur together.

"Private." The man scribbled something in his ledger after dipping his pen in the inkwell.

"Serial number?" he asked.

Ellwyne had already committed it to memory. "Eight oh two four two three."

"Right, then. Your sleeping accommodations, courtesy of the Canadian Expeditionary Force, is row D, tent four."

"Thank you, sir," said Ellwyne as he was passed the uniform and a small ledger book in which he would log his hours to receive his military pay.

"Off you go. NEXT!" blared the officer, rendering Ellwyne invisible.

Ellwyne turned away from the table and followed the line of boys making their way to the tents where they would set down temporary roots. His tent looked identical to all the others, except for the crudely painted number four posted on a stick at its entrance. Ellwyne peeled the heavy canvas flap open and entered. A musty smell, a combination of unwashed laundry, sweat, and mildew, hit his nostrils, making him gasp. Ten cots, each made up with a grey wool blanket and miniature pillow, lined each side of the tent. He chose the cot at the back and placed his things beneath it, producing a swirl of dust that rose and circulated through the tent.

"Hey there, mate." A cheerful voice filled the air. Ellwyne looked up to see who was behind him.

"Well, hello," Ellwyne replied, offering his hand to the tall, brown-haired man with the rosy red cheeks that Ellwyne had come to recognize as signalling Scottish roots. "Nice to meet you. I'm Ellwyne Ballantyne."

"I'm Alistair McPhie from Blyth. You know where that is?"

"I don't, but I expect you're about to tell me?" Ellwyne laughed, but he never grew tired of hearing about the origins of people, the places they called home.

Alistair grinned, revealing a gap between his front teeth. "It's a town just east of Lake Huron. Pretty as a postcard." He reached into his back pocket and revealed a hand-drawn postcard of Blyth's main street. "See?" He held it up for Ellwyne.

"That's a great reminder of home you've got there," Ellwyne said thinking of the quaint homestead in Carruthers Corners. "It's important to bring pieces of home with you, even if only in your mind." His voice trailed off.

Alistair put the postcard back in his pocket. "My family are sheep farmers. We have over a hundred head of Lincoln sheep." Alistair followed Ellwyne's lead and chose the cot next to his and began packing his few belongings under it.

"I've never seen Lake Huron. Is it nice?" asked Ellwyne.

Alistair blushed, his cheeks turning an even brighter shade of red. "I've actually never seen it either, but we all know about the lake and its bad moods, because it dumps heaps of snow on us in the winter."

"Is that right?"

"You got it. If they say there's a streamer coming in off the lake, expect to be blinded by snow." The laugh that followed sounded like two snorts punctuated by a wheeze. It was the oddest laugh Ellwyne had ever heard, but he liked it. He felt an immediate connection to Alistair. "I guess we'll soon get to see the ocean, though, and that will make Lake Huron look like a wee puddle."

"Yeah, once you see the ocean, you never forget it," said Ellwyne.

"What, you've seen it already? The ocean?" asked Alistair, a look of incredulity spreading across his face.

"Indeed, I have. I crossed the Atlantic with my stepfather when we moved here from Scotland."

"Is that so? Well, Ellwyne Ballantyne. Since you've already seen it, don't spoil it for me, okay?" He snorted and wheezed and slapped Ellwyne on the shoulder.

After completing his basic training at Niagara-on-the-Lake, Ellwyne returned to Carruthers Corners for a visit before embarking on the arduous ocean journey for the shores of Europe. He arrived in Ekfrid on a steamy Friday evening in July, 1916 after being granted temporary leave, his final one before shipping out.

Despite her objections to his decision to enlist, Betsy Jane had to admit that Ellwyne looked dapper in his khaki CEF military uniform. The tunic buttoned up smartly with seven shiny brass buttons. His ankle boots were polished to a gleaming, glass-like shine, and his leg wraps, which he explained were referred to as "put-tees," spiralled up his calves like the tight coil of a spring. Five-year-old Archie was mesmerized by Ellwyne's changed appearance. The little boy was used to seeing him dressed in overalls, a button-up shirt, and a straw hat, and appeared a bit star-struck by the soldier who had replaced Ellwyne. Sensing that the little boy was awed by the uniform, Ellwyne removed his tunic and hat.

Ellwyne (left) stands with a chum in front of the homestead circa 1916.

"Come here, Archie," he said gently. He held out the arms of the tunic, and Archie awkwardly placed his tiny limbs inside, struggling to find the arm holes. Ellwyne plopped the hat on his head, and it dipped over his eyes so that the little boy couldn't see. The tunic swam past his knees like a skirt. Ellwyne adjusted the hat so that it rested above his eyes, and Archie stood proudly on the verandah and twirled in a slow circle so that James A. and Betsy Jane could admire him. Everyone laughed, which only encouraged Archie to twirl twice more before James A. fetched the Brownie camera and took a photo of him as he posed on the verandah.

Later that evening, the community gathered at the local schoolhouse to bid farewell to the young man who had become a respected fixture in the community for his fine character and contributions to the Carruthers clan. After the group had finished eating, Charlie Reath, a close friend of Ellwyne's, rose and asked for everyone's attention. Normally a gregarious person, Charlie's outlook was more formal for this occasion.

"I'd like to say some words on behalf of everyone here who has gath-

ered, if I may?" he stated. The group quieted immediately. He glanced at Ellwyne, who was seated in
between Betsy Jane and James A. near the head of
the largest table.

"Dear friend. We, your friends, have gathered
here tonight on the eve of your departure overseas,
to express our sincere admiration for your loyalty
and devotion in giving your services at this time
to our country," he said as several men chimed in
unison, "Hear, hear."

"You have the assurance that you are doing so
in defence of the British flag, which is symbolic, in
the truest sense, of right and justice. We wish also to
bear testimony to your good moral character, and

Little Archie Carruthers
models Ellwyne's tunic
circa 1916.

we feel convinced you will retain unimpaired your temperance and other
principles in the face of every temptation. We trust God in His infinite
wisdom and mercy will return you to us in due time, in full health and
strength," he continued. At this moment, Betsy Jane reached out and
touched Ellwyne's cheek.

"As a remembrance we ask you to accept this small token of our regard,
that in wearing it you may be reminded that the thoughts of your friends
follow you …" He cleared his throat, now choking up, "wherever you may be."

Charlie put his hand into his breast pocket and removed a small wooden
box. He walked over to Ellwyne's table, bowed his head, and handed it to
his friend.

Ellwyne lifted the lid of the box and stared at the glimmering gold
signet ring inside with a scrolling intertwined E and B knotted together in
an intricate pattern. The members of the settlement had donated generously
towards a rather extravagant going-away gift for the young man, who had
left a deep impression on them. Carefully, Ellwyne removed the ring and
slipped it on his little finger, lifted his finger to his lips, and kissed the ring.

The group applauded. From behind her tears, Betsy Jane marvelled at
how Ellwyne had matured into a fine person, the kind of person worthy of
such a send-off from the community. She was bursting with pride at the

man he had become, but also quaking with uncertainty about what might happen to him.

People crowded around Ellwyne, one by one, to say their personal good-byes and wish him well. Charlie stood back waiting until everyone else had finished before he approached Ellwyne, then clasped him by the shoulders and gave him a firm shake. The two friends who had first met while haying at Carruthers Corners were now about to part.

"I still can't believe that you're actually leaving us, Ellwyne," Charlie said. "I thought you'd settle down in Ekfrid, become a farmer."

"I can't say it didn't occur to me to stay," Ellwyne explained. "But there's a big world out there, and I'm ready for some more adventure." He laughed, catching himself in the irony of having already lived on three continents in his short lifetime.

"Father says he needs me on the farm, or else I'd be signed up right along with you," Charlie explained. Only sons who were needed as farm hands could expect an exemption from the conscription that was sure to come, so that they could continue to keep the food supply chain moving at home.

"Well, I sure will miss you, especially if we have to do any haying over there." Ellwyne laughed at the thought, recalling the time he gave Charlie his straw hat.

"Promise me you'll write once you arrive?" Charlie's eyes misted up.

"You bet."

"Take care over there, Ellwyne. Just …" He paused. "Take care."

The two friends embraced in a hug.

Saying goodbye had never come easy for him. There was a finality to the word that Ellwyne wasn't comfortable with. He had, after all, said goodbye to so much in his short lifetime: his mother, his grandmother, his home in India, his half-sister, his innocence. Now, he was saying goodbye to the one place where he felt at ease, Carruthers Corners and the farm and its people in Ekfrid Township that he so dearly loved.

Ellwyne had to catch his train at four o'clock sharp. Before leaving for Glencoe, he gave Archie a bear hug, patted him on the head and told him to be a good boy for his mother and father. The little boy looked up at Ellwyne.

"Momma tells me that you're leaving. I don't want you to go away," he pouted. The two had become like brothers. Ellwyne dreaded missing out on the milestones of Archie's childhood. He also hated that he didn't know how long he would be away.

"I know, Archie. Someday, you will understand why I had to leave," he patiently explained. "I know it's hard for you to see why I have to do this."

The little boy's lower lip began to quiver.

Ellwyne embraced Betsy Jane. They stood locked together, his head buried deep in her shoulder, for a minute before she finally released him and said, "Come back to us, that's all we ask. Stay safe and come home."

"Of course I will, Betsy Jane," he replied. "This *is* my home. You've helped make it my home. I can never thank you enough for that."

"The way to thank us is to remember what we've taught you. Though you may face temptations …." She didn't finish. She didn't have to. She knew he understood.

James A. pulled up to the verandah with the buggy, ready to go. The horse stomped to shoo the flies from its legs. "Are you ready, then?"

"I almost forgot something," Ellwyne exclaimed, and rushed back into the house, leaving Betsy Jane and James A. shaking their heads with confusion. Once inside, he removed the gold signet ring from his finger and put it in the wooden box. He opened the top drawer of Betsy Jane's Hoosier cabinet and placed it inside. As he held onto the drawer, reluctant to let go, he silently told the ring, *I love you so much. You're made from the love of my family and friends here in Ekfrid. I want to take you with me, but I need you to stay here … with my family. I'll try even harder to come back, knowing that you're waiting here for me.* He closed the Hoosier drawer and wiped his moist eyes. "Wait here for me."

He re-emerged from the house, blinking away his tears. Ellwyne hadn't imagined he would ever be ready for this moment, but the time had arrived. He climbed into the buggy and sat beside James A. on the seat they had shared so many times before.

"Goodbye, Betsy Jane. Goodbye, Archie," Ellwyne said, seated next to James A., his eyes now brimming with tears.

"Do you know what 'goodbye' means?" asked Betsy Jane, unable to stop the tears that were now falling like leaves in autumn. She didn't wait for him to answer. "It means '*God be with ye.*' Always remember that. God will be by your side, Ellwyne, even when we can't be."

As the democrat moved down the laneway and turned onto the gravel road, Ellwyne looked back over his shoulder a final time. He drank in all the familiar sights that had become "home" to him: the wooden homestead with its scalloped eaves, the post-and-beam bank barn, the front paddock that housed the horses, and the chicken coop with its colourful flock. In the distance, he spied the rippling wave of trees from the corner woodlot, their leaves whispering muted words in the gentle breeze. He recalled the day so many years before that he and James A. had worked on clearing that woodlot and smiled because it still remained and had not yet been turned into a field for planting. He strained to see the buttonwood sapling with its broad leaves and unusual bark that he had discovered that day, but as the democrat pulled farther away, he only saw the larger maples and hickories. Although his ears could not detect it, a vibration encircled his chest and pulled him back a little in the seat. When the democrat reached the next farm's laneway, the vibration was drowned out by distance.

It was the longest ride he and James A. had ever shared. Birds chirped and the rhythmic rattling of cicadas filled the humid July air. The slight breeze made the wheat growing in John McDonald's field ripple and sway. James A. had the observant eyes of a hawk; he constantly scanned his surroundings looking for almost imperceptible changes. Wordlessly, he nudged Ellwyne's side and pointed to the field. Just visible over the wheat, a white-tailed doe's head lifted. She stood still as a statue, her eyes transfixed as she monitored the threat. Though deer were common in the area, seeing them still gave Ellwyne a thrill. As the democrat approached, the doe pivoted and, as if lifted by wings, floated out of the field in three long strides, her tail waving like linens hanging on a clothesline to dry. The doe slipped into the cover of the bush next to the field, leaving a ripple of wheat in her wake.

At the station, James A. pulled up to the hitching rail. Ellwyne hopped off the seat and tied the grey mare to the rail. He paused for a moment to acknowledge the horse, now covered in sweat. He had grown to love all the animals on the farm, but this old mare held a special place in his heart.

"Goodbye, Old Grey. Take care of James A. for me," he said as he patted the mare's forehead. She exhaled and pressed her head into his hands. They stood for a few moments until the spell was broken by noise coming from the station. Several more people were waiting to catch the same train. Words of goodbye fluttered through the summer air like butterflies.

James A. was now standing next to the buggy. He reached into his pocket and checked his watch. It was half past three.

"Do you want me to wait with you?" asked James A. He secretly hoped that he'd be asked to stay.

"No. I think I have to do this by myself," said Ellwyne, now feeling less sure about his decision than ever before. "Goodbye, James A., and thank you for …." Ellwyne offered his hand, but James A. pushed it aside and embraced Ellwyne.

"God be with ye, Ellwyne," James A. said, his voice cracking.

He meant it.

One month later, in August 1916, Ellwyne Ballantyne and one thousand other members of the 135th Battalion of the Canadian Expeditionary Force recruited from the farms and towns of Middlesex County departed the port of Halifax, Nova Scotia. They set sail for Liverpool, England, aboard the White Star liner RMS *Olympic*. Although many aboard had never ventured outside their own hometown, let alone their province or country, it was Ellwyne's second ocean voyage.

"Let's hope this gal is better at avoiding icebergs than the *Titanic*," joked one of the men after they had boarded. The *Olympic* was only slightly smaller than *Titanic*, but it looked almost identical to its ill-fated sister ship. In the years since the 1912 disaster in the North Atlantic, the *Olympic* had undergone multiple safety improvements, including the addition of more lifeboats, but thoughts of disaster still danced in the minds of some of the men. U-boat attacks were a new and constant threat.

"Old Reliable will get us there," someone else chimed in.

"What do you think of Lake Huron now?" Ellwyne asked Alistair, noticing that beads of sweat had formed on his friend's brow.

"We signed up for an adventure, right? So, here's our adventure," he replied.

"That's the spirit, Alistair," said Ellwyne. "We'll make it through."

Unbeknownst to Betsy Jane at the homestead in Carruthers Corners, a small wooden box containing a gold signet ring was tucked away in the top drawer of her Hoosier cabinet.

37

WITLEY CAMP, GODALMING, ENGLAND

THE MEMBERS OF the 135th Battalion wisely used their time aboard ship socializing and forming friendships as they sailed across the Atlantic. The tight living quarters aboard encouraged them to form the bonds of brotherhood they would carry into the battlefield.

Ellwyne spent most of the voyage chumming with Alistair McPhie from Blyth and a young guy from London, Ontario, who had enlisted in the army the same week he did.

"You got a girl waitin' for ya at home, Ellwyne?" Isaac asked as they were resting in their bunks.

Thoughts of 'home' flooded his mind. First, the crowded, vibrant streets of Calcutta and his grandmother's luscious garden, and the green fields and corner woodlot of Ekfrid Township and the homestead with gingerbread-scalloped eaves on the 16th Sideroad. Two images of home, both evoking the same feeling of warmth and belonging. "Not really. Do you?"

"Yup. Her name is Maria. Prettiest thing you ever saw." Isaac's voice changed from its normal gruff tone to a more lyrical one as soon as he talked about his love. "When I get back, we're gonna get married. She said she'd wait for me." His voice trailed off as if lifted into a dream. "Before I left, I told her all I ask is to remember me, and if she can't, please forget she ever knew me." Isaac nodded, recalling the conversation in his head.

"I'm happy for you. Have you written her a letter yet?"

"Two already, and another one I'm jotting right now. I'm hoping to have a few from her waiting for me when I arrive."

"If I'm lucky, I should have a letter or two waiting for me," said Ellwyne. "My adopted mom will have written to me. She writes a lot of letters. I know she'll keep me updated on the goings on at home."

"Where is 'home' to you anyway? You mentioned that you were born in India, but you enlisted with the CEF in Middlesex County. So, where's home?"

"Tough question. I mean, I'm from India; it's where I was born. But it's way more complicated than that. My parents are both passed now, but my grandmother still lives in Calcutta, and I would have stayed with her, but I had to come to Canada with my stepfather in '09, and that's how I landed in the farmland of Ekfrid Township. My stepfather's wife is related to some farmers who settled there. We lived with them for a while. They even built a house for us on the farm.—"

"Really?"

"Yeah, but I wasn't getting along with my stepfather, so I was taken in by the Carrutherses. And, they're like my family now."

"Wow, so they took you in and let you stay with them, even though you weren't related to them?"

"Yeah. I was working for them as a farmhand and I started staying with them at their house. I know that might sound strange, but it's really not. When my stepfather and his wife left Ekfrid to go to Toronto, I stayed behind with the Carrutherses. Now, I feel as close to them as I do my own blood relatives. It's like, we fit, you know? Like a hand fits in a glove, that's how we got along right from the start."

"It's like you were adopted?"

"Unofficially adopted, but yeah. I never knew my own father. He died when I was a baby. So, James A. is kinda like the father I never had. You'd love him. He's witty and he always sees things on the sunny side up. Know what I mean?"

Isaac nodded. "So he's a glass half-full kind of person."

"Yeah. And Betsy Jane is a force of nature. She has a tough exterior, but she's kind and loving, as long as you don't cross her. She doesn't take sass from anyone. Probably why she and my stepfather didn't see eye-to-eye. He got used to having servants do everything for him in India, and he likes to push people around. And you can't boss around Betsy Jane Carruthers." Ellwyne laughed out loud at the notion of Betsy Jane Carruthers being intimidated by Duff Ballantyne. An image of a matador waving a red flag in front of a raging bull came to mind. "Their son, Archie, is an adorable little fellow. He walks around with this sunny smile on his face. He's the type of kid who falls but, unless he's really hurt, he doesn't cry. Always smiling. He's like a little brother to me ...." His voice trailed off as he thought about Archie posing for the camera while wearing his army tunic on the homestead's verandah.

"Sounds like you have people back home who will miss you, Ellwyne."

"I do. And I already miss them right back."

In England, the men were transported to a temporary training camp while awaiting their first battlefield assignment. Witley Camp in Godalming, forty miles southwest of London, was teeming with more than forty thousand Canadian soldiers who had enlisted in the Canadian Expeditionary Force. The rows upon rows of white canvas tents outnumbered the permanent structures. It was an area in transition. The camp had a canteen area called "Tin Town" where the men could buy cigarettes and alcohol and also get the chance to interact with the young English women of the area, who were drawn to the camp as a potential source of boyfriends (and future husbands).

Each Canadian soldier was provided with a field kit upon arrival in England. The essentials they needed were packaged up, ready to be brought with them upon deployment. Ellwyne was looking through the contents of his rucksack: a first-aid kit, a gas mask, and a steel helmet. He reached deeper into the sack and rapped his finger on a small object tucked into the bottom. He pulled out a small, hard, clothbound book with an ivory-coloured cover. He read the title and felt his heartbeat speed up. The miniature New Testament fit perfectly into the breast pocket of his tunic, along with the little notepad containing mailing addresses, which is where he placed it. *Close to my heart and forever more you shall be,* he thought as he patted his pocket.

Ellwyne used his spare time at Witley Camp to write letters to his loved ones in Canada and India. His aching muscles, sore and stiff from rigorous physical drills, left him with little energy to do much else. His first letter home was addressed to Betsy Jane, to fill her in on his arrival and circumstances at the camp. He knew she would be eager to find out how he was doing.

August 1, 1916
Mrs. James A. Carruthers
Ekfrid Township
R.R. #4
Glencoe, Ontario
Canada

Dear Betsy Jane:

As I have a little time, I thought I would write a line. I hope this finds you well and having pleasant weather. I am in the best of health, I have never felt better physically. We are getting enough to do to keep us busy. There are only half the men here, the rest are all away on leave, they have to be back by September 13th at midnight. Then it will be our turn to go. I think I'll go up to mighty London for a day or two and come back to camp. I don't think I'd care to put in the six days, I feel as though I've done enough travelling for a while.

There isn't much done here in the line of farming, the farmers seem to spend the biggest part of their time trimming hedges. Every field and along both sides of the road they use hedges for fences. The country is not free and open, it's all hedged or walled in, every house has a high wall or hedge around it. But, the roads are grand: no mud or dust, all paved with asphalt.

We were inspected by the Premier of Ontario. He gave us a long lingo of a speech after the inspection. We were also inspected by General Fox. We see aeroplanes quite often, some are giant machines and go fast and fly high.

There are lots of villages and towns around here, and there are more liquor stores than any other kind of shops. The bartenders are all girls, and the women are getting drinks as well as the men. I've seen more than one drunk woman. There are an awful lot of our men drunk every night.

*There is a beer shop right in our dining hall and it's open till 9 p.m., even
on Sundays.*

*We have an Imperial man giving us our physical drills. It's getting
harder all the time; our drills will soon be with the full packs. Seventy-
five pounds! That's the pack without our entrenching tools and other
equipment. Our full load is over 100 pounds and it's some load to run
and jump with. Tell James A. that I'd be the best worker for haying season
now.*

With love and best wishes to all.
Your loving Ellwyne

After composing his letter, Ellwyne ventured outside his tent and knelt
to pick a piece of English heather. The bright purple colour reminded him
of Betsy Jane's lilac tree that grew near her back stoop at the homestead. He
pressed the heather between his fingers to flatten it and enclosed it in his
envelope and sealed it. He wanted to send a piece of England to Betsy Jane.
He instinctively knew that England already had a piece of her heart.

After posting his letter to Betsy Jane, Ellwyne headed back to his tent. As he
passed Tin Town, he heard the melodic sounds of an upbeat ragtime tune
being pounded out on the piano. He couldn't help but stop and tap his toe
in response to the rhythm. He heard gales of laughter coming from the men
inside who were gathered to have a pint, punctuated by the intermittent gig-
gles of women, so he decided to step inside and take a look. Too much time
alone wasn't good for the soul, and he was thirsty.

The smell of sweaty bodies and stale beer hit him as he wandered through
the door. He saw his new mate Jack Etherington waving to him from across
the room. Jack was an affable lad from Surrey, England, whom Ellwyne had
met on his first day at Witley during one of the running drills. They completed the gruelling five-mile run together, encouraging each other to keep
going when they both wanted to quit.

"Ellwyne, over here!" Jack was surrounded by a group of boisterous
Canadians who were drinking ale and slapping each other on the back as
they chortled and guffawed.

Ellwyne first approached the counter, leaned on it with both elbows, and yelled his order over the noisy group at Jack's table. "I'll have a Coca-Cola." The bartender, an older woman with heavy eye makeup and reeking of perfume, retrieved a glass bottle from the cooler, and slid it to Ellwyne across the counter. He paid and walked towards Jack's table.

"Everyone, this is Ellwyne *Valentine*," slurred Jack, thumping his chest like a beating heart. "Ellwyne *Valentine*, this is everyone." The men laughed and began thumping their chests and repeating his name, using high-pitched falsetto voices. Ellwyne wasn't used to being around drunks and found it both unpleasant and uncomfortable. He took a seat at the table and took a few sips of his cola. He was thinking about leaving when the door opened and a group of five women entered Tin Town.

"Well, would you look at that," said Jack. "Look, boys. The entertainment showed up."

"Finally. They brought us some candy!" proclaimed one of the men. "I haven't had candy for weeks," he said with a low-pitched, throaty growl. The others laughed. Ellwyne smiled faintly, feeling even more uncomfortable and wanting to disappear.

"Come over here, dolls," the black-haired man yelled to the women. He put his fingers in his mouth and let out a loud whistle that pierced the air. Four of the women walked towards their table, the men whooping and clapping as they approached. The background noise dulled in Ellwyne's ears and he remained transfixed on the fifth woman who didn't join the others. She stayed at the door, her eyes scanning the room. Ellwyne knew that this was his chance.

"Excuse me, miss. Are you looking for someone?" He noticed that she had striking auburn hair, emerald green eyes, and a button nose. He was dazzled by her beauty.

"Aye. I'm looking for me grand-mum. She works here." He recognized her accent as Scottish from his time spent there before he moving to Canada with the Ballantynes. Ellwyne felt his heart speed up and his palms begin to sweat.

"Can I help you find her?"

"Nope. There she is." She pointed towards the older woman tending the bar. A look of relief swept over her face. "I'm going to walk home with her when she finishes up but thank you."

Ellwyne was close enough that he could smell the woman's faint perfume, which he found enchanting. He hadn't smelled perfume since he had left India. Normally, the farm women of Ekfrid Township did not wear fine clothes, and perfume was a luxury not invested in. Ellwyne quickly decided that she was the most beautiful woman he had ever seen, and he felt self-conscious. His face turned crimson.

A drunken soldier approached the woman. "Come sit with me, darlin'!" he demanded in a slurred voice, and attempted to take her arm. She stepped backwards.

"Please! I'm not interested," she snapped.

"What's wrong? Too good for me, ya think?"

Ellwyne felt the hair on his neck rise. He stepped in front of the woman and blocked the drunken soldier's pathway forward, giving him no choice but to head the other way. "She said she isn't interested. Leave her alone." He glared at the man, and pushed him on his way towards his next victim, which happened to be a burly man with broad shoulders and permanent scowl. Ellwyne turned to the woman and said, "I'm sure sorry about that. Some of the boys left their manners at home."

"No, thank you for sending him on his way." She fidgeted with the button on her coat. "It can get a bit rough in here, so it's to be expected."

"There's no excuse for treating a lady like that, though."

She blushed. "I haven't seen you 'round here before," she said.

"I've just been at Witley for a few days. Some of my mates are over there," he said, pointing towards Jack and the raucous gang, who were now attempting to get the four women to dance with them.

"Ahh, that's why I haven't seen you before. I'm Rose Anderson." She extended a delicate hand towards him. "And thank you for not being like the rest." She smiled at him, which made his heart skip two beats. He clasped her hand between his and shook it lightly. He wished he didn't have such rough calluses on his hands.

"Pleased to meet you, Rose. I'm Ellwyne Ballantyne. I'm Canadian—"

"Yeah, I figured that one out," she interjected as she looked at the pin on his uniform's collar and flashed him a smile. Ellwyne was new to life in uniform and often forgot that he was wearing it, or that it identified his nationality to civilians. "Where in Canada?"

"The prettiest place I've ever seen."

"Oh, and where's that?"

"The green fields of Ekfrid Township. That's in Southwestern Ontario." She stared at him blankly.

"Ontario is a province, kind of in the centre of the country."

She continued to stare at him blankly. He continued. "The biggest city is Toronto."

Her eyes finally lit up with recognition.

"I've an aunt who moved to Toronto."

"And where in Scotland are you from, Rose?" he asked.

"How did you know I'm Scottish?" she asked incredulously.

"I know the accent. I spent some time in Scotland a few years back, with my stepfather. I didn't fancy it, but because of the company I kept, not because of the place itself."

"I see. I'm from Glasgow. I've been in Surrey for years, though."

"What brought you to jolly ol' England?"

"It was me and me mum, but she got sick and died. I was raised by me grand-mum."

"I understand. My parents both died by the time I was eleven. I wanted to stay with my grandmother, but my stepfather insisted that I go with him to Scotland."

"I see me grand-mum's almost done, so I should run along."

Ellwyne felt a surge of disappointment that she was leaving.

"It was wonderful to meet you, Rose," he said. "Roses are my favourite flowers. I used to pick them in my grandmother's garden in India."

"Wait a minute. Scotland. Canada, India, and now England? You really get around, don't ya, Ellwyne Ballantyne."

"You have no idea," he said, laughing. "Someday, I'd like to stop travelling and settle down."

"Maybe you could tell me more about it sometime, Ellwyne Ballantyne?" Rose was impressed by his gentle nature and good manners.

"Let me at least escort you out of the camp. You know, in case you run into any more problems." He glanced at the rowdy boys and grinned.

"That would be lovely, thank you."

He walked along the path with Rose and her grand-mum and made sure that they made it safely onto the street. As he had done with his mother, grandmother, and his sister in Calcutta, he made sure that he walked closest to the road traffic.

"Goodbye, Mrs. Anderson. Goodbye, Rose." He usually hated saying goodbye, but in this instance, he hoped to see Rose again soon.

"Do you know what goodbye means, Ellwyne?" Rose asked.

"As a matter of fact, yes I do." He smiled, thinking of Betsy Jane. "And God be with ye as well."

The next day, Ellwyne showed up at Tin Town around the same time. Just as he'd hoped, he spotted Rose standing near the drink counter. He fixed his tunic and straightened up, a wide smile breaking across his lips.

"Hello again, Rose," he said as he approached her. "I was hoping I'd find you here."

She blushed. "I'm here to walk home with me grand-mum."

He handed her a piece of purple English heather that he picked from the grassy field near his tent a few minutes before. "For you," he said as he handed it to her. "I'm sorry I couldn't get you something fancier, but I don't have leave until tomorrow. Until then, this will have to do," he said.

She sniffed the heather and placed it in her red hair behind her ear.

"May I escort you again through the camp?" he asked.

Her face turned an even deeper pink, which he noticed complemented the heather in her hair. "I think that'd be lovely."

"It would be my pleasure," he said.

The following morning, Ellwyne received his leave and made plans to walk into the nearby town. With his army pay in hand, he knew exactly what he was looking for. He headed into the market and found a shop selling flowers. The shopkeeper was an older woman with hunched shoulders and a weathered face.

"I'm looking for roses," he said. "Could you find the nicest ones you have, please?"

She floated across the shop and disappeared into the back, emerging a few minutes later with an armful of thirteen radiant red roses. "These just came in. Will they do?"

His mouth gaped at the sight of the delicate flowers. "They're perfect. I'll take them all," he said. The captivating floral scent wafted to his nose as the woman passed them to him. It had been years since he had smelled roses, and it filled him with both joy and nostalgia for his home in India and the time he had spent in his grandmother's walled garden, carefully choosing the prettiest rose for his mother.

"What a lucky gal," said the shopkeeper.

"The luck is all mine," he said, with a broad smile and bright eyes.

Ellwyne stood at the lamp post and waited. He watched as the carriages and cars passed by him. The scent of fresh bread filled his nostrils. It was nearly four o'clock. He checked up and down the street, trying not to appear over-anxious, but inside, butterflies were swirling in his stomach. From across the street, he saw her. Her green coatdress tapered at the waist, accentuating her slender figure. He waved, unable to contain his joy.

"What a coincidence finding you here," he said when she finally reached him.

"Yes. Fine happenstance, isn't it?" she mused. The day before, Rose had discreetly asked him to meet her at the lamp post by the apothecary.

Ellwyne handed her the wrapped bouquet. "I picked these up for you. One for every day that we've known each other."

Rose raised the bouquet to her nose and breathed in deeply, and exhaled. "Thank you! The scent is beautiful!" she marvelled. "I love roses."

"Beautiful. Just like you," he said.

"But," she said, counting the blooms, "there are more than three roses here." She laughed.

"One for every day I've known you, and another for every time I've had to stop myself from thinking about you since we met."

She tucked the bouquet under her arm, and then looped her arm through his. "Let's go for a wee walk, Ellwyne Ballantyne."

They strolled together for hours and chatted about their pasts and their dreams for the future. Ellwyne told Rose about his childhood in India with his loving mother, his grandmother and her garden, his mother's death, the conflicts with his stepfather and his wife, and of course, about Betsy Jane and James A. and farming at Carruthers Corners. Rose told him about how she never knew her father because he had left the family before she was born. After her mother died of a fever when she was ten, she moved to live with her grandmother, and now she was working as a housekeeper for a wealthy family in Guildford. As the afternoon light faded into evening, Rose stopped and turned to him. "I need to go back soon, or else Grand-mum will begin to worry 'bout me."

Ellwyne didn't want the day to end, but he knew that their time alone together was short. They returned to the lamp post, which was now casting a golden light on the street where they stood.

"Thank you for spending some time getting to know me, Rose."

"It was my pleasure." The pink colour rose in her face again. Ellwyne leaned towards her, and his lips softly brushed against hers. In the distance, a clock tower chimed eight times.

"Meet me tomorrow, Rose?" he whispered.

She nodded, then hurried up the street without looking back.

Ellwyne watched until she disappeared, turned, and walked towards Witley Camp. He wasn't sure if his feet were actually touching the ground, but somehow, he floated back, his head filled with images of a beautiful red-headed lass.

He received his battlefield orders six weeks later, and the boys of the 135th Battalion were told to prepare to ship out across the channel. Only one thought entered his mind. As soon as he could get away, Ellwyne made his way to Tin Town and hoped to find Rose there to tell her the news that they both dreaded. They had spent every available moment stealing time together, chatting in the noisy hall, or walking her home. He found her, as usual, at the counter, waiting for her grandmother to finish her shift.

"Hello, Rose," he said, breathless from the dash across the camp.

"Ellwyne! I didn't expect to see you so soon." She looked surprised to see him.

"I know. Can we speak for a moment?" he asked. "Let's step outside, away from the noise." He took her arm and guided her through the room to the door.

"What is it?" she asked, though she already suspected. Her green eyes filled with dread.

"Rose, I received my orders. We leave in two days." His lips were pursed. "We're headed across the Channel to France."

"Oh no," she said, her eyes moistening. Her gut filled with dread.

"Yes. But give me your address, and I'll write to you as soon as I can."

She nodded, unable to speak, sick with worry.

"You will be in my thoughts constantly," he said. He reached out and embraced her, holding her to his body close enough to feel her heart beating against his. He nestled his head into her shoulder, brushed his lips across her ear, and whispered, "I promise I will come back. Knowing you're waiting for me, I'll come back. I swear."

They kissed for only the second time. Ellwyne's heart raced. He took her hands into his and squeezed them gently. "Promise me you'll write?"

The tears were streaming down Rose's cheeks uncontrollably. "I already have," she said as she handed him an envelope sealed with pink wax. "Open this later," she said.

He caressed the ivory envelope between his roughened fingers that now knew not only how to hold farm implements but also how to load and fire a rifle and stab a straw-filled torso with a sharp bayonet. Not three hours earlier, he had been holding Rose's delicate fingers within his own. Her mesmerizing scent was still fresh in his nostrils. And this envelope contained an important message. He both wanted to rip open the envelope and devour its contents immediately and savour it for later. *What could she have said?* he wondered.

When he wasn't thinking about the green fields of Ekfrid Township, he thought about the captivating green eyes of Rose Anderson. He could get lost forever in either vision.

38

CARRUTHERS CORNERS, ONTARIO, CANADA

LIFE ON THE farm continued as it always had. Every season had a different set of tasks to complete, dependent on weather and available hands. Fields still needed harvesting, chickens never stopped laying eggs, fruit needed canning, wood needed piling, water needed to be pumped and carried, and the routine ground on. But something profound had been missing at the homestead since that dreadful July evening when Ellwyne left for Europe. At times, the gaping hole left by Ellwyne's departure was nearly unbearable for Betsy Jane. Her slight frame didn't have much weight to spare, but she just couldn't force herself to eat. Her stomach rumbled with knots of worry.

Each morning, her initial thought as she opened her eyes was the same. *What a terrible dream,* she would think, only to have her thoughts switch to the stark reality. She was living the nightmare of every mother whose son was far away, fighting in a dangerous war. She was a mother who wasn't certain she would ever see her beloved son again. Without question, she had grown to see Ellwyne as her own son, in the same way that she saw Archie. Her mothering instinct had kicked in nearly the moment that she set eyes on Ellwyne Ballantyne. She had sensed that he was the weakling chick, the chick the stronger ones pecked at. In Betsy Jane's world, the weakest chicks were removed from the flock and placed in a safe area until they were strong enough to fend for themselves.

Under her watch, the strongest didn't peck apart the weakest.

Under her watch, the weakest were given what they needed to thrive.

Under her watch, Ellwyne had bloomed into an independent, strong-willed man.

Before he left, Ellwyne had presented Betsy Jane and James A. with a framed portrait of himself wearing his Canadian military uniform, with his heavy rucksack slung across his shoulder, taken at the training camp in Niagara-on-the-Lake. The oval-shaped wooden frame was made from a striking tiger maple and had a convex bubble of glass covering the photograph that Betsy Jane dusted each time she passed it. The Carrutherses chose a prominent place in the parlour to hang the picture, and Betsy Jane moved her rocking chair so that it now faced the portrait. In the evenings, after chores were complete, Betsy Jane headed to the parlour, sat in her chair, and gazed upon Ellwyne's face before opening her Bible.

In difficult times, Betsy Jane leaned on her faith in God to help her though. These were indeed difficult times. She found herself

The framed portrait of Ellwyne Ballantyne that Betsy Jane kept in her living room.

relying often on Psalm 91:1-4. She read it repeatedly. She found the words soothing and uplifting, even though she often felt dispirited and downcast.

He that dwelleth in the secret place of the most High shall abide under the shadow of the Almighty.

I will say of the Lord, He is my refuge and my fortress: my God; in him will I trust.

Surely he shall deliver thee from the snare of the fowler, and from the noisome pestilence.

He shall cover thee with his feathers, and under his wings shalt thou trust: his truth shall be thy shield and buckler. (Psalm 91:1-4, King James Version)

Her baby bird had left the safety of her nest. She now entrusted his safe passage to God.

To God, and also the Canadian army.

"He has to make one more trip across the ocean, and *then* he can forget about travelling," she said as she prayed, thinking about his latest letter. "Please, Lord, keep him in good health. Although I want him to return, I know that my wants are selfish and I trust that You will oversee him for us," she said as she closed her book and once again focused on the portrait.

She didn't know what prompted her to open the top drawer of her Hoosier cabinet that day. Maybe it was the vibrating sound she had been hearing intermittently for weeks. When it was quietest, the sound would ring in her ears, and she would shake her head, wondering whether it was real or imagined. She walked towards the Hoosier, opened the drawer, and reached inside. She felt a hard, smooth box and lifted it into her palm. She recognized it as the box that Charlie Reath had presented to Ellwyne at his going-away dinner in July. She opened it, expecting it to be empty, but a familiar shiny ring caught her eye.

"No!" she gasped, feeling the breath escape from her lungs. Her heart pounded and her palms began to moisten with sweat. "You were supposed to take it with you!" She strode into her parlour, sat in her rocking chair, and opened her Bible to Psalms.

Thou art my hiding place; thou shalt preserve me from trouble; thou shalt compass me about with songs of deliverance. (Psalm 32 7, King James Version)

🍁

Oh, Ellwyne. Why didn't you take us with you? She felt a gnawing worry building up in her stomach, which growled its discontent once more.

39

THE ENGLISH CHANNEL

ALONG WITH THE boys of the 135th Battalion of the Canadian Expeditionary Force, Ellwyne solemnly boarded the ship headed from England across the channel to France. Tensions were high. The smell of sweat mixed with anxiety permeated the salty air, punctuated by the caws of seagulls. Their basic training at Camp Niagara and Witley Camp had increased their physical fitness, taught them how to load and fire weapons, and given them rudimentary expertise in hand-to-hand combat with bayonets, but no one knew exactly what to expect. The lingering highs from the frivolity and fun they had experienced in Witley Camp dissipated when everyone focused on their impending task. The weight of not knowing caused the most anxiety. What would they see? What would they be expected to do? And the most uncomfortable question of all: Who wouldn't return?

Ellwyne busied himself with thoughts about France, ticking off one more country on the list that he would visit. Would he smell the aroma of fresh baking wafting from the villages that they marched through? Would the sights and sounds of the French markets compare to those he knew from Calcutta? The spices of India still tickled his tongue as he recalled walking the streets of Calcutta with his mother. Would the French landscape resemble the rolling hills of lush green he had seen in Scotland? Or maybe the French farmland would remind him of the green fields of Ekfrid Township, where the hay wavered as the wind teased the growing crops? The images of places he had known and loved bounced about in his mind as he contemplated the coming days and weeks.

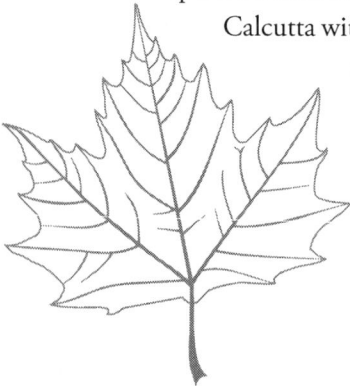

His thoughts were interrupted, and he was returned to the rocking of the ship.

"Whatcha got there, Ellwyne?" asked Alex Robertson, a fair-haired man with broad shoulders and a gap between his front teeth. He had been twiddling his thumbs for the past half hour and decided to speak to Ellwyne.

Ellwyne was clutching an envelope that was now weathered and dog-eared from the sweat from his hands.

"It's a message from my girlfriend," he said, smiling as he pictured the green eyes that had beguiled him.

"Aye, you're lucky."

"She told me not to open it, so I'm waiting."

"Waiting for what?"

"The right time."

Later, when he was in his bunk, he tore open the ivory envelope and unfolded the delicate page. A single red rose petal fell onto his cot. With trembling hands, he read the contents of the treasured envelope he had so carefully guarded.

October, 30, 1916

Dearest Ellwyne

You will be headed to France by the time that you read this. Goodbyes are difficult for me to say, so I needed to write this one. These past few weeks have been as close to heaven as I can imagine. You have given me hope that people can find happiness in the most unexpected places. I will keep the memory of the days we spent together in my mind as we begin this terrible separation. But know that although we are physically apart, you remain fastened to my heart, forever. This is my address. Write whenever you can. I shall be waiting for you, always. The lamp post is our very own and I'll always be standing beneath it waiting for your return.

Your loving Rose
Portsmouth Road
Guildford, England

Ellwyne picked up the rose petal, now delicate and dried, and pressed it to his lips. He placed it in the right breast pocket of his tunic.

40

BATTLEFIELD, SOMEWHERE IN FRANCE

802423. THE STRING of numbers now rolled off his tongue easily. That is who Ellwyne Ballantyne had now become. Just a number. He was 802423.

After the weeks in England training at Witley Camp, the 135th Battalion of the Canadian Expeditionary Force was commissioned to the fields of France. When he had enlisted in Glencoe on that snowy December day, he had been promised the chance to work on engines and mechanical things, to expand his mind, to become more worldly, to become a man. He had been promised an adventure, the chance to travel, and perhaps to get closer to India once more. Now, looking at the mud and mayhem that unfolded all around him, Ellwyne realized the promise had been empty. It certainly did not match the reality.

As soon as he had signed his name on the attestation paper's dotted line, Ellwyne had surrendered his liberty to His Majesty King George V, whom he had sworn to defend. Once again, he found himself in a situation where he had no choice.

🍁

The battlefield assaulted the senses. It was the opposite of what he'd imagined: the soldiers were not heroes marching in front of cheering crowds, welcomed and thanked by grateful citizens. Instead, his battalion was holed up in a muddy, filthy trench, no matter the time or temperature. The first thing that struck all the new arrivals was the overwhelming stench. The stench of death, in all its starkest manifestations, hung in the air like a fog. It was over-powering. Some men wore handkerchiefs over their noses and mouths in an attempt to block or muffle the odour, in vain. You breathed it in, and soon it became a part of you. The reek of rotting food, sweaty, unclean bodies, animal waste, human excrement from overflowing latrines, and worst of all, the odour of decaying bodies and animal carcasses, engulfed the air and hit the nose like a slammed door.

As on the farm, life in the trenches followed a predictable routine. Each morning, the infantry had to "stand-to" at dawn to guard their front-line trenches. For this exercise, each man had to stand on the trench fire step, with his rifle loaded and bayonet fixed. The soldiers expected an enemy attack as the sun rose, an attack of either machine-gun fire or, worse, the creeping greenish mustard gas that blinded and choked to death those unfor-tunate enough to be exposed to it. The Germans, who knew the Canadians were waiting, never actually attacked at dawn, but they performed this same exercise every morning anyway. Day in, day out.

Daylight hours were filled with work in the field. The troops had to clean latrines, fill sandbags, and repair damage to trenches or dig new ones. Even though life on the farm had prepared him for hard manual work, Ellwyne found it exhausting. Digging to fill sandbags. Digging to build trenches. Digging to bury corpses. So much digging on so little sleep. During the day, they kept mostly underground, in the trenches, to stay clear of a sniper's sight. Because the trench system was a zigzagging maze with no clear direc-tion for in or out, the men of the battalion came up with a naming system to keep them oriented while they traversed its passageways. The snaking pat-tern of the trenches provided a modicum of protection for the men. Should a trench take a direct hit from a mortar shell, the walls would absorb the percussive force and save more lives than if it were constructed in a simple grid pattern. The trench names were plucked from the familiar and beloved places of Middlesex County, from which the battalion's men had originated. Ellwyne had offered up "Ekfrid" as a name for one of the trenches, and he was honoured when it was adopted by his new friends.

Ellwyne dreaded nights the most. At night, the rats appeared. Thou-sands, as if poured from an overhead pail, slithered through the trenches like a walking carpet of vermin. They stole food. They gnawed on the living and the dead. They crawled over the men as they slept. They carried fleas and gave the men lice. They carried diseases that made the men sick. They caused misery and suffering. When Ellwyne closed his eyes, he saw rats scattering in front of his feet. When he felt something brush against him, his thoughts flew to rats crawling on top of him, and he jolted awake and jumped to his feet.

It was the closest thing to hell that Ellwyne and the others could imagine. Oh, how Ellwyne longed for one more walk up Betsy Jane's narrow staircase in the flickering light of her coal oil lamp.

Ellwyne was sitting in the trench listening to the sounds of war around him. The men who found it possible to sleep snored, others laughed and yelled, and distant gunfire popped. A horse whinnied. He leaned back and rested his head against the muddied wall. The night was clear, and he could see stars twinkling in the sky. He closed his eyes and drifted off into a restless sleep. In the morning, the routine would begin again. Day after miserable day, night after terrifying night. No end in sight. Digging a deeper hole.

On a cold morning in April, as the men stood waiting for their orders, the commanding officer passed out light green postcards to each of them. "You can fill these out before we get started today, or not. I actually don't care what you decide to do with 'em, but I'm obligated to at least make sure you have one." he said. "Don't write anything else on 'em, or they won't get sent. The censors will toss 'em in the bin. Just check off what applies and sign it. I'll collect 'em from you after lunch." He was a tall man with an angry, red face, who spit when he talked. Behind his back, the men joked about getting splattered by his saliva when he yelled at them. "Say it, don't spray it," they said when he was out of earshot, causing everyone to chortle at the C.O.'s expense.

Ellwyne scanned the postcard, which provided a few multiple-choice responses that he could either check off or strike through, depending on what message he wanted to send home.

I am quite well.
I have been admitted to hospital

$\begin{cases} \textit{Sick} \\ \textit{Wounded} \end{cases}$ $\begin{cases} \textit{and am going on well} \\ \textit{and hope to be discharged soon} \end{cases}$

I am being sent down to the base.

I have received your $\begin{cases} \textit{letter} \underline{\hspace{2cm}} \\ \textit{telegram} \; " \underline{\hspace{2cm}} \\ \textit{parcel} \; " \underline{\hspace{2cm}} \end{cases}$

Letter follows at first opportunity.
I have received no letter from you

$\begin{cases} \textit{lately} \\ \textit{for a long time.} \end{cases}$

The options were limited, but at least it was a way to reach out. Given that it was too wet to write letters, this was a stopgap measure until the pouring rain stopped. Like everything else in the army, the truth was buried deep in the mud, and as long as no one dug any deeper, the truth remained far below the surface and festered like an infected wound.

"There aren't very many options here, are there?" he said to Alex.

"You're just noticing that now?" Alex laughed and jabbed Ellwyne in the ribs.

"Ha ha, very funny," replied Ellwyne. "No, I mean with the postcard. When I say that 'I am quite well,' is it implied that the lice are happily eating me alive while I'm awake and that the rats are chewing on my ears while I sleep? I don't see options for 'rats' and 'lice' on the list."

Alex paused. "I think as long as your heart is still pumping blood and you can form a simple sentence, the only possible option is, 'I am quite well.'"

Ellwyne shrugged. "I don't want my family to know about the dirty rats anyway," he said. "They'd be horrified." He took his postcard, checked off that he was quite well, that a letter would follow at the first opportunity, scratched off everything else, and, in a shaky hand now stained with a mixture of tobacco, blood, and grime, signed his name. "There, that ought to do it. Not much more to say than that. I mean, what else *can* we say?" He addressed the postcard to Mrs. James A. Carruthers and tucked it behind his piece of wood in the trench until the C.O. asked for it after lunch. He felt anything but well, but he didn't have the will, or the strength, to dig up the truth from the mud. No one did.

❦

Despite the barbaric conditions under which Ellwyne lived in the trenches, when he was able to write more detailed letters, he never told the whole truth about his discomfort or fears to his loved ones. He didn't want to worry them. So, he held back the most graphic descriptions of the carnage and horrors that he saw. He kept those memories tucked well away into the back of his mind, and they surfaced only when he let himself go to that dark place. Instead, in his letters home, he focused on his yearning for a return to life as he once knew it, to peace and tranquillity, to green fields.

April 1, 1917
Miss Rose Anderson
Portsmouth Road
Guildford, England

My dearest Rose

Thank you for your latest letter, my darling. Receiving one from you uplifts me. I feel my spirit soaring above when I see the envelope from you. You cannot know how much it means. To know that you're thinking of me brings light to the darkness and chases away all the sadness and uncertainty that might be. Know this: We will be together someday.

On my next leave to London, I promise that we will spend time away from this chaos. We will talk about our future. Walking the streets together, hand-in-hand, searching for lamp posts to stand beneath, we can express the beauty of our love, the love that keeps me going each morning when sometimes I feel too weary to continue. Your love sustains me.

I keep all your letters and read them over and over again. You are always here with me. Please write again soon.

Your loving Ellwyne

He sealed the envelope and held it close to his heart, not quite ready to let it go. "Keep beating," he said aloud as he patted his heart.

On the battlefield, each day stretched and then overlapped into the next. Ellwyne no longer had a clear idea what day of the week it was. He counted down the days until his next leave, but the calendar had lost its meaning for him. He was thinking about meeting up with Rose in London on his leave when he heard the crash and snap of timbers breaking as they twisted against the ground. He heard the sickening sound of a bone breaking in two and cries of agony. Finally, he heard groans and the muffled whinnies of a horse as its legs thrashed in the thick mud.

"Help! Come quick! Is anyone there?"

Men dashed past Ellwyne and emerged from all directions to assist. Ellwyne put down his rifle, abandoned his post, and raced towards the sound. It was carnage. The entire landscape was a mixture of mud, blood, and waste, making it difficult to imagine how things could get any worse.

Ellwyne assessed the scene. A wooden wagon had overturned, spilling bags of sand into the muddy track they used as a supply line. The wagon's driver was trapped beneath the heavy load, his legs turned at an unnatural angle as he screamed in pain. The horse, still harnessed to the wagon with the load, was struggling to get up and escape. If the horse stood and bolted with the wagon still attached, it would crush the driver and kill him.

"Stop movin', ya nag!" yelled one man at the horse, prompting the terrified beast to thrash even more violently.

"Arghhhhhhhh. Fer goddamnsake." The trapped soldier's face was ghost white, his lips turning a light shade of blue. He clutched at the mud as if trying to dig himself out. "Hurry the hell up." He continued to moan.

A memory flashed through Ellwyne's mind. Within a second, he pushed past the men who were gathered by the horse, whose legs flew in all directions as she tried to extricate herself from the thick soup of mud that trapped her. Getting too close was dangerous, and one risked getting hoofed, but Ellwyne knew what he should do. Instinctively, he approached from her back, dropped to his haunches, and sat down on the horse's neck. He shielded her eyes and began to stroke her powerful head and neck.

"Attagirl, whoa, girl. Stay calm. We're here. We'll help you. Easy now."

Although calamity continued to envelop them, a level of calm washed over the horse. Her legs stopped thrashing. As if put under a spell, the horse became still. Only the furious expanding and contracting of her chest and the flaring of her nostrils showed that she was still alive. Bystanders buzzed around the horse and unbuckled the harness so that the horse was no longer attached to the wagon. Sensing release, the horse exhaled and snorted.

After several minutes, Ellwyne heard the words he had waited for. "She's free."

He stroked the horse's neck. "Okay, slowly, girl. I'm gonna stand up and you're not going to kill me. Okay?" From his days in Carruthers Corners, he knew that horses could be skittish when threatened. He slowly rose from his seated position. The horse, now weakened after her fight to stand up, struggled to stand. "Come on, girl, you can do it." He pleaded with her. With a final loud grunt, the horse pushed herself to her feet and wobbled. She took a few tentative steps and swayed with exhaustion; head lowered nearly to the ground. "That's a good girl. You did it. Easy now." Ellwyne patted her forehead and led her away from the scene. She had a deep gash on her withers and across her shoulder. The whites of her eyes flashed as she scanned the horizon and jumped with fright in response to every loud sound. *I know how that feels,* he thought. But she was alive. And so was the driver, who was now being freed from beneath the wagon and loaded onto a stretcher.

A soldier approached Ellwyne. "I'll take her now. She needs to see the field vet."

"Take good care of her. She's a good horse. She wasn't going to hurt anyone, she was scared and fighting for her life."

"We will, man. Thanks for helping her."

Later, the men gathered around Ellwyne and offered him a cigarette and a light.

"What possessed you to sit on the horse's head?" they asked.

Ellwyne drew in a long drag on the cigarette, feeling more calm wash over his body. "I knew that if she managed to get up and pulled the wagon sideways, it would crush the driver caught underneath it."

"But sitting on her like that?"

"It's a trick I learned from a fearless farm girl many years ago." Betsy Jane's slender face flashed in his mind.

"Well, thank God. Well done, mate."

Ellwyne felt his heart beating inside his chest. His pulse had now returned to near-normal following the adrenaline rush. "Thank God, indeed." He looked up at the sky and thought again of Betsy Jane and the lush green fields of Ekfrid Township.

41

THE CORNER WOODLOT, EKFRID TOWNSHIP, ONTARIO, CANADA

AT THE EDGE of the northwest corner of the Carruthers farm, the button-wood tree continued to grow taller. Its mottled bark, now flaking off in large chunks as it shed its outer skin to make way for pending expansion, displayed the tell-tale patches of silvery white, brown, grey, and green for which button-wood trees are known.

On a battlefield thousands of miles away, as aeroplanes soared overhead, miserable men camped out in the muddy trenches scarring the fields of France and Belgium. The reconnaissance flights once easily identified the French soldiers because of their bright-coloured uniforms. But they had abandoned the traditional blue, red, and white and changed to colours that blended into the landscape, to help them hide from and confuse their enemy. Patches of brown, grey, and green, like the mottled bark of a buttonwood.

Hoping to survive.

Struggling to hang onto life, even in its misery, where many did not.

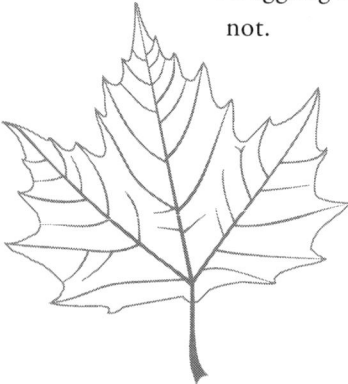

42

CARRUTHERS CORNERS, ONTARIO, CANADA

THE FIRST TRIMESTER of her pregnancy passed without any morning sickness, for which Betsy Jane was grateful. If she had been sickened, she wouldn't have been sure if it was from the pregnancy or from the heartache of missing her boy. Her belly was becoming more prominent, and the baby was now kicking regularly. She talked to the growing life inside her daily, telling stories about how Ellwyne had come to the family. She wanted the baby to know about Ellwyne so that when it arrived, it would already be well-versed in the history of the dark-haired boy who had come to the homestead all those years ago. Family is not always those you are born to; it can also be those you choose to let into your heart. Ellwyne had chosen them. He was family to them, and they were his.

Betsy Jane approached the Hoosier cabinet in her kitchen. She inhaled sharply, opened the drawer, and removed the small box containing the signet ring. Not many months ago, Ellwyne had been sitting beside her at the schoolhouse send-off, opening that box for the first time. Now, he was nowhere near, and she physically ached for him, missing his presence, and worrying about his safety. She had noticed a change in the tone of his letters now that he was at the front. *You should have brought this with you, Ellwyne. It was for safe passage*, she thought, running her fingers around the smooth edges of the ring. The heat of her hands warmed the metal. She had found herself looking at it more and more often, the longer Ellwyne was gone. She desperately wanted him back home, but each time remembered to place her faith in God, knowing that He would ultimately decide whether that happened.

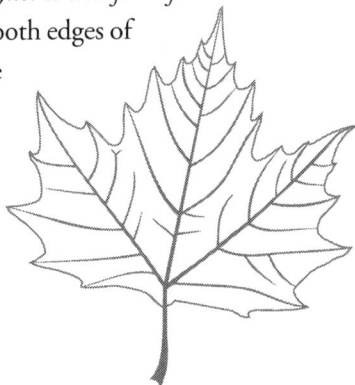

43

BATTLEFIELD, SOMEWHERE IN FRANCE

THOUSANDS OF MILES away, Ellwyne was lying outstretched in a muddy, damp trench, looking up at the stars and thinking, for the thousandth time, about the homestead in Ekfrid Township with its gingerbread trim and cookstove, where Betsy Jane heated up bricks in the winter to wrap in a blanket and put into bed with him to keep him warm at night. When he closed his eyes, he had a vivid picture of the green Ontario pastures. He could hear the cracking and snapping of the corn as it simmered in the sun, growing on a hot July afternoon, and he could feel the warmth enveloping him from the unconditional love he had received from James A. and Betsy Jane. He hungered to return and pick up where he had left off.

"I can do this," he said to himself. "I will see them again."

As he closed his eyes, a shell exploded in the distance, making his teeth rattle as the ground shook. He inhaled, letting the air expand in his lungs, to help settle his nerves. No matter how frequent, the blasts shook him to his core. In fact, he had become jumpier with each passing day. The slightest unexpected sound made him startle and snap. He felt like a jerky puppet on a string, no longer in control of his own movements.

Keep breathing. Just keep breathing. He thought of Rose and her mesmerizing green eyes. He had memorized all her letters and, when especially stressed, recited them to himself. *Keep breathing for Betsy Jane and for Rose.*

Nothing excited the troops more than mail delivery

day. Humble pieces of paper scribbled with inky sentiments were their lifeline to home, a reminder of happier, quieter times. The letters gave them the most valuable commodity, now in shortest supply: hope. Hope that they would reunite with their families. Hope that they would be able to brush away all the horrors surrounding them and forget the terrible sights, sounds, and smells of war. Hope that they would escape with their lives. With each letter they sent to a loved one, the men expected to receive at least as many in response. Correspondence was what kept many of them going. Thoughts of the life they used to have. The wish to return to it.

Ellwyne regularly wrote letters to Betsy Jane in Ekfrid Township, Rose in London, his grandmother in Howrah, India, his sister Valetta in Toronto, and postcards to six-year-old Archie Carruthers. They were all signed "Your loving Ellwyne."

He usually received a letter (or two) from Betsy Jane on mail day. It was the one certainty in this war that he could depend on: a letter from Ekfrid Township. Letters from Canada usually took about two weeks to arrive, so all the news Ellwyne received about home was outdated by the time he read it, but he didn't mind. At least he hadn't been forgotten. Not even close. She wrote often, telling him of the mundane details of happenings on the farm with the Carruthers clan. News about a maple syrup jar that wouldn't open, the people who visited them, or about her sister's apple tree and the pies that they made from it. The letters were addressed to Pte. Ellwyne A. Ballantyne, No. 802423, 4th Battalion, France, and always signed "Your loving Betsy Jane."

He kept all the letters from home stashed in between wooden supports in the trench. He was living in one named Delaware, whose name was offered up by a chap who hailed from the small town southwest of London, Ontario. He thumbed through his letters often, memorizing their words, imagining the writer's voice while he read them to himself. It felt to him that the letters were the only thing keeping him sane. Angus McDougal was an affable lad from a farm in Lobo Township, close to where Ellwyne had spent the happiest days of his life. Angus rarely received mail. When all the other men from the battalion clamoured to line up for their letters, Angus hung back in the trench, whittling the wooden handle of his knife into an elaborate series of interconnected channels, whistling to himself.

"You know, if you wrote letters to home, you might receive some back, Angus," Ellwyne remarked one day.

Angus's face instantly turned as red as his hair.

"I can't," he stammered.

"You can't write letters?" asked Ellwyne.

"I, I can't write at all," he muttered. "My *da* died when I was young, and I had to quit school to work on the farm." Angus' red face revealed his shame.

Ellwyne knew immediately what to do.

"Do you want to learn?" asked Ellwyne.

"I do. If I *can*, that is."

"Of course you can. You hold your pencil like this." He demonstrated how to clasp the instrument between the second and third finger, and the thumb. "You press the lead to the page, but not too hard or you'll break the lead." Ellwyne began writing the alphabet in capital letters on the paper, using oversized letters. When he was done, he passed the paper and pencil to Angus. "Now you try. I'll help you."

Angus smiled, picked up the pencil, and pressed it to the page. He started with the first letter and traced over the capital A that Ellwyne had written.

"That's the first letter of the alphabet," said Ellwyne.

"A is for Angus," Angus declared. "I know that much." He beamed as he traced it again.

And angel, Ellwyne thought. *A is also for angel*. His thoughts drifted thousands of miles away to the fields and farms of home.

🍁

Some of Ellwyne's fondest memories of the homestead involved the animals he had tended to. As a boy, when he was feeling lonely or sad, he had found refuge and solace in listening to Old Grey and the other horses munching on hay. When he felt homesick now, he let his mind wander back to the places that had given him the greatest comfort. In the midst of unspeakable carnage and chaos in France, he found himself needing refuge once more.

The European battlefield had brought immense suffering not only to the human beings but also to the animals that served alongside them. Shortly after the war began, Britain had scoured the land for horses to add to its military campaign. Most were work horses used to pulling a plough or a wagon. Being subjected to constant shell blasts and explosions wore on their nerves, just as it did the men. Ellwyne felt sorry for the beasts living in these same conditions. Underfed and overworked, the horses and donkeys toiled in impossibly cruel conditions. They were living beings treated like machinery, thrown aside when no longer usable.

When possible, Ellwyne liked to walk among the harnessed horses and spend a few moments rubbing their ears and whispering calm words to them. He found scattered moments of peace with the war horses; they reminded him of home. He found himself naming them, even though they were usually nameless.

"How are you doing, Daisy girl," he said as he patted the emaciated chestnut mare on her forehead. Although she was a large draft horse, hard work had whittled her size, and her hip bones protruded so that they were sharp points. He called her Daisy because of the white star shape on her forehead that reminded him of the flower. She had been harnessed without respite for months on end and had developed angry, oozing welts on her chest from pulling heavy loads that became heavier the weaker she became. Ellwyne knew that Daisy would die from exhaustion shortly. Her hollowed eyes had that tell-tale look of surrender in them. After months in the field, he recognized it well among both animals and men.

"I'm not going to have this today, so you might as well enjoy it," he said as he reached into his pocket and removed a coveted sugar cube. He had been saving it for his next mug of hot chocolate, but Daisy's forlorn eyes reached into his soul. He flattened his hand and offered the horse the sugar cube. She sniffed it gently, and gobbled it up, and smacked her lips with satisfaction. Her eyes brightened at the taste of sugar coated with kindness. "I'll bring you another one tomorrow if I can," he said. "You need it more than I do." He patted her velvet nose, and the mare exhaled her warm breath on his hand, which James A. had taught him was a sign of affection from a horse. "You're welcome, girl," he said as he turned away and headed back to the trench.

The next morning, Ellwyne grabbed two sugar cubes, put one into his tea, and stowed the other in his pocket for later. In the afternoon, he looked

for Daisy but could not find her. A younger and fresher-looking white geld-
ing was now hitched to the wagon, but Daisy was nowhere in sight. Ellwyne
yelled out to John Brown, one of the drivers.

"Hey, John! Where's the large chestnut mare?"

"Which one?" he asked.

"The one with the white patch on her forehead. She was pulling a wagon
loaded with canvas tarps on it yesterday. I saw you working with her."

John winced, shook his head, and pointed westward. Ellwyne saw a
mound that could have easily been mistaken for freshly dug earth in the
fading light. He breathed in deeply, then exhaled, blinking away some tears
that were welling against his will. He walked towards the mound, dreading
what he knew he would find.

"Oh, Daisy." He kneeled beside her, stroked her patchy chestnut fur,
easily feeling her ribs underneath his fingertips. Her body was still warm,
her brown eyes and mouth open. He unbuckled her bridle and removed the
metal bit from her mouth and placed it on the ground beside her. He wanted
to give her her freedom.

"I guess you're at peace now, poor girl. I'll find someone else to give this
to," he said as he felt around in his pocket for the sugar cube. He placed his
fingers on her lids and closed the mare's eyes. "Rest now, Daisy. You worked
so hard for us."

As he headed back to the trench, he stopped and patted the white geld-
ing on the muzzle. His nose felt like luxurious velvet to Ellwyne's roughened
hands. "Hi, Snowman," he said gently. He offered his flattened hand holding
the sugar cube to the hungry horse.

He felt a mix of sadness and rage boiling in his gut. How many more
innocent things would this war destroy? And for what? He could not shake
the image of Daisy from his head. He was now thinking about Old Grey
and Billy, the foal that he had named after James A. invited him to the stall
to see him stand a few minutes after his birth. How he missed them and
the simplicity of life back at the homestead! He did the only thing he could
think of: took out a piece of paper and began penning a letter to Archie.

May 9, 1917
Master Archie Carruthers
Ekfrid Township

R.R. #4
Glencoe, Ontario
Canada

Dear Archie:

Thank you for the recent note. You're becoming quite the letter writer! I see that your mother has also begun to teach you how to write beautifully as well. She made sure I knew how to write perfectly, and I've been able to teach a man here how to write because of the lessons she gave me.

How is Fanny? And what about Old Grey? We have a lot of horses here. I have been naming them and giving them sugar cubes whenever I can. I have a favourite named Daisy. She did such a good job helping us that she will soon be sent back home because her farmer needs her back. She misses him, too. I will miss her, but I'm happy for her that she has been called home.

It's good that you have all the kittens to keep you company. Maybe you could send me one here. We have a lot of rats, and a kitten would prove useful, I'm sure.

Take good care. Write again soon.
Your loving Ellwyne

A tear dropped onto the paper, smudging the ink. Archie was too young to understand the truth about Daisy, but Ellwyne did believe that she had been called home.

"I'm scared, Momma," he said, loud enough for others to have overheard. "I hope you're here with me now." Feelings of dread and fear raced up and down his legs, making them feel wobbly and weak; it reminded him of the day he had seen Billy the foal first standing a few minutes after being born. He swayed and then steadied himself. He recalled the conversation that he had had with Betsy Jane years ago about fear and courage. She had advised him that it was okay to feel fear—natural, in fact—but that courage was present when you were able to put your trust and faith in God. Another tear formed and spilled onto his cheek.

I'm afraid, but I'm going to leave my fate in Your hands. As he closed his eyes, he saw a vision of a glorious chestnut horse, its coat gleaming in the morning light, racing across a lush pasture. The sound of horse hooves pounding the ground resonated in his ears. *You made it home, Daisy.*

44

CARRUTHERS CORNERS, ONTARIO, CANADA

"ISN'T SHE PRECIOUS?" Betsy Jane cooed.

Neil's wife, Maggie Belle, a petite, brown-haired woman with tanned skin and rounded cheeks, reached out and took the babbling baby into her arms. The two half-sisters, who lived on neighbouring farms, relied on each other for many things, not the least of which was midwifery duties. The labour had been swift. Betsy Jane's second baby, a dark-haired girl named Elizabeth, had arrived without fanfare, a textbook birth.

"I must write Ellwyne and let him know that we now have a baby girl," mused Betsy Jane, gazing at her new daughter cradled in the arms of her sister.

"At least give yourself a bit of time to rest before you exert yourself," Maggie Belle said, though she knew her advice would not be heeded. If she knew anything about Betsy Jane, it was that she would get out of bed and write that letter today. She had done little else in the months since Ellwyne had left but pray for his safe return. It consumed her thoughts and her conversations. Not that she blamed her in the least; the whole community was praying for him and all the other boys who had enlisted.

45

LENS, FRANCE

OVER TIME, HIS senses dulled to the assault of sound, the pounding of explosions and the stutter of machine-gun fire, but the silence that followed as the men waited for the next attack leeched beneath his skin, and terrified him. Bangs and whizzes punctuated the air with an intense but uneven rhythm that prevented anyone from figuring out a safe path, day or night. But it was the waiting, the brief silences, the knowledge that lulls never lasted, that made Ellwyne tremble.

Ellwyne was crouched in the Parkhill trench (named after the small town where Jimmy Decker grew up) when he heard the whiizzzzzzzzzzzzzzz that signalled an incoming shell. Before he could react, there was a thunderous bang and a metallic singing as whirring shrapnel tore up the mud around them, somehow sparing their flesh. "All clear?" came a voice, a survivor a few yards away asking if anyone else was still with him. "Still here," said one voice. "Yup, here," said another. After recovering from the surprise of the explosion, Jimmy said, "At least we know why they call it a "whiz-bang." The men laughed, though there wasn't anything funny about it. The explosion had cost them one more piece of their sanity.

The ferocity of the blasts stripped the formerly lush, green fields of France to barren, muddy wastelands. Once past the initial shock, the men became blinded to the devastation and destruction around them. It was a Tuesday in July when Ellwyne realized that the tall poles protruding from the mud and barbed wire in no man's land were once tall trees that must have

been elegant, with leaves that rustled as their branches swayed in the breeze. And then it hit him. That's what he was missing: the soothing sound of leaves blowing in the wind. But explosions and fire erupting all around the enemy lines had sucked the life out of the trees and spit their remains into the mud below. The only audible sounds were disturbing, disruptive, and plunged fear deep into his bones. Any abrupt noise made him jump involuntarily. After many weeks of exposure to battle and its barrage of assaultive noises, jumpiness became contagious among the men. They startled at the slightest of sounds. Their nerves were rubbed raw, and the energy required for constant vigilance, combined with lack of sleep, sapped them. The officers, however, did not accept fatigue or fear as an excuse to shirk duties or ignore a command. When ordered to run over top of the trenches, the men were expected to sprint, even if it meant rushing into the enemy's machine-gun fire.

"Cowardice is the greatest shame you could ever bring to yourselves or your families." The commanding officer barked at the men lined up for the dawn ritual stand-to. "I needn't remind you, but yellow bellies will be shot." His venomous words cut through the morning air.

"Why did we get warned about being cowards?" Ellwyne asked Jimmy later that morning when they were digging a new trench line. "We're out here wading through shit and breaking our balls." Ellwyne's casual use of coarse language had developed since his enlistment. Sometimes the words that now flew out of his mouth shocked even him. He knew that Betsy Jane would not approve, but he was far from home, and she would never hear those words escape his lips.

"You didn't hear?" Jimmy set down his shovel and stretched his arms and shoulders.

"I don't think so. What happened?"

"A few days ago, a young lad from Manchester didn't go over the top with the rest of the 162nd. When everyone else ran, he didn't. The C.O. later found him hiding out, pissing his pants. The next morning, they lined him up and shot him." Jimmy picked up his shovel again. "Firing squad," he added. "A shame to waste our target practice drills, eh?"

Ellwyne gulped. "That's h-harsh."

"Yeah. So, if you're a deserter, they'll shoot you. If you get scared, they'll also shoot you. Oh yeah, and the enemy? They wanna shoot you too."

That evening, as he sat in the trench, Ellwyne grasped the wooden stock of his rifle and ran his fingers over its smooth surface, heating it under his touch. He recalled the day he had begun carving a piece of firewood into a boat, on the verandah at the homestead. In his hand was a smooth piece of wood that could have been sculpted into an object of beauty but instead was part of a deadly weapon. His days at Carruthers Corners working on the farm were so long ago, though it was mere months since he'd last stepped foot in Ekfrid Township. His heart ached for old times, so he reached out the only way he could. He picked up his pen and paper and wrote a letter.

August 1, 1917
Mrs. James A. Carruthers
R. R. #4
Glencoe, Ontario
Canada

Dear Betsy Jane:

Thank you for all the letters you've written to me. I appreciate receiving them on mail day. Most of the boys here get letters, but I'm lucky because I get an avalanche of them. I keep them all and re-read them when I have spare time, sometimes in the early morning before dawn, or sometimes late at night when I have a bit of alone time. Turns out, we often have lots of spare time when we're not digging holes in the dirt.

I realized something today. I was wondering if you could check on that buttonwood tree in the corner woodlot? Remember the day that James A. and I were clearing underbrush and we found it and decided to let it stay? I'm hoping that it's still there and growing and getting stronger. The trees here have mostly been burned to matchsticks. I miss hearing the wind rustling through the leaves. It's strange the common things you miss when they're not there. It's strange the things that you begin to accept as normal.

Give Archie a hug and tell him he's a good boy.
Your loving Ellwyne

After folding the paper and putting it in an envelope, he reached for his last remaining piece of paper. He wouldn't receive more until the next day unless he traded some of his cigarettes, but he wasn't willing to give any of those up yet. Using his tiniest script, which gave his hand a cramp, he jammed as much information as possible on the page.

August 1, 1917
Miss Valetta Ballantyne
Toronto, Ontario
Canada

Dear Valetta:

I realized that I'm long overdue for writing you a letter. It's sometimes hard to find the time to pen them. We do a lot of digging and clean-up during daylight hours, so I'm stretched to grab a free chunk of time to write when we're not working. Thank you for sending me so many, I am fortunate to receive piles of letters from home. I get them from India, Scotland, Canada, and England, if you can believe it.

Have you written to Grandmother lately? I write to her as often as I can. She tells me that her garden has more peacocks now than ever before. The lemon tree had a fungus and didn't produce any fruit last year. I wonder if you still think about India. When I close my eyes, I can feel the sun beating on my head and the taste of lemons and mangoes. I miss the warm weather, especially now that we've had two solid weeks of rain. That means my feet are constantly wet and have become swollen and sore, it's quite painful.

If you travel back to see James A. and Betsy Jane at Carruthers Corners, make sure you walk through the woodlot on their farm. Do me a favour and please go find the buttonwood tree. It was a sapling when I last saw it, but it must be getting tall now. Ask James A. to take you to it if you're not sure where to look. We don't have any trees here in France. They've all been either burned or cut down. Knowing that my buttonwood tree is still growing would bring me some joy and something to look forward to when I return.

This is my last piece of paper and I'm running out of space, so I'll close for now. Know that I think of you often and cannot wait to see you again.

Your loving brother,
Ellwyne

Ellwyne's 135th Battalion, made up of Middlesex County boys, had long ago been absorbed into the 125th Battalion, and next into the 4th Battalion, due to mounting casualties. Because so many men he had befriended had already been gravely wounded or killed, Ellwyne went against his nature and learned not to become too attached to anyone. Now, instead of doing work tasks to keep the supply line moving, his battalion was stationed at the front line. Mere feet from the enemy, only barbed wire, land mines, and snaking trenches separated them. With this change, his life was in immediate danger. The risk of being killed had skyrocketed, and Ellwyne began to obsess about it.

The list of dead and wounded read like a tragic roll call from school days. He played it back in his head:

Robert Anderson, one of the oldest men in the group. Referred to as "Pops." Shell blast.

Alexander Brown, the battalion's best storyteller. Shell blast. They retrieved only pieces of him.

Alistair Jones, the ruddy-faced jokester. Sniper bullet. When they pulled him back into the trench, he tried to speak a few words, but he choked on his own blood.

Samuel Stocker from Lancaster, England. Wounded in a blast and taken away on a stretcher, probable fatality. So much blood. No word yet on his condition, but such announcements were rare.

William Stokes, the friendly lad from London who shared his cigarettes with his mates. Shell blast. William's screams of agony before he died still rang in Ellwyne's ears when he closed his eyes.

Charles Watt, working on a magnificent shell carving. Machine-gun fire. His body was ripped in half in the assault.

Cliff Wiseman, the quiet loner whom no one really got to know. Sniper bullet. Tore through his throat, and death came swiftly.

The nameless private, just a sixteen-year-old kid, shot at dawn by firing squad because he didn't obey an order, one that probably would have killed him anyway.

The last death haunted him.

I just have to make it to the next day, Ellwyne told himself as he took a long drag from a cigarette. Orange embers fell from the tip onto the mud at his feet. He had never smoked before joining the army but had picked up the habit in the past three months. It was necessary. He found that it helped calm his nerves, but the taste of nicotine also helped dampen the stench of rotting flesh no one could escape. Like many of the men, he relied on whatever he could get his hands on that might keep him from making a foolish move that would get him killed. Sometimes, though, when he felt defeated, he wondered if the escape of death might be easier than finishing this tour.

He tried to brush aside defeatist thoughts when they crept into his mind, but when he was being honest with himself, he had to acknowledge his fears were founded. Picking up body pieces, the random hands, legs, and torsos of those ripped apart in blasts, had shattered a part of him, perhaps forever. They buried the bodies usually where they fell, or sometimes, when the death toll mounted, in a mass grave behind the trenches.

Being a soldier was not what he had expected.

Digging to try to stay alive.

Digging to cover up the dead.

He wondered if the hole would ever go deep enough.

Had he understood what he knew now, he never would have volunteered to take part in this mess.

※

In August 1917, the Canadians were attempting to take back a hill in Lens, France, to move their front line forward and push the German line back. The troops were battered, weary, and filthy. They struggled with the itch caused by lice. They fought against boredom, mingled with adrenaline rushes when explosions or enemy fire interrupted it. Death was a part of everyday life, and nights were the worst. Ellwyne often thought about the promises the army recruiters had made to him in Glencoe so many months ago. Despite their lofty assurances, he had not once been given an opportunity to work on an engine or learn anything about mechanics. Instead, he'd been forced to the front lines, where his life was in extreme peril at almost all times, but especially at night. That was when they were sometimes ordered to venture into no man's land to repair the barbed wire that separated the opposing trench lines. Ellwyne dreaded this duty. He had done it twice before, and for days afterwards had quaked with fear, feeling lucky to still be alive but wondering how long his luck would hold out. If he was a cat with nine lives, he had used up too many already.

His thoughts drifted to the gold signet ring stowed in Betsy Jane's Hoosier cabinet in her kitchen. Wondering if he would ever get to wear it again, Ellwyne choked back a lump in his throat. What he wouldn't give for one more walk through the fields, one more sing-along led by Betsy Jane on her pump organ, one more made-up bedtime story about a fox and a fawn. He ached to go home. For the second time in his life, he understood with absolute clarity where that was.

That night, a ringing sound resonated deep inside his ears, as though a bumble bee was trapped inside. He shook his head to try to make it stop. But it only became louder. *Too many shell blasts,* he thought.

No matter how he tried to ignore it, the vibration didn't let up.

46

THE EUROPEAN CONTINENT

AS THE FIGHTING raged on, the toll of the war was becoming incalculable. Limbs were ripped apart by artillery and bombs. Lungs were poisoned by toxic gases, brownish clouds of death that descended on the men and blistered their lungs when inhaled. Minds were permanently scarred by the trauma that surrounded them. Although humans were the instigators of the conflict, they were far from the only victims of it. The damage and suffering inflicted on the trees and forests of Europe was equally immeasurable. Trees were engulfed in flames and burned to the ground during bombing attacks. Their trunks were riddled with bullets. Limbs and leaves were ripped off and destroyed. Old-growth forests, already at risk before the war, were obliterated. A few burned trunks devoid of foliage or limbs or life were all that remained after a battle. The forests, once green and vibrating with life, were dying.

Hope was being exterminated along with thousands of lives.

The vibration weakened but did not stop entirely.

In their final moments before dying, even the trees called out for an end to the suffering. *Enough!* they said as they vibrated.

47

CARRUTHERS CORNERS, ONTARIO, CANADA

RITUALS BRING A sense of calm and peace precisely because they enable a person to do the same thing repeatedly during times of stress and uncertainty. For Betsy Jane, letter writing was one of the rituals that helped ease her mind while Ellwyne was gone. On a humid day in August, when the cicadas were buzzing and the field corn was snapping from the heat, Betsy Jane sat at her oak dining table and stole the few quiet minutes available to compose a letter to Ellwyne.

August 22, 1917
Pte Ellwyne Ballantyne
802423
4th Btn
France

Dear Ellwyne:

It's been a few days since I sat down at the table to write you a letter, so I figured you might want to hear some more news from Carruthers Corners. We've had a dry summer and the corn didn't grow as high as usual, nor as plentiful. I think by the end of August, it was only up to my shoulders, which isn't as tall as it has been in the past.

Neil and Maggie Belle give their regards. They were over last Sunday, and we sang a few songs

together. My foot was tired after pumping the organ, but the music filled the house, and probably beyond. The Munsons have a new bull, a great stocky Hereford that looks like a mean one. When I'm walking to Neil's place, I always keep my eye on it even though it's behind the fence. Archie discovered the green beans in the garden and helped himself to nearly a whole row before I found him. Needless to say, we'll have fewer canned beans this winter. James A. finally repaired the seat on the democrat. He ripped a big hole in his work pants on that loose board. So, I got darning to do and he had to find some wood and straw to replace the seat. And now it's as good as new. Elizabeth is growing quickly and has learned to babble in full sentences. We are all eager for her to speak in sentences that we actually understand.

I am nervous to hear that you're seeing action at the front. I try not to think about that, but instead fill my head with happy thoughts. You know how I am.

I'll end this now. Know that we think of you often and keep you in our evening prayers. I'm proud that you have managed to avoid the temptations that face you. God will be with you.

Your loving Betsy Jane

She sealed the envelope and addressed it to Private Ellwyne A. Ballantyne, 802423, CEF, France. After applying the postage on it. she waited for James A. to take it to the Glencoe post office later that day.

When broken, rituals also cause enormous pain.

48

THE CORNER WOODLOT, EKFRID TOWNSHIP, ONTARIO, CANADA

A GROUP OF five turkey vultures circled in the sky above Carruthers Corners. Their long wings extended as they soared in smaller and smaller concentric circles, like water circling a drain. Earlier, a raccoon had been in a vicious fight with a larger raccoon over some scraps of food they found. The swipe to his chest had opened a deep wound that bled heavily at first, then slowed, but his wound had become infected. He weakened as he continued to crawl through the brush, looking for a place to hide and rest. The raccoon sent out the invisible signals of dying that only vultures are tuned to pick up. He finally nestled beneath a fallen tree. An hour passed and he stopped moving, then he stopped breathing altogether. A gentle breeze rippled through the trees, causing the branches to sway and the leaves to rustle.

The buttonwood tree stood watch.

A small piece of bark fell from its trunk and landed on the grass below.

49

LENS, FRANCE

ON A CHILLY September night, hours before the sun would rise, Ellwyne had just finished his night-time sentry duty. After two hours of sitting motionless, watching and scanning the darkness of no man's land for any movement or threat from the nameless enemy, he stood to return to the trench. It was Angus' turn to take the post next. His shift was over, and he might be able to get a few minutes of restless sleep before the impending dawn. He thanked God that he had made it through another night. He patted his right breast pocket, as he always did, to ensure that he had his clothbound army-issued Bible, the address book containing names of his loved ones, and his sweetheart's rose petal next to his heart. As his fingers pressed onto his tunic, he felt it.

Thump-thump. Thump-thump.

His heartbeat gave proof that he had survived one more round of this lethal match.

When he lowered his hand from his chest to his side, it happened.

He felt the sharp pierce of a bullet entering his chest through his breast pocket and exiting through his back. He knew immediately that he had been hit. His worst fear, and what he had managed to avoid for over twelve months of deadly battle, had been realized. He took three enormous steps backwards, and his body crumpled to the ground. Despite the eruption of sound around him, everything grew quiet to him. Time stopped. His senses dulled. The rush of those around him faded into emptiness. He didn't hear their voices or yells for help. He didn't see them scurrying around him to tend to his wound.

Instantly, his mind filled with visions, blurring in and out of focus, of the people and places that he loved most.

He saw his mother Eliza, restored to full health, seated in the red velvet chair, arms open and waiting for him to bound into her lap.

He saw his grandmother in India offering him a rosebud from her garden.

He saw his sister Valetta placing her small hand into his as they walked together on a dusty street in Calcutta.

He saw Rose from across the smoke-filled room at Tin Town, her brilliant green eyes shining in the dim light.

He saw the green hay fields of Ekfrid Township, the tall grass rippling in the breeze as it welcomed him to the gingerbread house with its scalloped trim.

He saw Archie, the boy he considered his little brother, peering out from beneath his CEF uniform hat as he posed for the camera on the verandah at the homestead.

He was riding on the democrat buggy seat beside James A. as they headed to Glencoe to the feed mill. He heard the clip-clop of Old Grey's hooves on the hardened road.

He was sitting in Betsy Jane's kitchen at her oak table, practising his cursive writing. He could feel the warmth from her woodstove and smell the aroma of warm bread. He saw James A. and Betsy Jane walking towards him, mouthing words that he could not yet hear.

Their images faded into black.

A beam of light pierced the darkness and the images of his mother and father came into focus. They were several hundred yards away from him, embracing on the familiar Hooghly River Bridge that connected Howrah to Calcutta. Edward Dacosta, dressed in a dark suit and top hat, placed his arm around Eliza's shoulder and motioned towards Ellwyne. Edward called out to Ellwyne, but he could not hear the words. As he strained to hear his father's voice, Ellwyne said, "I'm being called home."

Their images faded into black. He blinked once more. The breath expelled from his chest, and it did not rise again.

❧

Angus was the first to reach Ellwyne's crumpled body, which was lying face up with eyes fixed. A torrent of blood gushed from the bullet hole in his chest. Angus, without thinking, jammed his index finger into the hole to try to stem the bleeding, hoping to buy his friend some precious extra time. He had to get Ellwyne away from the front line to get him treatment. If Ellwyne could hold on long enough, there might be a chance to save him.

"Over here, boys! He's hit!" Angus yelled. Feeling his heart fluttering in his throat, he realized he was in full-blown panic mode. "Come on, Ellwyne. Stay with me," he pleaded. Ever since Ellwyne had helped him write letters home, the two had become fast friends. This wasn't how Angus wanted to see their friendship end.

Samuel Ball rushed from the trench and crouched beside Angus. "Looks bad," he said to Angus. "Get us a stretcher!" he yelled over his shoulder to the men gathered in the trench. Two men soon appeared with a canvas-covered stretcher and scurried back into the relative safety of the trench. Angus lifted Ellwyne's head while still keeping his finger jammed in the chest wound, while Samuel lifted his legs and they placed him on the stretcher. Angus removed a handkerchief from his pocket and stuffed it into the wound. Samuel covered Ellwyne with a wool blanket. "Let's get him out of here," he yelled. Gunfire erupted around them.

Samuel and Angus lifted the stretcher and began their hobbled walk towards the medics.

Ellwyne's eyes fluttered once, but his body did not move.

Ellwyne felt the warmth of a wool blanket being placed over him. His eyes fluttered, and then stopped moving. He felt his muscles relax.

He saw a young doe dipping her nose into a river and taking a small sip. Around her, unusual broad-shaped leaves fluttered from the magnificent white and grey-barked tree, falling from the branches like tears cascading down a cheek.

WHIIIIIIIIIIIIZZZZZZZZZZZZZZZZZZZZZZZZ!

BANG!

The buttonwood tree cried out in pain.

An enemy mortar shell exploded nearby, spraying up mud and water to coat everything around the three men. A brilliant light flashed in the blackened sky. Ellwyne's body hit the mud first as the stretcher bearers let go of the wooden handles.

Angus loosened his grip and collapsed from the concussive force of the shell blast.

Samuel never knew what hit him.

Ellwyne saw the doe startle, leap backwards from the river, pivot, and soar into the woods, her tail waving like a white flag of surrender until she disappeared. He felt himself twirling as if dropped from above. His body twisted and turned as he tumbled through the darkness. After a few moments, his fall was broken by the downy softness of a furry coat. He felt himself moving forward, rocking up and down.

He heard the inhale and exhale and felt the expansion and contraction of lungs beneath him.

He felt the branches of trees brushing his shoulders as he hurtled past them. Faster, faster.

It darkened even more.

He felt a vibration. A humming surrounded him and echoed through his ears. Quietly at first, then growing stronger and more distinct.

It faintly called out. "Home."

A few hours later, after the casualties were being assessed, the men of the 4th Battalion were huddled in the Springbank trench following the early morning attack from the other side.

"How many men did we lose this morning?" demanded the commanding officer. His reddened face looked angrier than usual. A purple vein popped at his temple and pulsed as he spoke. He awaited the tally from the battalion's chaplain, who was tasked with figuring out how many they had lost and who they were.

"Three in that shell blast," Reg Lovell's voice cracked as he spoke. He stood with his arms pasted to his side, struggling to contain his grief from the attack's outcome. "Three men called home, sir."

No one moved. They had lost three popular mates in one chaotic explosion. The only audible sound was Reg fumbling with the three metal dogtags he had removed from the neck chains of the deceased men, whose bodies were laid out on the ground and covered by grey wool blankets.

"Well, what are you waiting for?" The commanding officer's scream snapped the man to action. "Pick up a shovel and dig." And with that, the bedraggled men reached for their shovels and headed to the mass burial site.

50

THE CORNER WOODLOT, EKFRID TOWNSHIP, ONTARIO, CANADA

AS THOUGH A switch had been flipped, an unexpected chill filled the mid-September air, dropping the temperature by five degrees within minutes. Black and grey clouds swirled ominously in the darkened sky and moved aggressively, as a predator does when pursuing its prey. A long band of dark clouds formed a distinct line, almost as if two opposing sides of an atmospheric conflict had been separated by force. As the dark clouds burst open and pelted cold rain onto the hardened ground, the wind whipped and whirled, lashing the trees and forcing them to dance in frenetic, uncontrolled rhythm. First, the brilliant flash of fingered bolts of lightning charged down from the clouds and hit the trees at the corner woodlot. As it struck, the explosion of electricity raced into the thick clay soil. Two seconds later, a crack of thunder erupted and rattled the windows of the homestead at Carruthers Corners. The fury of the storm continued until the trees at the corner woodlot were drenched with the sudden downpour.

The buttonwood tree stood amidst the crackle of electricity. Its limbs reached out to the neighbouring trees for support. As the wind swirled furiously, the buttonwood branches grasped desperately at the air, like wet fingers trying to hang onto something that kept slipping through its clutches.

Slipping.

Fading.

Falling.

The buttonwood's vibration sound weakened as

it clasped the air. Its limbs began to droop, and handfuls of leaves fluttered into the air and twirled as they fell to the ground and blew away.

The vibration grew in intensity and desperation. The other trees at the corner woodlot began to join in a humming chorus. They swirled and streamed their limbs towards the buttonwood tree and leaned in towards it, forming a leafy barrier between it and the ravages of the storm.

Enough! They said. *Enough suffering!*

PART 4

SPREADING SEEDS
1917–1960

"In nature, nothing is perfect and every-thing is perfect. Trees can be contorted, bent in weird ways, and they're still beautiful."

—Alice Walker

51

EKFRID TOWNSHIP, ONTARIO, CANADA AND CALCUTTA, INDIA

ON A CHILLY day in 1917, when the cerulean sky stretched infinitely above them, Betsy Jane and James A. took delivery of information no wartime family ever wanted to receive. The telegram was delivered to the homestead at Carruthers Corners and also to Ellwyne's grandmother in Howrah, also listed as his next-of-kin. It read simply:

ID. No. 802423
Private Ellwyne Arthur Ballantyne
4th Battalion
Date of Casualty: 14-9-1917
"Killed in Action"

Deeply regret to inform you that, while on duty, this soldier was instantly killed by the explosion of an enemy shell.

Officer in Charge, Record Office.

James A. read the telegram first. His eyes scanned the message twice, before he dropped the paper from his fingers. It floated to the floor and landed at his feet.

In the wood-framed homestead, watching James A.'s eyes cloud over, Betsy Jane knew instantly that she didn't need to read it. Her mother's intuition already knew. She wailed and hugged her arms to her chest to keep it from imploding. She cried out,

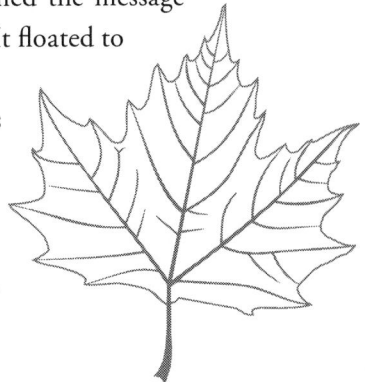

"No! Not Ellwyne!" in a pitiful yowl that echoed throughout Carruthers Corners. The tick-tock tick-tock of the gingerbread clock was the only sound in the room.

1. NO.	2. RANK OR RATING	3. SURNAME	4. CHRISTIAN NAMES
802423	Private	BALLANTYNE	Ellwyne Arthur

5. UNIT OR SHIP	6. DATE OF CASUALTY	7. H.Q. FILE No.	8. RELIGION
4th Battalion	14-9-17	649-B-20197	Not stated

9. CIRCUMSTANCES OF CASUALTY	10. NAME, RELATIONSHIP AND ADDRESS OF NEXT OF KIN
"Killed in Action" While on duty, this soldier was instantly killed by the explosion of an enemy shell.	

11. LOCATION OF UNIT AT TIME OF CASUALTY
Cite St. Laurent Sector.

Excerpt from Private Ellwyne Ballantyne's service records.

Time stopped for James A. and Betsy Jane.

In the corner woodlot, the humming of the buttonwood tree stopped momentarily, then changed frequencies and wailed in agonized harmony with Betsy Jane.

🍁

In a doorway halfway around the world, Bessie Smyth cried out with grief at the loss of her only grandson. "No! First my daughter, and now Ellwyne! Nooooooo!" She crumpled to the ground in a heap, sobbing and clutching at her chest as she tried to keep her heart from bursting through her rib cage.

🍁

No one had forecast it. The wind whipped through Ekfrid Township like an unexpected and unwelcome guest, toppling trees, ripping roofs from barns, and knocking over wagons. At the height of the storm, a lower branch of the buttonwood tree was torn from its elegant trunk. It crumpled at the base of the tree and its withering leaves soon began to shrivel and dry up as it died. It blew away, tumbling down the road and into a ditch.

The buttonwood's leaves fluttered in the wind, their rustling harmonizing like a symphony with those of all the trees surrounding it. As if hypnotized by the melody, the lone white-tailed doe wandered to the corner of the wooded property, approached the buttonwood tree, feeling back home, safe and where she belonged, and bedded herself beside the tree to wait out the storm.

She felt protected. The tree hummed.

After thirty minutes, the rain stopped, and the wind died down. The black clouds broke up and a beam of sunlight broke through them and shone on the doe's back. With the warmth of the sun radiating across her, the doe stood, stretched, and shook the dampness of the storm from her coat.

The buttonwood tree's lowest branch reached downwards as a final gust of wind blew through the woodlot.

Thump-thump. Thump-thump.

It began first as a subtle note. As the rhythm of the heartbeat reverberated through the corner woodlot, it picked up strength and continued to build as it repeated over and over again.

Hoooooooommmmmmmmmmmmeeeeeeeeeeeeeeeeee.

52

GUILDFORD, ENGLAND

HE DIDN'T SHOW up.

Rose kept repeating under her breath, "He'll be here any minute, you silly goose," as a way to soothe her frazzled nerves, but it didn't help. She was eager to see him again, and the thought of missing a chance to reconnect with Ellwyne left her torn up inside. The young lovers had planned another rendezvous in London for his leave, slated in late September. Rose had counted the days, crossing them off with an X on her wall calendar. When the anticipated date arrived, Rose waited by the lamp post for her handsome soldier to appear. She pictured his familiar saunter, the way he swung his arms when he walked. Her hand tingled as she remembered how he clasped it in his as they strolled the streets. She couldn't wait to hear him say her name. Having been brought up in both India and Canada, he had a peculiar mix of British and Canadian accents, and the way he pronounced "Rose" was unlike anything she had heard before. She had dressed in her favourite pale blue skirt, the colour Ellwyne had said made her green eyes sparkle. She had picked some purple heather from the field across the road from Tin Town and weaved it into her red hair.

As she stood waiting, Rose tapped her toe and hummed a few bars from her favourite hymn. It was already past noon; she could tell by the length of her shadow. He had promised to meet her there by eleven. As time passed, she grew impatient, and her heart sagged.

He didn't show up.

In her gut, Rose knew something was wrong. His polite manners had elevated him above the crowd

among the rude, unruly men at Tin Town. In a short period, although time seemed to be measured differently in wartime, Rose had learned that he was a man of his word. If he said he was going to meet her at a set time and place, he would be there if he possibly could. And if he didn't show up, something had gone wrong. But what? Was it a simple case of being delayed? The army constantly changed directions and plans for its soldiers, after all. Had his leave been rescheduled, and he hadn't yet been able to reach her? Or …. But she couldn't let her mind wander to the other possibilities. The thought of Ellwyne being injured and unable to let her know yanked at her heart. A tear streamed down her cheek as she pondered the other devastating possibility. "It couldn't be that, could it?" she whispered to herself.

The unspeakable 'other option' plagued her. After waiting for Ellwyne for two hours, Rose trudged home.

At her writing desk, she removed a single piece of writing paper and began to scribble a letter.

September 18, 1917
4th Battalion, CEF

Dear Commanding Officer:

My name is Rose Anderson and I am looking for information about the whereabouts of my boyfriend, Pte. Ellwyne Ballantyne (Serial number 802423). He was meant to return for leave on September 14th, but as far as I can tell, he did not return. As of now, I have not been able to reach him.

Can you kindly inform me of his status or how I may reach him?

Yours sincerely,
Miss Rose Anderson
Guildford, England

She folded the paper and placed it inside an envelope, uncertain that she wanted a reply. The war had created many uncertainties; not knowing the whereabouts of Ellwyne was one she hadn't wanted to deal with.

"Please come back to me," she said.

53

CARRUTHERS CORNERS, ONTARIO, CANADA

HER LIFE WAS now divided into two parts, with a clear line demarcating the middle: life before receiving the dreaded telegram, and everything that followed. The first part was life in colour with cerulean skies, harvest gold fields, and trees splotched with infinite hues of green. The second side was monochromatic, everything in dull shades of grey.

Betsy Jane's intense grief at the loss of Ellwyne, the dark-haired boy who had become a part of their clan, was dramatic. She didn't eat for days on end and became so thin that others gossiped and worried about her health. But life on the farm continued. Her new baby girl still needed nurturing, animals still needed feeding, crops still needed harvesting, and chores didn't get done on their own. So, she did the only thing that she could, the only thing she had ever done. She carried on. Tapping once again into her tough Scottish roots, she picked herself up and pushed through.

Betsy Jane had a secret she wasn't ready to share with anyone yet.

She knew she had to build her strength in the coming weeks.

She was expecting another baby.

And, although she celebrated that another life was about to enter the world, she was deeply mourning for the one that had just left it.

After finishing her morning chores, Betsy Jane decided she needed to clear her mind. With Archie and Elizabeth spending time with James A. while he visited Neil and Maggie Belle, she'd finally have some alone-time. She admitted to herself that she'd been in a fog. Nearly every minute of the day was occupied with thoughts of Ellwyne: things she didn't say but had wanted to, things she should have done but hadn't, and how much she missed his presence at the homestead. It was a slow-motion torture that played through her mind from dawn to dusk. Even sleep provided no escape. Sometimes she awoke from dreams so vivid that she needed to touch her sleeping husband's shoulder to ground her again. And she kept replaying in her mind the way they were informed of Ellwyne's death. When she closed her eyes, she envisioned the telegram and its devastating words. She often repeated them, sometimes saying the words aloud. "Deeply regret to inform you ..."

She closed the house door and narrowed her eyes against the brightness of the sun. Standing on her verandah, she scanned the horizon, taking notice of the expanse of mackerel sky. A ray of sunlight twinkled in the direction of the corner woodlot. It had been years since she'd walked through it; the last time she had taken time to visit it, she and James A. had planted hickory tree seeds the day after their wedding. "No time like the present," she thought as she strode down the laneway towards the trees.

As she walked, she noticed the birds twittering, their melodic conversations filling the morning air all around her. Having spent so much time with her beloved chickens and ducks, Betsy Jane had a natural affinity for birds, and she particularly enjoyed hearing songbirds. Turning her ear, she listened and recognized the trill of the cardinal.

Birdie birdie birdie, it called out.

Silence.

And then again. *Birdie birdie birdie.*

It was waiting for an answer. Betsy Jane breathed in and answered the songbird's call with her own whistle, imitating its joyful trill.

The cardinal responded with *Cheer cheeeeeeeer cheeeeeeeeeeeeeer.*

Message received.

Feeling her spirit lift, Betsy Jane smiled and started to hum a favourite hymn. It'd been far too long since she'd allowed herself to smile. She reached the edge of the corner woodlot and paused. Feeling a weight lifted off her shoulders, she stepped off the gravel road and scrambled through the ditch and into the stand of trees. The temperature changed as soon as she stood amidst the trees. The sounds around her changed. The fluttering of leaves in the breeze filtered around her. Instantly, her mind cleared, the way a storm cloud evaporates after it unloads its rain. *I've missed being around trees*, she told herself, recalling her beloved mulberry tree at her mother's old farm and reminding herself to check on it the next time she was gathering hickory nuts.

The sound cascaded from above and swirled around her.

As she stood still, breathing deeply the oxygen offered up by the trees surrounding her, the faint rhythm took hold.

Thump-thump. Thump-thump.

She shook her head, unsure that what she was hearing was real.

The beat rattled through her chest.

Thump-thump. Thump-thump.

It didn't let up. It seemed unmistakable now. She noticed that it was synchronized with her own gentle heartbeat. She turned her head. Standing twenty feet away, the doe eyed Betsy Jane, deciding whether to freeze or flee. Its ears flicked forward and back, assessing the potential danger of the intruder. Sometimes, the most trivial things decide whether you live or die, and the doe was weighing her options.

"You don't have to leave. I'm in your home, and I'm visiting. I won't hurt you. Please don't leave," she whispered.

The doe kept her gaze focused on Betsy Jane, ears continuing to flick back and forth, as she headed towards the white-and-grey-barked tree standing in the corner of the woodlot. When Betsy Jane's eyes locked on the unusual-looking tree, she felt instant weakness in her knees and a shock of electricity running up and down her spine. Compared with the other trees, this one looked as if it were cloaked in the magnificent robe of a queen. With the doe still standing near the tree, Betsy Jane took a few tentative steps and reached out to touch its bark. She wrapped both hands around the tree's trunk and felt a vibration jolt into her palms and then run up her arms and into her chest. She leaned in and embraced the tree, giving it a passionate hug and pressing her face into its mottled bark. The coolness of the bark warmed against her cheek.

"I never wanted you to leave," she sobbed.

A subtle hum vibrated through the corner woodlot, swelling up from the ground and fluttering through the leaves as it floated away with the wind.

54

CARRUTHERS CORNERS, ONTARIO, CANADA

HE WAS AN optimist. It took a lot to dampen the spirits of James A. Carruthers, but a telegram delivered to Carruthers Corners from across the Atlantic Ocean had managed to break him, at least temporarily. Although he had been working the farm without Ellwyne's help for many months, James A. had expected and hoped that he would somehow return, if not to his farm, then at least to Ekfrid Township. He had looked forward to welcoming Ellwyne back, telling him how much they had worried about him, and reassuring him that they had never stopped thinking about him.

Before he left for the war, Ellwyne identified James A. as the executor of his estate should anything happen to him. In November 1917, James A. received notification of a shipment from Europe. Dread and anticipation overwhelmed his thoughts. "What could it be?" he thought.

He hooked up trusty Old Grey to the democrat and drove to the post office in Glencoe to pick up the package. The empty seat beside him on the wagon was a constant and painful reminder that the man he had grown to see as his son was never coming home. He purposely moved to the left side and sat partially where Ellwyne would have sat, in a feeble attempt to get closer to him. It didn't help. The pain was pro- found.

After picking up the package, James A. turned around and headed back to the familiarity of Carruthers Corners. At least there, he wouldn't have to worry about running into someone and having to discuss the undiscussable or explain the inexplica-

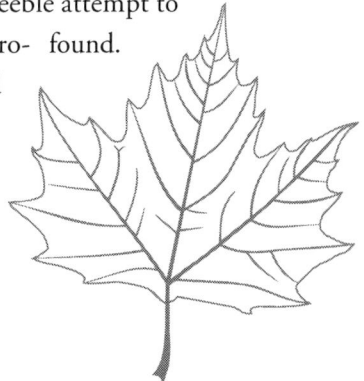

ble. He wanted to be left alone, to cocoon himself with his grief until he was ready to re-emerge.

With shaking hands, James A. cut into the box using his jack-knife. He slit it open and reached in to remove its contents. Ellwyne's final belongings from the battlefield were wrapped in brown paper, marked with dirt and smudges.

This is as close as I'm ever going to get to Ellwyne again. These items were the last things on earth that he touched.

A tear welled in his eye. He blinked it away and steeled himself to continue looking. He removed a series of handwritten letters, all still contained within their original envelopes, enclosed in a larger file folder. The letters represented all the correspondence that Ellwyne had received while he was overseas. Judging by the dirty fingerprints on the envelopes and the dog-eared nature of the letters, James A. could see that he had read and re-read them countless times. The final letter that Betsy Jane had written to him was unopened and stamped with "DEAD SOLDIERS OFFICE" in red capital letters. Ellwyne had never had a chance to read her last letter. A stinging sensation jabbed his heart. He noticed another brown unopened envelope addressed to Ellwyne, with handwriting that James A. didn't recognize. The return address was Guildford, England. Tears blurred his vision, and he wiped them away with the wrinkled cuff of his shirt.

We had so much more to tell you, Ellwyne, and you had more to tell us.

He next removed a tiny, clothbound book. Its cover was grimy from the mud of the trenches and had brown stains on it that he assumed was dried blood, Ellwyne's blood. The thought nauseated him but also made him feel a connection to Ellwyne. The corner of the book was crudely shorn off, as if it had been caught in the gears of a slow-cranking machine. James A. rubbed his finger across the roughened burr.

A jolt of pain seared through his chest and made him step back.

He dropped the book as if he'd been stung by a poisonous barb.

The sound of it hitting the floor snapped him back to the present.

You had so much more to tell us, Ellwyne. My boy. My dear boy. He sobbed before catching himself and sucking back the grief, deep into his chest.

He bent over and picked up Ellwyne's book and put it back into the shipping crate. He lifted the crate and carried it upstairs into the second bedroom. The clothes closet had a half-door that James A. had to crawl through to get into the cramped space above the first floor of the house. In the attic, he placed the crate in the farthest corner, behind a trunk that contained Betsy Jane's wedding attire and other keepsakes she was saving. Treasured memories. Another time, another day, he would tell Betsy Jane about it.

"It wasn't supposed to end this way," he said as he crawled back out through the half-door. He knocked his shoulder on the door frame, which sent a searing pain down his arm and into his fingertips. "Blazes!" he exclaimed as the pain continued to shoot through his shoulder.

55

CARRUTHERS CORNERS, ONTARIO, CANADA

THROUGHOUT HER THIRD pregnancy, Betsy Jane had constant visions of Ellwyne. Memories of him picking peas from the garden or walking behind the plough with James A. flashed in her head, usually at unexpected, and sometimes unwanted moments. When this happened, she had to breathe in sharply to regain her composure. As the baby grew larger inside her, it forced her to think more about the future, something she had been reluctant to do now that Ellwyne wasn't a part of it. It was too painful to think about a life without him in it, but she knew she had to. Mornings were most difficult, because it meant accepting for another day that Ellwyne was not going to return.

"I will never forget you, dear, sweet Ellwyne," she said to his portrait that morning as she passed it in the parlour. She walked to her comfortable rocking chair and took a seat, sighing. Her feet were swollen and sore, so she decided to rest for a while before starting her chores. She picked up her Bible and opened it to the book of Ruth.

And Ruth said, Intreat me not to leave thee, or to return from following after thee: for whither thou goest, I will go; and where thou lodgest, I will lodge: thy people shall be my people, and thy God my God:

Where thou diest, will I die, and there will I be buried: the Lord do so to me, and more also, if ought but death part thee and me. (Ruth 1:16-17, King James Version)

The morning sun was streaming through the window and warming her back as she read in her

rocking chair. A few years before, before Ellwyne had arrived in Ekfrid Township, Betsy Jane had convinced James A. that the wood-framed house needed to be rotated a quarter-turn so that her parlour could have better sun exposure. Farmers are problem-solvers, and soon James A. proposed a solution that involved lifting the house from its foundation, putting wooden rollers beneath it once it was lifted, and hooking up Old Grey to the rollers. The mare used her incredible might and power to turn the house to the preferred position, after which it was lowered and reset on a new foundation. The Carruthers clan participated in this exercise together during a work bee, and despite the skepticism about the project at the outset, everyone agreed afterwards that the house looked far better after it had been turned. And, as Betsy Jane had predicted, it gave the parlour more sunlight in the morning. Betsy Jane's tiny homestead, her nest, had followed the source of light, like a tree that grows towards the sun.

"Your people shall be my people," she repeated, then sighed. She looked up at Ellwyne's framed portrait and noticed that a glint from the morning sun was illuminating the right breast pocket of his tunic.

56

CARRUTHERS CORNERS, ONTARIO, CANADA

IT HAD BEEN a few weeks since James A. retrieved the crate from the post office in Glencoe, but it had occupied his mind since then. He needed to tell Betsy Jane about it. On a Friday, he mustered the strength after she had finished her morning chores.

"I was too upset to tell you at the time, but you should probably know now," said James A., his brows furrowed and eyes downcast.

Betsy Jane was seated in her rocking chair in the parlour. She waited, motionless, for him to elaborate. Elizabeth was seated on her knee, babbling as she sucked on her finger. "What is it?"

"We received a crate full of Ellwyne's belongings a few weeks ago. The army shipped them to us."

"Why did they come here?"

"Ellwyne put me down as his guardian, remember? Anyway, I looked through a few of the things, but I put them upstairs in the attic for safekeeping."

Archie was playing with homemade wooden blocks on the floor of the parlour. The little boy sensed the change in the air in the room, paused, and looked up at his mother.

"I'd like to see them." She clenched her jaw.

"Today?" he asked.

"Now."

Her hazel eyes penetrated him. He knew that look.

James A. climbed the creaking stairs to the second floor and walked into the bedroom. He crouched onto his hands and knees and crawled

through the closet's half-door to enter the attic. Streams of dust floated in the rays of sunlight that peeked through cracks in the wood siding. The crate was as he had left it. He dragged it across the bare floor, which made a scraping sound that resounded through the house.

"Here you go," he said as he placed the crate before the rocking chair, at Betsy Jane's feet.

"Can you please leave me alone? I think I need to do this alone."

Without saying a word, James A. picked up Elizabeth and took her to her cradle. The baby seemed to understand and sat in the corner, sucking on her thumb. "Give your mother a few moments, Elizabeth. She'll come back for you soon." He stuck his head into the parlour and said, "Come with me, Archie."

He took his son by the hand. As he closed the screen door, he heard the first sob.

🍁

After James A. left, Betsy Jane strode to the Hoosier cabinet and retrieved Ellwyne's gold signet ring from its box and slipped it on her finger. She returned to her chair in the parlour and stared at the wooden crate for minutes, unable to blink. On the one hand, she longed for the floor to swallow it up and bury it so she wouldn't have to deal with it. On the other hand, she was anxious to see what secrets it held. She touched it. A shock of electricity raced up her arm as if it were ignited by an unknown energy source.

"Blazes," she said to herself.

She opened the crate and inhaled, holding her breath as she looked at its contents. Books, papers, letters, envelopes, and file folders. A musty smell enveloped her; the odours of damp things released into the homestead. This humble crate held the final worldly possessions of Ellwyne Ballantyne. She picked up a stack of his letters and fanned through them. She recognized some of the names and addresses. She recognized her own writing. Letters from India, Canada, England, and Scotland. People from three continents had been writing to Ellwyne as he holed up in a muddy trench. It made sense—he had stepped on three continents himself.

"You touched so many people in your short time on this earth," she said. Her heart beat with both overwhelming sadness and pride. The feelings worked in opposition: as soon as she swelled with pride, the grief sucked it back in and squashed it. She saw her own opened letters and recalled the moments she had spent sitting at her oak dining table penning letters to her dear Ellwyne, trying to keep him updated on the happenings at Carruthers Corners, sending a morsel of common everyday life to him across the ocean. She noticed that the letters were smudged with the mud from the fields of France.

Unopened envelopes were stamped with bright red ink shouting out the angry words of Ellwyne's death. "DEAD SOLDIERS OFFICE" it blared, like a cruel reminder of the finality. Knowing that he hadn't had a chance to open them before he was killed, Betsy Jane wept. Recognizing again the incompleteness of his life sent fresh waves of grief flooding through her body. It was like an unfinished sentence. *How does it end?*

A brown envelope postmarked Guildford, England, caught her eye. She held it for a moment, then tore it open, taking care to preserve the return address.

Dearest Ellwyne

Your latest letter sent a flurry of emotion fluttering through my heart. Despite the miles that now separate us, I feel a closeness to you that I simply cannot explain. I think of you every waking moment, and when I close my eyes at night, you also appear in my dreams. You're with me with every beat of my heart. I long for the day when you will again meet me under the lamp post. I am waiting for you. I will always wait for you. I love you endlessly.

Your loving Rose
Portsmouth Road
Guildford, England

With warm tears streaming down her face, Betsy Jane stood from her chair and walked into the dining room. She wiped her eyes on her sleeve. She retrieved her stationery and pen, sat at the oak dining table, and collected her thoughts. *What do you say to someone whose heart will be forever shattered in a million pieces?*

In her trademark beautiful cursive, her thoughts streamed from her heart and onto the page.

October 29, 1917

Dear Miss Anderson

We have never met, but I feel compelled to write to you. I have determined that you are an important person to Ellwyne Ballantyne. I found your name and address among his possessions in an unopened letter. It causes me great pain to have to write this, but we received word in late September that Ellwyne was killed in action in Lens, France. I am so sorry to tell you this, but in case you haven't received word, I wanted you to know. Your letters were among the items we received from the army upon his death. Although we were not related to Ellwyne by blood, he became a family member after living with us on our farm in Ontario, Canada. We will forever mourn him and question the futility of his death. It does, however, bring me some solace knowing that he experienced love, and was loved, so deeply. I feel that he would have returned to you, had he been able to. I am so sorry for our shared loss of Ellwyne.

He was special to so many.

Sincerely yours,
Mrs. James A. Carruthers

For the remainder of the day, she couldn't get the thought of Rose out of her mind. Now she had two people dominating her thoughts. "Ellwyne, you were supposed to come back." She sensed heat from the signet ring on her finger.

57

CARRUTHERS CORNERS, ONTARIO, CANADA

TOWARDS THE END of her pregnancy, Betsy Jane had a stirring dream. She woke up, sweaty, her heart pounding, on a stormy January night. The rhythmic breathing of her husband's sound sleep filled the bedroom, making her feel trapped and uncomfortable. She was slender, but her now ballooning belly restricted her mobility. Knowing that she would not be able to fall back asleep, she rose to check on Elizabeth and then on Archie, who was sound asleep in his own bed in the room he once shared with Ellwyne. Clutching her abdomen, she treaded down the narrow staircase towards her parlour, pausing only to check out the window to see how deeply the snow was drifting into their yard.

She lowered herself into her rocking chair, wrapped herself in the patchwork quilt, and rocked to soothe herself. The dream that had awakened her was about Ellwyne. She had replayed his departure from Carruthers Corners over and over in her mind. The what-ifs sometimes tormented her. What if she had been firmer with him about her views on guns? Maybe he wouldn't have felt compelled to volunteer in a faraway battle that didn't really concern him. What if she had hung onto him and refused to let go? What if, what if.

What-ifs didn't solve anything; they simply caused her more anguish. As the baby kicked inside of her, she had a thought.

"I will always remember you, dear sweet Ellwyne," she thought to herself. "I know how I will carry you forward with me. Forever."

She patted her belly and felt a kick.

Life, like the changing seasons, always moves forward.

Later that morning, Betsy Jane felt the first strong contraction. Within hours, the contractions became stronger and more frequent. Instinctively, she knew the baby was coming quickly. After another smooth labour, four hours later, Betsy Jane was holding her new baby boy on her stomach as Maggie Belle brought in warm water and clean sheets and wiped the sweat off her sister's brow.

"Please tell my husband that he can come in now and meet his new son," said Betsy Jane. Maggie Belle quietly left the room to retrieve James A.

He peered around the opened bedroom door first before entering. He saw Betsy Jane cuddling their new baby and felt a warm glow engulfing his body. He was so proud of his wife, knowing how difficult it was for her to become pregnant, and because she had shown such strength during her deepest sorrow.

"Looks like he's going to be a good helper around the farm," chuckled James A. as the newborn gripped Betsy Jane's thumb. She smiled and looked up at her husband, noticing for the first time how grey his temples had become. Since Ellwyne's death, James A. had aged prematurely.

"Meet your son. This is William Carruthers." She paused. "William *Ellwyne* Carruthers," she whispered. A white beam of light flashed through her mind as she said the name aloud for the first time.

James A. felt a shot of warmth filling his body from head to toe. "It's perfect," he replied. Unlike their disagreement over Archie's middle name almost a decade before, this one was an obvious and fitting choice.

On January 6, 1918—the Christian Feast of the Epiphany—William Ellwyne Carruthers was born. On that same date, Betsy Jane's epiphany, her sudden flash of insight, started an astounding legacy of remembrance.

58

CARRUTHERS CORNERS, ONTARIO, CANADA

WHEN THE GREAT War ended on the eleventh hour of the eleventh day of the eleventh month in 1918, the world collectively breathed a sigh of relief and looked towards healing the gaping wounds left by the conflict. It had been four years of maiming, in body and mind. Four years of death leading to unspeakable grief that spilled out from the families who had lost so much. Four years of unimaginable cruelty and inhumanity. Four years of continual bad news. But after feeling so much sorrow, when the conflict ended, people no longer knew how, or what, to feel. Their lives had been consumed by the constant worry that accompanies armed conflict and chaos. The world had forever changed.

For many families, it had been years of waiting, hoping, and praying, but they could now rest knowing that their beloved soldier was going to return home. For other families, it marked the beginning of a lifetime of coping with dashed hopes and futures permanently altered. It had been a cataclysmic event.

The Glencoe boys who had signed up to serve in the Canadian Expeditionary Force began returning from Europe in early 1919, in dribbles, like a small leak in a large bucket. Moving thousands of troops across the ocean was no small logistical task, and it would take months to return everyone home. Hearing of other boys coming home to their families brought more waves of grief for Betsy Jane and James A. Recognizing the finality of it—that Ellwyne would never return—devastated them all over again.

One day, James A. walked into the parlour and found Betsy Jane seated in her rocking chair. She was staring ahead at the framed photo of Ellwyne, rocking in a slow, methodical rhythm.

"Did you know that a few of the local boys returned from Europe this week?" he asked her.

She shook her head. "No. Who else has come home now?" She continued to stare at the photograph. James A. was not sure she had heard him, but he continued anyway.

"Reg Lovell is back. He's asked if he could come see us sometime. What do you think?" Reg was a twenty-three-year-old man from Glencoe who had volunteered to serve around the same time that Ellwyne had enlisted. An eye injury he had received as a boy in England, however, had disqualified him from active duty, but he had still volunteered to go to Europe and served as a chaplain in the 135th and 4th Battalions of the Canadian Expeditionary Force. Part of his grim duty was gathering up the belongings of the casualties and packaging them for the Dead Soldiers Office so they could be shipped home to their loved ones.

"I suppose that'd be fine."

"He wants to come on Sunday after service. How about that?" He hesitated. "Shall I tell him to come? Are you ready to see someone?"

Betsy Jane lowered her head, wiped a tear from the corner of her eye, and nodded. "Yes, that'll be fine. Please tell him to come."

James A. exhaled. He knew that, however much Ellwyne's death had devastated them both, extended isolation wasn't good for the soul. Having someone visit might give Betsy Jane the pick-me-up she needed. He craved for the storm clouds to clear. He missed his bubbly Betsy Jane.

* * *

When Sunday arrived, Betsy Jane laid out her tea set and freshly baked tea biscuits in anticipation of the company. It had been quite some time since she'd had outsiders over to visit. During the war years, people retreated into their own cocoons to wait out the storm. She still had regular contact with Neil and Maggie Belle, of course, but neighbours from farther afield didn't stop by like they did before the war broke out. And since the news of Ellwyne's death, Betsy Jane hadn't felt much like visiting others. The knock at the door was preceded by Fanny's high-pitched barking.

"He's here, Betsy Jane," James A. said as he walked towards the side door to greet the visitor. The door swung open, and sunlight filtered into the dining room and spilled across the oak dining table.

"Mr. Carruthers, so nice to see you." Reg held out his hand, which James A. shook with enthusiasm. "There were days I never thought we'd see each other face-to-face again," he said. His Sunday suit was pressed, and Betsy Jane noticed that he had a row of colourful medal ribbons decorating his breast pocket. He appeared to have aged beyond his twenty-three years, with white hair appearing at his temples.

"We're so grateful that you're back," James A. said with a smile. "Thanks for coming, Reg. It means a lot to us that you'd want to come see us."

"Thanks for having me over." He turned to Betsy Jane. "Nice to see you again, Mrs. Carruthers," he said as he bowed his head towards her in reverence.

"Please, do come in." She pointed towards the table. "Make yourself at home." Betsy Jane felt tension all through her body. She didn't know what to expect from this visit. She could feel her chest tightening with anxiety as she took a seat too and turned her head to listen to Reg.

"You must have so many stories to tell," said James A. "And we have news to catch you up on, too. Although I'm sure things move a lot slower here than they do in Europe."

"Even though I wasn't gone for all that long, it feels like decades, to be honest. So much has changed." Reg patted his breast pocket, which he found himself doing more and more since he had returned to Canada. Knowing that the medals were there gave him proof that he wasn't losing his mind. The nightmares and flashbacks he experienced felt as real as the day they happened.

James A.'s voice broke through Reg's thoughts. "Before we get started, maybe we could take a moment and pray?" James A. reached out his hands and joined them with those of Betsy Jane and Reg around the table.

"I find myself giving thanks at every opportunity," said Reg. "Please lead us."

James A. closed his eyes and searched for the inspiration within to produce a meaningful prayer. "Almighty Lord, we thank you for giving us this chance today to spend with one another and for giving safe passage home to

Reginald. Blessed Lord, You commissioned Your disciples to continue the work which the Father sent You into the world to do. You supported with Your word and spirit those who ministered in the armed forces. We thank You for giving them the grace to preach the gospel boldly and for giving them courage in the perils of their calling, that they might glorify You before all people, through Jesus Christ, our Lord. Amen."

"Amen," said Reg and Betsy Jane in unison.

Betsy Jane passed the teapot to Reg, and he poured himself a steaming cup of tea, which he immediately wrapped his hands around, gripping it to steady himself.

"Sometimes, it doesn't seem real, that I'm back. Everything is the same, and yet it's all so different," said Reg. "Even the roads and the trees. Everything is ... different."

"Life doesn't move fast around here, but there are some changes," said James A. "The trees keep growing, even if we don't see it."

And with that, the mood in the room shifted, as if a window had been opened in the deep of winter. Reg tightened his grip on the teacup, afraid his tremoring hand might drop it. "I have something to share," he said in a lowered voice.

"Oh, and what is that?" James A. knitted his eyebrows in concern. He didn't know what to expect from someone returning from battle, and he felt the trepidation of walking on a not-yet fully frozen pond.

"This isn't easy for me," Reg said, choking up and lowering his head to his chest, eyes closed.

"Just take a breath." As if to demonstrate, James A. himself took in a deep breath and relaxed his shoulders.

Reg opened his eyes and continued. "I, uh ..."

"What is it?" James A. asked again, with a quieter voice.

"I ... was there when Ellwyne, uh ... died." He looked up at the couple as Betsy Jane gasped. The air left the room. The only audible noise was the tick-tock of the wall clock behind them. He didn't speak for several long seconds. "It was chaos, complete chaos." In his mind, Reg saw the blackened night sky punctuated by bursts of flares and explosions, and the sounds of machine-gun fire erupted around him.

James A. nodded and winced. "It must have been terrible for you."

Reg nodded. "Do you want to know the details, or shall I … spare you?"

Betsy Jane felt a chill run up her spine and the hair stood on her neck. Before James A. could answer, she spoke up. "Tell us. We need to know. Knowing might bring us some peace."

Reg's throat felt locked as it dried up. He felt his palms begin to sweat. He took a long sip of tea and cleared his throat. "We were losing so many boys. Night after night, the numbers were dwindling. There was so much gunfire and explosions. Ellwyne was doing the night-time lookout duty, like a sentry. While everyone else slept, someone had to stand guard to make sure we weren't attacked in the night. He never complained, just did his job. You know how he was."

James A. nodded. "Yeah, he was never one to complain, that's for sure."

Reg continued. "He was sitting at his post when he was hit by a sniper. He must have moved, maybe he dozed off. Something put him in the sights of that gun. I think it happened near dawn; there was a bit of light to guide us. We heard the shot. Two guys raced out with the stretcher to get him. As they were loading him up …" Reg stopped and took another long drink of tea, tears rolling down his face.

"Take another breath," said James A., reaching his hand across the table towards Reg. Betsy Jane was frozen in her seat, almost unable to move, dreading the next words, but knowing that she needed to hear them.

Reg continued. "As they were loading him onto the stretcher, the Germans launched a bomb at us and the blast killed all three of them. They never stood a chance. We lost all of them to that blast."

Betsy Jane let out a high-pitched sob, which made Reg gasp and hold back a sob too.

"No one suffered. I guarantee you that. It was over … quickly." In his mind, Reg knew there had been little recognizable left of the three men to retrieve, but he kept that detail to himself.

Tick-tock tick-tock. The clock continued to count the passage of time, even if it felt like it had stopped for Betsy Jane.

"We appreciate you telling us …." James A.'s voice trailed off. He imagined the scene, a muddy field where Ellwyne had taken his last gasp, and he felt a tear welling in his eye and trickling down his cheek.

"I wanted you to know. It must be so difficult not knowing details."

After several long seconds of silence, Betsy Jane finally spoke up. "It's better to know than to always wonder." She offered Reg her hand, which he clasped. She squeezed it tight. "Thank you for telling us the truth. We needed to hear it."

Reg's face, reddened with tears and anguish, relaxed with Betsy Jane's words. "We couldn't save them," he whispered.

"Thank you for telling us," she said. "It really does help."

"I am God's messenger. He sent me to tell you this news, but only if you were open to hearing it."

The three sat at the oak dining table in silence for several minutes. Betsy Jane processed the information that Reg had told them. She preferred not to think about the horrors that Ellwyne surely had witnessed in his time as a soldier. It was too painful to think of her sweet boy enduring such unimaginable hardship and pain. So, instead, she focused on the positive, what little she could muster up. Ellwyne had died while watching out for his friends. And when he needed them, his friends had, in turn, tried to save him. And now his friend had returned home to convey his final moments to them. The bonds of friendship had allowed all these moments to take place; the unbreakable bonds of friendship held her together.

"Come on, let's go to the parlour," she said as she stood and led the way into the next room. Once there, she took a seat at her pump organ. Touching the ivory keys, she knew which hymn she was going to play. "Abide With Me"[2] was the only hymn that seemed appropriate for this occasion. In the absence of a proper Christian funeral service for their beloved Ellwyne, this was the next best thing. After she began playing the chords, she sensed James A. approaching and standing behind her bench, and she heard Reg join in. Together, all three sang the chorus that flowed from her fingers and floated out of the organ.

> Abide with me, fast falls the eventide
> The darkness deepens, Lord with me abide.
> When other helpers fail and comforts flee,
> Help of the helpless, oh abide with me.
> Swift to its close ebbs out life's little day
> Earth's joys grow dim, its glories pass away.

2 A Christian hymn written by Henry Francis Lyte in 1847.

Change and decay in all around I see.
O thou who changest not, abide with me.
I fear no foe, with Thee at hand to bless
Ills have no weight, and tears no bitterness.
Where is death's sting?
Where, grave, thy victory?
I triumph still, if Thou abide with me.
Hold Thou Thy cross before my closing eyes
Shine through the gloom and point me to the skies.
Heaven's morning breaks, and earth's vain shadows flee.
In life, in death, o Lord, abide with me.
Abide with me, abide with me.

The music from the homestead drifted towards the corner woodlot.

Thump-thump.

Like the beating of a drum, it swelled up from the ground and drifted through the air. The rhythm from the corner woodlot flooded towards the homestead and encircled it, wrapping around the homestead the way a vine climbs a downspout and clings to it.

Thump-thump.

The beating heart, pushing the memories from the roots to its newest branches, feeding them the nourishment, soaked in love, that they needed to grow and survive.

59

THE CORNER WOODLOT, EKFRID TOWNSHIP, ONTARIO, CANADA

NATURE HAS AN infinite capacity for healing itself, and for renewal.

When branches break, new ones grow. In the death of one being, life is sustained for another. Following the vicious storm that took down its branch, the buttonwood tree began repairing itself. Tiny shoots, soon to become the start of a new branch, appeared in its place, and the buttonwood tree sent nourishment from the roots upwards.

Thump-thump, its heartbeat resounded.

In the spring, a bright red bird with black wings found its way to the wooded lot at Carruthers Corners and landed on a lower branch of the buttonwood tree. It surveyed its surroundings, flitting about from one tree branch to the next. It then landed on the ground, picked up a piece of dried, dead grass that was stuck under the snow for winter, and flew back to the buttonwood tree. This time, it selected a branch that was further out from the trunk. It placed the dried grass in the crook of two branches, flew to the ground, picked up a twig, and returned to the branch. It did this repeatedly, until a compact, cup-like nest made of grass, dried leaves, twigs, and weeds was perched in the crook of two buttonwood tree branches.

In spring, the cycle starts anew.

Healing.

Renewal.

60

CARRUTHERS CORNERS, ONTARIO, CANADA

IN THE LATE spring of 1933, it started as a slight abdominal ache, persistent but easy enough to ignore. Until it wasn't.

James A. was tending to his livestock for evening chores when he found himself doubled over and gripping his stomach as he gasped for air. Within a few moments, the pain lessened. He steadied himself on the stall door before continuing with his work, brushing it off as a bout of the flu. He didn't tell Betsy Jane about it because he didn't want to worry her unnecessarily.

A few weeks later, it happened again, this time while he was driving home from Glencoe after a visit to the post office. He had to pull over to the side of the road, get out, and walk around the car a few times before being able to continue. Betsy Jane noticed something was awry when he refused a piece of her burnt leather cake. The man, whose heart had been ruled by his stomach, was not known to refuse food, and particularly not a sugary delight like the burnt leather cake that had always been his favourite dessert.

"What's wrong? Why don't you want a piece of cake?" she asked him with a look of concern.

"I don't feel like it," he explained.

In the light of the dining room, she noticed that his complexion was a little pallid. "That doesn't sound like you. I've never known you to pass on dessert." Her brow furrowed deeper.

"I know. I've been feeling funny lately. I've had some sharp pains in my stomach."

"For how long? And why didn't you say something sooner?"

"I didn't want to worry you. I don't think it's anything to be concerned about." But in his mind, he was starting to get concerned. He didn't feel like himself.

"Well, if it keeps up, I want you to go see the doctor."

When he finally made an appointment to see the doctor in Glencoe, James A. couldn't keep any food down except a few morsels of bread and his morning tea. His sixty-two-year-old body had been in peak shape, but now his well-muscled frame was starting to wither from the lack of calories. Despite feeling poorly, he never neglected his responsibilities on the farm, so he continued to work as hard as ever, but with no energy to fuel his body. He found himself gasping for air when the pain struck, and he knew he had to get himself checked out.

After the exam, he couldn't help but ask the question before the answer was offered.

"Well, what do you think it is?" James A. asked. He was sitting on the cold metal examining table wearing a cloth gown, his muscled legs dangling over the side of the table. He wanted to hear that it was nothing and that he would be back to normal within a few weeks.

The doctor, who had known James A. for over twenty years, was scribbling notes on his pad. "I'm going to give you a prescription for the pain, but that doesn't solve the problem, it just addresses the symptom. I think we'll need to send you to London for some further tests," advised the doctor. "If I arrange something for tomorrow, can you make it?"

James A. had purchased his first motor car a few years earlier, which made trips to the larger city, London, possible. On the hour-long drive to the city, James A. couldn't decide if he'd rather know the answer or continue to live in an uninformed fog. Sometimes, it was best not knowing the truth. He kept a brave smile on his face, despite feeling scared and unsure about what he might learn. It was the first time in his life that he hadn't felt in control, and he didn't like it.

After a brief preliminary exam, the surgeon decided that he needed to open him up to see inside to diagnose the cause of James A.'s abdominal pain and unexplained weight loss.

When he awoke from the surgery, he received the news that he had been dreading.

"Unfortunately, I'm so sorry to have to tell you this, but we discovered a tumour. It's cancer," the doctor told him. "And we weren't able to remove it due to its advanced state."

"So, what does that mean?" he asked.

"It means that there's nothing more we can do to treat it. We can continue to keep you comfortable and make sure that you're not experiencing pain, but we aren't able to treat the cancer to extend your life. I'm so sorry."

The weight of that devastating news formed a pit in his stomach, and his face drained, becoming ghostly pale. "How much time do you think I have?"

"No one can say for sure. If I had to guess, we are looking at months, not years."

The pain twisted his insides further. Faced with his own mortality, James A. struggled to find the next words. "Hmmm. Not too long, then." His voice cracked.

His remaining days were now measured in the length of a growing season, the time it took for corn to sprout through the soil and reach towards the sky. He sensed that he wouldn't see the start of the next planting time. He was reminded of the Book of Ecclesiastes. In his head, he recalled the words from that scripture: "To everything, there is a season. A time to be born and a time to die. A time to plant and a time to harvest." The powerful words now seemed hollow.

"Again, I am so sorry to give you this news. I wish we could do more for you."

James A. wasn't certain how he was going to break the news to his beloved Betsy Jane.

He was released from the hospital a few days after the exploratory surgery that revealed his intestinal cancer. It took him a few days to recover from the surgery, but he was relieved to be back home. Archie, now twenty-five, assumed his father's duties and took care of the livestock and any other chores that needed tending to. He had partnered up with his uncle Neil to start the next season's crop of winter wheat.

Although he was devastated by his diagnosis, James A. didn't want anyone else to worry. Betsy Jane had already suffered so much loss in her life. Losing her husband was going to be one more hardship for her to face. He would try to soften it as much as he could. He knew his wife was strong, but even the strongest of backs had a breaking point, and he didn't know when, or if, she would reach hers.

"Good morning, my love. How did you sleep?" Betsy Jane had his morning breakfast on a tray, which consisted of dry toast and a cup of tea, a fraction of what he used to eat before he became sick.

"Like a rock. It's so good to be home," he said. "This is where I belong and where I always want to be. But I'm not telling you something you don't already know."

She smiled. "The house isn't the same without you in it. Say, how about we take a drive today? The fresh air might make you feel a bit better."

"That sounds wonderful. I am still trying to wash the smell of the big city from my nostrils, so I bet a drive in the country would be just what the doctor would recommend. Let's take a drive past Macksville to the general store, perhaps?"

Betsy Jane sensed how hard her husband was struggling to keep up his positive outlook on his situation. It was a trait she had long admired in him. He tried to see the bright side, no matter the circumstances. And these were dire circumstances indeed. Ever since he'd told her of his diagnosis of terminal cancer, her world dimmed a little more. After recovering from the initial shock, she had decided to be grateful for every single moment she shared with him. She was intent on making his final journey as comfortable as possible, and to walk it alongside him. She owed him that. They were partners, and he needed her now more than ever before.

Elizabeth knocked at the bedroom door. "Can I come in?" she asked. She was now a young woman of seventeen, with long brown hair. Since James A.'s diagnosis, Betsy Jane had noticed her daughter taking on more responsibilities around the farm every day, picking up where it was needed without being asked. She was proud of the woman she was becoming. Ever since she was a little girl, Elizabeth had demonstrated a caring nature towards her family and strangers alike, which Betsy Jane had encouraged.

"Of course, dear. Come on in. We're talking about maybe going for a drive in the country later. Your father thinks it'd help him wash the stink of London out of his nostrils."

"I was going to ask what you wanted me to prepare for dinner," she said.

"You're such a big help, Elizabeth. Use the spare meat from the swing shelf in the milkhouse." In the days before electricity, the farmers used basements and cellars to keep their food chilled. At the homestead, they kept their perishables in the milkhouse. A suspended shelf, attached by a chain to the ceiling, similar to a child's swing, kept vermin away from the most prized items like meat and cheese. And in the depths of the Great Depression, food had become something to guard with care. "We'll be back before noon, so let's plan on eating at the usual time. Thanks, dear."

James A., born in 1871, had spent his entire life in Ekfrid Township, working the land and forming a close bond with it. He knew he was going to die here. He clung to his strong faith in God and his belief in everlasting life. On a crisp fall day, weeks after being given the dire diagnosis, he sat at the breakfast table sipping his morning tea. At least it was something he could keep down. So many of his favourite foods were now unappetizing to him, and he took little joy from eating.

"Let's take a walk, Archie. Just you and me."

"Sure, Pa," said Archie, who was already preparing to head out to the barn to do the morning chores. James A. pulled on his work boots and a heavy jacket. With the significant weight loss, he felt the chill of the morning cold and dampness more than usual. The path to the barn was well-worn. James A. had walked it thousands of times and was certain that he could do it in complete darkness. He had done it in blinding snowstorms and other terrible weather conditions, but the short jaunt always gave him joy. They walked together, wordlessly, towards the barn and into the pasture that still had some green morsels of grass left for the cattle and horses to finish up before the first frost ended the growing season.

"Let's go see Billy," said James A. The massive Clydesdale workhorse had been a resident at the homestead since his birth. He was the last foal born to their trusted old mare, Old Grey. Now twenty-four years old, and showing a grizzled muzzle from advancing age, Billy was rarely asked to work and had been retired, a privilege granted to the horses that had worked alongside the farmers and given so much to keep the farm and its people going.

Billy was grazing alone in the far corner of the pasture, distinguished by his tell-tale rear white socks. James A. put his fingers in his mouth and whistled two sharp blows. The old horse looked up, hesitated, and began a slow, lumbering march towards the two men. His hocks were starting to lock up from arthritis, a sign of the years of hard work that the horse had performed for the Carruthers clan, pulling ploughs and wagons in the fields, but his gait became more fluid as he walked.

"He knows you're calling him for duty," said Archie. "That horse always did love you, Pa."

They stood in silence and waited for the horse to approach. After a few minutes, Billy stood in front of James A. and exhaled his warm breath into the older man's face. James A. breathed in deeply, and blew his own breath into the horse's nostrils in return, patting him on the forehead.

"Atta boy. You've been a good worker, Billy. Thank you for always doing your best for me." The horse lowered his head further and waited for more pats. James A. reached into his pocket and took out a glistening white sugar cube and offered it to the horse on a flattened hand. Billy's lips grazed his hand as he took the cube, crunched it, and sighed.

James A. patted him on the neck and turned to his son. "Archie, make sure that Billy lives out the rest of his life in peace. He's been a good friend to us. He's the hardest working horse I ever had. The only horse I ever had that didn't work well in a team because he tried to pull too hard." James A. chuckled at the memory of the unsuccessful attempts to get Billy a suitable workmate, all failures.

"That's saying something, because you've had a lot of horses over the years," said Archie.

"Yup. Sure have. Couldn't have done any of this without the horses. And when it's his time, please bury him over there," he said, pointing towards the corner woodlot. "That's where I'd want him to be. He belongs to this farm. Forever. Just like I do. Just like your mother does. We all belong to this land."

"Yes, Pa." Archie wiped away a tear from his eye.

As they walked back together to the house, Archie looked over his shoulder. The old horse stood watching them. Both Archie and Billy sensed that James A. had taken his final walk in the green fields of Ekfrid Township.

The walk in the pasture had exhausted him.

"I'm going to have to go lie down for a while," James A. said to Betsy Jane as he walked into the dining room, through the parlour, and into their bedroom.

Betsy Jane sighed, realizing that the short trek to the pasture with Archie had probably used up all her husband's energy for the day, and maybe the next one as well. It was difficult watching the man who had worked like a machine for over fifty years slowing down due to this terrible sickness that was eating away at his insides.

After she had finished cleaning up the dishes and fed her flock, Betsy Jane stood outside the bedroom and listened to her husband's rhythmic breathing. She crept into the room and eased herself to sit on the edge of the bed without disturbing its occupant. James A.'s eyes fluttered open, and he smiled when he saw his wife seated next to him.

"I shouldn't be sleeping the day away," he said in a gravelly voice. "I'm going to get fired from this job."

"You rest as long as you need to," she said, wiping his brow that was now covered in sweat. She took up his hand in hers and caressed it. The familiar calluses were starting to soften up now that he wasn't using his hands much.

"You know how much I love you, right?" he said, looking at his wife.

"Of course. And I, you."

James A. closed his eyes. Several seconds passed before he spoke again. "I think it's getting closer, Betsy Jane. Ellwyne was here. He came to see me."

"Oh?" Betsy Jane recalled hearing that the process of dying often involved "visits" from departed loved ones. She sensed the door starting to close on this chapter of their story.

"Yeah. He was standing right there." James A. pointed towards the corner of the bed. "He says he's waiting for me, and to hurry up because time's a-wastin'." James A. smiled, and closed his eyes again. His breathing slowed to a rhythmic pace, but Betsy Jane could hear a slight rattle in his lungs, the approaching sign of death swirled from within.

A tear spilled from Betsy Jane's eyelid and fell onto the bedspread. "We've been together through so much. We've learned a lot about each other. And here's what I know. Even after you leave, I know that we'll see each other again," she said.

"I know that, too," he said. "I believe."

A few days later, on a bitterly cold morning, James A. Carruthers, surrounded by his wife and three children, took his final breath, and departed.

The thumping sound from the corner woodlot, undetectable to most human ears, continued to beat. Although a winter's frost had set in, to all things there was a season. The buttonwood tree, humming a melody of grief, prepared for the eventuality of spring and new beginnings.

61

THE CORNER WOODLOT, EKFRID TOWNSHIP, ONTARIO, CANADA

TRAILS OF DUST, like a swirling tail, followed the vehicles as they drove on the gravel roads, giving drivers an advantage to spot approaching cars. The faster the car travelled, the larger the plume of dust that followed. After checking both ways and making sure it was all clear, the driver of the pickup truck turned the corner.

"Look, that's Ellwyne's tree!" proclaimed Valetta as they cruised past the corner wood lot at Carruthers Corners. It was 1950, and Valetta was in her late forties. She wore her long, straight hair, once blond but now a chestnut colour, wrapped in a loose knot at the top of her head. Makeup covered any signs of wrinkles that might have started to appear. She pointed towards a lone silver-barked tree with large, broad leaves facing the road, surrounded by the more common maples, oaks, basswoods, and hickory trees. After moving to Toronto with the Ballantynes when she was a child, Ellwyne's half-sister had returned to Ekfrid Township as a young woman and had spent some time living with Betsy Jane and James A. at their Carruthers Corners homestead. In her early twenties, she married a handsome farmer from the area and settled down permanently in Ekfrid Township, retaining her close connection to the Carruthers clan that had so lovingly raised her half-brother so many years ago.

Valetta's husband, William McFarlane, stopped the truck and rolled down the window to take a closer look. He had to admit that it was a stunning specimen.

"What do you mean, it's Ellwyne's tree?" he asked curiously. William, of course, knew about the tragic and senseless loss of Valetta's half-brother in the Great War decades ago, but he had never heard about the tree or Ellwyne's connection to it.

"Years ago, Ellwyne and James A. Carruthers were clearing fields together and they came across that tree when it was a bit taller than they were," Valetta explained, feeling transported back to a time that caused her great pain. "Ellwyne liked it. He felt a connection to it and wanted it to live. They decided to leave it be," she explained. A tear welled in her eye and streaked down her cheek at the memory of a beloved brother lost so long ago. "He even wrote to Betsy Jane and me while he was in France and asked us to check up on the tree."

"Is that so?"

"Yes. Can you imagine? Of all the things that he missed about home, he also missed his tree."

William let out a long sigh and nodded his head knowingly as he eyed the tree from top to bottom.

As the years passed, the tree shot upwards, taller and stronger, and the memory of "Ellwyne's tree" and how it had come to be known as his filtered through the Carruthers clan families.

The tree hummed with appreciation.

62

APPIN ROAD, EKFRID TOWNSHIP, ONTARIO, CANADA, 1952

HER LONG HAIR, once chestnut brown, was now a snowy white, but still pulled into a tight knot and fastened at the nape of her neck. Betsy Jane held her head high and her shoulders back, but her advancing age, now seventy, and the effects of time were starting to stoop her posture, so that she wasn't nearly as tall as in her younger days. Life's most important job, mothering, still came effortlessly to her. She had taken care of children her entire life, which now stretched into its seventh decade. As she sat at the front window of her parlour waiting for her elder son, Archie, to drop off his son James, her grandchild, for a much-anticipated weekend visit, Betsy Jane nodded to herself. It was time. He was old enough.

A few minutes later, the light blue car pulled into the grassy laneway and stopped at the verandah. The back doors popped open and six-year-old James C., whom everyone called "JC" for short, jumped out of the backseat and leapt onto the grass, barely stopping himself from toppling over before redirecting himself towards the chicken coop. Archie, now a grey-haired man in his early forties, still had the happy eyes of his youth and an easy smile. *He was such a beautiful baby*, Betsy Jane recalled as she watched her son amble to the side door. When James A. died of cancer two decades before, Archie had stepped up and assumed the duties of farmer on the homestead, seamlessly picking up where his father had left off. He and Betsy Jane had worked together

to keep the farm going, and Betsy Jane had only relocated to a smaller house nearby after Archie married.

"Ma? We're here!" he yelled.

"In the parlour, dear," she answered back, smoothing out her long house dress.

"There you are," he said with a huge grin.

A blur of energy blew past Archie and bounded towards Betsy Jane. She braced herself for the impact.

"Hi, Grandma! When do we feed the chickens?" JC already had grass stains on his knees and a smudge of dirt on his rosy cheeks.

"You know the routine, JC. We feed them after supper. Now, go get your grip and take it upstairs to the bedroom."

"Yes, Grandma." The little boy sprang up and let the screen door slam shut behind him as he raced towards the car to get his overnight bag.

"I'll be back for him on Sunday after service, if you can handle him that long," said Archie.

"Don't you worry about that. We always have fun together." Betsy Jane enjoyed having someone else in the house with her to fill up the empty spaces.

"Well, I sometimes worry about you being here all alone, Ma." Betsy Jane's smaller, wood-framed house was on Appin Road, not far from the homestead on the 16th Sideroad. Though other homes in the area were installing electricity and indoor plumbing, Betsy Jane had resisted those modern upgrades and continued to hand-pump her own water, heat her house with a woodstove, and use coal oil lamps for lighting. She had also shunned the idea of purchasing a car and getting a driver's licence, instead continuing to rely on a horse and buggy to get her where she needed to go. She had allowed herself two luxuries. The first was a white cast-iron claw-foot bathtub. She still had to draw her own water for her weekly baths, but she got to enjoy them in her own deep soaking tub. The second was her telephone. To get service installed at her house, she had to purchase shares in the local municipal phone company, but she did so and was one of the first homes in the area to have telephone service.

"Now, Archie. You know where I come from. I was raised by the people who cleared these fields and turned them from wild forests into farms. It's been twenty years since your father died. I think I can manage but thank you for your concern."

An older widow living in a house alone caused worry, though Archie and his wife Verna lived only a few miles away at the old homestead. "Okay, but I worry."

"No need to worry, dear. I've got my telephone and if there's ever any trouble, I know who to call."

"Okay, Ma."

"While you're here, would you mind tightening up the latch on the gate to the paddock? It's jiggling."

"Sure. Give me a sec to get my toolbox from the car." When he was done, he headed back into the house. "All done," he said with a smile.

"Thanks, dear. You're so helpful." The endless list of farm chores never stopped, but Archie, even from a tender age, had always known intuitively which ones to do without being told. "Say, do you remember when your father and his brothers turned the house so that I could get better daylight?"

"I do," he said. "That sure was a long time ago."

His mother laughed. "And when people would visit us, the first thing you'd say was 'Old Grey turned the house!' at the top of your lungs. Not 'hello' or 'welcome,' but 'Old Grey turned the house!' And then everyone would laugh."

Archie chuckled. "I wanted to let people know that we used real horsepower, Ma."

"She was a good mare, wasn't she?" Betsy Jane felt herself moving back in time.

"The best. Say, do you remember her colt, Billy?"

"The big bay Clyde horse?"

"Yeah. The one that didn't work well in a team because he pulled too hard."

"I remember Billy. He was your father's favourite horse."

"Really?"

"He thought the world of that horse. Maybe it's because Billy, like your dad, worked so hard."

"Maybe so, but I think there was another reason, too."

"Oh, and what's that?" Betsy Jane was curious about Archie's impressions of that time.

"Well, I think it's because of his name. Do you know who named him Billy?" Archie's eyes moved towards the portrait hanging on her parlour wall. It had been a fixture for as long as he could recall.

Betsy Jane sighed. She had forgotten that James A. had offered the honour of naming Old Grey's colt to Ellwyne. "He always did love the farm, didn't he?"

And at that moment, Archie was unsure whether his mother was referring to James A. or to Ellwyne. It applied to both men. He hugged his mother. Since he was a young boy, he had longed for his mother's hugs.

After supper, Betsy Jane placed a few of the scraps from the canned fish dinner that she and her grandson had shared into the slop pail in the kitchen.

"Are you ready to feed the chickens, JC? It's time."

The little boy bounded into the kitchen, grabbed the slop pail, and disappeared. *A hard worker who doesn't need to be asked twice, just like Archie and Ellwyne*, she reflected.

At nightfall, as the sun disappeared below the horizon, Betsy Jane lit an oil lamp and set it on the oak dining table.

"It'll soon be time for bed, James. Let's go wash up and get ready."

"Grandma?"

"Yes, dear?"

"Tell me again about the man on the wall."

Betsy Jane sighed. The burled oak framed portrait of Ellwyne Ballantyne was prominently displayed on the northern wall of her parlour, in front of her rocking chair. It was a centrepiece of the room that she looked at every morning as she came down from the bedroom and every night before she retired to bed. Even though it had been over thirty-five years since he'd left Carruthers Corners and never returned, she had never stopped thinking about him or wondering what might have been.

"You want to hear about Ellwyne Ballantyne?" she said, a tear glistening in the corner of her eye. She understood that JC's questions were a stalling tactic before bedtime, but she was happy to oblige her grandson with a story.

"Who was he again?"

"He was a beloved friend of the Carruthers clan."

"A friend?" asked JC.

"Actually, more like a son to me than a friend."

"Where is he now?" Her grandson's questions came rapid-fire, but Betsy Jane appreciated his curiosity.

"He's in heaven with his mother and father and with your grandfather." Betsy Jane blinked the tears from her eyes. "Enough questions for now, dear."

"Well, when I grow up, I want to be like him," said JC. Although Betsy Jane did not often speak about Ellwyne anymore, his presence remained in her home, in the framed portrait but also in casual comments and comparisons she made to Ellwyne. The "just like Ellwyne would have done" or "that sounds like something Ellwyne would have said," were not lost on her grandson. He knew that the man in the photograph was revered, and he wanted that same light in his grandmother's eyes cast upon him.

She stood up and walked across the dining room with the lamp in her hand, radiating warm light in her path as she strode. The little boy, not wanting to be left alone in the dark, fell into step behind her and followed as she led him up the dark, narrow staircase to the bedroom. He climbed into the bed and settled under the colourful hand-quilted cover that Betsy Jane and Maggie Belle had stitched at a Carruthers Corners quilting bee some forty years before, using scraps of throwaway material.

"Can you tell me a story?"

"A new one or an old one?"

"A new one, please."

"Okay. A new one it is." Betsy Jane sat on the edge of the bed and rubbed JC's back in large, comforting circles. She was stalling while thinking about a new story to share. She closed her eyes, and the familiar handsome face came into focus in her mind's eye. The dark hair, brown eyes, and the eyebrows arched, as if about to ask an important question. She knew in a flash which story to tell.

She cleared her throat and started speaking, in her seasoned storytelling voice.

A beautiful young doe was out looking for food and water near the river. Feeling thirsty, she decided to take a drink. As she bowed her head to the rippling water, she heard whimpering and crying. She turned her head and looked around but didn't see anything. She continued to suck up the cool water, but the crying sound continued.

"Will you help me?" a voice finally asked.

"Who are you?" the doe said.

"I'm a fawn."

"Where are you?"

"I'm hiding in this bush."

The doe walked towards the bush and saw a set of large brown eyes staring at her.

"What are you doing in the bush?"

"My mother hid me here while she left to find us some food. She told me to wait here until she returned."

"Then you should do that," said the doe and turned to walk away.

"But she's been gone for days," said the fawn.

"She will be back. If she said she'll be back, she will return."

The next day, the doe returned to the same spot at the river to take another drink of the cool water. She heard whimpering and crying again.

"Will you help me?" the voice asked again.

"Little fawn, is that you?"

"Yes, I'm still here."

"Did your mother come back?"

"No, not yet."

"She will. Wait there for her."

"But I'm quite hungry and thirsty."

"Stay there until she comes for you. If she said she'll be back, she'll return."

At nightfall, the doe was settling for a sleep beside a tall tree. She had closed her eyes when she heard dogs barking and howling in the distance. She heard two loud bangs, and the dogs stopped howling. She heard laughter. And she heard the voices of men. She trembled as she closed her eyes and tried to sleep, but she couldn't stop thinking about the fawn she had met. When it was daylight, she wandered to where she had heard the commotion the night before. She saw the hoofprints of a deer, the pawprints of dogs, and the footprints of men.

Turning like a top, the doe raced back to the river. Her white tail waved like a flag as she dashed over logs and fences.

Breathless, she arrived at the river where she had taken a drink two days before.

"Are you still here?" she asked.

"Yes. I'm still here."

"Good boy."

"Did you find my momma?"

"I did. She sent me for you. She told me that you should come with me."

"But she told me to wait here until she returned," he replied.

"I know she did, but now it's important that you come with me."

"I'm not sure if I should. You said I should wait for her."

"And you did, like a good boy. But now your mother has sent me to take care of you."

The doe reached into the bush and nudged the fawn. He finally stood and joined her at the river's edge. His legs were wobbly and unsteady. "Take a drink first, and then we'll go find some grass and leaves to eat."

So the doe led the fawn to the riverbank, and then they went to eat some leaves and grass. They ate and ate and ate until they were both full. And they spent the summer wandering the fields and bushes together until the fawn was old enough to head out on his own. And when he finally did, he said, "Thank you for helping me."

JC sat up and tapped his grandmother on the arm. "I have a question," he said.

"What is it, dear?" she asked.

"What about the fawn's mother? What happened to her?"

"She wasn't able to return," Betsy Jane explained.

"Why not?"

"Sometimes bad things happen in this world. But that's why a different mother stepped in to help."

"Really? That happens?" he asked with incredulity, his eyes widened.

"I've seen it for myself. Countless times." She tucked the quilt up around JC's ears. "Have a wonderful sleep, dear. Dream about does and fawns." She picked up the coal oil lamp and left the room.

In the morning, Betsy Jane was already making breakfast when JC awoke and padded down the stairs.

"Guess what?" he asked his grandmother.

"I can't guess. What is it?"

"I dreamed about deer, like you said I would. Maybe we can go looking for some today?"

"Not today. I have something else I want to show you. Eat up and we'll get started."

After JC finished his breakfast and they washed the dishes in the basin, Betsy Jane took his small hand in hers and sat him on the chair at the oak dining table.

"You know the photograph on the wall in my parlour of the man that you're constantly asking questions about?"

JC nodded enthusiastically. "The man on the wall."

"Today, we're going to go look at some of his things. You can learn all about him and ask me questions. Come on, let's go up to the attic. It's going to be a special day."

"The attic?" JC asked with a bit of apprehension.

"The very one. Let's go up and see what's in there."

"What if there are ghosts in there?"

"So what if there are?"

"Then I'll be scared." He covered his eyes with his hands.

"Not all ghosts are bad, you know." She offered him her weathered hand and together they climbed the narrow staircase to the second floor. Once in the attic, she led JC over to the trunk containing Ellwyne's belongings. The old steamer trunk was covered in a thick layer of dust, its leather straps wrinkled and worn from decades of enduring the extremes of the attic. "This is a sacred spot to me, James. The things in this trunk are special to me. I'm going to show them to you because I think you're old enough now to start learning about them. Plus, I want you to know the stories so that you can someday tell them to others."

"You want me to tell stories?" he asked with widened eyes.

"Yes. But they're not made-up stories. They're real stories. They're the stories about what happened to me, to your grandfather, to your father, and to Ellwyne Ballantyne. Do you think you're ready to learn?"

"Yes, Grandma," he said, his eyes wide with anticipation. "I wanna hear the stories."

"Okay, then." She opened the lid of the trunk, reached in, and pulled out a carved wooden boat and rubbed her hands across it. It was smooth to the touch. She lifted it to her lips and kissed it.

"What's that?"

"It used to be a piece of firewood that was headed for the woodstove. It would have burned and been tossed away in the ash pile, long ago forgotten. But that man in the photo on my wall, Ellwyne? He was just a boy, but he looked at a piece of firewood and he saw something else. He saw that this gnarled old piece of wood that was destined to be thrown away and burned had potential. He saw that it could be something else, something beautiful. He knew that if he gave it some time and attention, he could make it into a thing that people would look at and admire." She held it out for JC to look at. His eyes followed her hands with magnetic attention.

"Can I touch it?"

She nodded and handed it to him. "Handle it carefully. It's special."

"I'll be careful with it." The little boy's hands caressed the wood.

"The same thing can happen with people, you know. There are people on this earth who no one expects much from, but then someone else comes along and sees potential in them that no one else can see. And with a bit of time and attention, they can turn out to be pretty special."

JC's focus shifted from the carved boat to his grandmother. "I really want it. Grandma … can I keep it?"

She reached over and took back the boat from his hands, and shook her head. "Special things aren't meant to be owned, James. God shows them to us, and we get to take care of them for a little while. And with special things like this, we have to put them back in the trunk so we always know where they are and that they're safe." And with that, she placed the wooden boat into the trunk and caressed it before taking out the burlap bag inscribed with the initials E.A.B.

After a few hours of storytelling, Betsy Jane decided that they had covered enough ground for the afternoon. "Well, JC, you've been a terrific listener, but I think we've done enough for one day. It's time to get ready for supper and then we have to go feed the chickens." She gave her grandson a pat on his shoulder, turned her head away and sniffled.

"Grandma, what's wrong? Are you crying?" he asked with concern and reached out to touch her long skirt.

She paused and dabbed her nose with her handkerchief. "I am. But it's only because I'm pleased that you're interested in these things, JC. It brings me great comfort to know that you're curious about Ellwyne and that he won't be forgotten. You see," she paused while she blinked through the teardrop now blurring her vision, "he was very special to me and your grandfather."

The little boy extended his arms and waited for a hug. He loved his grandmother's hugs. She wrapped her arms around him and squeezed.

63

AIX-NOULETTE, FRANCE, SEPTEMBER 14, 1960

THE TRIP WAS decades in the making. She had dreamt of taking it since she was a little girl and had first heard the name "Ellwyne Ballantyne." She was fulfilling a promise to her mother. Clutching the cemetery map, she searched for his plot among the hundreds of white limestone markers.

"Can you help me?" she asked the guide, who was standing nearby.

"How may I assist?"

"I'm looking for plot I.R.6, and I don't know where to begin." She had tried to research the cemetery layout before the trip but met many roadblocks in her quest for information.

"You're almost right in front of it." He pointed to the next row. "This is Row I, count six markers in, that should be the one you're searching for."

Her long legs carried her a few steps to the white cross, indistinguishable from the hundreds of others. "I can't believe I'm this close to you," she said loud enough for the guide to overhear.

He strode over and knelt beside her. "He's not actually buried here, miss."

She gasped.

He placed a hand on her shoulder to show his support. "During the fury and chaos of the battles, the armies buried their dead either where they fell, or in mass graves behind the trench lines. These cemeteries contain the grave markers and the soldier's dog tag, but most of the bodies themselves remain buried in the battlefields throughout Europe."

"Oh," she gasped. "I didn't realize."

"I know. I'm sorry to share that. It was a brutal war, gruesome really." He rose to his feet and left her alone to sort through her muddled thoughts.

8-0-2-4-2-3. She ran her fingers over the white limestone once more, feeling each carved numeral and committing them to memory. The limestone was rough to her touch, sharp edges catching her fingers as they moved across the cool surface. Her dark hair cascaded over her shoulders and hid her face from the view of others as she knelt at the headstone and read the inscription aloud:

802423
PRIVATE E. BALLANTYNE
4TH BATTALION CANADIAN INFANTRY
14TH SEPTEMBER 1917 AGE 21

Her eyes lowered. At the base, where brilliant red poppies sprouted, she read the verse, which she recognized from the Book of John:

GREATER LOVE HATH NO MAN THAN THIS, THAT A MAN LAY DOWN HIS LIFE FOR HIS FRIENDS

"We thank you for your service and sacrifice, Private Ballantyne," she said. She removed a single red rose petal from her pocket and placed it at the base of the headstone, anchoring it with a grey pebble she had picked up on the pathway. "I promised to give you this, Ellwyne. A love note from my mother, Rose, your one true love. She has never forgotten you. She said she wanted to die herself after receiving the terrible news that you'd been killed, but she had to go on anyway. I know all about you, too. I heard the story about how you

The grave marker of Private Ellwyne Ballantyne in Aix-Noulette, France.

stepped in to protect Rose at a pub when a group of rowdy soldiers was getting out of hand. And how you walked my mom and my great-grand-mum home to make sure they made it safely. She showed me your lamp post, and how you two shared your first kiss underneath its yellow light. You made quite an impression on my mother, Ellwyne. All my life, I've heard your name. I only wish I could have met you in person."

The mourning dove's wail broke the silence. The cemetery was serene, though it was alive with the motion of many people from her group exploring the rows upon rows of white crosses, each representing a life lost in a long-ago conflict. The cheeriness of the bright green grass belied the horrors and pain the muddy ground had long ago swallowed up. Fluffy clouds obscured the sun, bringing a cool breeze that made her plunge her hands into her sweater pockets for warmth. Unexpectedly, a chill travelled down her neck. She turned her head as she heard the thunderous sound of pounding hooves coming from beyond the distant hill. The clouds broke open again and a brilliant ray of sunshine warmed her back, evaporating the chill from the late summer air.

She stood and returned to the tour bus. Once seated, she peered out the window, straining to see any sign of the horses she'd heard.

She saw nothing.

"Did you hear horses? Galloping horses?" she asked the tour guide, a younger man named Evan who wore a blue suit coat and carried a clipboard that he kept referring to throughout the trip.

He shook his head. "Ahhh, so you're one of them."

"What do you mean, I'm one of them?"

"You're one of the people who hears galloping horses. You're not the first to say that you've heard them in this cemetery. I've never heard them myself, though."

"That's odd. It sounded like they were so close," she said, giving her head a slight shake as if to test her hearing.

"Millions of horses died in the Great War," Evan explained. "Even after the fighting stopped, the horses continued to suffer. Up to their knees in mud, pulling heavy loads, worked to death. The stronger ones, even they didn't fare so well. After the war ended, many of the surviving horses were slaughtered to feed starving people."

"Slaughtered?"

"Yup. Not much of a payback for their loyal service, huh?"

She shook her head. "Not at all."

He continued. "Locals believe that some of the war horses still roam these green fields to this day. Maybe that's what you heard?"

"Maybe." She let out an audible sigh. "Just maybe." She lifted her hand to her chest and felt the beating of her heart.

64

APPIN ROAD, EKFRID TOWNSHIP, ONTARIO, CANADA, 1966

BETSY JANE HAD grown tired. The world, it seemed, kept speeding up, but she herself was slowing down as her age crept up. In her almost eighty-four years, she had witnessed so much change: houses with electricity and indoor plumbing, news and entertainment delivered by the radio and now television, and automobiles that had replaced horses. She had also survived the world's most crippling economic downturn, the Great Depression, which was sandwiched between two bloody world wars. Yet, despite the signs of progress all around her, most parts of her life remained as they always had. She kept the rhythm of tending her dwindling flock at the start of each day and closed out each evening by reading the Bible. Her favourite passages were from the Book of Psalms; she had relied on them to survive the darkest days of her life. This simple routine was what she craved—living a quiet life in a modest home, buoyed by her faith in God.

With her beloved book on her lap, she reached over to tune her radio to the gospel station and awaited the broadcast of Sunday service. She was no longer strong enough to attend in-person services at the church in nearby Appin, though her son Archie had offered to stop by and pick her up. She missed worshipping at the church, but she couldn't command the energy to propel herself to and from town. Even minor tasks, the kind she had done with ease all her life, were becoming arduous. Life took too much out of her. Her hands, with painful joints gnarled by arthritis, fumbled through

the pages of her book as she followed the readings. She listened dutifully to the minister's words and sang along with the hymns.

After the service concluded, she hoisted herself out of the rocker, making an audible groan as she lifted her body to a standing position and hobbled towards the kitchen. Her dinner, which she ate in the late afternoon to accommodate her early bedtime, consisted of canned herring mixed with tomato sauce and spread on crusty white bread, cut thick just the way she liked it. She dumped the scraps from her fish dinner into the slop pail for the next morning's feeding. *The chickens will be fighting over that*, she thought. For the last few weeks, she had found it increasingly difficult to make her way up the narrow staircase to bed. Her joints ached, and she was becoming unsteady on her feet. *Tonight*, she thought, *I'll sleep in the rocker*.

She made her way back to her favourite chair and burrowed beneath the colourful hand-made quilt she and Maggie Belle had created from leftover scrap material so long ago. She sighed, wriggling herself into a position that partially eased the throbbing pain in her lower back. Looking at the portrait directly in front of her, she noticed that the bubble glass held a fine layer of dust, but she could still make out the CEF tunic and cap. *My dear Ellwyne*, she thought. She turned and looked at her framed wedding portrait, which hung beside it. How fancy her hair had been that day. And her handsome husband. His brilliant eyes were his most striking feature, she thought. Surrounding herself with the love and memories of the two men so long ago lost, Betsy Jane closed her eyes one last time. *Thank you, dear God, for one more day. Your mercy endureth forever*, she thought as she drifted into sleep.

The door of the homestead creaked as it closed. Betsy Jane had finished baking one of her sourdough loaves that was now cooling on the counter. The aroma of bread wafted from the kitchen into the dining room. "Don't forget to take the sandwiches I made with you!" she yelled.

James A. stuck his head into the kitchen, his brilliant eyes twinkling with mischief. He scooped up the basket containing the roast beef sandwiches wrapped in paper. "How could I forget your sandwiches?" His appetite for her nutritious meals was stoked by the hard work from toiling in the fields. "Hey, you got any cake left?" he asked. "A piece of that sugar cake finishes it off so perfect." He licked his lips for dramatic effect.

Betsy Jane had intended to share the cake with Maggie Belle when she visited later in the afternoon for their quilting project. She tsked, as she removed the pan from the pantry shelf and cut her husband a healthy slice of the crumbly cake, wrapped it in a cloth, and tossed it into his basket. "There you go. Eat it up then. You and Ellwyne enjoy it."

James A.'s smile widened. He turned away and headed towards the door. As he stepped onto the verandah, he shouted at the slight figure headed towards the barn. "Ellwyne! Wait up."

Ellwyne turned to face James A. and lowered his straw hat over his eyes to shield them from the rising sun taking its place in the eastern sky. "What's up?"

"You won't believe it, but I panhandled and got us some cake!"

Betsy Jane, who was watching from the screen door, snickered at her husband's antics and snapped the tea towel against the door. He had always been crazy for her cooking, ever since she had wowed him at the Glencoe Fair with her jar of cabbage beet relish. "Be back by supper. It'll be waiting here for you both."

James A. caught up with Ellwyne and handed him the basket containing their lunches, a commodity more valuable than gold. He wrapped his arm around the boy's shoulder, gave him a squeeze, and the two disappeared from her sight as they entered the barn. *There go two pieces of my heart*, she thought. She returned to the kitchen and began cleaning up.

She didn't hear it at first, but soon the faint hum enveloped her; she paused from her chores and stood still to identify its source.

Thump-thump. Thump-thump.

She tried to ignore it, but the sound increased in volume, making Betsy Jane shake her head with disbelief.

🍁

Archie was worried.

Wrinkles formed on his brow as he considered the possibilities. He phoned his mother once a day to check on her, and even though she protested his protectiveness and concern, he knew that she enjoyed their ritual. That Monday, however, she hadn't answered his call. He let it ring twelve times before hanging up. When he tried again half an hour later, he received the same result. "I'm going to check on Mom," he said to his wife as he grabbed the car keys and his coat and headed to the door. "She didn't answer the phone this morning."

"She has slowed down in recent weeks," A look of concern washed over Verna's face. But Archie was already out the door and headed to his car.

The drive took only five minutes, but Archie couldn't get there fast enough. *Please let her be all right*, he said to himself. He turned onto the grassy laneway and threw his car into park and shut off the ignition. Bounding onto the porch, he rapped on the door. "Ma? You in there?"

Only silence answered him. He removed the key from his pocket and turned it in the lock. "Ma, are you here? It's me, Archie." He saw the remains of last evening's supper still in the slop pail, a hint of fish smell still lingering in the kitchen. Oh no. He knew that Betsy Jane would never neglect her flock. Archie entered the parlour, which was dark with the curtains drawn. Only the portrait of Ellwyne Ballantyne greeted him. "Ma?" he said more quietly. He was startled when he saw his mother in her rocker, wrapped in the colourful quilt.

"Ma?" he said again. He gazed at his mother's shrunken figure. Betsy Jane's eyes were closed as if she were asleep, but her chest was not rising. Her long, white hair cascaded over her shoulders. "Are you okay, Ma?" he whispered. Archie reached out and touched her pale cheek, which was stone cold.

"Oh, Ma," he gasped. His shoulders began to shake as he held back the torrent of sobs building up in him.

Thump-thump. Thump-thump.

On that chilly Monday morning in April, when the final frost of the season painted the blades of grass a glistening white, Betsy Jane had gone home.

PART 5

REGROWTH
2012–PRESENT

Trees

I think that I shall never see
A poem lovely as a tree.
A tree whose hungry mouth is prest
Against the earth's sweet flowing breast;
A tree that looks at God all day,
And lifts her leafy arms to pray;
A tree that may in Summer wear
A nest of robins in her hair;
Upon whose bosom snow has lain;
Who intimately lives with rain.
Poems are made by fools like me,
But only God can make a tree.

65

THE CORNER WOODLOT, EKFRID TOWNSHIP, ONTARIO, CANADA, NOVEMBER, 2012

Full circle

THE GROUP HAD been rapt while listening to the tale of the boy and his tree.

"And that's why we still talk about Ellwyne." JC had just spent the last hour spinning the complex story about Ellwyne Ballantyne, told to him by his grandmother Betsy Jane, detailing his arrival at Carruthers Corners, working first as a farm hand, and then becoming a beloved son. The shimmering trunk of the buttonwood tree, with its unusual white and grey bark, was now adorned with a glorious piece of hardware, centred like a buckle on a belt. Visible from the roadside, it alerted all who passed that the tree belonged to Ellwyne. It read simply:

> In memory of
> ELLWYNE BALLANTYNE
> LENS, FRANCE 1917
> BUTTONWOOD

"Thanks for the story, JC. I'd heard pieces of it, but it's sure nice to get the whole thing." The white-haired man reached out to grasp the shoulder of his adult son, who was cradling his own four-year-old

boy in his arms. "I'm glad we did this today." The grandfather, son, and grandson made up one branch of the Carruthers clan family tree known as "the Ellwyne branch."

"Me too, Dad. It's up to us to carry this forward."

"Your great grandparents, Betsy Jane and James A., wanted us to remember," he replied. "That's why they named your grandfather William Ellwyne. It's why he and Mother named me Ronald Ellwyne. It's why your mother and I gave you the middle name Ellwyne. And I'm so proud that you've carried on that tradition with your own son." The proud grandfather clasped the chubby hand of his grandson. "Isn't that right, Quinn?" The little boy squeezed his grandfather's hand and giggled.

"I'll send you copies of our group photograph once I receive it from the photographer," JC told his white-haired older cousin.

"Thanks for organizing this event, JC. It's important for us clan members to get together as often as we can."

"I agree. And now we've identified this buttonwood as Ellwyne's tree. We've always known it was his, but now everyone else can see it as they pass by." JC sighed. "It's long overdue."

Ellwyne's buttonwood tree in 2024,
still standing on the corner woodlot in Carruthers Corners.

Like a buttonwood tree passing its seeds to grow and start anew, the Carruthers clan continued to honour Ellwyne Ballantyne by including his name as the middle name of one son from each succeeding generation.

Locals say that if you stand quietly at the base of the magnificent buttonwood tree, growing where it should not have been able to take root, and listen with a loving heart and an open mind, you can faintly detect a distant humming sound, singing the melody of love, faith, and remembrance.

Members of the Carruthers clan gather in front of Ellwyne's tree in 2012 to remember him and dedicate the tree to his memory.

66

MIDDLEBIE HEIGHTS FARM, MIDDLESEX COUNTY, ONTARIO, CANADA, 2020

Lest we forget

WHEN HE RETURNED to the wood-framed farmhouse from his wood shop, he noticed the flashing red light on the answering machine that indicated a message waiting. He pressed the button and listened to the unfamiliar voice on the recording:

Beep

"Hello there, this is a message for Mr. James Carruthers. You have no idea who I am, but I got your name and phone number from your cousin in Glencoe. I've been trying to track down some details that you might be able to help me with. Harold said that you might have information about a World War One soldier named Ellwyne Ballantyne that has some sort of connection to your family? I'm looking to learn more about Ellwyne, and possibly write a short story about him and the memorial plaque on that unusual tree out on McArthur Road. I first read about this story a few years back in the Glencoe newspaper article about a dedication at the tree. I was wondering if you might be willing to speak to me and tell me what you know about Ellwyne Ballantyne? I'm leaving my number if you'd like to call me back. I hope to hear from you. Have a wonderful day."

Beeeeeeeeeeeeeeeeeep

JC arched his eyebrows and cocked his head to one side. *That's interesting*, he thought. A random phone call out of the blue was unusual, but it was about a subject that had fascinated him his entire life. Since he was a young boy, he had admired the sepia-tone photograph of the uniformed man on his grandmother's parlour wall. His curiosity had been stoked further when his grandmother had finally begun to teach him about the man by showing him his belongings that she safely stowed in her attic. Now seventy-four, JC had spent decades researching Ellwyne Ballantyne, cataloguing the photographs of him, and labelling and preserving Ellwyne's artifacts that he had received from his father and grandmother. "Very interesting indeed," he said aloud with a nod.

Later, he took a stroll through his farm and paused to further think about the mysterious phone message as he looked over his pond. Frogs croaked their evening symphony as he stood and let his eyes wander across the Southwestern Ontario landscape. He felt a deep connection to the land, an appreciation passed on by his father and grandmother. He had lived on his farm, Middlebie Heights, since the 1970s and had planted an arboretum of native trees and designed a magnificent garden as fine as any open to the public.

"I wonder what that person really wants? Should I call her back?" Thoughts tumbled through his head, memories fading in and out of focus. He thought about his grandmother and how she had so carefully guarded Ellwyne's memory and kept it alive through the next generation. He recalled the wood-framed homestead with the gingerbread trim where he and his father, Archie, had both been raised. And he remembered the framed portrait of the man on his grandmother's parlour wall and how his life had been cut short by the Great War.

As he pondered what to do, a large green leaf, broader than it was long, floated from the branch above his head, twirling as it fell, and landed at his feet. The buttonwood tree that he had planted on his property, close to the pond to give it an ample water source, shivered in the breeze and relaxed.

Thump-thump. Thump-thump.

"I think I'll call her back," he said. "Some stories are best when shared."

THE END

AFTERWORD

The buttonwood tree is one of the largest hardwood trees that grows in eastern North America, reaching heights of 150 feet and with trunk diameters of seven to eight feet. They can live between 450 and 600 years. Buttonwoods are easily identified by their leaves, which are broader than they are long, and their distinctive bark, which is strikingly mottled and sheds frequently in large, thin pieces during periods of growth. New tree growth has white bark, which shimmers and is iridescent in moonlight, giving buttonwood trees the moniker "the ghost of the forest."

The buttonwood tree, visible by its white bark, surrounded by its neighbour trees in the corner woodlot at Carruthers Corners.

Scientists studying plant bioacoustics have discovered that trees emit vibration sounds, and that the frequency varies based on whether the tree is experiencing optimal growing conditions or is under stress (such as occurs during a drought). In this manner, trees can (and do) communicate with one another and, as some believe, with us. Trees also have a pulse, indicating a type of heartbeat crudely similar to a human's, and pump water through a system from the roots to the branches and leaves.

This work of historical fiction is based on Ellwyne's life; most characters and circumstances are real, but some characters (such as "Rose Anderson") are entirely fictitious or composites, and details have been embellished where information was either unclear or lacking altogether. Ellwyne's story was shared through oral storytelling, handwritten letters, newspaper articles, genealogical documents, cemetery headstones, artifacts, and photographs that were carefully preserved and passed on from one generation to the next.

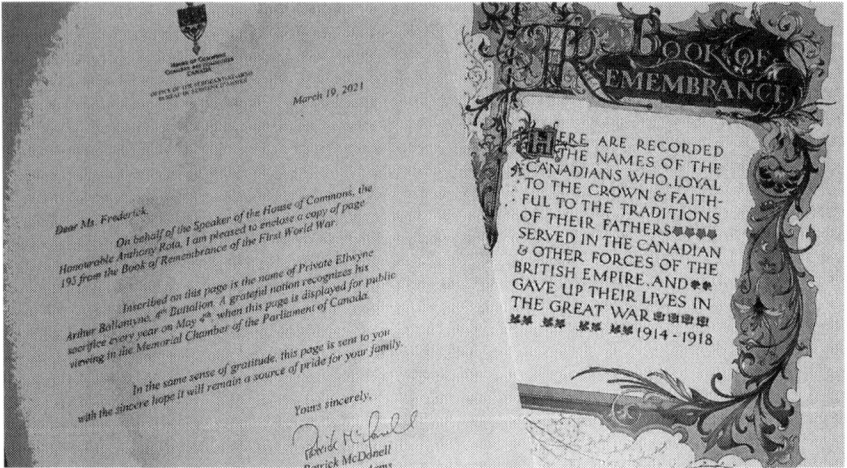

Letter from Sergeant-At-Arms enclosed with the
Book of Remembrance page for Ellwyne Ballantyne.

Ellwyne Ballantyne was born Ellwyne Arthur Dacosta before being given the surname of his stepfather following his mother's remarriage. The Portuguese surname "Dacosta" means "by the riverbank" or "on the slope of the river," like the buttonwood tree that grows best when close to a river. Ellwyne Ballantyne died in action near Lens, France, on September 14, 1917, two weeks before his twenty-second birthday. At the Remembrance Day ceremony in Glencoe, Ontario, each November 11th, his name is the first read from the roll

representing local citizens who gave their lives in World War I. A memorial banner with his photograph is displayed outside the Reg Lovell Branch of the Royal Canadian Legion in Glencoe each fall. His name is also included in Canada's Book of Remembrance for the First World War, housed in the Peace Tower on Ottawa's Parliament Hill. Each day at 11 o'clock, the pages of these sacred books are turned by a member of the House of Commons staff. Ellwyne Ballantyne's name is printed on page 195 and is displayed in the Memorial Chamber every year on the fourth of May.

William Ellwyne Carruthers (known to many as simply Bill or "W.E.") was the last child born to Betsy Jane and James A. Carruthers. William lived his entire life in Ekfrid Township, Ontario, where he raised prize-winning black Aberdeen Angus beef cattle and played fastball, after being encouraged to follow his passion by his mother, Betsy Jane. He died in 2007 at age 89. William's son, grandson, and great grandson all share the middle name Ellwyne and were present at the base of the buttonwood tree when the clan dedicated the tree to Ellwyne Ballantyne's memory in 2012.

William's older brother, Archie A. Carruthers, also became a farmer, prize-winning breeder of poultry, and a beekeeper after being encouraged to follow his passion by his mother; he died in 2003 at age 93. Archie's son, James C. ("JC") Carruthers, provided the factual details for this story and has been fascinated by the legacy of Ellwyne Ballantyne since first seeing the portrait on his grandmother's wall and hearing the stories about him as told by Betsy Jane. He lives on a farm southeast of London, Ontario, where he has planted several buttonwood saplings that he found growing along the Thames River. They now tower more than one hundred feet and serve as reminders to him of his roots. His son, Christopher Carruthers, was the first clan descendant to visit Ellwyne Ballantyne's gravesite in Aix-Noulette, France in 2005.

Elizabeth Mae Carruthers, middle child to James A. and Betsy Jane, married William May. Her mother encouraged her to follow her passion for helping others. She became a noted nurse in the Glencoe area, known for her community-mindedness. She died in 2002 at age 86. Her son, James May, was also told the stories about Ellwyne Ballantyne by his grandmother, Betsy Jane; he was the second Carruthers clan ancestor to travel to Aix-Noulette to visit the grave. In 2012, James May and his wife, Jane, sponsored a memorial banner for Ellwyne Arthur Ballantyne that is displayed on the streets of Glencoe, Ontario, each November, along with banners of other soldiers. Ellwyne's banner hangs from a lamp post near McRae Street, close to Branch 219 of the Royal Canadian Legion, the Reg Lovell branch.

Valetta Ballantyne McFarlane, Ellwyne's half-sister, returned to Ekfrid Township from Toronto, Ontario, in her late teens and joined the nest of Betsy Jane and James A. Carruthers at the homestead, just as her half-brother had, before marrying a farmer from Ekfrid

The memorial banner for Ellwyne Ballantyne that hangs on the streets of Glencoe, Ontario every year in preparation for Remembrance Day services.

Township. She claimed that she learned her remarkable baking skills under the watchful eye and caring hands of Betsy Jane. Valetta died in 2001 at age 99.

Duff Ballantyne never owned another company. He and Donalda Elliott Ballantyne moved from Carruthers Corners to Toronto, Ontario, and lived there for the rest of their lives. Duff died in 1968 at age 93, and Donalda in 1970, also at age 93. As he was not listed as next-of-kin in Ellwyne's enlistment papers, it's unclear how (or when) Duff Ballantyne found out about his step-son's death during the Great War in 1917.

James A.'s favourite horse, Billy, named so by Ellwyne Ballantyne, was the hardest-working draft horse that he ever knew. Billy pulled with enough force to break the leather harness and needed a special metal bit to control his power. That bit, now rusted and age-worn, is still a part of the Carruthers clan artifacts and is stowed safely in an attic.

Although he lost his best farmhand, James A. Carruthers continued to farm and lived the rest of his life on his homestead in Ekfrid Township.

James A. died at age 63, at the height of the Great Depression in 1934, from bowel cancer. Despite the lack of treatment options available at the time and the pain he endured as the disease progressed, people say that he never lost his optimistic outlook and sunny disposition.

Betsy Jane Carruthers lived the remainder of her life alone in a wood-framed house with an attic where she stored her most treasured artifacts, including a trunk filled with handwritten letters, war medals, photographs, wood carvings of boats, a gold signet ring, a New Testament, and other mementoes belonging to Ellwyne Arthur Ballantyne. She often hosted her grandchildren for visits, including overnight sleepovers (complete with bed-time stories), during which she led them up the narrow stairway lit only by flickering lamp light. She invited them into the attic with her to explore the special items contained in the trunk so that they, too, could learn about the man whose military portrait hung prominently on her wall. In a 1950s photograph, she is pictured with all her grandchildren gathered around her rocking chair in her parlour, and the oval-shaped portrait of Ellwyne Ballantyne is proudly displayed on the wall behind her. Although not officially a family member by blood, Ellwyne Ballantyne was considered family by the Carruthers clan. Betsy Jane never stopped mourning the loss of her adopted son. She died in her sleep from complications of old age in 1966, at age 84.

James A. and Betsy Jane Carruthers are interred, side by side, in Eddie Cemetery near Appin, Ontario, in Southwest Middlesex Township (formerly known as Ekfrid), a few miles away from their former homestead on McArthur Road and the corner woodlot where a stunning and remarkable 125-year-old buttonwood tree still stands.

Family crests and coats of arms are powerful symbols passed down through generations that put people in touch with "who they are." The Carruthers clan family crest contains a seraph with three sets of wings and the motto *Promptus et Fidelis* (meaning "prompt and faithful" in Latin). In Christianity, seraphim are the highest order of angels, sent to earth to do God's good work.

Sometimes the most ordinary people among us on earth do the most extraordinary things.

AUTHOR'S NOTES

Stories ripple all around us, if only we're willing to hear them. In 2012, I first learned of Ellwyne Ballantyne and the astonishing relationship he forged with two strangers after reading a short newspaper article about the dedication of an unusual tree to a long-dead soldier from World War One. With obligations to work and family filling my time, I wasn't yet ready, or able, to hear his story. It took a global pandemic, with the prospect of lockdowns and unexpected forced time at home, for me to open my ears, mind, and heart and be ready to explore the roots of Ellwyne's story that took place more than a century before.

I grew up in the 1980s in a wood-framed farmhouse built by Scottish settlers, situated on a dead-end road that terminates near the winding Sydenham River. In 2000, this road was renamed from a numbered concession, a holdover from the time of British colonization to Buttonwood Drive. The name reflects the stand of buttonwood trees gathered at the river's edge, where they most comfortably grow.

I attended school in the nearby community of Glencoe. My high school English teacher, Mr. Donald Johnson, a farmer turned teacher, drilled into us the significance of Remembrance Day. His message about respect for veterans from both world wars hit close to home for me. I had learned about the Great War from artifacts and tales relayed to me about my grandfather, who had volunteered at age eighteen and served overseas in Belgium, France, and Germany with the 162nd Battalion of the Canadian Expeditionary Force. Given this deeply personal connection, I have had a natural and intense curiosity about World War One and what it must have been like to live through such a cataclysmic global event.

In 2020, I began reflecting on the fallen soldier and his extraordinary buttonwood tree that grows near my childhood home. My curiosity eventually led me to the doors of Carruthers clan descendants, where I begged to have a conversation about Ellwyne and his connection to the tree. Thinking it might have the makings of a short story, I began putting together the pieces of Ellwyne Ballantyne's brief life. But, with each photograph, letter, and artifact shared, I became more engrossed in the tale of an orphan who had stepped foot on three continents and was taken in by strangers who came to love him as their own. At the outset, I did not anticipate that it would bloom into a novel, but as I learned more details about the characters and events, I believed that each nugget was fascinating and intriguing. I hope that Ellwyne's story and his connection with the Carruthers clan touches people with its message of love, faith, and remembrance. It's only through storytelling that those who carry memories, and decide to share them, make history come to life.

In listening, we let storytellers plant roots.

Through sharing them, we remember.

Lest we forget.

The cenotaph in Glencoe, Ontario where Remembrance Day ceremonies are held every November 11th.

PHOTO CREDITS

Thank to all who shared their photographs for this story.

Photo of the Carruthers Corners sign © 2021 Butch Frederick. Used with permission.

Multiple archival photos of Ellwyne Ballantyne, Betsy Jane, James A., and Archie Carruthers provided courtesy of the Carruthers family photo albums. Used with permission.

Photo of the 135th Battalion pennant © 2020 Mike Reintjes. Used with permission.

Postcard image of Glencoe's Main Street, courtesy of the Glencoe & District Historical Society.

Image of Ellwyne Ballantyne's circumstances of death register courtesy of the Canadian Virtual War Memorial – Veterans Affairs Canada. Source: Library and Archives Canada. CIRCUMSTANCES OF DEATH REGISTERS, FIRST WORLD WAR Surnames: Babb to Barjarow. Microform Sequence 5; Volume Number 31829_B016715. Reference RG150, 1992-93/314, 149. Page 761 of 1072.

Image of the Book of Remembrance page (page 195) courtesy of Veterans Affairs Canada.

Photo of Book of Remembrance page and letter from Sergeant at Arms © 2021 C.J. Frederick. Used with permission.

Photo of Ellwyne Ballantyne's grave marker in France © 2021 Kurt de Tavernier. Used with permission.

Photo of the memorial plaque on the buttonwood tree © 2024 Kristi White. Used with permission.

Photo of the buttonwood tree © 2024 Kristi White. Used with permission.

Photo of Ellwyne Ballantyne's banner displayed on Main Street in Glencoe © 2020 Patrick Bianchi. Used with permission.

GLOSSARY

This glossary defines some of the unique words, phrases, and places used in this story.

Books of Remembrance	Canada honours its war dead with eight separate Books of Remembrance, containing more than 120,000 names of Canadians who have given their lives in service of the country. These books are kept in the Peace Tower on Parliament Hill. Ellwyne Ballantyne's name, on page 195, is displayed in the Memorial Chamber every year on the fourth of May.
buttonwood	Also known as the American sycamore, one of the tallest deciduous trees that grows in eastern North America. Named for its early use in making wooden buttons for clothing and shoes. Buttonwoods are also sometimes called buttonballs. This species of tree is most often referred to as a buttonwood in southwestern Ontario.
Calcutta	Calcutta is the anglicized version of Kolkata, the capital city of the Indian state of Bengal.
Canadian Expeditionary Force	Also referred to as the CEF, the designation of the field force created by Canada for service overseas in the First World War.
Carolinian Forest	A biologically diverse life zone in eastern North America characterized by its broad-leaf deciduous trees.
Carruthers	A Scottish clan and surname originating in Dumfriesshire, Scotland. Its original pronunciation was kridders.
Carruthers Corners, Ontario	An intersection of two roads in the former Ekfrid Township in Middlesex County, Ontario, Canada, where four Carruthers brothers and their father owned five farms. Christopher (Kersty) purchased the initial one of three farms in 1867 and helped his sons buy their own farms close by. Although no Carruthers families live at the intersection in present day, it is still known by that moniker.

Colonel Thomas Talbot (1771–1853)	An Irish-born Canadian colonial administrator who served under John Graves Simcoe. Colonel Talbot was responsible for settling the Thames River area in Ontario (Upper Canada) by offering land grants to settlers.
democrat	A light farm wagon with two or more seats that is drawn by horses.
Ekfrid Township, Ontario	A township in Southwestern Ontario, Canada, established in 1820. It merged with its southern neighbouring township, Mosa Township, in 2001 to form the amalgamated Township of Southwest Middlesex.
Gaelic	A Celtic language native to the Gaels of Scotland. In 2018, Scottish Gaelic was identified as one of the world's endangered languages, at risk of disappearing.
Glencoe, Ontario	A tiny hamlet in Ekfrid Township, Ontario, Canada. Named after a settlement in Scotland.
grip	An overnight bag, similar to a duffle bag.
homestead	A wood-framed farmhouse, usually one built on a grant of land.
Hooghly River	The 260 km eastern distributary of the Ganges River in West Bengal, India. Ellwyne Dacosta (later Ballantyne) was born near its banks.
jack-knife	A small foldable pocketknife, often carried in one's pocket or on one's belt.
Kersty	A Scottish nickname for the masculine first name Christopher.
Mosa Township	A township in Southwestern Ontario, Canada, known for its rolling hills and heavy, clay soil. Established in 1821, it merged with its neighbouring township, Ekfrid Township, in 2001 to form the amalgamated Township of Southwest Middlesex.

Niagara-on-the-Lake	A picturesque town in southern Ontario, Canada, that sits on the shores of Lake Ontario, at the mouth of the Niagara River. In the early twentieth century, it served as a military training base camp for members of the Canadian Expeditionary Force.
No man's land	The narrow, muddy, treeless stretch of land, characterized by numerous shell holes and barbed wire, that separated German and Allied Powers trenches during the First World War.
puttees	Strips of cloth, worn wrapped around the lower leg in a spiral pattern, from the ankle up to below the knee. Puttees provided ankle support to World War One soldiers and prevented debris and water from entering the boots or pants.
reel	A social folk dance popular in Irish and Scottish communities.
Remembrance Day	Originally called Armistice Day, a memorial day observed in the British Commonwealth to honour those who have died in the line of duty. It is held on November 11th and began observance after the First World War.
RMS Olympic	A British ocean liner of the White Star line. Although originally a passenger ship, it was dedicated as a troopship in 1915 to transport Canadian and American troops from North America to England.
stook	A group of sheaves of grain stood on end in a field. Pronounced "stew-ck."
Sydenham River	A 165 km river that flows from its source near London, Ontario, and empties into Lake Saint Clair near Sarnia, Ontario. It is the only river located entirely within the Carolinian Forest bio-diverse area. Carruthers Corners and the homestead where Ellwyne Ballantyne lived are located within several miles of the Sydenham River.
trench foot	A painful and serious ailment that results from the foot being immersed in cold water for extended periods. In WWI, many soldiers developed trench foot from having wet feet with no change of clean socks or boots to help keep their feet dry.

whiz bang	A nickname for WWI German artillery shells that landed without much warning, causing much devastation and casualties among the allied forces.
Wolseley Barracks	Established in the 1880s, in London, Ontario, this base is part of the Canadian Forces Base establishment. Also referred to as Wolseley Hall.

FAMILY TREES

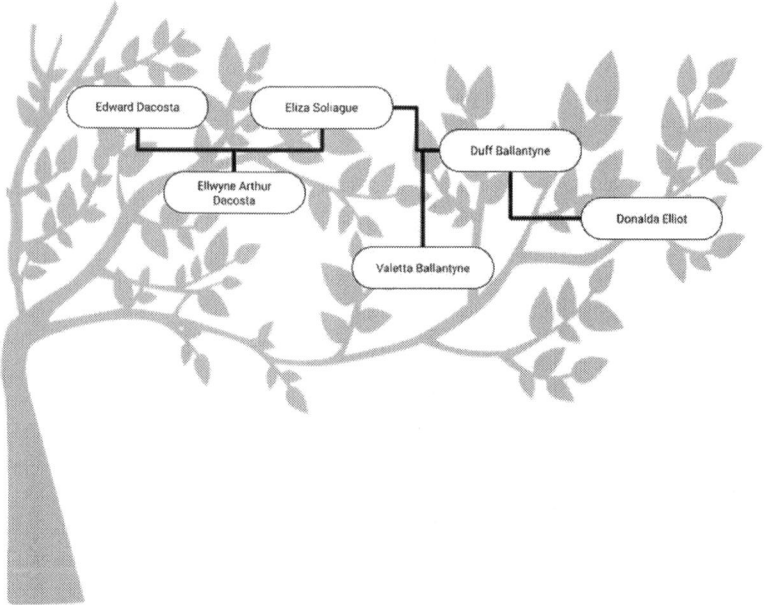

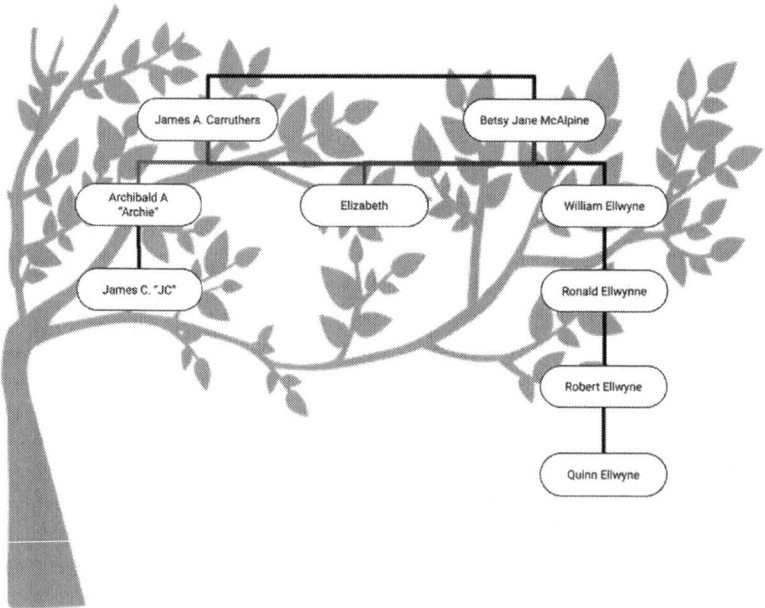

RECIPES

Food and nourishment are an important part of any family's story. These recipes, referenced at various points in Ellwyne's story, were compiled by the descendants of Betsy Jane and James A. Carruthers and first published in a recipe book lovingly put together by, and for, Carruthers clan members.

Fried Cabbage Recipe

This recipe is one that might have been shared at a schoolhouse community celebration potluck supper.

> 2 tbsp. butter
> 4 c. chopped cabbage
> 2 tbsp. vinegar
> 1 tsp. salt
> ½ tsp. pepper

Melt butter in a cast-iron frying pan. Add cabbage. Cook and stir for about 3 minutes. Add vinegar, salt, and pepper. Fry until the cabbage is limp, about 5-10 minutes. If the cabbage comes too dry, add water.

Salad Dressing Recipe

> 1 egg, beaten
> 1 tsp. dry mustard
> ½ tsp. salt
> 3 tsp. corn-starch
> ¾ c. white sugar
> ½ c. cider or white vinegar
> ½ c. whole cream or whole milk

In the top of a double boiler, mix egg, mustard, salt, cornstarch, and sugar. Add vinegar and milk/cream. Boil and stir until thickened. Serve over grated green cabbage.

Wedding Cake Recipe

This fruit cake recipe has been a part of many Carruthers family weddings. You'll notice that the oven heat doesn't give a temperature in degrees. This cake was baked in a wood-fired oven and the baker had to understand the temperature based on the type of wood burning inside.

Fruits/Nuts:

2 lbs. seeded raisins

2 lbs. currants

2 lbs. dates

½ lb. mixed peel

½ c. maraschino cherries

10 cents blanched almonds and walnuts

Batter:

1 lb. butter

1 lb. brown sugar

6 eggs, separated and beaten separately

½ c. strong coffee

½ c. buttermilk

1 c. homemade strawberry jam or jelly

1 lb. sifted flour

1 tsp. baking soda, dissolved in 1 tbsp hot water

1 tsp. cinnamon

1 tsp. nutmeg

1 tsp. cloves

Grated rind and juice of 1 orange and 1 lemon

Combine fruit and nuts and dredge with ½ cup of the flour. Beat egg whites separately and add to batter before fruit is added. Bake in a slow oven for 3 to 4 hours. Use a shallow pan of water in the bottom of the oven during baking time to retain moisture and prevent the bottom of the cake from overcooking. This was cooked in a wood-burning oven, which requires constant vigilance.

Hickory Nut Tarts Recipe

Betsy Jane Carruthers made recipes with the readily available ingredients she had easy access to in her area. Hickory nuts and walnuts were always used in her baking. She gathered these nuts from the roadside trees in Mosa and Ekfrid Townships.

¼ c. butter
1 c. brown sugar
1 c. corn syrup
3 eggs
1 scant tbsp. vinegar
Dash of salt
Hickory nuts
Unbaked tart shells

Mix the first six ingredients well. Place the desired amount of hickory nuts in individual unbaked tart shells. Pour filling into each shell about three-quarters full. Bake at 375 degrees for about 10 minutes, reduce heat, and bake until done.

Sourdough Starter Recipe

A sourdough does not require store-bought yeast. The yeast is grown organically.

1 c. flour
2 tbsp. white sugar
1 tsp. salt
1 c. warm water

In a large bowl, mix the ingredients. Let stand, covered, at room temperature for two days. It becomes a spongy mass and develops a yeasty aroma. Cover and refrigerate. To keep starter activated, feed at least once per week by stirring in the following ingredients:

1 c. flour
1 c. milk
¼ c white sugar

Be prepared to use the starter often. If you do not, cover and freeze. When needed again, thaw and feed before using.

Cabbage and Beet Relish Recipe

This is Betsy Jane Carruthers's own recipe, created due to a bountiful crop of red sugar beets. It was shared in the Carruthers clan heritage recipe book. This relish can be enjoyed with any meat or poultry dish. It continues to be served today by her descendants.

    8 c. raw shredded cabbage
    8 c. cooked mashed beets
    3 c. white sugar
    1 ½ c. vinegar
    ½ to ¾ c. ground horseradish
    1 tbsp. salt
    1 ½ tsp. black pepper

In a large bowl, combine the cabbage and beets. Add the remaining ingredients. Add horseradish to taste. Mix well and fill pint jars. Cover and refrigerate. Makes 8–9 pints. No canning is required.

Burnt Leather Cake Recipe

This is Betsy Jane Carruthers's own recipe, shared in the Carruthers clan heritage recipe book. White sugar and boiling water create a burnt syrup, dark brown in colour, which lends to the cake's name. With its hint of caramel flavour, this cake was a family favourite at Carruthers Corners, particularly in the 1920s and 1930s, when refined sugar became less expensive. James A. Carruthers was particularly fond of this recipe, which continues to be enjoyed today, on special occasions, by Betsy Jane's descendants.

    Syrup
    ½ c. white sugar
    ¼ c. boiling water

    Cake
    ½ c. butter
    ¾ c. white sugar
    3 egg yolks, beaten
    3 tbsp. scorched syrup

1 tsp. vanilla
2 ½ c. all-purpose flour
½ tsp. baking soda
Pinch of salt
3 egg whites, stiffly beaten

Icing

1 c. icing sugar
1 tbsp. scorched syrup
¼ c. butter

For the syrup, stir and scorch sugar in a saucepan until it has a caramel appearance. Add boiling water, boil and stir until syrup thickens. Set aside to cool.

For the cake, cream the butter and sugar, and add egg yolks. Mix well. Add the first amount of scorched syrup and vanilla. Mix baking soda with cold water and blend in. Sift in the flour, baking powder, and salt. Mix well. Lastly, fold in the beaten egg white. Bake at 350 degrees until the toothpick comes out clean.

For the icing, combine the icing sugar, butter, and the second amount of scorched syrup. Mix well and spread on a baked, cooled cake.

War Bread Recipe

This recipe is from a series of wartime menus issued by the Office of the Food Controller, printed in the *Kingston Daily British Whig* on October 29, 1917. The recipe was meant to be an economical yet nourishing staple when common bread ingredients were lacking.

2 c. boiling water
½ c. molasses
½ tbsp. salt
1 tbsp. dripping
½ yeast cake dissolved in ½ c. lukewarm water
1 c. rolled oats
4 ½ c. flour

Add boiling water to the oats and let stand for one hour. Add molasses, salt, butter, dissolved yeast cake, and flour. Let rise, beat thoroughly, turn into buttered bread pans, let rise again, and bake.

Lye Soap Recipe

This is an old heritage recipe for making the type of lye soap used at Carruthers Corners in the 19th and early 20th century.

5 lbs. pork fat
5 quarts of soft water (use rainwater or melted snow)
1 lb. of lye

Boil ingredients on the stovetop until it thickens (3 to 4 hours). Keep an eye on it because it will boil over.

ACKNOWLEDGEMENTS

Pulling this project together required teamwork for the labour of love that it represents. It began because my father, Butch Frederick, alerted me to an "interesting story" that he read in the *Glencoe Transcript and Free Press* newspaper years ago. He loves nothing more than a good story and pushed me towards researching this one specifically. He has spent every step of this journey with me. My mother, Yvette Frederick, provided encouragement and context on how a mother mourns the loss of her son. My parents cycle through the rural intersection of Carruthers Corners nearly every day in good weather, and spend time engrossed with thoughts about Ellwyne Ballantyne as they pedal past his mighty buttonwood tree. *Thump-thump.*

My partner, Patrick Bianchi, provided me with oodles of encouragement and feedback during the writing process; his help as a beta reader and newly minted buttonwood tree admirer has been invaluable.

Two editors helped me with developmental edits of the story. Susan Fish took the first round and helped point out holes in the plot. Catherine Muss took the second round and gave pointers for additional character development and plot. Both editors provided invaluable feedback that only improved the tale. Doreen Martens provided a substantial copy edit. Liza Levchuk proofread the final version.

Beta readers provided invaluable feedback as the manuscript took flight. I am especially indebted to Suzanne, Geoff, Marilyn, Jeff, Celia, Patti, Angela, Telma, Liza, Susan, and Bob, who set aside time from their schedules to give my first novel a whirl. Thank you.

Mostly, I am indebted to Mr. James Carlyle ("JC") Carruthers, who spent countless hours with me in person and on the phone to provide background about his ancestors. In preparation for each meeting, he wrote pages of notes (in beautiful cursive!), summarizing memories of events or stories he had been told. JC educated me on the Carruthers clan family history and shared details about key aspects of the story from photographs, letters, and his memory. Each in-person meeting occurred at his home, where we sat at a grand oak dining table next to a wood cookstove. His generosity cannot be easily repaid, but as I soon learned and you've discovered, the Carruthers spirit embodies giving and faith. I thank him for entrusting me to tell this important story. His thoughtful and elaborate descriptions of his beloved grandmother, Betsy Jane Carruthers, affirmed that storytelling is how history comes to life. It is through Betsy Jane's own storytelling that JC first learned what he knows of Ellwyne Ballantyne, and it is through JC's retelling of her stories that I received the details needed to construct this tale. I believe he would have made his grandmother proud in his passion for preserving and sharing valuable stories. I am delighted to now call JC my friend.

Finally, I offer my heartfelt thanks to the memories of Betsy Jane Carruthers and Ellwyne Ballantyne. I was not privileged enough to meet either, but I feel as though I've forged an unbreakable bond with them both. A significant portion of my creative life for the past four years has been dedicated to reconstructing this tale. Betsy Jane, your nurturing spirit vibrates in the subsequent generations of your clan. Ellwyne Ballantyne, you have become a symbol of perseverance and remembrance. Thank you for your sacrifice. We shall never forget you. Stand down.

BOOK CLUB QUESTIONS

1. How different do you think things were for children who lost their parents in the early 1900s than it is now?

2. What similarities do the buttonwood tree and Ellwyne share?

3. In what ways are Betsy Jane and Ellwyne alike?

4. The Carruthers clan worked as a team. Why do you think this approach appealed to Ellwyne?

5. Why do you think that Ellwyne decided to enlist in the Canadian Expeditionary Force?

6. How does Betsy Jane's faith get her through difficult times?

7. What does the "called home" metaphor mean to each main character?

8. Is home a place or a feeling?

9. Letter writing plays a large role in the story. Which letter impacted you the most?

10. As a society, what have we lost by abandoning the art of letter-writing and written correspondence?

11. In how many ways does the Carruthers clan remember Ellwyne? Which way is the most meaningful to you?

12. Which character would you most like to meet in real life?

13. To you, who was the protagonist of the story?

TO MY READERS

I hope you have enjoyed this family story. Reviews help other readers discover my books (and keep me writing) so consider leaving an honest review on Goodreads or your favourite review site. It's the easiest way you can support my continued writing efforts.

Manufactured by Amazon.ca
Bolton, ON